IMPOSSIBLE PEOPLE

ANNA LYNDSEY

The right of Anna Lyndsey to be identified as author of this
book has been asserted in accordance with the Copyright,
Designs and Patents Act, 1988

ISBN 978-1-7384119-0-0

Published by Rootling Books
www.rootlingbooks.co.uk

A CIP catalogue record for this book is available from the
British Library

Typeset by Coinlea Services

Cover design by PD Photography

For Sarah, Sarah, Roger, Rod,
Pete, Laura, Helen,
Julia, Sue and Sue

and in memory of Julie, Jason, Wendy and Lisa

"You see, I am fate," it shouted, "and stronger than your puny plans; and I am how-things-turn-out and I am different from your little dreams, and I am the flight of time and the end of beauty and unfulfilled desire; all the accidents and imperceptions and the little minutes that shape the crucial hours are mine. I am the exception that proves no rules, the limits of your control, the condiment in the dish of life."

F. SCOTT FITZGERALD

The Cut-Glass Bowl

PART 1

CHAPTER 1

On the screen it gleamed palely, with its black stripes of text, the thing that could not be true but at the same time was true, the paradox that was fusing all the circuits of Tom's brain. He gave it the chance to disappear, to slink discreetly back into the void. But when he'd logged out, logged in and reopened the site – the thing was still there.

Tom grabbed the laptop and rushed into the corridor. As he loped along, he was aware of the thing under his fingers, smug, shining, almost amused. When he reached Ed's office he knocked once and pushed at the door, but it resisted him. So he shoved it with his body and as it flexed reproachfully about its lock he remembered that his supervisor would not be back in the physics block until noon.

He had an hour to wait.

Cursing, Tom turned round and walked back to his own room. It felt cramped and foetid, like some farmed creature's pen. On the desktop monitor, numbers flowed, calculations he had been running before he'd stopped for a coffee and that idle fateful surf. Had they come out as he expected? He could no longer be bothered to look.

In offices around him, work went on. PhD students like him, diligently probing small portions of the universe. Industrious, contented. He could feel the vibrations, the harmonious intellectual buzz. And here he was with this enormity lodged in his head, his thoughts no longer proceeding in a logical linear fashion, but writhing back on themselves in some wild perpetual churn.

He wanted to smash his fists into the plasterboard walls.

Time to get out. Quickly he walked past lines of pale blue doors and hurried down three flights of lino-covered stairs. One of his undergraduate tutees, coming up towards him, gave him a smiley greeting; he managed to grunt something in response. On the ground floor he burst out into the bright mid-October morning; the air was too mild – it cloyed like spring. He headed through meandering gaggles of students to the large lawned square that formed the centre of the Northington campus. Around its edges, various unadventurous modernist buildings in shades of brick squatted like phlegmatic spectators. The neat grass was crisscrossed by tarmac paths lined with stocky cherry trees, their leaves subtly suffusing with orange, pink and red.

Tom sagged onto a bench. Closing his eyes, he leaned back and let the low beams of the post-equinox sun warm the clenched muscles of his face. In his mind he took hold of the impossible thing, began breaking it down into its component parts:

Title of paper: Proposal for a new calculational method for modelling the collisions of black holes.

Date of publication: 7th October. A week ago. On ArXiv.net, where researchers published things early to establish their authorship, before submitting them to the formal journals' lengthy processes of peer review.

Author: Dr Ed Torrios, Department of Theoretical Physics, University of Northington.

Subject: The solution to a problem Tom had come up against in the course of his PhD. The solution which – although he had discussed it with Ed, who had been helpful – Tom had believed to be his own.

And finally – Ed himself. Brilliant, kindly, nerdy, otherworldly. Loved by his students. Respected by his peers. Known and trusted by Tom, since his undergraduate days.

Ed who would never…

Would never…

Tom's mind kept swerving the word.

When he opened his eyes, the girl was an abstract shape across a corner of his vision, a black bar of stillness amid the brightness and the movement, like a shadow that had peeled itself up from the ground. She was standing with her back to him and she was tall, almost as tall as he was, and wore an old black parka with the hood up, faded skinny jeans, and biker boots which were scuffed and down at heel. She clutched a sheet of paper as though she had difficulty reading. In front of her, at a junction of paths, angled signposts waved their arms.

'Hey – can I help you?' Tom called out, glad of a break from his thoughts. Her body went rigid, but she didn't turn round. Unfolding himself from the bench he walked a few paces towards her. 'Where are you trying to get to?'

After a pause, she appeared to decide something. Squaring her shoulders, she spoke in a firm voice: 'Thanks, I need to find the psychology department.' And then she did turn round and stopped Tom in his friendly well-meaning tracks when there was less than six feet between them, because the black parka hood framed a silvery blank.

The girl did not have a face.

Tom's mind ran wild, hunting madly through archives for points of reference, retrieving only alien astronauts and emissaries from Mordor. And those made no sense – how could they? They were fiction, and fiction did not leak.

Shock and confusion must have filled his own features, because the girl said dryly, 'Don't worry, I'm human underneath. Can you help me find the psychology department? Please don't come any closer.' When she spoke, Tom detected the movement of her lips, and noticed veiled eyes observing him. So the moonlike blank was semitranslucent, not opaque. And soft – a sort of silvery mesh, worn over her head like a bag.

'Left here,' he said, recovering himself. 'Past the main admin block, turn to the right. My friend works there.' He pointed at the paper in her hand. 'I can show you where you are on your map, if that would help.'

The girl stepped back, thrusting one palm out towards him. 'No, stop. I can find it. When I said don't come any closer, I meant it.' She turned to go, then, relenting, swung back. 'Look – thanks. I'm sorry about...' And indicating her face with a quick embarrassed gesture she moved swiftly away to the left, passing between the rows of bright-leaved trees, her head bowed as though she walked into a storm. Students coming in the opposite direction, if they noticed her, jerked round and stared at her retreating back; others, heads bowed themselves, noticed nothing, intent on their phones.

Was she – contagious? If so, why had she come onto the campus at all? Disfigured? The outlines of a normal face lurked beyond that mysterious helmet, as far as he could tell. And why the psychology department? An anxiety disorder involving an extended sense of her personal space? Something dry and amused in her manner made that seem unlikely. Tom shrugged and checked the time: nearly midday. He drew a long breath: Ed would soon be back. Setting off towards the physics block he took the right-hand path between the regimented trees, and the image of the tall, black-clad, hooded girl, materialised on campus like a visitor from another world, went with him. What did she want here?

Ed Torrios' wide tanned face with its silver-framed aviator glasses always gave the impression of being broader than it was high, helped by the big straight-line grin that stretched across the lower part. He was wearing a white polo shirt, blue jeans and bright white trainers with thick bouncy soles, and sat casually on the front of his desk, hands in pockets, ankles loosely crossed. His springy grey hair, which grew upwards from his head like heather, meant that even when sitting down, he seemed to have a lot of upward momentum. Outside physics, Ed's great love was birdwatching: on the back of the door hung a camouflage anorak and binoculars on a leather strap, and along the wall behind him, a series of framed prints showed the different species of native British owl. Tom found himself the focus of five stern, wide-eyed glares.

'Ah, Tom – I'm glad you've come by. I came across some papers about gravitational waves that made me think of your work.' Ed widened his letterbox grin, which made avuncular crinkles appear at the corner of his eyes. He swivelled round and began rummaging in one of the piles on his desk. 'I definitely put them here somewhere, marked them out for you especially…'

'The paper I came to talk about is this one, actually.' Tom held out his laptop. 'This paper here.'

Ed took it and peered. 'Oh. Yes. My recent submission on ArXiv.'

Tom scanned the figure in front of him for any hint of foreknowledge, or frisson of shame. The man seemed totally relaxed and unconcerned.

'It's my calculational method.'

Ed said, 'Your calculational method?'

'Yes, you know – the one I devised to solve the problem with my thesis. So I was…kind of surprised.'

Ed's straight grey eyebrows tilted upwards like a bridge opening and his heathery hair seemed to bounce higher with astonishment.

'Oh dear,' he said. 'I don't think so.'

'But it was so,' Tom persisted. 'Remember – it was back in March, I'd hit this snag, we had a discussion about it, you suggested various ways forward, then I went away and had the idea. You said it was a really good one.'

Ed closed the laptop, carefully placing it on the desk beside him.

'I'm very sorry, Tom. I don't remember it like that. I gave you pointers in the right direction. I like to do that; I don't spoon-feed my graduate students. You did well to work it out. But I don't think you can then claim it was original. I don't think that's fair.'

Tom's hands were clenching at his sides, the palms slippery with sweat. Did Ed even realise what he had done? Had he simply held down the delete key in his brain until all the inconvenient memories had vanished, and typed out a shiny new text?

'Anyway – there's another reason I'm pleased you've come by,' Ed was saying. 'I've got good news.'

I have to look back, Tom thought frantically. To the time when we had the discussion, and I had the idea. There must be something that would prove it – to me as much as to him.

'The Department gets to nominate one graduate student to go to the Warwick conference…'

They had to get this untangled somehow. He couldn't go on with the rest of his doctorate with the article hovering over every discussion like some intrusive drone.

'…I'm recommending we nominate you.'

What had Ed been talking about?

Warwick. Warwick would be an amazing opportunity. He'd get to talk to all sorts of people in similar fields. It would be really useful and stimulating, but—

'So – what do you think?'

'That…would be fantastic,' Tom stammered.

'Not a difficult decision,' Ed smiled. 'After all, you are one of the Department's outstanding students.'

Desperately Tom wondered: Is this some sort of quid pro quo? Some sort of not-so-subtle message: look what great opportunities can open for you if you don't make a fuss? Or was it just an innocent straightforward offer – the kind that conscientious and supportive supervisors make to promising PhD students every single day? Reality seemed to shimmer and twist, to tease him with multiple perspectives, as though he looked at the scene in Ed's office through a series of distorting lenses. Ed had power over his future: that was what it came down to. He could be helpful or unhelpful, for the rest of Tom's PhD. And after it was finished, he could be instrumental in securing Tom post-doc work.

Or…not.

So – let him get away with it? Tom shuddered. This peculiarly intimate harvesting – at that moment, he could not think of another, more suitable, term – if it had happened once, would it happen again? The top of his head felt tender and bruised, as though he were an egg and someone had dug at his skull with a spoon.

He had to go and teach soon, needed to get out of there with his options intact. He said, 'Thank you, Ed. I'd be proud to be nominated. I'll take a look back at the notes on the calculational method, see how it evolved.'

Taking his hands out of his jeans pockets, Ed tipped his chin right back as though the ceiling had become a fascinating object of contemplation, and for a moment Tom had the illusion that above the white and pristine polo collar emerged a stunted, featureless, tanned stump. The chin came down again as Tom turned to go, and Ed beamed and said, 'Of course all I can do is make a recommendation. The Head of Department makes the final decision…'

CHAPTER 2

Number 37 Honey Lane was the last house in a terrace of six, grey stone, narrow-faced, with a pocket front garden and a red front door. It stood on the outskirts of the little town, north of the university, and Tom had cycled home across the moor, through shadowy expanses of heather and gorse, as the sun had subsided hazily behind the Pennines to his left. Now he manhandled his bike into the cramped hall and propped it up next to Marianne's – there was nowhere else to store it so it had to live there, entangling handlebars with everyone who passed. He went into the kitchen, where Marianne herself, an elfin figure in leggings and a royal blue tunic, stood stirring a huge stainless-steel pot. The atmosphere was moist and pungent with spices. She was trying out a new recipe, Tom remembered, and his friend Kevin had been invited to help eat the results.

'Hey – you look like a sexy witch,' he said. 'What's in the cauldron?'

'Oh, all sorts of mysterious stuff,' she laughed. 'But mostly lentils.' She smiled up at him, her dark eyes lustrous, her usually pale, delicate features, with their sprinkling of freckles, rosily flushed by the heat. Her neat pixie-cut hair, a rich reddish brown, had lifted into tufts of concentration on the crown of her head.

Tom pulled her to him. She was barely five foot, while he was six foot two, rangy, long and blond, all arms and legs and outsize feet, as his mother used to say, with hair that only behaved itself if he had it cut close to his scalp, and then only until it got its breath back and started sprouting again in twisting yellow question marks. 'I must get it from my father,' went through his mind, but as usual he shook away the thought. His mysterious Australian father, whom he'd never known, the great Antipodean blank, who had slowly over the years become the necessary repository of all those things that were *not his mother*, but about whom his mother remembered or would reveal so frustratingly little.

He grasped Marianne's perfect round backside, lifting her up until she twined her legs around him. As they kissed and the golden gloop seethed in the pot he decided that tonight he would try to put aside what had happened with Ed and give himself the evening to relax. Tomorrow he would start looking back, comb through the exchanges about the calculational method, begin amassing his proof.

12

'Hey, put me down,' Marianne said, when the doorbell broke in with an assertive ring. 'That'll be him. I need to make some poppadoms.'

'Fantastic curry, Marianne.' Kevin, comfortably filling his trademark leather jacket and jeans, sat halfway down the folding table, his dark slicked-back head bent forward in concentration as he expertly corralled remnants of rice.

Four months before, when Tom and Marianne had first moved in together, the living room had been a particularly dismal shade of tobacco, with mysterious stains. Marianne had charmed the landlord into letting them paint the walls a warm deep orange. She had found seventies curtains in an overlooked pile in a charity shop and altered them to fit, so the window was framed with an orderly riot of stylised flowers. On Freecycle she had tracked down a squashed scarlet sofa, which lazed along one wall like a slack contented mouth.

Kevin's head reared up from his plate. 'Hey – did I tell you – we started the first exposure sessions in the lab last week.'

'That's great,' Tom said. 'At last. So you sorted your recruitment problem.'

'Well…sort of. At least enough to get going. It's not the people for the control group – we've never had any problem recruiting them. It's the…the other lot. I've been worried, you know.' Kevin put his elbows on the table and tilted his stocky body forward, speaking in a confidential tone. 'Loads of times I said to myself, "Just your luck, mate. First post-doc research assistant post" – after I'd applied for loads and got nowhere, you know what a struggle it's been – "great group of colleagues from different disciplines, proper funding, all very prestigious – and it's all going toes up because you can't persuade enough of...that...sort of person to come and get tested" (and I'm the one who's supposed to do that part, you see, I'm the dogsbody, most junior member of the team).'

'What do the participants have to do, exactly?' Marianne asked. 'I can understand why people might not be keen to be experimented on.'

Kevin settled himself back in his chair. 'Each participant has to attend our special lab for three separate hour-long sessions, about one week apart. That's their only commitment. *And* we pay them expenses.' He raised his bottle of beer.

'But what happens to them during those hours? If it is distressing or unpleasant...' Marianne's large brown eyes prepared to widen in reproach.

Kevin clinked the bottle down on the table and waved his arms dismissively. 'They just sit comfortably in a chair while the radio transmitter is turned on. They can't see anything, it's built in behind a screen. Every fifteen minutes they write down any

14

physical symptoms they're feeling and score their severity on a scale of 1 to 10. After three quarters of an hour, they fill in a brief psychological well-being questionnaire. Then, fifteen minutes after the end of the session, they note down their physical symptoms again.'

'Hang on,' Tom said. 'Don't they also have to say whether they think the transmission they've just experienced was real or fake?'

'Yeah, yeah, that too. Each participant gets a high strength, low strength and a blank transmission, in a randomised sequence, over their three sessions. We ask them which they think they've just had.'

'And then you work out whether there is any difference in the responses between the normal people in the control group and…' Marianne trailed off. 'I don't quite know how you'd refer to them…'

'The people who think they're *not* normal,' Tom said roughly. 'People who think they can detect stuff that the rest of us don't notice, because – hey – scientifically – it's too weak to detect.'

Marianne gave her sweet airy laugh.

'You two can be flippant,' Kevin said, 'but I have to stay objective here. They call themselves reactors. And they don't exactly claim they can detect it. They say it makes them ill.'

'What – the stuff from normal phones and masts and Wi-Fi?'

'Just that stuff. Radiofrequency radiation. RF for

short. That's what we're testing them with in the experiment. The transmitter gives out radiofrequency radiation of broadly that type and strength.'

'Which,' Tom cut in, 'is completely different from the kind of radiation that has been shown to cause anyone any harm.' People reacted oddly to the word *radiation*; he didn't want Marianne getting all environmental and outraged based on a misunderstanding. 'Firstly, because it's non-ionising radiation, not the ionising kind like x-rays or gamma rays which are much higher frequency and mess up your cells, and secondly because it's very low power, well within the safety limits.'

Marianne rose from the table. 'Does anyone want any more? We might as well finish the rest of it.' Tom relaxed as she trotted out of the room, dainty feet padding over the wooden floorboards. When she came back, she was clutching the cooking pot against her chest. 'It's the fresh coriander which makes the difference, I think,' she said, wrinkling her nose judiciously. 'I'll convert you both to vegan cooking yet!'

'I just love vegan cooking,' Kevin replied, drawing his chair back to the table and preparing to concentrate once more on his plate. 'So long as I can still eat cheese on toast and fish and chips.'

'Next time,' Marianne said, 'I'll make you a vegan pizza. And I bet you hoover it up.'

'Vegan pizza? How does that even work?'

'Kevin, you are such a Luddite.' Marianne laughed again. 'At least try the pizza before you start making objections.'

In the fridge, Tom still had his shelf of animal-product sin. Marianne treated it with the same indulgence she would have shown an ancient teddy bear or some other relic of Tom's childhood, held onto through nostalgia or sentimental loyalty, destined, one enlightened day, to be inevitably outgrown.

'What's in vegan cheese anyway?' Kevin demanded, and when Marianne had recited ingredients he grunted, 'Hmmm. Sounds like flavoured rubber to me.'

'I think you are letting your preconceptions influence your judgement,' Marianne replied primly. 'If you're convinced it's going to be horrible then it will be. You should know that, being a psychologist.'

'Make him two pizzas,' Tom said, 'one with normal cheese and one with vegan cheese. Serve him slices in a random order, make him eat them with a blindfold on, and see if he can tell what he's got.'

Kevin roared with laughter. 'Nice one, mate. Just like my experiment. And maximum pizza for me. What's not to like?' He went on, 'Actually, the experiment goes a step further. The transmitter's linked to a pre-programmed computer producing a randomised sequence of exposures. So the subject doesn't know what type is happening in each session – but neither does the researcher. Removes any possibility of subtle clues or differences in our behaviour skewing the results. That's what makes it "double-blind". Nothing for it, Marianne, you'll have to be blindfolded too.'

'I won't be doing any of it,' Marianne said. 'It all sounds disgustingly messy. And anyway, it's a matter of principle, not just taste. It's about moving to a sustainable food system that can support everybody on the planet and not wreck the climate at the same time. You'll see' – she winked at Tom – 'it's just like one of your equations – it's the only answer that makes sense.' She stood up, graceful, serene and untouchable. 'Sorry – I know I go on. Pass me the plates, if you've finished.'

'I'll wash up,' Tom said. As he followed her into the kitchen, he had a vivid memory of the day they'd met. Marianne had been dressed as a polar bear, in a big white coat and a white hat with ears, a patch of pure furry brightness lighting up the dank November drizzle. She'd been standing with about thirty other protesters at the entrance to the Central Admin building. 'DON'T FOSSILISE OUR FUTURE – No to tainted Arts!' said the green fabric banner behind her, and when he'd gone up to ask what the protest was about, she'd explained that the university was proposing to fund a new Arts Centre through sponsorship from an oil company and that this was outrageous and had to be stopped.

'Do you really think it matters that much?' he'd

asked her. 'If they're prepared to give us a big chunk of cash, shouldn't we just say thanks very much and take it?'

'It's part of their strategy of *legitimation*,' she'd said fiercely. 'Trying to look like normal mainstream companies, while applying to drill for oil and gas which has to stay in the ground if we want to keep climate change to within manageable limits. It's climate vandalism – people need to call it out.'

'But people still use oil and gas,' he'd said. 'I expect you have central heating. Somebody has to supply it. If this company didn't do the drilling, other companies would.'

'Well, people should be protesting against them then.'

He'd asked her if, when she'd finished protesting, and wanted to warm up, she would like to persuade him further over a coffee, and she'd looked straight up at him from under her sweetly arching brows and said, with great earnestness but a delicious undertone of mischief, 'You mustn't think I only talk about climate change, you know. I do do other things.'

She had been an undergraduate, part-way through an English degree; Tom had been in the first year of his PhD, researching black holes, those dark pitfalls in space where gravity was so intense that nothing that entered could escape, not even light. He'd liked the way she'd argued with him, her commitment, her principles, how undaunted she was by the difficulty or size of a task, the way her eyes fired up and her cheeks went pink, how later, in the coffee shop, she'd gestured passionately with her spoon.

Tom thought: she is the most ethical person I know.

What gave one person serene certainty and someone else complex doubt? You could show two people the same set of evidence, and they'd come to radically different conclusions. Marianne was convinced she was the future, and who knew, she might be right. The world was changing fast. There was disruption everywhere. Assumptions people had grown up with for years – that you ate roast animal on special occasions; cars ran on petrol; there was ice at the North Pole; law and accountancy were solid careers; all were dissolving, you could almost hear the crack and split and ooze.

And so much that had been unrecorded, transitory, unquantified and mysterious was now being pulled into the light. Cameras and satellites and sensors and smart devices sucked in data like electronic vampires, radio waves communicated it wirelessly over distances, and data centres shared and combined and crunched it to make new knowledge. And at the same time, people being what they were, tides of triviality, misinformation, obscenity and violence swept erratically through it all.

He scrubbed at the plates in the foamy water as Marianne darted about, drying things and putting them away. Kevin had wandered in, to sit stolidly at the small pine table with his beer. 'Not much space in here,' he commented. 'Best I stay over here, out of the way.'

Tom said over his shoulder, 'Kev, you know your reactors?'

'I do.'

'In a weird intuitive way – they're kind of right?'

'About what?'

'Radiofrequency radiation. It's the thing beyond everything else that's setting technology free. Letting it rip to career into the future. Disrupting and transforming so many aspects of life.'

'I suppose so, but –'

'So – to fixate on it as a source of illness and pain – well – it makes creepy poetic sense.'

Marianne said brightly, 'Oh so you were listening when I was talking about metaphor. You mean it's a metaphor for modernity. Or to be more accurate – metonymy, which is where a part of something is used to signify the whole.'

'Definitely listening.' Marianne was currently studying for a Masters in English literature; he reached out to hug her as she trotted past. 'Anyway, it's kind of saying: stop the world, I want to get off.'

Kevin stared at the label on his beer, rotating the bottle on the table in front of him. 'The thing is,' he said after a pause, 'they're not all *old*. Nothing like. Some of them are young. They'll have grown up with wireless. Never known anything else. Digital natives. Just like us. And – there are more and more of them. That's why we got the funding. It's a rising tide.'

Suddenly an image flashed into Tom's mind. The black-clad girl, her hood framing the silver blank of her face like a spacesuit in reverse. Her dry, firm voice. Her palm thrust out, keeping him determinedly at bay.

He turned to Kevin, saying slowly, 'Do you know, Kev, I think I met one. On the campus at lunchtime. I helped her with directions to the psychology department. She wouldn't let me come near her. Must have assumed I had a phone.'

'The whole campus is full of phones,' objected Marianne. 'Everyone's got one. And tablets. And Wi-Fi – they've just upgraded that, thank goodness – it was really rubbish before. Radiofrequency whatnot would be all around her.'

'I think she knew that,' Tom replied thoughtfully. 'She was wearing…something…over her head. A sort of metallic mesh bag. She'd got the physics completely right, actually. That would provide some degree of protection…' He scythed the air impatiently with his arm. 'If, of course, there was anything she needed protecting from.'

He let a handful of dripping cutlery clatter into the rack, suddenly inexplicably irritated. 'Look, I'm not an expert on the sources of neuroses, okay? Who knows what happened to screw her up? I leave that to the psychologists.'

'Not to me,' Kevin said. 'I'm not a clinical psychologist. There's a difference. I'm just testing their perceptions.'

'Yeah. Well. You just get on with doing that and prove it's all in their heads.'

'You are being very judgemental,' Marianne said. 'Anxiety disorders and phobias are real conditions – just as real as physical illnesses. And just as distressing and disabling. Kevin' – she turned to him – 'I hope your team can show what's really going on, and then everyone can be given the right support.'

CHAPTER 3

The following Thursday, Tom had arranged to meet Kevin at quarter to four at the psychology department so they could walk over to the football game together. The game was informal but regular; the players, mostly postgrads and postdocs from various departments, shared a dislike of repetitive solitary workouts and a preference for getting out of breath collectively, with the occasional release of a goal. They met each week on the most distant, lumpy and unloved of the university's football pitches, divided whoever turned up randomly into two teams and played enthusiastically and energetically in mud, heat or rain.

The psychology building was new and swanky; the whole place smelt as though they'd just ripped the packaging off. The downstairs lobby where Tom waited had a double-height glazed front with glass swing doors. The walls were pale lilac, and plump grey velvety seating units crouched in low feline groups. Tom was the only person sitting on one.

In the few free intervals of his busy week, he had continued combing through his notes and records from that time last March. But so far, he had failed to find a smoking gun. The evidence was ambiguous, open to interpretation. When Tom had emailed his new method to his supervisor, Ed's electronic reply, looked at with hindsight, was almost suspiciously bland. Had he had something in mind, even then? But around the electronic records there had been warm, living words; chats, praise, commendations....

Tom had been in two minds about coming tonight, had told Kevin at lunch that he might have some sort of bug starting (his head was aching at the top again), but Kev just said, 'Oh come on mate, man up, what you need is to run up and down a field a few times, and you'll be sorted. Trust me, I'm a doctor.' Tom took a long swig from his water bottle. Where was Kevin? On the back wall of the lilac lobby twelve raised silver bars formed an outsize clockface; the blade-like silver hands now indicated three minutes to four. He texted crossly, 'I'm downstairs. Where R U?' and had just pressed SEND when the left-hand door at the back of the lobby crashed against the wall and Kevin rushed out, looked wildly around, spotted Tom and hurried over. 'There you are,' he gasped, 'I'm sorry, mate, I can't come tonight, we've got a bit of an emergency here.'

'Why – what's happened?'

Kevin's black hair, usually neatly slicked back, had divided into multiple crests and hung down over his ears. 'One of the participants – had her second session this afternoon.' He stopped to draw breath. 'Halfway through she threw up on the floor in the testing room. And her nose began bleeding. Then she threw up again. Mate – she was bent over' – he gestured a swift incredulous arc – 'she was on her hands and knees.'

Out of the door through which Kevin had come a girl emerged, moving erratically as though the floor beneath her heaved. The smell of her came before her, expanding like a noxious gas into the tasteful lilac lobby: the acrid stink of vomit, the sour musk of unhealthy sweat, the metallic sweetness of blood. Her face was chalk white except for a viscous red trail that led down from one nostril to the side of her mouth. Her tangled hair was long and brown, with a fringe which stuck up ragged and disordered. Both her hair and her skin shone with perspiration under the discreetly recessed lights. The front of her pale blue shirt was stained with drips and patches, and strands of her hair were caked.

Kevin stepped in front of her, putting a hand on her arm. 'Sarah – please – there's a sick room here. We can get one of the University Medical Centre staff to look at you – if you won't let me call an ambulance.'

'Let me go.'

'I can't do that. You're my responsibility.'

Her face, freed from its silver covering, was new to Tom – he registered deep-set brown eyes under strongly marked brows, a bony but shapely nose; guessed her age as late 20s, a few years older than him. But her voice, her height, her strange defiant yet shrinking manner, the shabby parka slung over one arm – he remembered them all. It was the black-clad girl.

The girl caught sight of Tom and a spasm of recognition passed over her damp exhausted face. Shoving Kevin to one side, she lurched towards him, reeling as though she was drunk. 'Here's the man who knows his way around. I need the nearest place away from buildings and people, where there are trees. I need to get there now. Will you help me?'

'On the far side of the sports fields,' he said. 'There's a wood.' In his early days with Marianne, she had persuaded him to go on campus wildlife walks. 'I could take you there. But are you sure you don't need a doctor? Wouldn't it be better...'

For answer she grabbed his elbow and dragged him through the glass swing doors. He barely had time to glance back at Kevin with a helpless 'what else can I do?' shrug.

'I know when I need a doctor, okay?' she growled, as she propelled him onto the tarmac path. 'I'm a nurse. Which way here?'

'Right.'

The grip on his elbow released and she stepped

away. 'OK, you walk ahead with your phone and I'll follow you. I'm not going to wear my headnet while I'm actually feeling this sick. Just keep going. I'll be about ten paces behind.'

So their weird walk through the campus began. Tom glanced back, now and again, to check she was still there, hadn't collapsed or thrown up. She kept palely trudging forwards, in her grotesquely stained shirt.

As they reached the sports fields Tom saw the footballers congregating on a distant pitch, stretching their hamstrings or pulling at their quads, or doing humorous high-stepping runs. Laughter and indistinct banter floated over the air. He slid his phone out of his jeans pocket and fiddled as he walked. 'It's off,' he shouted back, stopping and waving the device, 'if that makes you feel more relaxed.'

She glanced up quickly. 'Thanks,' she said dryly. 'Every little helps. Although feeling relaxed has nothing whatever to do with it. Anyway, you've probably got a smartwatch or a Fitbit. They also emit.'

'Actually, I don't.'

'Oh. Okay.'

He slowed his pace, letting her catch up. 'God, I stink,' she said, when they were level, sniffing the front of her shirt and giving it a shake. 'Sorry. You'd probably prefer me ten paces behind.'

'It's fine.'

Side by side they went on, easily falling into

28

step, their equal shadows stretched by the low sun over the golden-green grass. Perhaps she really is ill, Tom thought. But instead of going to the doctor and getting checked out and properly tested, she's become convinced that radiofrequency radiation is the cause of her symptoms. That's why she volunteered for the experiment. Then, coincidentally, in the testing room the second time round, she's had an attack of...well – whatever it is. Or – more fantastical, but there are such cases – she is so convinced that RF will do her harm that her terror and distress have created violent physical manifestations, even though there is nothing physically wrong with her. The vomiting and the bleeding are – what is the word – psychosomatic. In *New Scientist* he'd read an article which pleaded for greater and more sympathetic recognition of psychosomatic disorders. People who suffered them were so often cruelly judged, believed to be 'faking it', making it up. But their symptoms were real – unconscious, uncontrollable, unchosen. The only difference was the way the symptoms needed to be treated – with careful psychiatric assessment, and a gradual untangling of the emotional trauma that lay beneath.

The wood on the far side of the sports fields was a remnant of what must have been there for centuries before the campus had arrived and spread itself over the land. It was mostly made up of beeches, ancient, broad and muscular, their leaves forming a shimmering golden band between the green of the grass and the blue of the late afternoon sky. As they came closer, Tom saw grey branches, curving downwards in elegant concave arcs, which forked and forked and forked again like enormous compound hands.

There was no obvious way in. He lifted a branch so that she could duck under it. Beneath their feet, innumerable biscuity leaf layers crunched, and a complex smell of growth and decay seemed to emanate from everything around them.

Tom walked a few paces forward to a clearing where two old-fashioned wooden benches stood at a conversational angle.

'Benches! Wow – you picked me a really good spot.' The girl sat down heavily on the nearer seat and flopped forwards, propping her head in her hands. 'At least' – she forced herself to sit upright again – 'I think it's pretty good. I should check, to be sure.'

Tom was astonished to see her slide a slim black rectangle from the pocket of her coat. She pressed a switch on the side and peered at it as she held it in front of her.

'Hey…how can you…'

Her brown eyes flicked contempt from under her thick brows. 'It's not a *phone,*' she muttered. 'For God's sake.' The gadget gave off a gentle hissing sound with intermittent overtones of a higher hum. One green light came on, the first in a line of ten tiny LEDs, and a second green light flashed on and off. Intrigued, Tom bent closer. Beside each LED was a number, some sort of measurement in volts per meter; the numbers got higher from the bottom up.

'Wow. That's really not bad at all,' the girl said, sounding pleased, as she clicked off the device and stowed it away. 'What was that thing?' asked Tom.

'My pocket oscilloscope,' she replied. 'A meter that measures the level of ambient RF. It's good here. As I thought.' She swung her legs up to the bench, arranged her black backpack against the wooden arm at one end, spread her parka over her and lay down with her knees bent. As she did so she exhaled an enormous breath of relief and her eyes fell shut.

Tom said, 'Are you just going to stay here?'

The girl opened one eye. 'It's the best thing for me. Don't hang around – there's no need.'

'But how long—'

'As long as it takes for the aftermath to calm down. Could be a few hours. Or longer. I don't know. I need to be well enough to travel.'

'But that'll be the middle of the night...'

She wriggled her shoulders dismissively, as if to say 'what of it?'

He stood watching her taut features soften and relax. Unshouldering his backpack, he searched inside. 'I've got some chocolate here.' It was a bar of organic Fairtrade dark, the kind Marianne always insisted they buy. 'Would you like it?'

Her eyes flashed open and her wan face was transformed by a huge curvy smile that flowed up her cheeks and outwards towards her ears. 'Hey,' she said, laughing, 'chocolate always helps. Even when the person giving it thinks you're nuts.'

'...I don't...' He cursed himself – too slow, too weak.

'Of course you do.' As she took it from him their fingers briefly brushed; he felt a cold corpse touch.

'God, I was stupid to take part in that stupid experiment,' she said with sudden vehemence, snapping off a chunk. 'But that's what happens I suppose, when you're desperate. I just hope it hasn't... had any long-term effect.' She looked directly up at him as she pulled away the foil. 'If I get away with it, it'll be thanks to this place. Thanks to you.'

She seemed to hesitate, debate something within herself. Then she came to a decision.

'Look – I'm sorry – I'm on the edge, and pretty far gone. There's only one thing I can do to thank you, and you probably won't like it, but I'm going to do it anyway.' She wriggled backwards to sit up straighter on the bench, her long fingers clutching the black parka. 'This thing is real. It's real and it's happening to more people. If you ever think...if you ever start to suspect...that you – or anyone you love...don't ignore it. Don't mess with it. Act – don't delay.'

Her eyes. Ferocious, passionate, burningly sincere. They held him – he couldn't look away.

'I'm not trying to recruit you. Believe me' – she gave a dry percussive laugh – 'I wouldn't wish this on my worst enemy. But you should be informed.'

She had reached out and pinioned his hand. And now – what the hell? – she was writing – *writing* – on the back. The point of the pen crawled over his skin like a ticklish insect, leaving a fine black trail. 'Hey!' Tom freed himself with a violent disgusted lurch. 'What d'you think you're doing?'

Already she was rearranging herself on the bench, lying back uninterestedly. 'That's the website. In case you ever need it.'

'I'm not going to need it.'

'Good.' She closed her eyes. 'You can wash it off.'

He was suddenly, overwhelmingly angry. This is what happens, he told himself furiously, this is what happens when you pander to these people. Try to be considerate, give them chocolate, turn off your phone. They get their claws into you, twist things round inside your head, drag you through the mirror into their impossible, inconceivable world. He wanted to pick her off her bench and shake her, shake her hard until her delusion slid stickily out of her brain and fell to the leafy ground with a sickly thud. He could almost imagine it, grey, deformed, rat-like, scuttling away.

Time to get out. He sensed his life calling him, messages heaping up in the cloud like drifts of soft petals, each a tiny caress of pleasurable connection.

Marianne would be texting him, sending him kisses and sweetly indecent proposals, wondering why he hadn't replied. Kev would be worrying, feeling responsible, wanting to know what was going on.

Tom focused his eyes on the distant campus buildings beyond the lattice of intersecting leaves. He spoke as calmly as he could:

'I don't need it and you don't need it. *Believe me*' – a low blow, he hadn't meant to mimic her, it had just come out – 'I hope you can get some proper help.'

She said nothing, lay passive and quiet, but as he walked away, he caught a flick of pale movement in the corner of his eye. She was giving him the finger.

Once he was out of the trees he began to run, thundering over the damp grass, fumbling at his phone as he went. When the screen lit up it illuminated the marks on his hand and he couldn't avoid the information transmitting instantaneously to his brain: reactorrights.org was what it said but he was more absorbed by the notifications pinging through as he pounded along.

Kev had been texting incontinently. 'Tom where are you? What's happening?' 'Is Sarah okay? Let me know.' 'CALL ME when you get this. I'm worried.'

He did call, and Kevin answered immediately, exclaiming, 'Thank God it's you. What's going on?'

'Calm down Kev. Everything is fine. I had my

phone off for a while, that's all. Nobody died.'

'What happened to...'

'She's fine. She is in the trees, won't move, insists she'll stay there till she feels better.'

'But...'

'Look, we've both done what we can, okay?' Tom said roughly. 'She's obstinate as hell. I don't see how you can be blamed.'

'I'm still at work.' Kevin sounded doleful. 'I had to clean everything up in the testing room. I just couldn't get rid of the smell of vomit, which isn't exactly good for business, so I apologised to the next participants and rescheduled them. Then I tried to fill out a report on the system, which was complicated because she did 90% of the responses but not the final bit, and the system isn't set up for that, it wasn't envisaged in the design, apparently. So the IT fell over and I had to call tech support. By the way,' – his voice dropped to an anxious murmur – 'd'you think she'll be back?'

'Who – Sarah?'

'Yes. For her third session. This was only her second.'

Tom gave a bark of laughter. 'What – after today? Somehow I don't think so. She's too freaked out.'

Silence at the other end, then a gale of white noise as Kevin sighed heavily down the phone. 'No. Well, I can't blame her, I suppose. But that means...'

'Means what?'

'Oh...none of her results will count. They'll all

have to be thrown away. Can't be helped, I suppose. I'd better go and finish up.'

The football match was underway, well into its second half. No point in joining the game now. The sun had dropped below the university buildings and the air was becoming clammy and cold. Time to cycle home to Marianne, warmth, dinner, sanity, sex – and sleep.

And everything had happened as Tom had predicted – except for the sleep. He had lain on his back staring up at the shadowy ceiling. Had rolled onto his left side, with his arm crooked under his head. Had rolled onto his right, with his knees drawn up. Tried his back again, crossing his ankles this time in case that made a difference (it didn't). He must have changed position at least fifty times, marvelling at the sheer variety of shapes that the human body could assume, and still fail to find rest. Next to him, Marianne lay, breathing peacefully, her neat pixie-cut head perfectly aligned on her pillow as it always was, mainlining great effortless draughts of the stuff he craved.

This thing with Ed. It had truly got to him. He had always considered himself a laid-back character, able to take a detached, objective attitude to the ups and downs of life. Certainly not a person who would be kept awake by worry. Everything seemed to be rushing through him too fast; blood careering impatiently along his veins, thoughts burrowing round his brain like supercharged worms. His heart kept hopping with pointless anticipation, as though he was about to kick a crucial penalty rather than lie here in a bed.

All week different courses of action regarding the article had done formation dances inside Tom's head, first one then another advancing itself as the only obvious, rational, sensible choice, until he would sigh with relief and say to himself, 'Yes, that's settled. That's what I'm going to do', and as soon as he'd said it the option would start to shimmy and retreat, and all the potential downsides would leap out from behind it, looking solid and convincing.

He gazed at the faint outline of the window. Already, it was Friday. In a few hours the streetlit darkness would drain away and he would have to put this blighted night behind him, get back to campus and face it all again. He yearned to shove time forwards twenty-four hours, spin the planet swiftly just once on its axis, so that he would not have to do that, and the weekend would start immediately, now.

CHAPTER 4

On the north side of the big lawned square in the centre of the campus, one bulky brown building housed a café on its first two floors. The café sold an eclectic mix of food which would never have been replicated in the world beyond the campus, the menu an archaeological record of waves of campaigns and counter-campaigns for the exclusion, inclusion or reinstatement of various dishes or ingredients. The café had floor-to-ceiling windows along the side which looked out over the square, so that as you approached you saw twelve sideways-on vignettes of people sitting at tables, six above and six below, and could wonder at the content of intense conversations, the cause of glazed looks, or admire eating while texting undertaken with unusual dexterity.

Tom sat by himself beside a window in the corner furthest from the till, reading a physics blog on his tablet while he ate a baked potato. The fug of coffee, the scraping of cutlery, the surges of chatter and laughter surrounded him with a companionable haze. Today was Monday and all his feeling of malaise had gone, wiped away by the weekend; on Saturday night and Sunday night he had slept well.

In the morning he'd had a brief meeting with Ed. They had both carefully avoided the subject of the calculational method. Tom grinned sourly to himself: it was as if they'd had some massively ill-advised one-night stand and were both trying to forget it had ever happened. Nothing more was said about the Warwick conference; Tom had found out that the deadline was not until the start of December. He had decided he would talk to some of his colleagues, Ed's other supervisees, and to postdocs whom Ed had supervised in the past. He would be discreet, subtle and hypothetical, but alert to any sign that they may have had an experience something like his own.

'All right?' A loud cheerful voice cut through the ambient buzz. Glancing up, Tom saw Kevin pivoting his stocky figure through the crowded tables carrying a Coke and three sausage rolls on a tray; he weaved his hips with surprising grace. He was wearing – optimistically for the end of October – his favourite wraparound shades. With his slicked back hair and black leather jacket, they gave him the look of an amiable CIA agent.

'All right mate?' and 'How are you doing?' and ''Scuse me' he shouted as he passed through. Kev knew an unfeasibly large number of people, having worked in one of the town's student pubs after he'd finished his PhD while he had applied all over the country for job after job after job. 'Something I'm doing in the interviews. Or something I'm not doing,' he had said dolefully to Tom. 'Must be. Puts them off. Like they can smell my dad's a brickie, or something.'

'That's rubbish,' Tom had told him. 'You're being paranoid.'

'I love the Hat and Feathers, mate, you know that, it's my happy place. But I can't do it forever. Not after all that work. My dad laughs at me, when I go home.'

Tom had tried to reassure him. 'You'll get there – I guarantee it. It happens to lots of postdocs. It just takes a bit of time.'

Kevin was putting down his tray and shimmying onto a chair opposite Tom. 'Come on mate, it's lunchtime. Stop working for five minutes. Smell the sunshine. Feel the coffee.'

Tom grinned as he pushed his tablet to one side. 'How do you know it was work? I might have been looking at all sorts of things. Like – hey – drunk psychologists singing Abba songs. To take a totally random example.'

Kevin had been stoked when he had finally landed his job. He hadn't even had to move – it was right here in the university, where he'd done his PhD. He had celebrated his success by buying several rounds in the Hat and Feathers, and singing 'Take a Chance on Me' with the karaoke machine. Someone had filmed him; he had become a minor YouTube hit.

'Yeah, but you weren't, were you?'

'Okay, I was reading about gravitational waves.'

Kevin shook his head in mock despair. 'I know you too well, mate.'

Tom calculated how long they'd been friends. He had moved into the large ramshackle shared house at the start of his second year, and found Kevin ensconced in the largest and most desirable downstairs room. On that first day Kev had been lounging in an armchair with his feet up on a bookcase, cartoon-socked ankles crossed, headphones on, a thick textbook balanced on his paunch. A spider doorstop with revolting black hairy legs kept the door of his room wedged open so he could keep tabs on what was going on in the hall.

'Hi...' Tom had ventured as he struggled towards the staircase carrying bulging bin bags and a guitar case.

Kevin had removed one headphone. 'You got an actual guitar in there?'

'Well...yes.' And had thought, 'Who is this idiot?'

Strange how things turned out.

Kevin picked up one sausage roll and bit off a substantial chunk, which he chewed abstractedly. When he had almost finished, he sighed and said, 'D'you know, I envy you, only having to deal with the forces of nature.'

'Why – what's happened?'

'I got this this morning.' He turned the screen of

his phone towards Tom. As Tom read, Kevin watched him and chewed.

To: Kevin Corden

From: David Redmond

RE: Withdrawal from experiment

Dear Kevin

I'm writing this on behalf of my wife Sandy. Unfortunately her first session resulted in a severe reaction the next day, and her sensitivity has subsequently become worse. So she won't be able to participate any further.

Apologies – hope you will understand.

Regards

David

'It's the fourth.'

'The fourth dropout?'

'Yeah.' He sagged forwards, his lower lip hanging down.

'But Kev – surely that always happens with psychology experiments. It's a free country. People sign up for these things voluntarily and they're free to pull out. Some of them always will.'

'You're not getting it.' Kevin spoke with uncharacteristic vehemence, clenching his fists on the table. 'All the dropouts are from the reactor group.'

'Okay, so – not the control group. Not so far. That

could just be random variation. I see your problem though. If too many reactors drop out, the study won't be valid. But four surely doesn't get you to that tipping point.'

Kevin said, 'Tom, get your head out of your arse and think like a human being.'

Tom swung back in surprise. 'Hey, calm down. What do you mean?'

'All the reactor dropouts give the same reason as… this Sandy person. And Sarah. They can't carry on because the sessions are making them too ill. Worse. More…sensitive. It's' – he shifted uncomfortably on the chair and his voice dropped to an undertone – 'it's making me feel weird about the whole thing.'

'Kev – that's exactly what's bound to happen. Don't you see?'

'See what?'

'Those so-called reactors are totally convinced that RF makes them ill. They've just had what they believe to be a dangerous exposure, so hey – surprise – they start to feel ill afterwards. It's a psychosomatic effect.'

Kevin said, with some bitterness, 'Yeah. And it's even got a name. The nocebo effect.'

'I didn't know that,' Tom admitted. 'Why nocebo?'

'Nocebo comes from nocere which means 'to harm' in Latin. It means you believe something will harm you, and so it does. The opposite is the placebo effect. Which is when you believe something will make you better. And it does.'

'And the placebo effect can be really powerful,' Tom said. 'I read an article about it. People with bad backs took part in a controlled trial and were told they were going to be getting a supereffective new painkiller, and the ones on the dummy pills made massive improvements and started playing tennis and climbing mountains and refused to believe it when they were told they were not getting the real thing. They insisted on continuing the dummy pills even after the trial was over.'

Kevin bent forward into the table and gripped his head with both hands. He spoke hoarsely, his broad friendly features screwed up as though he was in pain. 'But how am I to know which one it is?'

'That's obvious. You have to complete the experiment.'

Suddenly Kevin was on his feet. 'Okay mate, have to go now.' He wrapped the third sausage roll in a napkin and stuffed it in his pocket. 'I'm irradiating another one at half-past two.'

'Come on, Kev, that's not even accurate. You're not using…'

Kevin cut in. 'I know. We're not using ionising radiation like gamma rays or x-rays which are super-high-frequency and cause your electrons to pop out of your atoms which will eventually kill you. We are using non-ionising radiation which has much lower frequencies. All it can do to cause damage is heat you up as though you were a pie in a microwave – and then only if its power is strong enough. And all the stuff we're testing with – and all the stuff used by Wi-Fi and phones and so on – is far, far below that thermal level. So – *no heating, no problem.* Isn't that what you were going to say?'

'Well – yes it was...'

'I've heard it,' Kevin snapped, and turned his back on Tom. As he made his way towards the café exit, people greeted him – they always did – but he responded only with mechanical grins and nods.

Tom stared after him. An outburst like this could only mean one thing: Kev was getting seriously stressed. He'd always had a tendency to jump to conclusions that were dramatic or interesting, in advance of the facts. There had been the incident in the shared house with the boy called Sean, or was it Dean. Small, twisted, bony, nervous-looking, shaved head with prominent bumps. He had lived in the attic room and mostly stayed there, never hung out in the big kitchen/living area in the basement like the rest of them, just skulked in occasionally to abstract mysterious wrapped parcels from his section of the freezer and smile placatingly before he slipped upstairs. Kevin had asked one day in a friendly way, 'Hey mate, what's in the packages?' and the boy had jumped two feet and stammered 'N-n-n-nothing' before he'd scampered from the room. Kev had become completely obsessed. 'What's he doing up there?' he had constantly asked. 'I bet he's got one of those disorders when he can't eat in front of other people. Or he eats really weird food. Or perhaps he's murdered someone and the packages are body parts, cut up small and neat…'

The reality had been more prosaic. The tenancy agreement had a no pets clause: Sean/Dean had been keeping his beloved lizards surreptitiously in his room. The packages were frozen mice, purchased to feed the lizards from the reptile section of the pet shop.

So here Kev was, at it again – believing he had discovered some exciting new phenomenon, rather than confirming a boring accepted truth. And anyway, if he thought that dealing with the forces of nature was free of human complication, well – Kev was wrong.

CHAPTER 5

The tutorial room had white walls and a hairy blue carpet. It was on the top floor of the physics department – the fourth – with a south-facing window stretching along one side. Pigeons would perch on the outside sill, and gaze through the panes with unnervingly single red eyes, cooing throaty critiques of the equations scrawled on the whiteboards. Beyond the pigeons arched the swaying tops of trees, a mysterious fractal sea. Tom liked this room, its height, the sense it gave of a rare privileged glimpse into another, inaccessible world.

Four tables were pushed together in the centre of the room and around them sat six first-year physicists. Over the last week they had attempted a set of problems about simple harmonic motion, and now waited with the usual range of expressions on their faces: smugness, boredom, bemusement, terror.

A keen, pure-voiced girl called Rachida, who wore tortoiseshell spectacles and a hijab, was eager to give an opening definition: 'Simple harmonic motion – it's when you've got a thing, an object, right, which moves backwards and forwards through an equilibrium point' – she drew arcs back and forth with her finger in the air – 'and the maximum displacement each side of the point is equal?'

'That's right,' Tom said. 'And where might you find simple harmonic motion in the real world?'

'A pendulum swinging.' That was from Jen, a large-boned, sporty girl, always in trainers and tracksuits and complicated vest tops, her crinkly red hair yanked into an explosive ponytail.

'A weight on a spring. When you pull down and set it in motion.' Rashida, miming expressively.

'Atoms in a molecule,' said someone else. 'They vibrate.'

'They do. Their movement can be modelled using the movement of a spring. So – when will the movement stop?'

This wasn't in the questions they'd been given. The tutees turned uncertainly to each other. Finally, Neil, square, blonde, pink-cheeked like a twelve year old cherub, with ears that glowed red each time he tried to speak, whispered tentatively, 'It…won't?' Tom nodded encouragement and Neil whispered some more: 'It will carry on…unless there are other forces that would cause some energy to be lost.'

'On and on and on…' A colourless drawl embodying the entire pointlessness of everything cut in from the table's far end. Dylan. Who else? Skeletal, black-clad, grey-skinned, his face obscured by an irregular dyed-black fringe. Intermittently brilliant, when he bothered to turn up. He always brought with him a faint animal smell, as though he curled up each night with dogs.

'Okay, we've got our object moving backwards and forwards. When's it going to be moving fastest – at its maximum velocity? And when is it going to be moving slowest? Would somebody like to draw out their graph?'

Rachida bounced up eagerly, pushing her spectacles higher on her nose and picking up a purple pen. 'So the object starts at one side and it's not moving at all and then it starts moving slowly but gets faster and then it's going fast fast fast through the centre' – her purple line rushed steeply upwards – 'but then it slows down' – the line began to curve over – 'until it reaches its maximum distance from the centre, and then it actually stops completely and then it gradually speeds up again and then whoosh through the middle and slows up again in the other direction.'

'That's it,' Tom said. 'Now, who can draw the graph of the acceleration – which is the rate of change in the velocity? Neil – you have a go....Yes, it's the same curve, but shifted along a bit. Because the maximum acceleration comes at the point when the velocity is actually zero – getting moving again requires the biggest *change* in speed.'

Dylan tipped back on his chair, levering one foul grubby trainer against the table edge, and began swinging himself backwards and forwards. The room seemed too warm this Friday afternoon, and Dylan's odour particularly pervasive.

To prove that something was moving in simple harmonic motion, it was enough to show that its acceleration was proportional to its distance from the centre point. The tutees wrote out the equations which demonstrated this, and then went through the problems, working out speeds and distances in different oscillating systems. As the class went on, the bruised feeling was starting again on top of Tom's skull, as though someone was digging, trying to breach the bone.

'I didn't do the next one,' Jen declared. 'I thought it had to be a mistake, because we haven't done anything like that yet.'

A snort of contempt from Dylan. 'God, woman, use your *brain...*' Seeing Tom's face he hoisted both palms in mock supplication. 'Hey, sorry, okay. Jen, I'm totally sorry. That was completely *unacceptable* and *inappropriate.'*

'Dylan. One more comment like that and you can leave. Now – this problem. It's presented differently to the others, but actually the tools we need to solve it are just the same. We know the final answer, and two of the earlier terms. So we use the same equations...

and then swap them round.'

'I did that!' beamed Rashida.

Jen wrinkled her broad freckled forehead. 'I think there should be a warning at the top,' she said, 'if there's going to be a different sort of question which we haven't done before.'

'The thing is, Jen,' Tom said patiently, 'when you're doing physics for real, often problems come up that you haven't met before in exactly that form, and you have to do a bit of lateral thinking to work out how to tackle them. So it's a good idea to practise.'

'It should say that, then,' Jen persisted. 'That there's going to be lateral thinking.'

'But there's always going to be lateral thinking,' burst out Rashida. 'That's what makes physics so... so...wonderful!'

Dylan's scornful guffaw had generated too much momentum. With a strangled yell he lurched forward, eyes bulging, fringe flying, avoiding by the finest of margins crashing backwards onto the floor. Titters eddied round the group. Dylan didn't blush, didn't comment, just stared blankly straight ahead.

Tom generally enjoyed teaching, but today it felt like trying to excavate a pit in a morass of agglutinating swamp. He kept flicking glances at the clock, and finding, on each occasion, that a shorter segment of time had passed. On top of his skull the digging had morphed into continuous pressure, a drill bit determined to bore through into his brain. Usually on

Friday afternoons he would expect to get in a couple more hours of work, but – not today. When this class was finished, he was heading straight home.

CHAPTER 6

'Oh, you poor old thing,' Marianne said, when she came back from her evening Green Group meeting and found Tom slumped on the sofa. 'You do look miserable. We ought to take your temperature properly, with a thermometer.'

'Have we got one?' asked Tom, vaguely.

'In the bathroom cabinet,' Marianne said, 'and I'll make you a hot lemon and maple syrup. That's much better than coffee.' She arched delicate eyebrows at the cluster of beige-rimed mugs.

'Thanks, you're a star.' Leaning back Tom smiled up at her and she bent down and stroked his hair.

'I've probably got it by now,' she said, 'but I won't actually kiss you, just in case. You don't mind?'

'Don't worry, I'll cope. We don't both want the lurgy.'

Marianne pouted when she took his temperature. 'Normal,' she said, shaking the thermometer. 'Maybe I'm not doing it right.'

'Perhaps it's a cold, or some flu that hasn't got going yet.'

'I know what I'll do,' Marianne said, her eyes lighting up. 'Garlic is antibacterial, antiviral and anti-inflammatory. I'll make garlic soup. There's a recipe online I've been wanting to try.' She paused in the doorway to wink at him over her shoulder. 'After all, we've established that it doesn't matter what either of us smells like, at present.'

Later, in the garlicky fug of the bedroom, Tom groped for a configuration of limbs which might grant him some rest. The drill on the top of his head started up and subsided, started up and subsided, in teasing sadistic waves. The whole of his upper skull felt tender now, as though hammered all over by some conscientious geologist. A sensation of pumping, of pressure, filled his torso and limbs; he could almost believe that he must be emitting a sound – a hissing or roaring, like a turbulent stream. But Marianne lay beside him, her sweet symmetrical nose pointing upwards, sleeping the sleep of virtue, entirely undisturbed.

By lunchtime the next day, which was a Saturday, he was tired, but all the pain and pressure had gone. Marianne was delighted. 'I'm sure it was the soup, Tom. You couldn't have got rid of such a nasty bug so quickly, otherwise. Please can I post about it? I've already done pictures of the soup, in those blue bowls we found at the car boot sale, with little croutons on top, and a blue flower beside them…'

'Yeah, they look great,' Tom said languidly from the sofa when she showed him her phone. 'Do it, if it makes you happy. But you can't be sure about the causation, from just one example…'

'Yes, I know that, Tom,' Marianne sniffed. 'I'm not submitting a paper to a physics journal. I'm just sharing an interesting case study that might help others. I'm not stupid, you know.'

Tom had been in his office after lunch on Wednesday when the thing in his head started up. Skipped the tapping stage this time, decided to go straight to the drill. Soon his eyes felt as though they were being fried, his throat as well as his nasal passages hot and dry. He'd got rid of the thing on Saturday, had been fine for the next three days. Why was it happening again?

I just don't have time for this, he thought.

For the next thirty minutes he braced himself defiantly in his chair, tried to concentrate on his notes. All that happened was the pressure on his head grew more intense and the heat in his mucous membranes began to mutate into scrapings, pricks and needles of pain. His heart surged as though he'd been running for his life.

He glued his gaze to the screen, lasered his thoughts onto letters and numbers, sliced his mind away from the maelstrom in his body, tried to make it float among the calm eternal regularities of the universe.

It didn't work. He threw himself back in his seat, dropped his arms to his sides.

I'll have to go home. Again.

He had no teaching that afternoon. At five he had been due to see Ed for a catch up: he had not been looking forward to it. The article hung over everything – a greasy smoke of ambiguity. He was ninety-five – ninety-seven – hey, ninety-nine per cent sure that his reading of the sequence of events was the right one. But he couldn't shake out that final one per cent of doubt; it persisted, like an awkward piece of grit in his eye. And if he was only ninety-nine per cent sure – what was the best course of action – to take a stand, or to grasp that conference pass with both hands? In his head the options were still doing their complicated dance routines.

Clattering out a message to Ed – 'Really sorry – have to postpone this p.m. due to flu' – he packed his backpack and left, walking slowly to the bike park, an anomalous figure moving through the studious hush of mid-afternoon.

'That's strange, Tom,' Marianne said, wrinkling her nose in delicate puzzlement when she arrived home. 'Flu doesn't usually come back like that. I'll make some more garlic soup. But you probably ought to go to the doctor.'

Doctor? He couldn't remember the last time he'd needed one. There was a University Health Centre, a semi-circular brick building with glass doors that lurked behind the central admin block. Presumably he was registered there? Lackadaisically he negotiated a jungle of drop-down menus on his phone as he lay on the couch, booked a slot on Monday with a Doctor Peter Trepanne. I bet by tomorrow afternoon I'll be fine again, he thought morosely.

It took a bit longer, in the event. Having spent Thursday at home doing some reading on his laptop, he found that by the evening everything had passed, apart from the residual bruised feeling over the top of his skull.

On Friday he went back to campus early. Settled into his office, got down to some useful solid work. After two and a half hours, on the top of his skull, that strange preliminary crawling tightness he had begun to recognise, and dread.

He yelled soundlessly at his body: stop. Stop it. Please. Please – don't do this. Don't let it happen all over again.

In response the thing picked up the drill bit and dug it in.

The thing was taunting him, mocking him, playing deliberate games. Lying low, so he assumed it had gone away, then leaping up to ambush him once more.

I can't go home *again*, he thought, I've got a class this afternoon.

Burning and scraping round his eyes, as though someone had handfuls of hot gravel, and was rubbing them well in.

I have to find another way to make it stop.

Think. Think back. Analyse. What do you know?

First occurrence: a Thursday. Felt he'd had a bug coming on. Wanted to cry off football; ended up taking Sarah to the trees. Hadn't slept well for a couple of nights.

Second occurrence: last Friday. Came on during his afternoon class, he had gone home at four. He'd been fine by Saturday afternoon. Marianne had made garlic soup.

Third occurrence: this week. Wednesday. Started after lunch, had gone home at 3.30, recovered by the following evening.

Fourth occurrence: today. Friday. Started two and a half hours after he arrived.

Looking at the evidence, he could draw three tentative conclusions:

The first – so far, it had only happened when he was on campus. It had not happened elsewhere. The second – if he removed himself from campus, he recovered the next day. (Great. But WHY for God's sake? Already this was sounding crazy.)

The third – and despite the drilling and the burning

a chill ran through Tom as he acknowledged it – the thing was not staying the same. It was – developing. Happening more frequently. Becoming more intense. Taking longer to go away.

On Monday he would explain it all to the doctor. Lay it out clearly and rigorously as he had just set it out to himself. But what about now, today, this afternoon? If his analysis held, he needed to remove himself from the campus straightaway, to stop the thing getting any worse. But he did not want to go far, so that he could come back to start his class at two p.m.

How far was far enough?

Time to experiment. By now, he had nothing to lose.

He logged out of the computer and picked up his backpack. The corridor outside his office was silent and deserted, lined with phalanxes of pale blue doors. Each sealed a warm white cell with its busy, contented occupant. At the end he hurried down the three flights of stairs, grasping the metal handrail; the aim was to move as quickly as possible, but at the same time not to keel over.

Outside the morning was a jet of iced water in his nostrils, the sky cleared of clouds as though they had been carefully vacuumed away. Low ornamental shrubs bordered the tarmac path; their leaves had turned a rich blood red.

When he arrived at the central grassy square, he

entered one of the avenues of cherry trees that crossed it from corner to corner. Along the south side the university library stretched, three stories of brownish brick striped like an unprepossessing mega-sandwich with two bands of black tinted glass. An elfin figure in a bright blue coat and a knitted ethical hat emerged from one of the central doors and trotted down the library steps.

Marianne. Tom stiffened within his lines of trees, pulled his head into the collar of his anorak. He found that he had a strong antipathy to admitting he was ill again. In particular, he did not want to explain what he was doing, perhaps because he was not entirely sure himself. Above all he did not want to *stop,* waste time, when every throb of his head and stab in his eye reinforced the message: you need to get out.

Risking a swift glance backwards through the trees, he saw that Marianne had turned to her left at the bottom of the steps and was moving away from him along the library's main front. The spike of tension in his chest released.

Down the shady side of the library. Past the Arts Theatre. He was in the farther reaches now, coming closer to the edge. Sports fields lay in front of him, acres of slick glistening grass. Rugby goals reached towards the sky, like the symbols of some mysterious cult. Football goals squatted, more baglike and prosaic. On the far side, awaiting him – the shimmering golden trees.

In the clearing, the two wooden benches had been decorated with a scattering of yellow leaves. Brushing one seat clear and arranging his backpack as a pillow, Tom lay down, bending his knees so that his long body would fit. For a while he looked straight upwards at the patterns made by multitudes of golden discs, moving infinitesimally against the blue. But soon his eyes closed. Here he had moderate distance from the campus, seclusion, and – most important – privacy. No one would ask him solicitous questions; he could conduct his experiment in peace.

CHAPTER 7

'Oh Tom – that's so lovely! You went forest bathing!'

Marianne lay propped up on one elbow on top of the duvet on her side of the bed, wearing her blue pyjamas with the bird and leaf pattern. Darting forwards, she planted a swift kiss on his lips.

'I did what?' Tom was nonplussed, but gratified by her reaction. Marianne smelt of lavender; her damp brown hair rose up in eager enthusiastic tufts.

'Forest bathing. It's a thing – really it is. It's Japanese originally, Shinrin-yoku. It's supposed to be so good for you. Claire put a post on the Green Group page about it. I'll show you…' She reached over to her bedside table for her phone.

'Well, I didn't do any of that,' Tom said, when they'd read the post together. 'I mean paying attention to my various senses. I just collapsed on the bench and lay there for nearly four hours. What was so amazing was it worked. I felt so much better. I went back in and took my Friday afternoon class which I thought

I'd have to cancel. And I didn't want to do that, not at present. I don't want any favours from Ed...'

'I'm so pleased for you.' Marianne leant over and kissed him again. 'I'll just post a comment about your experience – everyone will be so interested.' She sat up cross-legged, thumbing intensely. 'And I've made the point,' she said when she had finished, 'that it's another argument for our campaign against the proposed new bypass. People need green space with trees, it's vital for our well-being. The new road would go straight through Hollerby Wood.'

Tom smiled up at her. 'So you'll argue on behalf of people as well as rare bugs and birds?'

'On behalf of everything,' she said stoutly, 'and everyone. We're all part of the great web of life. Every form of life is precious and makes its contribution to the whole.'

'Hey – come here.' Folding her in his arms he pressed his face into the downy whorls in the nape of her neck. 'What bothers me is that you could convince everyone in this country to think like you, but there will still be people in India and China who want cars and meat and foreign holidays and are just getting to the point where they can have them. We could end up roasting anyway, despite having done the right thing.'

'Oh, it would make things a bit more comfortable though, don't you think? The inner chill of virtue...'

Tom yelled as she slipped a small cold hand inside

his pyjama top. 'Oi – hey – you…'

She was giggling helplessly as he erupted from the duvet, but when he was kneeling above her trying to pinion her arms she grew still and earnest again, her eyes huge and glowing as she put her hand up to stroke the side of his face. 'Tom, I know it looks bleak. But the future – it's not out there already. It's not fixed, it's not set. It's the outcome of millions of actions we're all taking, every minute, every day. Just influence a few of those actions, and they start to influence others. Habits and norms start to change, there's a tipping point, things that were once accepted just – fall away. And the world is getting more interconnected every day. Look' – she had her phone again, was scrolling through – 'we see stuff from people in America; here's how they stopped a road in California. Here are some climate change protesters in Strasbourg. And in India too. I have hope, Tom. I really do.'

My shining girl, he thought, and was very moved. She shone a light on the mess of the world, as she so often did, made the way through the labyrinth clear. She had clarity and passion, properly orientated; in comparison he felt complicated, lumbering, sceptical. But she took him by the hand and led him through.

He bent down and kissed her very deeply, hoping his tongue would convey at least a part of what he felt. She made small twists and happy moans.

*

The doctor was a youngish balding guy with a trimmed beard and a shaved head, who'd looked blandly at Tom through unnervingly rimless spectacles that seemed to float in place with no visible means of support. He checked Tom's neurological signs (normal) and sent him for an ECG there and then in the medical centre (also normal). Finally, he steepled his fingers and pursed rather pink lips, saying that Tom's symptoms sounded a bit like migraine, a bit like an allergic reaction, a bit like a panic attack. He would investigate further, arrange for blood to be taken to rule out other conditions. Did anything make things better or worse?

Tom told him about the campus and the trees, trying to sound very sane and rational and calm. He sensed the next question before it came: was he under stress at work? And because of the thing with Ed, he had to say yes, a bit.

Did he recall when the very first episode had occurred?

Tom thought back and something surfaced in his mind, which – up to that point – he had forgotten. He had been in Ed's office, his respected supervisor calmly offering to recommend him for a conference place. His brain had been reeling, his thoughts tangled, an obscure squirming sense of having been violated wriggling through his body – and among all of this the bruised feeling on the top of his head, as though someone had dug at his skull with a spoon.

That had been the first.

The memory brought him up short. Was he actually going mad because of Ed? Developing some weird stress reaction to the whole place, simply because of him? This needed thinking about before he'd be ready to admit it. 'Oh, somewhere on campus, definitely,' was all he said. The doctor suggested he keep a symptoms diary, note down what he'd been doing and what he'd been eating and what he'd been feeling when things got worse. There was an app he could get for his phone. There was also a prescription for anti-migraine meds, 'to try, and see how you get on.'

After he'd left the medical centre, he'd been at his desk for five minutes when – kapow – it had all started up. He'd checked the time and calculated quickly. Since he arrived on campus, he had lasted barely two hours. Two sodding pathetic hours.

So here he was, forest bathing all over again, sitting on a bench stained dark by overnight rain, listening to residual subdued dripping that started up and stopped, started up and stopped, as water slopped its way to the earth. Around him leaves stealthily abandoned the golden canopy; not enough, yet, to make a noticeable thinning, but it would come. There would be a critical mass: when it was reached, the absences would swiftly swallow up the final hangers-on.

Gradually the stabbing and scraping in his eyes

ceased and the thudding on his skull subsided to a dull ache. Soon he would be able to go back to the physics block, if his previous experience was correct. He wanted to scream.

CHAPTER 8

Marianne came trotting over the sports fields in her bright blue coat and stripey woollen hat, carrying over one shoulder a large red square canvas bag. The low autumn sunshine caught her and all her colours glowed.

Ducking and twisting deftly through the branches she arrived at Tom's bench, pink-cheeked, bright-eyed, softly panting. Without speaking he reached out and pulled her towards him, wrapping his arms around her, pressing his face into the rough material of her coat.

She leant down and kissed his hair. 'My poor boy. It must be awful. To have to keep running away to the trees – when all you want to do is work.' When she had freed herself from his hug, she put the red bag down. 'Now – let me show you what I've brought.'

With the proud air of a conjurer producing a whole litter of rabbits from a hat, she lifted out package after package and arranged them on the bench. 'I got two boxes of salad. I've got the spicy carrot cake you like. And vegetable crisps. And I filled up my flask with hot soya chocolate from the vending machine and borrowed an extra mug.'

That Thursday morning, Tom had come in late, having spent the first hour strategically working from home. He had lasted in his office from half-past nine until just after 11:15. (One hour 46 minutes. Down from one hour 57 minutes the previous day. One hour 59 minutes, the day before. A minor perturbation? Or a downward trend that was significant? He was becoming obsessed, had the stark black lines of a graph permanently tattooed on his brain.)

Just over an hour into his recovery, he did not feel like eating a large vegan feast. But she had made such an effort. 'Thanks Marianne. You're a legend, as they say.' He reached for a spoon.

'Ooh – before we start,' Marianne whipped out her phone, 'shall I take a picture – of us and the picnic? It's actually quite lovely here, in among the golden leaves.'

If she takes it, she'll post it, Tom knew. Hashtag forest bathing or some such. She had a lot of followers on Instagram now – over 4000, when he had last looked. 'Marianne – if you don't mind – don't. I'm… a bit embarrassed about what's happening to me. I kind of – don't want to publicise what I'm having to do.'

'Oh. I just thought it looked romantic.' She shrugged. 'But if you're sure.'

'Thanks.'

Tom spooned his way through half of his salad as Marianne munched companionably at his side. Birds flitted about in the canopy, and as the glade regained its stillness, some ventured to the ground. 'Look – I think those are bramblings.' Marianne pointed to five or six brown-headed small birds with striking orange breasts which were rummaging in the leaf litter among the long grey roots. 'They like beech woods, according to my app.'

'They've got the colouring for it,' Tom said. 'What about that one? He's different. He's got a blue head.'

'Chaffinch,' Marianne replied. 'Chaffinches and bramblings like to flock together. I think they're related.'

A noisy skittering made them turn round, a branch above them swayed, and a grey bushy-tailed form leapt to the outstretched limb of another tree. A second squirrel followed close behind and the glade was suddenly the centre of rustling, scampering movement as the creatures chased each other round and round. Tom and Marianne caught each other's eye. 'What's all that about?' she said, comically arching a delicate brow.

'Something really important in squirrel land,' Tom replied. 'Perhaps Squirrel A nicked the nuts off Squirrel B. Or the other way round.' Suddenly they were both laughing.

'I feel a bit guilty,' Marianne said, a while later. 'I

don't know if you've remembered, but I'm supposed to be going away this afternoon for a couple of days. It's the Green Network activist conference, near Manchester.' Her hand sneaked onto his thigh. 'But I don't want to go, if you're having a bad time.'

'Go,' Tom said, with decision. 'Honestly, you should. I'll manage okay. I'll work from home as much as I can, and come here to the trees when I need to.' I'll need an umbrella, he thought, or even a tent for when it rains. A flask for hot drinks. Hat and gloves – it's going to get colder.

'Thank you, sweetie. I am looking forward to it.' She darted a quick kiss onto his cheek. 'I'm hoping to get so many new ideas for Green Week. I'm on the committee this year and I'm a bit nervous about the responsibility, to be honest. You must text me all the time so that I know you're okay.'

'Sure.' He picked up her hand. 'Hey – I'll be fine.'

'Look – I'll show you some pictures of the venue. It's this really cool eco-lodge place, with straw bales as insulation…. Oh…. Oh, I can't…. Yes I can…. No, gone again.' She frowned as she fiddled with her phone. 'The super-whizzy new Wi-Fi upgrade works brilliantly everywhere else, but I suppose they didn't worry about the squirrels. Oh!…. Got it – look.'

Photos flicked past on the glowing screen, but Tom registered no more than a vague impression of tasteful creams and browns. He felt beyond himself, detached, everything fuzzy and unfocused as though some important control setting had been knocked massively out of alignment. Marianne's pure high voice spoke on in excited commentary but he could not distinguish her words. Part of her last remark had snagged on his brain, repeated itself over and over, the only clear thing in the fog. Deep in the core of him something began to pull apart, the tiniest tiniest slit, like a barely smirking mouth. He tried to press it shut, clamp it together, but things began to push their way out.

Questions – they were questions, with their sharp curved tails, hooked over like scorpions.

How many weeks….

When did it….

Can it happen like….

Stop. STOP. This is crazy. That mad girl got to you. Messed with your head. You are not one of them. You cannot be one of them. The thing does not exist. If it did – which it doesn't – it *could not happen to you*. Because….

Because?

Because I am not a phoneless freak.

Over that slimy questioning opening, slam a cover down. Nail it on, good and tight. Move mental furniture on top of it, so the edges can't be seen. 'Are you all right?' Marianne was asking, turning her face curiously towards him. 'It's an eco-lodge, Tom. You look like I've been making you watch a nasty video.'

'Oh!' He shook himself and forced a laugh. 'Sorry.

Look, I've just remembered…something I need to do. On my phone. Quite urgently.'

He hadn't meant to say it, it had just slipped out, because the questions under the furniture still moved, like an infestation under the floorboards; he could sense their muted rustling, and he'd realised in a spasm of unwelcome enlightenment that he had the answers, if he wanted them; they were there for the trawling, in the sleek black device in his hand.

Marianne checked the time. 'I ought to be getting back anyway,' she said, packing the picnic remains into her red bag. 'I've got a seminar on feminist readings of Milton this afternoon. Are you sure you're okay about the conference?'

'I'm good.' He kissed her goodbye. 'Have a great time. And thank you for lunch.'

He was scanning back through his emails as soon as she was out of the trees. And there it was. Yellow and red university logo. Picture of Vice Chancellor smiling oleaginously, with Project Manager, looking proud. Text full of excitable comparatives: better, faster, stronger signal, more consistent coverage. Part of our commitment to the most up-to-date telecommunications infrastructure. Demonstrating responsiveness to students' needs and concerns. Key enabler for the future. More powerful transmitters, newly installed campus-wide.

The title of the email was 'New Wi-Fi upgrade goes live TODAY!' The date of the email was 11th

October.

Tom switched to his texts, made himself start scrolling three months before that date. There were hundreds of messages, backwards and forwards, to Marianne, Kevin, his mother, other friends. *There at eight o'clock. Where R U? Gone to Tesco. Kiss kiss sexy beast.* Revisiting that innocent time gave him a strange sick feeling of vertigo; those weeks, so recently gone he could almost reach back and touch them, yet so different in quality to now, like silk compared to thorns.

He looked at his calendar. 14th October – his discussion with Ed. He'd already established that that was the first time. Back to his texts: *Kev – might have to cry off football.* Date – 21st October. *Have to cancel; sorry too tired; zonked; weird head thing* – more and more frequently. At first, on Thursdays and Fridays – the problem building up over the week, then improving at weekends: *weird head thing; sorry gone home.* Slowly sliding back to infect more and more of his week: *gone home; head thing again; in trees; gone home, in trees again, gone home, gone home, gone home.*

He had an impulse to fling his phone from him, lob it with all his strength, send it spinning end over end into the shimmering trees with its careful, patient, bloodless agglomeration of the data points of his existence. But, one moment later, the irony of such an action had him clutching the thing to his chest.

As he marched back across the turf the words beat in his brain to the thumping rhythm of his feet: 'Correlation is NOT causation. Correlation is NOT causation.' He was on his way to the physics block for his afternoon tutorial. To teach science, for goodness' sake. To get eager Rashida, and vile-yet-brilliant Dylan, and dogged bovine Jess to think in ordered structured ways. Not to jump to conclusions in advance of the evidence. Not put two and two together and make twenty. Correlation is not causation. Two apparently connected phenomena could be the purest coincidence – nothing more than sheer random chance.

Sitting at the blonde veneer table. Six pairs of eyes. Room warm, sunlight angling in. Pigeons cooing on the sill outside.

Fourth problem out of seven. Centre of mass in a rigid body.

Breathe. Keep breathing. Distract. You've been taking the migraine pills. They've surely got to kick in soon.

Blowtorch in the nose and throat. Hot gravel in the eyes – rubbed well in. Pressure down through the top of the head, like the bit of a pneumatic drill that has finally broken through.

Agonising, tearing, concentrated pain. Worse than it's ever been. Heart accelerating towards takeoff.

Arms, legs, hands tightening, swelling, pressing outwards.

Someone speaking. Dylan, asking a sneering question. Stand up, start to demonstrate on the whiteboard. No, not going to work. White walls slanting sideways, carpet rolling like a hairy sea. Best sit down quickly. Falling over not good.

A4 paper laid on table. Start writing, upside down. Necks crane to see. Figures and symbols dancing, changing partners. Unsustainable. 'I have to leave… you – Rashida – lead the group – discuss the rest – email your answers – sorry…'

Six mildly puzzled stares. Undignified stumble to the door. Push clumsily through. Silent empty corridor.

Escape.

Extrusion.

CHAPTER 9

For the first part of the journey home he walked his bike along pavements, didn't trust himself to ride. Drifts of dying leaves lay scattered over the ground, and once-bright fallen berries had squashed into brown smears. Thick porridge-like clouds were congealing close to the horizon, but in the part of the sky that remained clear floated the ghost of an afternoon moon.

'Do you want to see the moon?' his mother used to say, when he was small, and got restless at night in the stuffy, cramped South London flat. And when, as he always did, he indicated his assent, she would pick him up so that his head looked over her shoulder and she would carry him through the shadowy rooms that felt so different from the day to the window where, that night, the moon could best be seen.

Held in her arms, feeling her warmth, smelling her clean soapy familiar smell, he would gaze and gaze. The moon always calmed him. It shone so white and round and still, beyond the streetlights and the sweep of headlights and the neon shop signs that lined the high street where their flat perched on top of a bookmaker's. The moon did its own thing. You couldn't switch it on and off. It wasn't always there – it turned up in different places and it showed you different shapes: a glowing football or a ball sliced right in half, a shiny white banana, a thin silver smile. It gave him a sense that things went on, regardless of people – mysterious, bigger, impersonal things, and that sometimes you might glimpse those things, if you looked through the right window, at the right time.

Perhaps that had been the beginning. Or perhaps it had really started later, when he had had that extraordinary bit of luck in the charity shop two blocks down from the flat. Charity shop. He'd known the words since he was very young, recognising the interesting staccato rhythm long before he could say them, making the association with the whoosh and clatter of hangers pushed interminably along rails as his mother searched, patient, disciplined and thorough, the way she did everything, and with the smell, which was like the essences of lots of different people, pressed together and squeezed. Tom would run to the back of the shop where the toys and books were, and conduct his own search there. They went in so often that the manager and the volunteers got to know them. But his mother was never very chatty.

Other people would stand for hours regaling the shop with details of their fights with the landlords or with the Department for Work and Pensions. But his mother believed in *keeping your head down* and *not drawing attention to yourself.*

One day when Tom was ten he had been walking past the shop on the way home from school and a shape in the window had made him jerk to a stop.

Was it really that?

In the charity shop?

That would be – amazing. Slowly he turned his feet and crept towards the glass, as though any hasty movement might cause the shape to kick up its unwieldy legs and scuttle away. The shape had pride of place in a new display; instead of the usual dresses and shoes someone had mustered a metal-framed tennis racket, some balding yellow balls, a dartboard, board games, a large plastic water pistol – and *it.*

Three wooden legs, black, each with a butterfly screw at the knee joint, holding up an angled white cylinder. Tom twisted his neck sideways and pushed his face against the glass, which misted up from his breath. At the end of the cylinder he could just make out a glass disc.

Oh! It had to be.

He pushed through the door of the shop. Liam was the volunteer on the till, a thickset understated shy young man with spiky mouse-coloured hair, emerging from some unspeakable past. Tom went up to the counter. 'In the window – is it a telescope?'

'Yes.'

'H-how much is it?'

Liam went over to the window, reached in behind a screen of paper and examined a price tag around the telescope's leg. 'Fifteen pounds.'

Fifteen pounds!

All of the money that Tom and his mother had was divided into pots. There was the pot for paying the rent. The pot for gas and electric. The pot for Tesco's on Saturdays. Getting the bus. Lunch money. School supplies. Everything was calculated and portioned out. Tom had practised arithmetic with his mother, knew how to turn money per month into money per week, they'd worked it out together, 'so that he would understand,' she had said.

There was also a pot called 'fund for emergencies'.

Was this an emergency?

Tom felt desperately that it was. To buy a telescope new must cost hundreds of pounds. But while he waited to find out, the telescope might disappear. Racked by indecision he shifted from leg to leg. Liam had returned behind the counter and stood stolidly staring into space. Tom had a brainwave. On Saturday they'd been in the shop when a tall woman with knee-length boots and a commanding voice had strode to the counter holding an enormous cuddly lion cub. 'I intend to buy this for my granddaughter. She will absolutely adore him,' she had boomed. 'But

I can't possibly take it now. Can you keep it behind the counter for me and I'll buy it when I come back this afternoon?'

'Certainly,' the manager had said. 'We can keep it for you for twenty-four hours.' And the yellow thing had been jammed behind the counter to glare out at the customers with its bulging glass eyes.

That was the way to handle matters. Tom drew himself up and marched to the counter. His voice squeaked and quavered more than he would have liked, but he said, 'I want to buy that telescope. The one in the window. Can you put it behind the counter until I buy it tomorrow?'

Liam jiggled one finger in his ear. 'Leave a bit of a gap in the display.'

'Oh you could easily fill that,' Tom said, looking hastily round the shop for items with a sports theme. 'There's golf clubs – or... football boots or....' He tailed off. Liam climbed heavily into the window and jumped the short distance back to the floor with the telescope clutched to his chest. Tom gasped. Didn't he know? The tube was full of lenses – made of glass.

'Keep your hair on,' Liam said. 'Look. I'll put it behind here.'

When his mother came home that evening she told Tom he had done exactly the right thing. He'd been quick-thinking and resourceful and of course they would buy it tomorrow.

All that night the things he might see with his

telescope had danced through his head – planets, stars, galaxies, the close-up face of the moon. From that point onwards, space had drawn him in, and drawn him on – to work hard at maths and physics, to go to university, to explore the colliding black holes of his PhD.

And now – one hour. He'd lasted one feeble useless hour. Slowly, inexorably, the route to his future was closing, a heavy implacable barrier sliding stealthily across his way. Only a slim gap was left now, that he could barely wriggle through.

'This thing – it progresses.' Dark ferocious eyes under a sweat-caked fringe. A sadist's steel-like grip. He shoved the memory down, down into the weeds, but it kept bouncing to the surface, like an inconveniently buoyant corpse. He heard over and over again that urgent, passionate, reckless voice: 'If you ever think…if you ever start to suspect…don't ignore it, don't mess with it. Act, don't delay.'

The skin crawled on the back of his hand where she had left her mark. 'Act,' she'd said. That meant – if the thing were real, of course – there must be something he could *do*. Something that might halt the progression – keep that door jammed open, force it back against its apparently inexorable glide.

I can look, Tom thought. I can look tonight, quietly, without telling anyone. No acceptance, no commitment. Just – to eliminate the possibility.

CHAPTER 10

So – here he was, in the cheerful yellow kitchen at Honey Lane, sitting at the pine table by the radiator, while beyond the window glowed the remains of the November afternoon. In front of him his laptop yawned, an efficient compliant portal, baring rows of QWERTY teeth. Languidly the empty bar of the search engine stretched itself across the screen, and the cursor winked at him.

Mentally he scrolled through his other options one last time; found them as unpalatable as all the other times he'd checked.

He lifted his hands to the keyboard, clattered off the words that he had wiped from his skin but had stowed in some back pocket of his brain. Pressing enter he felt a nanosecond spurt of hope: there would be an error, the page would not be found. But the obedient web served it up: www.reactorrights.org.

Across the top of the screen appeared a blue band with a logo: two overlapping golden Rs within a protective golden ring. To the left of the ring was a red dot with a series of black concentric arcs – the international symbol for radiation. The same, reversed, appeared to the right. The longest arcs on each side brushed the outside of the ring. But nothing went inside.

Tom read the text in the centre of the page: 'Old, young, black, white, rich, poor. People who love tech. People who hate it. Intelligent people. Stupid people. Artists, scientists, cleaners, teachers, delivery drivers, engineers. Yes – becoming a reactor is a totally equal opportunities activity, and it's happening all over the world.

'Becoming a reactor is known as "turning", and each year, more people turn than the year before. Which means being a reactor is becoming more common, although still extremely rare. It's like a lottery win in reverse – your odds are hundreds of thousands to one.

'If it's you who's hit the jackpot, well – we can't exactly say congratulations. But you have come to the right place. Remember the "Hitchhikers' Guide to the Galaxy"? (If you do, you must be one of our older visitors. If you don't, it was a small chunky computer-type thing, full of useful info for the 1980s interstellar traveller, and on the outside it said DON'T PANIC).

'DON'T PANIC.'

This at least was obscurely reassuring. Tom clicked Read More.

'Why do some people turn and others don't? At present, we've got absolutely no idea. But for a particular individual, turning is often associated with the introduction of some new source of RF in their neighbourhood, workplace or home. People who turn get symptoms after exposure to RF. But the symptoms are different for each individual and within each individual they can vary over time. It's what gets called a "multi-system disorder".

'The type of RF which people react to can vary as well. Some people are fine with certain frequencies, but made violently ill by others. The most common reactions include head pain, sleep problems, heart symptoms, nausea, burning of the skin and eyes, visual disturbances and tinnitus. But there are many more.

'These phenomena are not new. From the 1930s onwards, thousands of workers in the expanding radar and radio industries began to present with collections of symptoms including headaches, palpitations, dizziness, sleep disturbance and fatigue. The condition was given a name, "radiowave sickness". NASA described the same symptoms in military personnel working near radar systems, in 1981.

'What seems to be happening now, as everyday RF exposure grows, is that a related form of sickness is developing in the general population. But perhaps not surprisingly, given the wireless industry is now worth around £4–5 trillion per year (that's around 5% of global GDP – somewhere between the percentage shares of Japan and India), it is now labelled psychosomatic.

'The telecoms industry argues that its products emit RF at power levels far below current safety standards, so no harm can result to anyone. But these safety standards, introduced in 1953 and never revised since, only take account of thermal effects. That is, they make sure that RF radiation is not powerful enough to physically heat up living tissue during or just after the period of exposure, the way microwave ovens heat up food. However there's actually a lot of evidence that RF can cause biological effects at power levels far *below* those which cause heating effects. These are known as "nonthermal effects".'

There was a link for a list of peer-reviewed research papers investigating nonthermal effects. When Tom clicked it, he found he had wandered into a half-strange, half-familiar world. He recognised at once the conventions of scientific publication. The names of the authors who had collaborated on each paper, making a kind of international poetry: 'Esmekaya MA, Ozer C, Seyhan N; Dasdag S, Akdag MZ, Erdal ME, Erdal N, Ay OI; Carlberg M, Hardell L; Chen Q, Lu DQ, Jiang H, Xu ZP'. The references to the volumes of the learned journals where the papers had appeared, so that other scientists could easily track them down: '*Biophysics* 55, p. 1054-1058;

Neurological Science 38 (6), p.1069-1076; *Review of Environmental Health* 2015; 30 (4): 251-71. Here were the precise descriptions of methods and materials; diagrams and graphs of results; the application of statistical methods to establish whether the results were significant; the careful, understated conclusions.

Used as he was to particles and gravitational waves, the subjects of the papers were new to him. He was introduced to rabbits with Wi-Fi antennae placed close to their right sides; followed rats round mazes designed to assess their spatial learning and memory; met mice, carefully exposed over an extended period to five hours of RF each day.

Compared to the control groups who received sham exposures, the rabbits had their heart rate variability and arterial blood pressure increased. The rats found the mazes measurably harder, and had more markers of inflammation in their brains. The mice showed more hyperactive behaviour, and inside their brains the sheaths which protect the nerve fibres were wearing away.

He learnt that 'sacrificed' is the term used when laboratory animals reach the end of their short but informative lives.

Rats again. Reduced melatonin in their pineal glands. Rats. Higher levels of two markers of oxidative stress in the tissues of their testes, liver, lungs and heart. Oxidative stress, which had been linked in humans with age-related diseases, like diabetes, and

Alzheimer's, and cancer.

At this point, the rats had a rest. Tom found himself reading about cells from the surface of the lens in the human eye. Exposed to RF, a type of unstable oxygen molecule increased. The result? Oxidative stress.

Ten studies analysed together, dealing with the effect of RF on human sperm. Some studies had exposed sperm samples in the lab, while some had observed the mobile phone habits of human subjects. The conclusion? How much the sperm moved – and how many were alive rather than dead – were both negatively affected by RF exposure.

The relentless stream of title after title gave Tom a vertiginous floating feeling, as though he had opened the back door and instead of the step down into the courtyard garden, had found himself on the roof of a tall building, with an unfamiliar city spreading out all around. He had scrolled through the detail of perhaps twenty or thirty papers; there were thousands. Not all had found evidence of nonthermal effects; but in so many categories, the site made clear, the majority did.

Why isn't this talked about? Why isn't this known?

The site went on to explain. 'Advisory groups on RF safety contain only experts who take an industry-friendly "thermalist" view. Other experts are available, but they don't get appointed. When the advisory groups write reports, the research showing non-thermal effects is dismissed as "not consistent", minimised as "not relevant to human health", combed over for minor flaws which are then held wholly to negate the results, spread around different sections to avoid it having to feature in the reports' conclusions, omitted entirely, or simply subjectively described as "not convincing".

'Don't just take our word for it. Here's Professor James Lin, formerly part of the key international RF advisory group, who in an article entitled "Science, Politics and Groupthink" deals with precisely this issue: "The tendency to dismiss and criticise positive results and fondness for and eager acceptance of negative findings are palpable and concerning."'

Okay, Tom thought. So being affected by RF at very low levels isn't totally physiologically implausible. But what does all this stuff mean in practice?

He clicked on a link which said 'So – if you are a reactor, what can you do?' and found at the top of the new page a big blue SORRY, shivering and weeping blue tears.

'Sorry – there's basically only one answer to this one and you probably won't like it. People out there will try to tell you to:
    – Try cognitive behavioural therapy!
    – Eat lots of fruit and vegetables!
    – Take exercise!
    – Switch to organic food!
    – Drink eight glasses of water a day!
    – Do yoga!
    – Take up mindfulness!

– Try relaxation techniques!

– Put crystals around your computer!'

Each item on the list of suggestions winged its way in from alternate sides of the screen, in a different coloured font with an appropriate image, and Tom wished the reactorrights designers had been less keen on their gimmicks. But on the other hand if you had to tell people something this unpalatable, you might as well have geek fun with the experience.

'All fine and lovely, but a total distraction. As we've said, there's basically only one answer: if you've turned, you need to avoid as much RF as you possibly can. Reduce your exposure in every practicable way. Give your body the chance to rebuild its resilience. You might find, in the future, you can tolerate small amounts of exposure once more.

'You might. If you're lucky. Unfortunately there are no guarantees. But we'd seriously recommend that you try it. Why? Because often, with cumulative exposure, the condition progresses. People start reacting sooner, more intensely, in more parts of their body. And they take longer to recover, afterwards.'

Tom sat upright, his fingers tightening over the plump backside of the mouse. This was what was happening. The progression. The intensification. That inexorable closing of the door.

But it was the next line of text that made his stomach coil: 'Also, the sensitivity can spread beyond the original trigger. So people start reacting to other wireless devices as well.'

Other wireless devices. Such a dry abstract phrase to denote such an unimaginable enormity. The world was full of 'other wireless devices'. It would be like being a fish who was allergic to the sea.

People who reacted to the radiofrequencies used by wireless devices to communicate were known as Phase 1 reactors. But something else could happen, when the condition became more advanced, and that meant there was also a Phase 2.

And when it became extreme – a Phase 3.

But these were so shocking that Tom deliberately steered his eyes away. What he had read was enough.

The digital clock in the corner of the screen flicked to 19:28. Powering down the machine and closing it, he took his phone from his pocket, and found texts from Marianne, asking if he was okay. 'Tough day, better now. Early night. Miss you.' he typed, taking refuge in vagueness. Then he switched it off and laid it down next to the laptop, so that together they formed two sleek black windows in the striped and knotted pine.

There is a way out of all of this, he thought. There is an escape hatch in the floor which can drop me back with a bump into the normal world. All I have to do is accept the thermalist position and dismiss everything else I've read.

He tried to nail the statement across his mind – the statement that had been welded there so firmly just a month ago – 'RF harms no one'. But the fixings were feeble and loose, the board kept slipping, the words would not stay in place.

It would be very strange. Almost unimaginable. Like giving up some physical capacity which had always been a part of him: his sight, his taste, his speech. Like having one of his limbs swiftly, cleanly cut away.

The end. The end – of gratuitous instant access, the gratification of anything, anywhere. Those infinite pleasurable micro-hits of connection knitted into the fabric of his days. What would it mean to be wired? He tried to imagine. To be tethered, to have particular places where you went to go online or to speak on the phone. The rest of the time to move about in a void, silent, mysterious, somehow chaste, in communion only with the people close by.

But it had to be worth trying. To make the campus friends with him again. Make it welcome him without vomiting him out soon afterwards as though he was some putrid piece of meat. Jam his foot in that door as it slowly closed on his future, brace himself against the frame and push push push until he'd shoved it open again.

If this was the mad ransom he had to pay for the return of his resilience – he would pay.

He stood up slowly from the table, steadying himself against the kitchen door frame, marvelling at the lump of resolution he now carried within him, that had formed itself so unexpectedly, like lava solidifying, within the last half-hour. Slowly he moved into the hall, like a person in a dream, preparing to perform surreal actions that he never would have contemplated in his life before – oh how the world had looked different than. Now, everything familiar was reversed, like images from an infrared camera: bright but empty sky rendered black, dark live trees aglow with silver light.

Tom walked into the living room and crouched down behind the couch. On the floor in the corner the discreet oblong router lurked, quietly exhaling the thing on which his contemporaries based their lives, that natural, normal, unquestioned good. He squatted and watched the router for a while, and it was black and sleek and slightly curved, and its four green eyes were unblinking as it breathed. Am I really going to do this? he wondered. But his resolution was firm and it held. He reached round to the socket where the router was plugged into the wall and clicked off the switch. On the other side of the room, the cordless phone for the landline sat in its cradle on a little table. He reached down and switched its power off too.

CHAPTER 11

'Oh Tom, it was wonderful,' Marianne said, hugging him in the living room when she arrived home. 'Some of the speakers were really inspiring. And I've picked up some great ideas for Green Week. But it's lovely to be home with you. How have you been?'

'Better,' said Tom. She was so small-boned and delicate, he lifted her easily off her feet as she wrapped her legs around his waist and they kissed for a long time. 'Goodness, you have perked up,' giggled Marianne, as she slipped down. 'Now, I must show you these' – sliding her phone from her jeans pocket – 'there's lots of photos of the venue, and the group, and where we went on the wildlife walk.'

'Marianne, there's something…'

'That's funny,' she said, her elfin face puckering, 'it says it can't access the Wi-Fi. I'll try again. Have you been having problems with it while I've not been here?'

'Marianne, stop.'

She looked up, unnerved by his tone. 'What's the matter, Tom?'

'Look, I need to explain something.'

'Explain what?'

'I'm sorry, I will explain, I promise. Could you turn off your phone, though?'

'But – don't you want to see the pictures?'

'I do – of course I do, but there's something I need to explain first, then you can show me on the laptop later. The Wi-Fi's off.'

Marianne stared at him. 'Off? But...why?' She cast hopelessly around the room, then remembered the router and advanced towards it. 'Look!' she said triumphantly, bending down behind the sofa. 'It's simple! It's just got turned off or something. It just needs switching back on.'

'Marianne, don't. Just stop. Just listen to me.' Tom grabbed her shoulder to pull her away and she fell backwards onto her bottom with a little cry. 'Please, Marianne. It's switched off because I switched it off. I'm sorry I grabbed you, I really am. I was just – well – I'm feeling so much better, I didn't want to wreck it.' Marianne came out slowly, her eyes great brown lakes of reproach; she crept round the sofa to its far end where she curled up, hugging her knees. Oh God, he'd just committed violence against women, or something. Everything seemed to be coming out wrong. He lowered himself onto the sofa beside her and sighed. Start again. From the beginning.

'You know the people Kevin is researching? The reactors?'

She nodded, still staring straight ahead.

'Well – I'm really sorry and all that, but – looks like I am one.'

Her head swung round, arched eyebrows leaping like a bird lifting its wings. 'Tom, whatever do you mean?'

'You know I've been feeling ill for ages – not sleeping, getting reactions on campus, having to hang out in the trees?'

'Yes, but…'

'Two days ago I did an experiment. I switched off all the RF in-house. All of it. And – oh Marianne – it was amazing. I just slept and slept, for nearly fourteen hours. It was quarter to eleven in the morning when I woke up. And I felt – I still feel – it's difficult to describe, but – kind of *clean* – as if I've finally had a really invigorating bath, got rid of layers of built-up muck. I just lay under the duvet, stretching out my arms and legs, thinking Wow. Just – wow. Because I recognise myself again. I'm back.' He grinned at her, willing her to join in. 'This is how I used to be.'

'Tom, I'm so pleased you're feeling better, but you said it yourself: reactors – the symptoms aren't actually real. They can't be real.' She reached out and earnestly clasped his hand. 'The levels of RF in Wi-Fi and so on are too low to have any physiological effect.'

'I know I said that. I was wrong. I've read stuff online, and – my symptoms – everything – it all fits. Absolutely.'

Marianne let his hand fall, giving a wriggling twitch of frustration. 'Tom, Tom – you know what the internet's like. It's full of crazies and every sort of conspiracy theory out there. Some people think the government is poisoning us with the contrails of aeroplanes. You mustn't jump to conclusions because of something you've read online.'

'It's not just that. Can't you see? I checked back, worked out when it started – which was just when they switched on the new Wi-Fi on campus. And there's the fact that I felt better in the trees, where the Wi-Fi is really weak – you told me that yourself, that was part of what put me onto it – I've got you to thank! Hey' – she looked so white and stricken, time to reassure her fast – 'it's not the end of the world. We can still have the internet. Come into the kitchen and I'll show you what I've done.'

'The kitchen?' Uncertainly she followed him. 'Look!' He'd bought an extra little table from one of her favourite second-hand shops, with a red Formica top and tubular metal legs. It fitted neatly against the wall by the door and his laptop sat at one end, a stout black ethernet cable emerging from its side. 'I've set up a wired internet connection. There are two ports on the router, so I can connect you up too, at this end of the table. It'll be fun – his and hers. Or if you think I'll put you off, I'll set you up in the living room instead. Oh – and I don't know if you spotted it – I bought a new landline phone as well, corded, to replace the cordless one. It's black – quite cool and retro, although we won't be able to take it upstairs. I've diverted my mobile calls to it and I'll do yours too, so we can keep the mobiles switched off in the house...'

'Tom...I thought...I thought we said...' She was propping herself against the table as if she was about to keel over.

He reached out, concerned. 'Hey, you look terrible, sit down.' He pulled out one of the pine chairs.

She shook her head, went instead to lean against the fridge with her back to him, one hand hiding her face. 'I thought...' Her voice was feeble and cracked, holding back sobs. 'We said we'd make decisions together...about the house...'

'I know, I know. I realise it's a shock. But what else was I supposed to do – go back to feeling like death, keep all the RF pumping away, because you might have views on the styling?'

'It's not the styling!' The words burst out in a modified shriek. 'All this "Oh let's just use the landline, go online in the kitchen, it'll be fine" – it won't be fine. It doesn't *work*, for all the things I do. For tweeting, texting, posting, campaigning, Green Week – everything, everything I'm involved in. I see a detail in our house – like the old junk shop vase in the living room window, with ivy and seedheads, and the sun on it. I take a photo with my phone, I post it, hashtag autumn bouquet. People like it. I reply to their likes, I say thank you, they share it with their friends, I follow them, comment on their stuff in return. Make sure I'm always pushing the environmental message. It's immediate, responsive. This is my life, Tom, it's me, it's everything I care about.'

'I don't believe I'm hearing this.'

'What?'

'Hello? Have you actually been living here the past few weeks? Here, in this house, with me? Your – hey – your boyfriend? Or have you been somewhere off in cyberspace harvesting Instagram likes?'

He was starting to shout, he knew it, but he consciously overrode his instinct to rein back.

'Of course I've been here.'

'Have you actually registered the hell I've been going through? That I've been this close' – he made a savage gesture in her face with finger and thumb – 'to losing my career?'

'Of course I have, Tom. It's been terrible for you, and really frustrating. I get that. But now you've been to the doctor and talked to him and he's on the case. You've got to give that a chance. Not hare off on some crazy theory that you yourself thought was crazy, just last week.'

'I did an experiment. And unlike those useless pills, it's working.'

'You think it's working.'

'And if the whole thing's so crazy, why has Kev's outfit got funding to study it? It must be at least convincing enough for someone to put the money up.'

Like a wounded waif Marianne drifted to the back door. She pressed a hand to the glazed panel and gazed through her splayed fingers to the whitewashed wall that divided their courtyard garden from the next cottage along. After a long spell of silence she turned back to him. 'I'll make a deal with you,' she said. 'I'll do what you want here, for one month, and we can see how it goes. I'll do my best not to use my phone. But you've got to go back to the doctor, and keep talking to him properly. Will you do that?'

Tom relaxed, swept his arm in a generous expansive arc. He would do whatever the doctor suggested, so long as he could keep the Wi-Fi off, keep feeling like this. 'Sure. You've got yourself a deal.'

'That's the first condition,' Marianne said. There was something else? Instantly he was on his guard again. 'The second is – oh, if you really are a reactor, you should prove it. Kevin can test you. As part of his experiment. You should volunteer to take part.'

Tom gazed into her earnest elfin face; beneath its sprinkling of freckles, it was pale, taut and determined. She knows me, he thought in wonder. We've been together for nearly two years. She knows I'm not a crazy person. If it's my word – my judgement – surely that should count for something.

'Tom, you know the mind can do extraordinary things. And you have been under stress recently, at work. You can't pretend you haven't – and it started at pretty much the same time as your symptoms. You'd be the first to say we need to be scientific and objective, if it was the other way round.'

Sure he would. He could practically hear himself saying it. But he found he was prevaricating: 'I'm not sure what the rules are, what's allowed…' What was his *problem*? It was the obvious way forward, but he felt a mulish resistance. Marianne was still looking palely resolute, her chin stuck out and her mouth set. Okay, if this was what it would take. 'I'll talk to Kev,' he said, 'if that's what will make you happy.'

Marianne gave a quick satisfied nod. 'It's such a huge thing, Tom. It's the only sensible way. I haven't actually unpacked yet,' she added. 'I'll go and do that now.'

After she trotted upstairs with her rucksack, Tom remembered the other piece of kit he'd bought. Not at the big out-of-town store where he'd picked up the wired router and the corded phone, but from a place online, one of various suppliers which had been listed on the reactorrights site. He switched the device on as he slipped it out of his pocket. Only one green LED showed now, since he'd made the changes in the house. But – what was this? This hadn't happened before. The thing was spiking now, up into the single red – now the double red zone. Over and over again.

Soft footsteps crossed the floor above his head, and he realised with a thump in his chest that Marianne had switched her phone back on.

He sat frozen, staring at the meter in his hand. Red – red – red. How long was she going to keep it on for? Where had she been going? The bathroom was above the kitchen. The bathroom, where she could lock herself in, not be disturbed, come out all innocent and wide-eyed.

Green. At last, green again. Thank goodness. His pent-up breath crashed out of him. But he watched the meter obsessively for the next twenty minutes, until Marianne came down. She smiled at him, and touched him gently on the shoulder saying, 'Hey, what have you got there – you look like a cat waiting for a mouse to peep out of its hole.'

He'd explained the gadget, then, and her pale cheeks had crimsoned. 'Well, I did put mine on earlier,' she said. 'Briefly. To let people know I was back. And of course to let them know I won't be so contactable. Just for the next four weeks.' As she went past him to pick up the kettle and fill it at the sink, she added, in a hurt undertone, 'You don't have to spy on me, you know. I said I'd do my best and I will.'

He was overcome with shame at her words, wanted to throw the gadget into the recycling bin which stood beside the back door. 'I'm so sorry, Marianne. You've been great. I'm – well – I'm being a paranoid tosser.'

CHAPTER 12

Ed was perching in his habitual position against his desk, hands in the pockets of his jeans, ankles crossed, white trainers gleaming. 'So you're feeling better? That's excellent news. I've been concerned.'

You've been concerned about whether I would say anything about the calculational method, Tom thought. But he said, 'Much better. I've worked out what the problem is.'

'Oh?'

'And it's something that can be easily fixed.'

Ed grinned his wide kindly grin. 'Hey – that's the best kind of problem to have.'

'If I'm going to carry on working here, I'll need all my classes and seminars and my office concentrated in one area, and the Wi-Fi transmitter that covers that area switched off.'

Ed's bushy grey eyebrows lifted to create space above his silver aviator frames. 'Wi-Fi? Then you're telling me you're a...'

'I'm a reactor. Yes.'

Ed folded his arms across his woolly blue jumper, rocked backwards slightly on the desk and let out a long whistle. 'My dear chap, that's – really unfortunate. But you know all this sort of RF stuff is only going to get more prevalent…'

Why did people keep implying he might have a choice?

'Yes. That's why I need to get my resilience back. It's already much better since I went RF-free at home. But when I talked to the campus IT people they were…not exactly helpful.'

Sherry Blakely, the IT manager, whom he had finally succeeded in winkling from her office after battering down ramparts of protective underlings, had stood before him with her feet rotated outwards in savagely pointed fuchsia-pink flats (they matched her lipstick) and her crest of black hair quivering. 'What you suggest is quite impossible.' Her voice had trembled with suppressed outrage as though he had made some indecent proposal. 'My team have an overriding obligation to provide seamless coverage. There cannot be not-spots. It is against the terms of business and the principles set out in the service document.'

'So it's not technically impossible, then?'

Her sallow nostrils had flared. 'That is irrelevant. Now if you'll excuse me, I have a Programme Board to attend.' And she had stalked away.

All in all, the encounter had not gone well. He said to Ed, 'I need you to back me up.'

'Oh. Ah.' Pause. 'Back you up.'

'Yes.'

Raising his left foot Ed thoughtfully brushed invisible mud from his trainers so that their eyes did not meet.

'Coming from you it would have some authority, that I need this in order to do my work.' Tom thought of an analogy. 'Remember when Steve had his motorbike accident? They moved his office nearer the loos, and widened the doors...'

'The thing is...Steve...everyone could see he was disabled...' Ed had his arms wrapped tightly around himself now, and he was shifting his buttocks on the desk. 'People might well say – not that I believe it myself of course – that I was indulging you, that you just needed to get some counselling.'

'They might,' Tom agreed. 'Hey – counselling – I could waste a lot of time doing that. Work through my traumas. Talk about stressful stuff at work. Go back over certain sequences of events. Get obsessed with them, perhaps.'

Ed must know what I'm talking about. He must – but he's not giving any sign. 'Would that be healthy? When I could be moving forward?'

You owe me, Tom added silently. You can put yourself out for me this one little bit. 'I can't see myself going to conferences for a while,' he said. 'I just want

105

to recover, get back to my routine of working here.'

He played his final card. If this was what it took…. 'Ed, if you can swing this for me, I'll be truly, genuinely grateful. For the rest of my PhD. I'll never forget it.'

A flicker – finally. So brief that Tom would have missed it, if he had blinked at the wrong time, or momentarily glanced away. A sort of hunger in the eyes, an intellectual salivation, as though Tom were an apple tree, not large yet, or in full growth, but from which one could expect in the future to harvest many tasty fruit.

Ed had stood up then, stretched his arms out, bounced a couple of times on his thickly cushioned toes. He nodded agreeably. 'Okay, I'll sort it out. It shouldn't be too difficult to arrange. After all, there's a study going on here into reactors. It's right you should be given the benefit of the doubt.' He sauntered round to the other side of his desk and tapped at an open laptop. 'Internal directory…' he murmured. 'Okay, who's Sherry Blakely's boss? Juergen…Humpenback?' – grinning broadly at Tom – 'Really, what an extraordinary name! Let's ring him now.'

Tom walked away down the corridor, dazed and lightheaded. He'd done it! Ed had done it! His supervisor had gone over the heads of the IT lot, got hold of the Director of Site. He'd explained the situation succinctly and persuasively, laying great emphasis on Tom's talent and potential – 'one of my truly outstanding students'. It would be a tragic loss to the university – indeed to physics itself – if this prodigy had to abandon his groundbreaking work merely because of some bureaucratic protocol in the IT department. He (Ed) was sure that Mr Humpenback would take a broader, more strategic view.

After some guarded enquiries regarding what exactly was involved, and an awkward period of waiting while Juergen Humpenback had checked with Sherry Blakely that one Wi-Fi not-spot would not cause the whole system to collapse (Tom visualised the downward swoop of her nose and the furious quivering of her crest), the Director of Site had agreed that such a view could indeed be taken. The necessary work would be carried out that afternoon.

Outside the physics block, Tom stood in the middle of the tarmac path and let the life of the place swirl around him, claim him again. A serious bearded type strode past, carrying an enormous zip-up portfolio. An ancient distinguished professor, bowed over like a brown tweedy tortoise, crept along with a placatory smile. An accusatory girl with blue hair, squinting at her phone, hissed 'Sorry' as she crashed into him. A smooth administrator, suited and shaven to minimise air resistance, tapped efficiently along in leather-soled shoes.

Tom looked up at the sky with its roiling grey clouds, and raising his arms he said out loud, 'I'm back!' It felt as good as winning a penalty shootout with the final kick of the game.

Home sorted. Work sorted. His resilience returning. Somehow, through chance and his own wild contortions, he'd flipped himself out of the mouth of the beast. Not for him that gradual agonising divergence that he'd read about online, had met, in fact, in scruffy black-clad Sarah. He was keeping his life, thank you very much, every last juicy scrap.

But as he walked on he realised something was different. The old Tom would not have made that grubby unspoken bargain. The new Tom had done it almost effortlessly, had found within himself an unsuspected capacity to scrap and hustle to survive.

At least he knew now. All those doubts about Ed and the calculational method – what he had seen in Ed's eyes, that momentary slavering gleam, had been an absolute and total confirmation. Tom himself had been right all along: the idea had been his own. Ed was a bastard. But a bastard he could use. When he had a really interesting idea in the future, Tom would be much more circumspect.

CHAPTER 13

The chair was the executive type, with thick padding covering the seat and back, and a lever to pull which made the seat shoot smoothly upwards to accommodate his long legs. A small plastic shelf attached to one of the arms held pencils, an eraser and some printed paper sheets.

The chair sat alone in the middle of hard-wearing grey linoleum. Originally there had been carpet, but it had been removed after incidents with bodily fluids. The walls were institutional powder blue, the ceiling a grid of white tiles, each about half a metre square. How many? Six along each side. Six by six. No – not thirty-six. Two fewer – thirty-four. In the far corner an anonymous inset had nibbled two away.

No windows. Light from above; three of the ceiling tiles replaced with misted glass squares, giving a diffuse milky glow.

The inset in the corner drew his eye. That must be where it was, the thing that he was here for, boxed in so discreetly behind those unassuming blue walls. The thing that was his opponent in this strange, fateful game.

On a shelf there was a little clock, to show him the time. 2:12 p.m. Twelve minutes gone.

After fifteen minutes, an alarm would go. They would ask him to assess how he was feeling; write down his symptoms, if any, their intensity, fill in the well-being questionnaire. How *was* he feeling? He did a quick scan of his body. The top of his head was tingling gently. Was this the start of something – or just a psychosomatic response to paying it attention? His heart – beating a little harder than usual perhaps – but that was surely a natural reaction to the stress of his situation.

'I am on trial,' he thought. The tension of the accused in the dock. He jumped, when the alarm did go, a shrill bleeping from somewhere outside the testing room. Tom glanced down at the paper log, scanned his body again for any evidence of change, detected – something? Nothing? Decided to write that he had no symptoms. Rubbed that out, wrote down a few and scored them as ones. Rubbed them out again.

He had had two weeks of Marianne's month. At first she kept reflexively sliding her phone out of her pocket, and her delicate hand would fly to her mouth: 'Oh! Sorry Tom, I forgot…' 'Oh! It's just…Laura will have texted me back by now…don't worry, it's fine.' 'I've GOT to show you this…Oh.'

Now she'd taken to leaving her phone on the little shelf by the front door. Her glance would stray towards it as they sat at the kitchen table. If she caught him following her gaze, she laughed, stroked his hand. 'Tom, don't look so worried. I can do this. It's fine.'

Tom found he was subtly performing his wellness, highlighting (in case it wasn't obvious) the contrast between his previous sickly decline and his current astonishing restoration. He bounded downstairs to make her coffee in bed on weekday mornings. He proposed energetic cycle rides on strenuous new routes. He hacked back the interlacing ropes of ivy overwhelming the flowerbeds in the courtyard garden so she could plant overwintering vegetables. He made love to her with imaginative dedication. Look what you've created was his message. By your abstinence you are restoring me. You are restoring *us*.

'It's wonderful that you're feeling better.' Sometimes she phoned him to say she would be staying over at Claire's. 'We had a meeting and it's finished so late – and I need to keep on top of the social media feeds. We've just gone crazy…' This wasn't unusual, in the run-up to Green Week. And this year, she was in charge – there was so much for her to do.

*

'Are you sure?' Kev had said, when Tom explained that he intended to volunteer. 'I mean – I know I need more reactors, but the whole thing makes me feel weird, and with you I'd be…doing it to a mate.'

'I've got to,' Tom had replied. 'I promised Marianne. I've got to prove it to her.'

Kevin had given him a strange, opaque look, rolling forwards onto the balls of his feet and then back onto his heels. 'Suppose….'

'*What*?'

'Suppose it does to you what it did to Sarah. Or to the others who got…worse.'

'Well…I get worse, I suppose, but probably only temporarily. I'm feeling pretty good at the moment. At least Marianne will be convinced. She'll have to believe me then.'

Kevin said, 'I believe you now. I kind of think – she should too, without' – he'd waved his arms at the surrounding psychology department – 'all this….'

'Just sign me up,' Tom had snapped.

This was the earliest slot Kevin had free. Tom would attend once a week for three weeks; his personal results wouldn't be available until well after the end of Marianne's month. He would ask her to extend, and she'd have to agree. He had already gone back to the GP to fulfil the first part of the deal. He had seen a different doctor from last time, a tweedy-looking type with a bow tie and large pale bulbous eyes. 'What can I do for you?' the doctor had snapped, staring at his monitor and clicking his mouse testily. 'I've had a lot of tests recently,' Tom said, 'for my headaches and heart problems and eye problems and so on, and the results have all come back normal.'

'Normal,' repeated the doctor.

'Yes. But the other doctor said I should come back if I still had symptoms. I tried the antimigraine pills but they didn't really do anything.'

'And do you still have symptoms?'

'Well…no. Nothing like as much. I keep them under control by limiting my exposure to radiofrequency radiation.'

'I'm sorry?'

Tom repeated himself, adding, 'I have started to react to radiofrequency radiation at levels that most people don't react.'

The doctor was still looking blank.

'Radiofrequency radiation – it's what makes mobiles and Wi-Fi work? It's how the message gets from your phone to somebody else's without any wires?'

The doctor was typing into his machine. 'No,' he said. 'Nothing on the database. Not in my bailiwick, I'm afraid.'

'Do you think I need psychological help?'

The doctor brought up another screen. 'I can tell you the answer to that,' he said, sounding much happier. 'Can you tell me how often, over the last two weeks, you have been bothered by the following

113

problems? The options are "Not at all", "Several days", "More than half the days", and "Nearly every day". Number one – little interest or pleasure in doing things.'

Tom said, 'Not at all. If I limit my exposure to RF.'

'Number two: feeling down, depressed or hopeless.'

Tom said, 'Not at all, if I limit my exposure to RF.'

'Trouble falling asleep, staying asleep or sleeping too much?'

'No, now that I am limiting my exposure.'

'Feeling tired or having little energy?'

'Much better, now I'm limiting my exposure.'

The doctor ticked 'not at all'. 'Feeling bad about yourself in some way – that you are a failure or have let people down?'

'Well...I did feel like that pretty much all the time, from October onwards when I started to feel ill, but now, not any more.'

'Trouble concentrating on things such as reading the newspaper or watching TV?'

'I did have, as I said before. Because I'd have a terrible headache and eye pain and racing heart and so on. But now I can concentrate fine.'

'And finally, thoughts of being better off dead or hurting yourself in some way?'

'No.'

'Your score is well within the normal range,' the doctor said. 'You don't meet the threshold for a referral for psychological therapies.'

Tom had grinned and leapt up from his chair. Here at least something to take home to Marianne. 'Cheers, doc.' He raised his hand in a cheerful wave as he loped from the consulting room. The doctor stared after him, bug-eyed.

The alarm bleeped again. That must mean half an hour. Nothing definitive happening, so far. He shifted in his seat. Again his eyes wandered to the anonymous inset which bit one corner from the cube-like room. The transmitter was in there, sending out its invisible waves – or not. Perhaps this was the blank transmission. Or the low-power one, and he was less sensitive to that. What are you doing? He posed the silent question to the thing inside the walls, staring intently as though his eyes could bore through plasterboard and paint. But it just kept on without answering, following its impeccable randomised programming.

They were testing to see if he was deluded, and now he was trying to communicate telepathically with inanimate objects. Relax, he told himself. Trust yourself, trust your reactions. You know you're right. It'll be fine. Think about the good stuff that's been happening. Revel in all that recovered normality.

He remembered his encounter that morning with Jen from his first year tutorial group. She'd waylaid him on his walk from the bike racks to the physics block, bouncing up on her complicated trainers, her red ponytail flicking from side to side with an admonitory swing. 'You're teaching us mechanics, right?' she'd said, thrusting a paper in his face. 'This problem that you've set – the last one – it's got optics in it too.' She sounded outraged, as though he'd mixed her sports drink with cocaine. Tom had pointed out that, as the group was also studying optics, and that real-world physics problems didn't always conform obediently to course boundaries, he'd included it to give them a taste of the later exams. 'You mean we have to do this sort of thing *in the exams*?' Her ponytail had nearly swung full-circle.

'Jen, you can do it. I'll prove it to you.'

'I've got a lecture at 10.'

Tom's personal dead zone was right at the back of the building, in the furthest corner of the ground floor. His office had been moved into an old windowless store cupboard and all his classes rescheduled into the seminar room next door. It would have taken a few minutes to walk there, and another few minutes for Jen to walk back. 'Let's have a look here then.'

There were a few low chairs near a drinks machine just beside the main entrance, so they had sat down to work the problem through. 'Oh. Oh, I see,' Jen had said, her habitual dour, cross, impatient expression abruptly transformed by a glorious, gleaming-toothed smile. Tom had spent more time than he had intended out of his dead zone, but he hoped he wouldn't have too many repercussions.

Too many repercussions.

And when might he expect to start feeling these repercussions?

Quite possibly – now.

Now. This afternoon. Here, while he was doing the experiment. While they were testing his reactions to that thing inside the wall.

He sat rigid in the executive chair.

So if I start to feel ill now, how am I to know which exposure I am reacting to? The one from this morning with Jen – or the one which could be happening now?

And the answer came back loud and clear, as if the thing in the corner had addressed him through the wall: *'You won't.'*

And if I won't know if I'm reacting to the transmitter or not....

Helpfully the thing finished his sentence: *'Neither will anybody else.'*

But in that case....

Sweat blossomed in his armpits and streamed down his back. He shoved the plastic shelf aside and the pencils and record sheets scattered over the grey floor. An instant later he was on the other side of the space, hammering against the door. 'Kev, Kev, get me out of here. Kev – let me out....'

The door opened smoothly inwards, and he was forced to stumble back. 'Hey, calm down. You only have to turn the knob,' Kevin said as he entered. 'We don't lock you in. Are you all right, mate? I'll get a bucket if you're going to be sick.'

'I'm fine.' Tom shouldered past him into the corridor and leant against a wall as horror flexed through him like a wave. 'It's your experiment that's fucked. Stop the transmission, or whatever it is. It's pointless to go on.'

CHAPTER 14

Kevin had scampered after him all the way back to the dead zone but Tom had scarcely heard his exclamations and pleas. Now they faced each other across Tom's desk, the bland fake wood a no man's land between them. Kevin was panting, his face was damp. 'Okay, I get it. You needed to get back here. Now we are here. So tell me what's going on.'

'I told you: the experiment is a pile of shit. You might as well put random numbers in the rest of your spreadsheet. Throw darts. Toss coins. Anything you like. I can tell you what the result will be – now.'

'What do you mean, tell me the result? I don't understand, Tom. You're not making sense.' Kev's slicked-back hair was divided into distressed dark chunks which flopped down over his ears. Tom was suddenly very tired: he wanted nothing more than to go to sleep, right there in his chair, in the warm cramped cupboard office, to go to sleep for a very long time and let someone else untangle this mess. This mess, this travesty, this monstrosity, which had somehow been conceived, had grown, had been vetted and agreed and funded, had bred rooms and staff and structures and budgets and institutional approval – all of which would now have to be unpicked. He leant slowly back in his chair, stretching his arms over his head. The ceiling tiles were punched with tiny circular holes, as though infested by some geometrically obsessed insect. He heard himself speak, as though he was observing the scene on a video feed from a long way off: his voice sounded cold, weary and detached. 'The experiment will find that the accuracy of the reactors' responses and the correlation of their reported symptoms to the transmission strength is no different to the control group. It will find both are no better than random chance. It will prove that reactors don't exist.'

Kevin gasped. His eyes went round and huge. 'But – how – does that mean....'

Tom stretched his mouth into a mirthless grin. 'And it will be totally, utterly and completely wrong.'

'But we took every precaution. You know how carefully it was all set up – the shielded room, the control group. Double-blind, placebo-controlled, the gold standard in research methodology. I admit I've had some qualms, because – well, you know, the effect it has on some people – but I kept going. You told me to keep going. And since you've become a reactor, every time I've had to mop up the room, or another one of them dropped out, I've said to myself, "Hey, I've got the opportunity to help my mate Tom, and all the people like him."'

Tom bowed forwards over the desk, rested his forehead in his hand. Oh God, the *mess*. And it couldn't have happened to a nicer guy than Kev. 'I know,' he said, 'I've been blind. And – oh – perhaps I wanted it to work too much. I really wanted there to be a way to prove it. So I didn't think, I didn't look too closely. But I understand now, stuff I didn't understand before. I understand what the condition is really like. And why your study won't find any trace.'

'So – explain.' Kev sat back in his chair and folded his arms.

Tom still felt so tired and detached and chilled. Somehow he had to rouse himself, express his thoughts clearly – now, more than at any other time in his life. He reached into a desk drawer and took out a large bound notebook, flicking through scribbled equations until he found a blank page. 'Okay. So –' He swivelled the notebook sideways across the desk and pointed with his pen. 'Your experiment is based on the assumption that if a reactor has an exposure, they get a reaction – which is fair enough, as far as it goes.' He sketched two symbols and drew an arrow between them. 'But the reaction isn't an on/off reaction. It's not like when you turn on a TV and it lights up and you get a picture, and then you turn it off again and the picture goes away. Your experiment assumes that an exposure at a given time – let's call that time t – results in a reaction at that time, or fairly shortly afterwards. We could write that assumption as $e(t) = r(t)$. But reactions don't always develop immediately, or even within the hour. Sometimes I've felt fine for a few hours afterwards but then terrible in the evening or even the next day. And in your study, these delayed reactions simply don't count at all. They're being missed.'

Kevin was poring over the notebook, his wide face pulled into an almost comical grimace of concentration. Tom went on. 'And there is the second problem: the whole extra dimension which reactors call "resilience". That means how much they react to any particular exposure depends on their prior state. So if they've been careful – and lucky – for a few weeks, and avoided things, they may get more resilient. So they might cope with the first exposure in the experiment without reacting directly – but it would reduce their resilience so that when the second exposure comes along, the next week, they react a lot.'

Tom was starting to relax now, warming to his theme. 'So r – reaction – is dependent on both e – exposure – and p, where p is prior level of resilience. But the experiment takes no account of that. And the third thing: well, it's a consequence of the first two, which are delayed reactions and prior resilience. You're not keeping the participants in a clean location for the duration of the study. If you did that, you would know for sure that the control transmissions are the only one they'll be getting the whole of the period. In the current design, you can't even start to control what the poor sods are exposed to in the days before each session, or on the journey there and back. That adds in all sorts of random exposures, which people could be having delayed reactions to in the session – e $(t - 3)$ = r (t) for example, not to mention the fact that these random exposures could be causing alterations in the p variable. That's what alerted me, actually,' Tom said, suddenly sombre. 'This morning, before my session, I ended up sitting in a Wi-Fi area with one of my students for longer than I'd intended. Then, there I was, sat in your hot seat, wondering if and when I'd get a reaction to *that*. And the whole absurdity of the thing hit me in the face.'

Kevin had taken the notebook and was tracing his finger thoughtfully downwards from the top of the page. Inside Tom's head a dry contemptuous voice said, 'God I was stupid to take part in that stupid experiment.' He saw again a pale taut face under a damp disordered fringe, smelled the mixed stench of vomit and blood and sweat. He said, 'Kev – there's also the thing that worried you right from the start. The reactors who are really sensitive – who are most likely to react quickly and strongly to the transmissions themselves – they get so ill that they can't complete. So their results are thrown away.'

Kevin finished his study of the page, and his rounded relaxed presence sagged. Slowly, dejectedly, he began to nod his head. 'You're right,' he said. 'It won't work.' He sounded utterly deflated, as though Tom had opened a valve and let out all his natural bounce. They gazed past each other into opposite corners of the tiny room. A minute or two passed. Neither of them spoke.

Suddenly Kevin lurched across the desk, gripping Tom's arm. 'Mate, I didn't do the research design. You know that, don't you? I was recruited afterwards, once it was all set up.'

'I know. I'm not blaming you. Let go of me, for goodness' sake.'

'My first job,' Kevin moaned miserably. 'My first proper academic job. And the research is dodgy. Just my luck.'

'Yeah – it's rotten. But Kev, we've got to stop it now. Or get it changed. We can't let it be published as it stands. It would be a disaster – for me and for all the reactors. You can see that?'

Kevin blew out his cheeks. 'Yeah, I can see that.' More time passed, dead, cold and flat. Tom tried to guess at the processes going on in his friend's head, hoped they were coming out at the right place. Eventually Kevin sighed and said, 'I suppose I'll have to talk to the Prof.'

Tom nodded, enthusiastic with relief. 'Absolutely. Best to go in at the top. What's her name?'

'Professor Mary Arrowsmith. Very distinguished.'

'What's she like?'

'I suppose – kind of sweet? Late fifties. Bobbed grey hair in a side parting, colourful hair slides. metal-framed spectacles. Chunky red shoes with – you know – a bar, like kids' shoes.' He was sketching with his hands. '*Caring*. A bit motherly. Keen on people's psychological well-being within the faculty. On the Well-Being Committee. Into mentoring – that sort of thing.'

'Do you think she'd listen to you?'

'She likes me, I'm pretty sure about that,' Kevin said, expanding again. People always did like Kevin – it was one of his greatest gifts. 'I gave her stick about going on the razzle at the Cambridge conference, made her laugh.' He chuckled at the memory. 'I'll go and see her.' All his old easy confidence was returning; the room itself seemed warmer. 'I'll set out the whole thing, end-to-end. You'll let me have your notes, mate? I'll put together a neat little presentation, get your input, of course. You should come to the meeting too, to back me up if she starts asking questions. After all, if I don't want to be associated with dodgy research, she won't want the department mixed up in it either.'

Something struck him then, and he looked up with a puzzled expression. 'But hang on, Tom – there is one thing I've got to ask, because she's bound to ask it: why are *you* the first person to point all this out?'

Tom had been wondering himself, more and more, as he'd become enthused with the elegance of his explanation. 'Perhaps I wasn't. You should look back, Kev, at the papers around the research design. Who did they consult? And what did those people say? You always had recruitment problems, right from the start. Reactors didn't want to play.'

'That's true,' Kevin acknowledged. 'Reactor numbers are way, way below what we expected.'

'And the ones who did take part – Kev, think what their lives must have been. Trying to create a safe space in their home, when other people there don't believe them; getting pushed out of their jobs; friends giving up on them because they don't have phones. The merest sniff of a chance of a possibility of validation, of being able to turn around and say to all the doubters, "I'm real" – it's the glint of silver in the desert for a traveller dying of thirst – you don't analyse it, you crawl towards it as fast as you can.'

And it had been just as much a mirage.

Then he thought of something else, and said, reflectively, 'The thing is, Kev, at the start, everyone tries to tell you that you're stressed, you're seeing patterns that aren't really there, you're drawing too many conclusions from coincidence. You have to mount a huge pushback against this great wall of incredulity to demonstrate that there *is* a connection: "Look, look, I turned the Wi-Fi off in the house and now I'm sleeping brilliantly!" The result is people take us crudely at our word. Act like we're machines with an on-off button. Ignore all the subtleties, which they wouldn't do with any normal health condition. Take...' Tom cast back through his ridiculously healthy life, searching for an example. 'A bad ankle – like I had after that idiot from Biological Sciences did a sliding tackle on me in the Thursday match. Some days, if I'd been careful, I could hobble a hundred metres fine, no pain at all. But then if you'd made me do it again the same day, I'd have been in agony after twenty. It wasn't as if every time I walked a hundred metres I got precisely the same degree of pain.'

'Mmmm,' Kevin said, nodding and looking much more cheerful. 'I can see why we might have ended up where we are, without it being anybody's actual fault. I'll set up a meeting and we'll get it sorted. Leave it to me.'

CHAPTER 15

They sat side by side in the corridor outside the professor's room, like two naughty school kids summoned to the headmistress. Passing psychologists gave them curious glances; Kevin attempted light-hearted banter with the ones he knew. But he'd seemed nervous, flicking through his slides with his chin sunk morosely into his chest.

'Do you think she's coming?' Tom said. Their appointment had been for 11:30 and it was now nearly 12. 'Perhaps I should go out to the trees and back... but sod's law she'd turn up.' He began to pace up and down, willing a dumpy bespectacled professorial form to materialise in his line of vision each time he turned round, as though his eyes alone could suck her into view.

'It's a bummer we couldn't do this in your not-spot. We could still get it moved....'

Violently Tom shook his head. 'We agreed − it might prejudice her. We don't mention me being a reactor. Not at all.'

'Okay, I know,' Kevin replied. 'I just say you helped with the equations. Calm down.'

'Well, boys, come in, come in. I'm so sorry I'm late.' Professor Arrowsmith had picked a yellow flowery slide that day, to pin back one side of her iron-grey bob. She had teamed it with thick-soled orange bar shoes sporting an appliquéd yellow flower on each toecap, and a knitted sunflower brooch pinned to her chest. But her lairy taste in accessories did not extend to her main garb. Her rollneck jumper was grey marl, and a mud-hued pleated skirt swung over her wide hips.

'Finance Committee,' she explained, bustling Kevin and Tom into her office. 'Really, the amount of time one spends these days on money. Dispiriting, but necessary, I suppose. Now, would you like to sit down on the comfy seats?'

These were at the far end of the large room, past the professor's formal wooden desk on which photographs of round-faced grandchildren and small Jack Russell-type dogs had rather excessively reproduced. Tom and Kevin ended up on a low rough-textured sofa with tubular legs while the professor sat at right angles on a higher, firmer chair. Kevin placed the laptop on the coffee table and turned it towards her. 'Okay, Prof,' he said. 'Thanks for seeing us.' All his former nervousness had gone; he expanded with the glow of the natural performer. 'Before I start, may I introduce my esteemed colleague soon-to-be Dr Tom Jenkins, from the physics department, who helped me out with the equations. (You'd have guessed they weren't original, you know maths was never my strong point.)'

The professor laughed and crossed her flower-toed legs at the ankle. 'Well, it's nice to meet you, Tom. Good of you to take an interest in our activities. I'm very much in favour of interdisciplinary work.'

As Kevin went through the presentation, Prof Arrowsmith nodded a lot and said, 'Mmmm' at various points. Tom tried to read her face, which remained a mask of empathetic interest. At the end, she rested her head on the high back of her chair and blew out gently through her nostrils. There were a few moments of silence. Then she sat up and said, 'Kevin, I can see you've worked really hard on this, and I'm so pleased you felt able to come to me with your concerns. That's absolutely the culture we are aiming to build in this department. Now, supposing we take your points one at a time....'

The first was the differential dropout rate. Tom squirmed in his seat as she advanced exactly the arguments he'd used himself: that people participate in psychology experiments voluntarily – archly, 'I don't think either you or I would want to live in a country where that wasn't the case, despite the advantages for us researchers' – and they can withdraw their participation at any point. 'And we have to be aware that what they *say* is the reason may not be the real reason.'

Kevin protested, 'But the reactors all say they're being made ill.'

'Kevin, we absolutely accept' – the professor was leaning forward, her hands clasped, her voice oozing compassion and concern – 'that the reactor group suffer more distressing day-to-day ill health than their counterparts. That's what's motivating us to undertake our experiment. We want to understand them so that we and our clinical colleagues can help them. And I'm sure that's what you want too.' She was so confiding that metaphorically she had her arm round Kevin's shoulders and her hand on his knee, although of course as one of the committee responsible for the university's codes of behaviour she would never have done anything remotely like that.

'Surely we can only help them if we get accurate data,' Kevin said. 'And as soon as the more sensitive reactors drop out, we junk theirs. That has to skew things.'

'It is very unfortunate that in a tiny number of cases we have to do that,' she conceded, looking sad and regretful. 'But, taking a broader view: this is such a novel area of study, our experiment has to be conducted so that it's on the same footing as other comparable psychology experiments. We don't want to ask for special treatment, do we, or our results just won't be respected. So – I'm sure you'll remember this

131

from your undergraduate days – clean data, rigorous data, complete data.'

Kevin still looked deeply unhappy. Tom had been trying to stay relaxed, concentrating on his breathing, studying the reflections of the overhead lights in the coffee table glass. He had intended to leave things to Kev as much as he could, but he could not keep silent any longer. He burst out, 'Okay, your data is clean, but it's completely meaningless. Does that not even worry you? It's like you're going fishing for sticklebacks with a net designed for sharks.'

'Ah, Tom. Yes. We've come to your equations.' Smiling warmly, she pivoted her whole body towards him. 'They're very ingenious. But I can assure you we didn't magic up this research design out of thin air. There was an initial information-gathering stage, before our friend here joined the team, and the people who claim to be reactors claimed that when they are exposed to RF they experience a reaction, either straightaway or a while afterwards. They didn't give us any *equations*.' A girlish laugh. 'Now – we can only respect what our participants tell us, wouldn't you agree?'

Tom said, 'But you didn't, did you?'

'I'm sorry?'

'You didn't respect what they told you. You made them carry on living their normal RF-dodging lives. Travel to your lab, getting exposed to all sorts of random RF en route, so that by the time they were sitting in the testing room trying to identify whether at that point they were being exposed to yet another dose, or not, they could have been at all sorts of stages in the reaction process. Then you made them travel home. You might as well put a person with asthma blindfolded into a smoke-filled room, and then ask if they can tell if someone has just lit up.'

Professor Arrowsmith's nostrils flared, white arcs appearing on her strong square-tipped nose. 'Our sponsors have made a substantial investment in this study,' she said. 'The shielded testing room is the most advanced of its kind in the world. What you are suggesting – if I understand you correctly – is that we should have kept all the participants – and it would have to have been all, the control group and the reactor group, you do see that, I suppose' – Tom nodded quickly – 'in entirely RF-free accommodation, for slightly more than their entire three weeks.'

'Yes,' Tom said. 'And even then, you'd still have the problem of cumulative effect.'

Shaking her head she gave a 'goodness me how naïve we are' smile. 'Oh Tom, Tom, Tom. I can see you haven't submitted many funding applications. Or needed to recruit real people for real life studies. What's your PhD in? Ah, black holes and gravitational waves. Well, I imagine you don't have to get their consent, ha ha' – he was getting a little sick of her arch humour – 'or pay them expenses for three weeks of lost time. Here, in this department, we have to strike a balance, between what would be ideally desirable and what is actually practical.'

Tom said, 'What you've just described – it has a name. The Streetlight Effect. It's a classic scientific fallacy.'

Something kindled briefly in the Professor's eyes, but was quickly doused. 'I think we'd all benefit, Tom, if we moderate our language,' she said, with ashy sweetness. 'Especially when commenting on research outside our own specialism. What is this Streetlight Effect?'

Kev was nudging him in the ribs, signalling, no doubt, that he was in danger of going too far. But he felt buoyed up, his mind extraordinarily clear, all the interconnected lines of argument laid out for his selection, as though he viewed the streets of a city from the air.

'The name comes from an urban myth. A drunk man is crawling around on the pavement at night under a streetlight. A policeman comes past and asks if he needs any help. "I'm looking for my car keys," the man explains. "Oh – where did you drop them?" The man points into the darkness. "Over there." "So why are you looking for them here?" the policeman asks, puzzled. "Because the light's better."'

Kevin guffawed, slapped his thigh. 'Hey, sounds like Saturday night outside the Hat and Feathers.' As an attempt to lighten the atmosphere, it didn't work. Professor Arrowsmith ignored him, focused her attention laser-like on Tom. 'And the relevance of

134

that is?'

'If you look where the looking is easy, settle for measuring what is easy to measure because it is easy, you will completely miss the truth.'

The professor gave a yelp. In the centre of each of her cheeks, a red spot appeared, as though two hot pokers had been neatly and simultaneously applied. Tom pressed on before she could speak, 'There's a famous example that shows how dangerous it can be. It's easy to measure heartbeats on a heart attack ward. A study of heart attack patients found that the ones with the most regular heartbeats had the best outcomes. So the doctors gave the patients with irregular heartbeats a drug to regularise them. Guess what happened.'

'No doubt you are about to tell me.'

'A ward full of lovely regular heartbeats. Unfortunately most of the patients died.'

'I don't accept that a medical analogy has any bearing on this case.'

'It does. Survival after heart attacks is a complex phenomenon. The study reduced it to a single, meaningless, easily measurable data point. People acted on the results.'

'You are being ridiculous, and as a scientist I am surprised at you. The natural world – the human psyche – all of them are complex phenomena. To study them successfully we have to break them down. Focus in on small circumscribed questions, tightly defined. Keep some variables constant, while we test others. Then, all these small, focused studies slowly build together to greater knowledge. Naturally, when we publish' – she blinked winningly at Kevin in a consciously inclusive way that said *of course my name will be the lead but don't forget yours will be on it too and in such distinguished company* – 'our paper will be open and honest about the limitations of the study, and include the appropriate caveats.'

Tom had to constrict the howl that surged up his throat. To choose – to make choice after plausible choice. To set up the study in one particular way, hobble it at each point, render it useless at detecting what it was supposed to detect, and then to stand back and say, 'Oh, we made the limitations of the study clear.' The thing took his breath away.

Quietly he said, 'Do you think people will read the caveats? When that central conclusion is so stark and so convenient?'

'Naturally, I cannot force them to….'

'This isn't some obscure study about memory, or learning, or whether people react faster to colours or words, where frankly – pardon me, I'm sure they are fascinating – no one else is particularly interested, outside academia. Your findings here will affect people's actual lives, hugely, irreversibly – whether they can stay in their jobs and their homes; whether others will or will not make any accommodation for them.'

Prof Arrowsmith laughed. 'Now come, surely you are being just a little bit melodramatic.'

'No. I am not. That is just what will happen. That is how …' *Shit.* He'd nearly said it: *that is how we live.* He'd screeched to a stop just in time. Beside Tom, Kevin cleared his throat. 'Prof, there's something I'd like to add here.'

Professor Arrowsmith turned inquiringly as though she'd just remembered he was there. 'Ah, Kevin. What do you have to say?'

Flicking a nervous glance at Tom, Kevin seemed to come to some kind of desperate resolution. He began to speak faster than usual, his words tumbling out. 'You know the dropouts, right, the reactors who only manage one or two sessions before they pull out? The ones we reckon may be particularly sensitive?'

'Yes. I thought we'd dealt with those.'

'Well – before I junked their data – the answers that they did give – I didn't mean to do it but the IT froze and I pressed the wrong button trying to get it working again…' – he swallowed – 'and…I unblinded their results.'

'You did what?' The professor reared up in her chair, her nostrils flaring.

'Unblinded them. And – they were right. All of them. No signal – guess – no signal. Symptoms – none. High-strength signal – guess – high-strength signal. Symptoms – severe. And so on. They were right – but we junked them all.'

When the professor had ushered them out, and smartly shut her door, Tom let out a long whistle as he and Kevin walked away. 'Wow, Kev. Thanks. I… didn't know you were going to say that.'

Kevin was putting one foot in front of the other and staring straight ahead as though, for now, these two activities were the absolute limit of his powers. 'Neither did I,' he said. 'When you nearly said…you know…it just kind of – jumped out.'

'I didn't know you'd done it.'

'Tom, I had to. Of course it wasn't the IT. But she'll never realise that.'

'She still came down on you like a ton of bricks.'

'Yeah. Unprofessional conduct. I shouldn't have looked at the screen. Why didn't I report the fault. Blah blah. I'm still shaking.' He held out his quivering hand, palm down, and gave a watery grin.

'You don't think…?'

'Nah. I'll be fine. Blow over. Don't worry.' He swept his hand to one side, brushing Tom's concerns away.

'I owe you one, Kev.'

'Anyway, we did it. That's the important thing. She said there would be a review.'

'They've got to change it,' Tom said. 'Logically, they can't do anything else.'

CHAPTER 16

Marianne had been asking him all weekend if he felt OK, and he'd just snapped 'I'm fine' and tried to keep out of her way. Now it was seven on Sunday evening and she was in the kitchen making a stew; the pungent smell of sautéing onions wafted up the stairs. The curtains were still open; he hadn't been able to rouse himself from the bed's embrace, although the sky had grown dark outside and the room was cold. In one corner of the window, he could just see the moon, a perfect, voluptuous circle, silvering the surrounding clouds. A faint swirl of music came through the wall behind his head – some sort of classical opera, he guessed, delicate quiet passages building up to stormy climaxes, then falling away again. A new guy was renting the refurbished cottage next door; Marianne had seen him in the front garden and said hello. Mid-thirties, she'd told Tom, posh voice, curly blond hair. His name was Oliver and he worked in TV, and he seemed nice, a great improvement on the previous occupant, who had died a couple of months before. Things had been a bit difficult with Ada Scholes; the old lady had had a number of brazen and incontinent cats, and Marianne had objected to them crapping on her herbs.

Supposing. Supposing – after all – his whole analysis had been flawed. Supposing all that stuff about being a reactor had just been totally, completely...*wrong.* He'd felt so sure, so confident; the contrast between the way he'd felt before and the way he'd felt afterwards had been so compellingly strong. But that had been before the last few days. Here he was, not doing anything differently. And yet the thing was back. Like an overstaying house guest he thought he'd shown the door. The pressure on his head, the revving of his heart. His fractured sleep.

His renewed longing for the trees.

It would be embarrassing to have to admit he'd made a mistake. And if he had – what did the future hold? Back to the doctor, tell his story again, try to explain about being ill whenever he spent time on campus without sounding like a neurotic who just didn't fancy his work? Come clean, finally, about that niggling coincidence, that first weird episode of pain, that had happened as his supervisor had been casually upending his assumptions about who and what he could trust? Admit the possibility he had developed a psychosomatic condition, requiring 'careful psychiatric assessment, and a gradual untangling of the emotional trauma that lay beneath'? Admit that the horrible closing door, which had been measurably, remorselessly shutting him off from the place where more than anywhere else he wanted to be, was something he was doing *to himself*?

The thing felt impossible, utterly ridiculous. But when first faced with a psychosomatic diagnosis, according to the article in *New Scientist*, that was exactly how patients often responded: total incredulity and ferocious resistance. Bold escapes had been staged from psychiatric facilities.

He couldn't say anything to Marianne. He didn't want to face her sad, I-told-you-so sympathy. And of course she'd have immediately put the Wi-Fi back on and started using her phone. And he would swear, he would have sworn – in fact, he was almost still entirely certain – that that would make everything worse.

Through the wall from next door came a discreet triumphal theme, brass instruments exulting in close harmony. Oliver plays his music at a reasonable, considerate volume, at least, Tom thought, I wonder whether he's streaming it and what kind of speakers he's got.

And revelation ripped through his consciousness like a bullet, jack-knifing him upright on the bed, annihilating at a stroke his supine lethargy. Of course. That was it – had to be. He'd bet a million pounds on it. And he could prove it – easily.

Launching himself from the bed, he thundered downstairs to the kitchen, seized his backpack and scrabbled inside for the meter. He jammed on the switch at the side, and watched the lights on the face light up: high amber, spiking regularly into red. In jubilation he raised it high above his head.

'I knew it!' he shouted. 'I knew it! It's changed. I was right!' Then the full enormity swept over him, and he folded abruptly onto a chair, putting his head in his hands.

Marianne laid down her wooden spoon and covered her stew very deliberately with a lid. She turned to him. 'Could you tell me, please, what all of that was about, Tom?'

'Oh God. It's obvious, when you come to think about it. I feel a total idiot for not realising before. You'd have to laugh, if it wasn't so awful.'

'Realising what?'

'Old lady – empty house – refurb – new tenant – hip young guy. Doesn't it say anything to you?'

'Only that I'm pleased those pesky cats have gone, and that Oliver seems a really nice person.'

Tom sighed exaggeratedly. 'What it means,' he said, 'is that the whole house next door is now full of the latest wireless kit and the RF is coming through the walls into here. Which is why I've been feeling weird all over again.'

Marianne looked through the kitchen window over the wall which separated the tiny back gardens of the two properties. The kitchen window on the other side was alive with light. 'Do you really think so?' she asked.

'Marianne, I know so. Look – a week ago, before he moved in, the RF readings in this kitchen were pretty negligible – and now....' He turned the meter on again, and held it out to her. He noticed his hand was shaking. A new neighbour. Such a casual, commonplace, everyday event – yet for him, the whole future was thrown into jeopardy. The yellow walls of the kitchen seemed to tilt, the pine tabletop slide to one side, the grey stone slabs of the floor lift his chair as though it were a boat on an unfathomable, uncontrollable sea.

'Well, I suppose it's natural that he's going to want to have the internet....'

'Yes, I know. The question is – what happens to me?' His haven – the haven that he had created – the reason he had been getting better – had gone. Just like that. Vanished. Destroyed. In the twinkling of a router's LEDs.

He would have to talk to this Oliver character, ask him to switch off. Not all the time – the man might not want to go wired – but at least at night, so that he could have some recuperation. And they could buy him one of those ECO cordless phones, that only transmitted when a call came through. Surely, once he understood what it meant for Tom, what hung on it, surely he would have to agree.

But when he said all this to Marianne, she looked genuinely shocked. 'You can't do that. He'll think we're – you're – he'll think it's madness.'

'Can you find me an alternative?'

She was really thinking, Tom could tell, biting her lip and fidgeting with the edge of her apron. But she did not suggest a solution.

'You could come with me, actually – he's met you. We could do it in a friendly neighbourly way… when's your stew ready?'

'It'll be about half an hour, but I'm really not sure…'

'Well, just time to do it now. Have we got any wine? We'll take round a bottle as a welcome to your new home.'

A tall blond stooping man in plush corduroy trousers and a cashmere V-neck opened the door of number 35. 'Marianne,' he exclaimed, 'how splendid to see you again. And you must be Tom. I'm Oliver.'

He shook their hands. 'We brought you this,' said Tom, 'to say welcome to Honey Lane.' He held out the wine. Scrupulousness made him add, 'And… we've also got a sort of favour to ask.'

'That's fantastic. Just the sort I like. How fantastically thoughtful of you. Come in and have a drink?'

'Thanks. That would be great. Just a quick one

though – we're having dinner soon.'

Oliver's front room had a stripped wooden floor with an expensive-looking abstract-patterned rug, two soft leather Chesterfield sofas, low lighting, a large, wall-hung flat-screen TV, and a trendy hi-fi system, with sleek black cylinders, from which music poured. Oliver switched it off with a remote and said apologetically, 'Götterdämmerung – I do hope I wasn't disturbing you?'

'Oh not at all,' said Tom and Marianne simultaneously, as they perched on a sofa's edge.

'So – are you settling in OK?' asked Marianne when he had served them with glasses of wine. 'It's a nice neighbourhood, we think.'

'Fantastic,' said Oliver again. 'Love the local shops – I had some panini from that artisan bakery which were quite as good as any I've had in London or Italy.'

'Do you like farmers' markets?' enquired Marianne. 'There's a really lovely one every month at Parrott's Cross.'

'Do they have goat's milk? I'm looking for a local supplier.'

Marianne and Oliver chatted on about local food. Say something, Tom told himself, with rising desperation. Tell him. But how to explain? Which were the best words? He had to get this right.

'Oliver,' he blurted, 'that favour we were going to ask.'

'Sure – please – anything I can do.' Oliver made an expansive gesture with his blue cashmere-clad arms.

'Well – I've been having health problems recently and I've worked out that they're caused by being sensitive to radiofrequency radiation – the stuff that comes out of Wi-Fi and mobiles and so on.'

Oliver looked perplexed. 'I beg your pardon?'

'Wi-Fi makes me physically ill. It's like – an allergic reaction. I get really bad symptoms. It's happening to more and more people, actually – they're researching it at the university.'

'Goodness. Well. That must be difficult for you.'

'It is. But I can just about manage if I've got a place to sleep that's Wi-Fi free. We've got rid of ours completely and got wired. But now yours is coming through the wall. So what I wanted to ask was – would you consider turning yours off at night? So that I can get a rest?'

Oliver lounged in his leather sofa and draped one arm languidly along its backrest. 'What an extraordinary request,' he said, arching his eyebrows.

Tom held his gaze. 'Yes, it is, I know. But it would make such a huge difference to me. To us.'

'Well, no can do, old chap, I'm afraid. Got to have connectivity, it's the way things are these days.'

Tom thought: How do I play this? The stakes are so high. Suddenly he was pleading with a stranger for his home, his career, his fate resting loosely in those long-fingered, well-manicured hands. If he begged too much, showed how much it mattered, Oliver would likely think him mad. The utter crazed imbalance of their positions floored him.

In the end he said, 'I'm really sorry to hear that. Could you tell me a bit more about why you couldn't?'

Oliver tilted himself elegantly upright on his sofa, placing both feet on the floor.

'I don't think it's actually any of your business, my friend. I have an extremely erratic schedule, with my TV work, and I often use my devices at night – for both work and play.'

'All night?' Tom asked, despairingly. He was thinking of the possibility of some sort of timer switch that could perhaps turn the router off at 2 a.m. and on again at 7. It would be something.

'Yes – all night. Or potentially at any time of night,' Oliver snapped. 'I don't sleep well. I like to catch up with…things, in bed.' He flushed slightly.

Time to play a final shot. 'Well, nice to have met you, Oliver. I hope you can reconsider what you've decided, because if you don't, I'm going to have to move. I actually won't be able to live here any more.'

Oliver raised a sceptical eyebrow. 'Surely that's a little melodramatic, old chap. An Englishman's home is his castle, as they say, each to his own – not really on to interfere with other people's household arrangements.' He got up, affable once more, and ushered them into the hall. 'Absolutely splendid to have met you both.'

And then they were outside, standing in the street in the chilly early December night, the row of cottages silvery-roofed in the moonlight, quaint, closely packed, neighbourly. From inside Oliver's cosy lair, Wagner stormed forth again.

Marianne's delicate hand crept into his. 'Come back inside, Tom, you knew it was very unlikely to do any good.' He shook her off like some importunate pet. He needed to think, before the pressure in his head turned his brain into mush.

Get away. Get right away, his instinct told him. No point in going to Kev's – shared house, three other guys, full of Wi-Fi, neighbours on both sides. Find somewhere properly low-RF, away from everywhere, in among trees. Sleep there tonight, hopefully start to feel better.

Then – tomorrow – try to work out what happens after that.

He rushed into the house, ran upstairs to the bedroom. Reaching his rucksack down from the top of the wardrobe, he stuffed a sleeping bag and a fleece inside. He pulled on some thick socks and his walking boots, an extra jumper, his anorak and a fleece hat, opened a drawer and added a torch to his inside pocket. Then he walked downstairs to Marianne. She was ladling stew into two bowls of brown rice.

'Marianne, could you put some of that in a thermos? I'm out of here.'

She stared at him.

'But…where are you going?'

'The moor,' Tom said shortly. 'There's a dip in the middle with trees, and no mobile signal. Remember – we found it on our walk.'

'But…it's cold. It's getting on for nine o'clock.'

'I'm going to sleep there. There's a bench.'

Marianne stood with her arms hanging by her sides, her mouth slightly open.

'You are mad,' she whispered.

'No,' Tom said, 'I am making an utterly rational choice.' He rummaged in a cupboard for a flask. 'Now please could I have some stew? I want to go now. I'll walk there – easier to carry all the stuff. I'll be back for breakfast.'

Tears welled in her eyes. 'You'll freeze…Look – if you're really serious – take my sleeping bag too. You can unzip it and use it like a blanket.'

'Thanks,' said Tom. He went towards her and hugged her. Marianne hung limply in his arms. 'Try not to worry,' he said into her silken hair. 'I know it's looking bad at the moment, but I'm sure we can find a way through.'

CHAPTER 17

The ground around the bench was, thankfully, dry, and scattered with fallen leaves. Sitting in a shaft of moonlight Tom ate his warm stew. Then he took off his boots and stowed them under the bench, and wriggled into his sleeping bag fully clothed. He put his rucksack under his head as a pillow and spread Marianne's sleeping bag over him so that it covered his face, a dark tent warmed by his breath. The bench was far too short for his long frame, so he lay flat on his back with his legs sticking out over one arm. The uneven edge of a slat dug into the base of his spine and a rucksack buckle poked his scalp. Shifting his body in search of a less uncomfortable position released an uncanny parallel memory from some storage vault in his mind. He was in the trees on campus, looking down at a figure preparing to sleep on a bench, looking down at first with puzzled, frustrated, irritated benevolence and then with fury and contempt.

Sarah. She'd given him the finger, quite understandably. How she'd laugh if she could see him now.

He woke up to change position several times. But between these wakings, when he would hear rustling in the trees and the quavering hoots of owls, he slept deeply and peacefully for the first time in several days.

He woke as the sun came up and touched the tops of the skeleton trees in the hollow with patches of peachy golden light. There had been a little rain in the night, and Marianne's sleeping bag was damp. Tom moved his limbs experimentally. He was extremely stiff and cold. His toes seemed to have disappeared, until he consciously wriggled them. A young woman in a brown duffel coat with a King Charles spaniel entered the clearing, and came to a brief halt when she saw him, before summoning the dog to her side and moving quickly past as far away as possible, her eyes fixed carefully ahead. 'Am I really that terrifying?' thought Tom, and then, 'But how is she to know?' and had a strange sense that in spending his night in the open, he had crossed some hidden boundary, passed beyond the pale, and was now on the outside of something that he had once been a part of, peering in.

He packed up his things in his rucksack, rubbed his stubbly chin and combed his fingers through his hair. He should go home, work out his next move, but he felt so much improved, compared to the last few days, that he was reluctant to leave his hollow. He was already developing an affection for it, for the way the trunks of birch encircled it like a protective stockade, and the coppery dead bracken mixed with shaggy yellowed grass.

He burst into the kitchen to find a pensive Marianne, her shoulders drawn up to her ears, her delicate hands wrapped around a mug of coffee. 'I've got it!' he cried, giving her a kiss and pulling a chair up to his computer table.

'Well, and good morning to you,' said Marianne. 'What have you got, Tom?'

He clattered at the laptop keys. 'I've worked out what we need.'

'What's that?'

'A van. We've got to get a van.'

'But...but...we said' – faintly – she sounded truly distressed – 'we always said we'd never own a car.... That...we should do without one. Hire one when we needed it.'

'Aha, ' said Tom, 'here's something.... I know we said that, but things have changed a bit, in case you haven't noticed.'

'I...well, yes I have. But why does that mean we have to have a van?'

'Because I've got to have somewhere to sleep. That bench nearly crippled me. I can drive to a place with low RF, and then spend the night there, and drive back again in the morning. Hmmm – I wonder if I could afford this one – could put it on my card, I suppose.'

'How much are you thinking of spending?'

'I can only afford a few hundred. It'd be an old banger, I'm afraid.'

'Oh Tom – they're the most polluting of all...'

It was amazing how little he cared, suddenly, about the future of human civilisation, that feeble, distant, anaemic postulate. The urgent present loomed in lurid close-up: the need for transport and shelter and warmth.

'Oh – this looks possible – hey – this could be really good – look.' He turned the screen towards her. 'It's an old transit. It's got space in the back to lie down in. I'll ring the number straight away.'

The van was still available, and after work he cycled over to the other side of town to pick it up, driving home with his bike in the back. The van was never going to be a looker; it was dusty dark blue on the outside, with patches of mottled orange rust like eczema. But inside, after he'd cleaned it, it wasn't too bad. Quite cosy, actually. Marianne might even be persuaded to make curtains to cover the back windows, and another pair to draw across behind the front seats. After all, he was upcycling something that could have gone for scrap.

*

'Listen, Tom…. This whole thing – it's making me feel a bit…unsettled. Can you tell me what your plans are? I mean – what's going to happen tonight?'

'Well, I'm here for dinner, and I think I'll have a bath, and then I'll drive to Hollerby Woods and sleep there – it's a bit more discreet than the moor – and then I'll be back for breakfast. Hey, do you want to come with me? You can have the camping mat, and I'll use the spare duvet to lie on. Come on, it'd be an adventure!' Marianne's mouth trembled. 'But of course it's absolutely fine if you'd rather not…'

She stood up bravely. 'Yes, of course I'll come.' she said. 'It will be an adventure.'

They left the house at ten o'clock and drove out of the town towards Hollerby Woods. The van had an old-fashioned radio, and they listened to the local radio station, which was playing an hour of classic songs, and they sang along to 'All you need is love' and 'Midnight Rambler' with the heater going full blast. 'Yes,' said Marianne, leaning back in the seat and stretching her legs luxuriously, 'I know it's not environmentally sound, but…well, there's something to be said for personal transport. Here, have a piece of dark chocolate.' She popped a square into his mouth. He laughed with relief; after all, it was going to be all right.

Soon they were driving on a narrow road with lines of tree trunks pressing close on each side, eerily delineated by the headlamps. A deer sprang across the road in front of them, and Tom had to slam on the brakes. A turning on the left led into an unmetalled side road, but as they prepared to pull over in a layby, a car already parked there flashed its lights. 'I wonder what that means,' said Tom. 'Perhaps they're not keen on company. Never mind, there's lots of other places.'

He swung the van round, drove back to the main road, and continued to the next turning. The equivalent layby was empty, and they parked up. 'Now,' said Marianne, 'I brought a flask of cocoa for a bedtime drink, and then we can sort out the beds in the back.'

'Good thinking!' said Tom enthusiastically. 'Hey, I'm so glad you came.' He squeezed her to him.

As Marianne fished in her backpack for the thermos, another car slid into the layby in front of them, parked – and flashed its lights. A man got out of the car, and sauntered over. He tapped on Tom's window. 'Got a light, mate?' he said, smiling. Tom lowered the window slightly. The man was wearing grey jogging bottoms, slip-on shoes, and a V-necked jumper over a shirt. His anorak was unzipped. His hair flopped from an unsuccessful combover and his breath smelt of stale beer.

'No, sorry mate,' said Tom, 'don't smoke.'

The man didn't go away. He looked over at Marianne, with an unmistakable leer. 'All right?' he said to her. 'You got a light, love?'

'No,' said Marianne.

'Nice evening for it,' said the man. 'Mild for this time of year. Haven't seen *you* before, though.' He continued to stand at the window, smiling expectantly.

Tom said, 'Look, sorry, we haven't got a light, and well, we're just having a drink and then we're going to bed.'

He wound up the window. The man did not go away.

'I don't like this,' Marianne said.

Tom suddenly gave a shout of laughter. 'Oh God,' he said. 'I think I've worked it out.' He wound down the window. 'Look mate, we really are just drinking our cocoa here, and then we're going to sleep.'

Another car drove into the layby and flashed its lights. 'I don't believe this!' he said. He handed the flask and his cup to Marianne, 'Here, hold that, drink it, whatever. We're going to have to go somewhere else.' This was the downside, he supposed, though he would absolutely never have guessed it, of trying to find low-RF places near a town.

'What on earth did that man want?'

'He thought...oh Marianne...he thought we were doggers. These woods...they must be some sort of dogging rendezvous. We're right in the middle of it.'

He accelerated out of the side road as another car turned in.

'You mean...he was waiting for us to...you know...'

'Er – yes – 'fraid so.'

'Eugh! What a sleazeball.'

The dark canopy of trees arched over the road and closed off the sky. Another car came towards them, headlights blazing, and sped past along the avenue of trunks.

'This is horrible,' Marianne said, shuddering. 'It doesn't feel safe.'

Tom turned right down a rough track. 'Look, the whole wood can't be full of doggers. I'll turn off the track under these trees, so people can't see the van. It'll be fine.'

'It's probably illegal to spend the night here anyway. It's not a campsite,' said Marianne. 'Have you thought of that? We might get arrested by the police.'

'If the police turn up, they will have other things on their minds. Anyway, I don't have much choice. I'm going to have to take the risk.'

They spent a tense but unmolested night.

CHAPTER 18

Marianne had not come with him for the next couple of nights. She had needed her sleep, because the preparations for Green Week were building to a climax. Each morning they had reunited over coffee and toast.

On Wednesday, Tom had been putting the breakfast things away when Marianne came down after her shower. She said, 'Tom, could you leave that for a bit? There's something I'd like to talk about.'

He smiled. 'Sure, no problem. Hey, you okay? Sit down, you look done in.'

Marianne drew out a chair and perched on it. She was wearing a fluffy green jumper and black trousers; her silky hair, damp from the shower, was combed back and her small elfin face was very pale and determined. She clasped her hands together.

'I've been doing some thinking,' she said. 'The thing is...all this living in the woods, and coming back here, and never knowing where you'll be, or

158

what you'll do next...it's...well...it's getting really difficult.'

She looked down at her hands.

'You're telling me,' said Tom. 'I know it's difficult. I'm sorry.'

'It's...well...it's affecting my uni work...and... other things for me as well.... Oh Tom,' she suddenly burst out, 'the point of having a house is to live in it... that's what they're for...I mean, it's just going to get harder for you, as it gets colder – have you thought of that? And...well...if you don't want to live here...do you think you should find somewhere else to live?'

Tom nodded; he was so glad she'd brought it up, he'd been thinking along exactly the same lines. 'I know. I know the van isn't a viable long-term solution. But I've realised now – trying to find another house or flat will be really difficult – it will be the same problem as with that prat next door. The only possible place would be some sort of detached house that's quite isolated. We should start to look for one. I'm really sorry, I know how much you like Honey Lane.'

Marianne was fiddling with the edge of the table cloth, weaving it between her fingers, head bowed. 'Tom, the thing is...I don't really want to move. This house – I love it, I've done so much to it, it's so convenient for the shops, and uni, and the Green Group and...my friends.'

Tom felt something tighten inside him, the first

stealthy turn of a screw. 'Hang on a minute. So what you're saying is…you want me to move out, and you to stay here.'

She nodded her head. 'Yes.' Quietly, eyes still on her hands. 'You wouldn't have to pay rent, or anything,' she went on hurriedly. 'Claire's looking for somewhere – she could move in.'

Tom sat back on his chair and stared. He felt as though he had been walking casually along a pleasant woodland path, and had suddenly, unexpectedly, walked into a wall.

'You're breaking up with me?' he blurted, incredulous. 'Because of…all this…?' He waved his arm in a vague gesture, encompassing the invisible ruination that pulsed, now, through all the rooms of their home. Marianne's face twisted and her eyes filled with tears. 'Oh Tom, I'm so sorry, I don't want to, I wish with all my heart that things were different, but I just can't see any other way.'

Tom gripped the sides of his chair, to try to stop the shaking that had taken over his limbs. He forced himself to speak in a calm voice. 'So – let's get this straight. We've been together for two years. We've had good times – or so I thought.'

'Oh we have,' Marianne sobbed. 'We truly have.'

'We've been acting like we've got a future together.'

'I know – I know, and that's what I wanted too.'

'And now I've developed a health problem, I'm

trying to deal with it as best I can, I'm still the same person, but you're not interested any more.'

'That's not fair.'

'Isn't it?'

She hung her head. 'It's not like it's just any sort of health problem,' she said quietly.

'So it would be different if I'd got ME, or irritable bowel, like ghastly Claire, or hey – terminal cancer?'

She shrugged hopelessly. 'It might be. At least then…well…it wouldn't be so disruptive, so weird. There would be something…'

Tom pushed himself out of the chair; it shrieked as it scraped across stone flags.

'So that's it. You'd rather have your gadgets than me.'

'Tom, I tried. You know I did. I've kept my mobile off for weeks now. Even after you walked out of the experiment which you promised would prove it to me, because you just decided that your judgement was superior to everybody else's. But it's not just the gadgets now, is it? It's the house, where you sleep, our whole life. Perhaps I ought to be able to cope, but I'm not.'

'So' – Tom pointed viciously through the window – 'if that twat hadn't moved in next door, with his hi-fi and his Wagner and his wireless kit and his total lack of empathy and his "oh I have to have connectivity at any time" attitude – we'd still be together.'

Marianne put her hands over her face. 'I don't

know, Tom. If it hadn't been him, I expect it would have been something else.'

And she was right. The thing that had been borne in on him over the last three days, since Oliver, was how utterly utterly randomly vulnerable he was, how at any time, someone could install some wireless thing – a new hotspot, an Xbox, a transmitter, a hub – that would force him to leave any place that he had started to call home, as easily and effectively as a casually marauding army could turn a settled community into refugees.

He was entirely dependent on the forbearance of random, unknown strangers, on successfully petitioning their active goodwill. It was like being forbidden by law to buy food, and to be able to find enough to eat only through the charity of others, which could change or be withdrawn at any point; a life of perpetual anxiety. How could he ask Marianne – ask anyone, for that matter – to join him in that bleak existence? It had been unreasonable of him to expect it – but oh God, so natural, to cling to love, to that one security, while around him everything else fell away.

Slowly he lowered himself back into the chair, his limbs stiff and cold as though he had aged fifty years. He put out one hand to Marianne, and took hers, even managing a feeble smile. 'Just my luck, then, hey? To get a health problem with no societal recognition.'

'But that's the thing,' said Marianne desperately. 'It's so awful – surely, if it was true, something would already be being done about it? Please – one last time, Tom – do you think you could possibly be mistaken about the RF? Would it be worth...looking at a different way forward?'

Tom dropped her hand; her knuckles made a hollow sound as they knocked against the wood. The chasm that had opened inside him when Marianne had asked him to leave began to fill with a bubbling anger, hot and viscid like a lava stream.

'You of all people, Marianne.'

'Me of all people what?'

'You, with all your campaigning about global warming and wildlife habitats, and all your experience of how unpopular causes have to push and push and push against the establishment to make their voices heard. Yet with this one thing, this particular inconvenient truth, a tiny minority who get screwed over by the stuff that makes money for the biggest commercial behemoths on the planet, you just can't see it. Or you won't see it. Because this time it's just that little bit too inconvenient for you. You've got feet of clay, my dear – great big feet of clay.'

Marianne was staring, huge-eyed, her lips forming a perfect silent O. She whispered, 'So that's what you think of me.'

'You'd better believe it.' Tom swung himself out of his seat. 'Right. This kind of changes my plans for the rest of the day.' He marched into the hall.

'Tom – Tom – I didn't mean...you don't have to

go straightaway…'

'As you helpfully pointed out, Marianne, this house is no good for me anyway.'

In the bedroom Tom flung jeans and sweatshirts and underwear and trainers into his rucksack. He found a sports bag under the bed, pulled books from the shelves, tore two posters from the wall. He found the case for his guitar. He stared at the soft furnishings – God, who had bought what? He couldn't remember, only a hazy sense of the general optimism of shopping trips in their early days at no. 37, and Marianne's liking for strong vibrant colours and insistence on organic cotton. He took his two pillows from the bed, the spare duvet from the top of the cupboard, some clean sheets and towels. How easy it was to dismantle a life. He went into the bathroom to get his shaving kit, and saw on the corner of the bath the small recycled plastic toy duck which Marianne had bought him as a cheeky Christmas present, because of his fondness for long soaks. He hesitated for a moment and then swept it up with the rest. He assembled his stuff in the hall, went to the kitchen to unplug his laptop and ethernet cable and grabbed some random cutlery and food. Marianne was making herself scarce in the front room. Tom looked at his watch – it was only eleven o'clock. He began to load the van, moving up and down the short front path through dank air that had been recently infused with rain. Wagner oozed from Oliver's house next door. Slamming the van's doors on his last load, Tom turned to see Marianne standing on the path, in her sloppy green jumper, her hair sticking out at odd angles, so pale and bereft and stricken that his heart went out to her.

'Oh God, after all we had, it's worth one more try,' he said to himself, and rushed into the garden of Oliver's house.

'Look mate, I'm really sorry to bother you,' Tom said, breathlessly, when Oliver answered his multiple knocks. 'But...'

'You again,' drawled Oliver, leaning on the doorpost with one hand on the door, as though ready to shut it at any time. He was wearing a silk dressing gown over paisley pyjamas, and pointed Turkish slippers. 'What do you want?'

'I wanted to explain things properly, and see if there's any way you could help us.' Tom indicated the van. 'I really am going to have to leave, if you can't.'

'Is this about my Wi-Fi again?'

'Yup – 'fraid so. Look – I have to leave. Marianne and I are going to split up. It's that critical. So I'm asking you...no, let's face it, I'm begging you. I'll pay you, I'll make any inconvenience worth your while.... If it's getting out of bed you don't like, I'll get you one of those remote control sockets so you can turn off the router from upstairs, but please, please...'

'Leave, please,' said Oliver. 'Now. And if you come back again it will constitute harassment, and I shall be calling the police.' He shut the door.

Tom stood outside, holding his arms rigid to stop himself from punching the fanlight, clenching his jaw to stop himself yelling. Eventually he turned away and walked slowly back to the van. So this was it, then. He and Marianne – finished. Their life together in this cute little house. Dead. Over. So final, and so unexpected. As if some dark chainsaw had lowered itself from the sky, and cut neatly all round him, and severed him cleanly from his previous world.

Marianne had retreated to just inside the open front door. Rage flared up inside Tom; *of course* she had, he thought, she didn't want to be part of the confrontation with Oliver, didn't want to get involved. If she'd been prepared to come with me, stand beside me, say it meant so much *to her*, flap her eyelashes on my behalf – but no, that would all be too *weird and embarrassing*. God, at least I found out about her now, before we had two kids and a mortgage. He flung himself into the driver's seat and slammed the door.

Marianne came running down the path. 'Tom, Tom, I – don't leave like this. Where are you going to go?'

'As if you'd care,' he spat, and gunned the van so that the engine's roar obliterated her reply.

He did know, of course, but was not going to give her the satisfaction. He'd thought about it as he'd done his packing, and realised that the 'detached house, quite isolated' was a pipe dream, for the moment – it would take him time to find one, and he could never afford it on his own. He needed time out, to sort the logistics, and while he did that he needed to be somewhere with a phone, and an internet connection, and heating, for God's sake, and the ability to wash. And there was really only one option, if he didn't want another night of wild camping in the van.

Just for a few days, he would have to go home – or what, improbably, since March, passed for home, though he had only visited it once. An elegant detached Georgian property, in the groomed Hampshire village where his mother was now so unexpectedly ensconced. He used the last remaining pay phone in a service station to ring Ed and negotiate some leave. Then he made another call. 'It's me,' he said when his mother picked up. 'You've got to help me. Everything's gone toes up.'

PART 2

CHAPTER 19

The road was grey and the sky was grey and the crash barrier that divided the carriageways stretched on into the distance like the spine of a huge dead animal, curving then straightening then curving again. Tom focused on the white slashes of the road markings, the flashing indicator lights of vehicles moving in and out of the lanes, the unnerving speed of cars hurtling towards his right-hand mirror every time he thought about overtaking. But soon he got used to the speed and relaxed – and found he could no longer keep his other thoughts at bay.

Disconnected chunks of what had happened moved round in his mind, like fragments in a boiling stew: Marianne's downcast eyes when she told him she didn't want to move out, his bitter tirade at her failure to follow her principles, her forlorn, martyred face. Should he have seen it coming? Were they doomed from the first time he'd asked her to switch off her phone in the house? Perhaps. But didn't he have a right – some right – to expect more, to expect a bit of support and adhesion, for her to stick around for a while when the going got tough? He'd thought people fell in love with people, with that unique themness that made them different from everybody else, and that their context, and circumstances, were, after that, unimportant.

Perhaps you fell in love with a package: a person and the lifestyle you thought you'd have with them – and you could fall out of love if that changed. And what had happened to him was certainly extreme. But he had been sorting it. At every stage, when things had looked bad, he'd found a way forward, and he would have done it again.

'I'll be back,' he said to himself fiercely. 'This trip south is a temporary stage. I'll finish my PhD. I'll be Dr Jenkins yet.'

He let himself imagine it, for a few minutes; even allowing Marianne to turn up in his thought experiment, throwing her arms round his neck and kissing him, and saying 'Oh Tom, I knew you'd do it.' But at that point the dream curdled and went sour.

If I was cured tomorrow, he thought, and could walk back into our cute little house, and sleep all night in the same bed as Marianne, without a care in the world, but knowing what I know now…could I do it? The thing that had hurt most, he now realised, was that tiny mental reservation, that delicate question mark, that had hovered there beneath all her compliance and concern, that implied, gentle 'Do you really *have* to do this?' at every expedient he was forced to adopt for his survival, the persistent, unspoken implication that he was somehow choosing his fate.

He slammed both hands against the wheel. If she could be with him for two years, and yet doubt his judgement about something so fundamental – had she ever really known him at all?

He switched on the radio to Radio 1, and listened to inane chat and songs about failed or failing love. Weren't there any other topics? But gradually his mood became more buoyant. He decided that he liked driving, and in his post–Marianne life, he was going to do more of it. In your little metal box, you were temporarily suspended from the rest of your life. No one could say you were wasting time, because you were busy getting from A to B – but you had the opportunity to think. And you could control your own environment, and have the music up as loudly as you wanted, and eat crisps and spill crumbs all over the seat.

He began to pay more attention to the country he was driving through, enjoying the sensation of inching down the map of England as he slid under the rectangular arches of road signs indicating turnoffs for obscurely named towns. The grey daylight faded, cars turned on their headlights and the cats' eyes on the road surface began to gleam.

Parking his van on the gravel drive, Tom looked back along the dark quiet road, at the lights of neighbours scattered at respectful distances. The place was, in its key aspects, as he remembered it, and he was overwhelmed with relief. The only time he'd been here before, back in March, he had come down on the train to attend the service of licensing, where his mother had taken her oaths and been anointed by the bishop with holy oil. As a result she was now the vicar of this group of rural parishes, the Reverend Janet Jenkins, and this was the house which went with the job.

It was a neat brick Georgian box, with walls weathered into a patchwork of muted reds and browns, three sash windows spaced evenly across the upper storey, and two more flanking the blue front door. It stood in a moat of tousled lawn, and along the back of the garden evergreen shrubs formed a feathery phalanx, and on the other sides were high mixed hedges of hawthorn and beech.

When he rang the bell the door was opened by his slim spare mother in her grey and white exercise kit, one foot grasped behind her as she stretched out her quad. He smiled. Ever since he'd been small, she'd been very devoted to exercise. He had an early memory of sitting in his buggy, black park railings and hedges and municipal flowers rushing past at high speed as his mother, pounding the tarmac paths, propelled him along. Luckily she was easy to keep clean, with short beige hair cut close around her skull, a smooth bony face and tanned unblemished skin; she had a knack of leaping into the shower and coming out ready to resume her public role with almost unbelievable efficiency.

'Tom,' she said, releasing her stretch. She must have been working out; in her study she kept the shining cage of a home gym. 'What a journey you've had. Come in. The Wi-Fi and mobile are off, as you asked. And I've bought the wired kit – we can set it up later this evening.'

'Oh Mum.' Tom leant over to hug her, tears bulging in his eyes.

He hadn't told his mother, at first, when he'd started to get ill, just been vague about headaches, not wanting to worry her – an early training in self-sufficiency, perhaps, from when the two of them were alone against the world. And when he had discovered that he had become a reactor, he'd been so blissed out by his returning health that he'd presented the whole issue to her in an absurdly positive light. But she had understood, instantly, when he'd phoned to explain that everything had gone wrong.

'My poor boy,' she said. 'This is a terrible thing.'

His mother had an incredibly beautiful voice, strong, sinuous, velvet-smooth, able to modulate any shade of emotion – yet always surprising, because it issued from such a slight bland frame. The seed had always been there, he supposed, but she had cultivated it, over the last few years, as she had trained for the Church.

He said, 'Thanks for all you've done, Mum.'

'That's fine – I understand. You can beat this, Tom, I'm sure of it. We aren't going to give in.'

He stepped back. 'I'm not giving in,' he said. 'I tried, you know, I was doing all right. I was in control, I was back at work – and then that…tosser moved in next door.'

'That was very unfortunate.'

'You know I slept outside for a few nights. It was freezing. It's just great to be back in a house again and know I'm going to be able to stay here.' He gestured around. 'Houses are great – look – central heating! Light bulbs! Hot water that comes out of taps!'

His mother smiled. 'Yes, I suppose it makes us count our blessings.'

'And no neighbours, thank God. I'm just so lucky. If it wasn't for this place I'd still be in the van. You're a lifesaver, Mum.'

She sat on the bottom step of the stairs to unlace her trainers.

'OK, Tom, I'm going to have a shower, and then over supper you can tell me about Marianne. I can well understand the circumstances must have put the relationship under strain.'

Tom grinned and stretched. 'You can say that

again. I could eat a horse, now I think about it. Shall I start making some pasta?'

*

Next morning, in the austere white guest room, Tom unpacked his books and files and arranged them on the small white bookcase. He set up his laptop by the window, on the console table with spindly legs. The room had something monkish about it, with its narrow divan bed covered by a pale blue candlewick bedspread – so appropriate for his unexpected single status – and on the wall opposite the room's only picture, a bloodless watercolour of different types of grass. But at least, after all the disruption, he had a base from which he could plan his next move. Until he got new accommodation sorted in Northington, this was going to be home; after lunch he would put his head out of the front door and explore.

It was a calm, cold, shining day. Thick frost still furred grass, hedgetops and rooftiles in pockets of shadow where the angled sunbeams had not reached. The church, grey stone with a red tiled roof and a stumpy spire, was along to his left, but he turned the other way, and wandered between houses set back from the road, with stately trees in their gardens. Their intricate branches were now almost empty of leaves.

For a while no cars passed him and he saw no one else about. His upper back grew pleasantly warm:

the afternoon sun, easing down behind him, held just enough heat. In the distance beyond the village the ground rose up in a radiant curve against the blue – the start of the downland hills. The air smelt of woodsmoke and wholesome decay, and of those mysterious expanses of sheep and grass.

A man was coming towards him, wearing a knitted multicoloured beanie, a parka and jeans. Thirties, quite hip – beard, but not a huge one, sharp foxy features, casual but determined stride. When the man was about ten feet away he nodded at Tom and said, 'Afternoon', so Tom smiled and said, 'Afternoon' back – this was what happened in villages, they were friendly places – and as the man passed by a skewer of pain twisted into the top of his skull.

What was that?

He turned to stare at the man as he sauntered away, and after he'd gone about fifty yards a hand snaked round in an easy practised movement to hitch his parka and slide his phone from his back pocket.

Tom started walking again. His head kept throbbing. Coincidence. It had to be. He would not allow it to be anything else.

A woman approaching this time, older, broader, green anorak, dyed black hair, long silver earrings, furry boots, stomping along.

He stepped off the pavement to allow the woman to pass and she winked and said, 'Thanks, love, I'm not as thin as I used to be' and the thing on his head grabbed its skewer and made another bid for entry and this time got a claw around the outside of his eye.

He nearly turned back then. But that would have been to give in, to acknowledge what was happening, to collude with the horror. Instead he soldiered on, past a pink-painted thatched cottage, a white house with two dark-windowed 4x4s nose-to-nose on its drive, an old brick terrace of cottages, the gardens full of arching rose stems bearing scarlet hips.

Four teenage lads came out of a side lane, about ten metres in front of him, jostling, laughing, hands out, clutching their magical oblongs. 'Bet you haven't seen what Kelly sent me, mate....' 'Phwoar.' 'You going to message her back?'

Four of them. He walked a few steps towards them, and the pressure in his head mounted, and the claw wrapped itself tighter round his eyeball, and his heart began to accelerate towards take-off.

That was when he turned like a rabbit and ran.

Bruised head, all over; in the innermost bones of his skull a sick, toxic, unwholesome ache.

Walls. Curtains. Bookshelf. Picture. All moving. White ceiling bulging, a looming avalanche about to crush him into the mattress.

'The sensitivity can spread out beyond the original trigger. So people start reacting to other wireless devices as well.'

What had caused him to progress? Why now?

His journey. It had to be. At some mysterious point on the road south, something had crossed over inside him, a threshold had been breached. Now he had descended – within twenty-four hours – to a more acute level of sensitivity.

To a lower circle of hell.

He hadn't realised how well off he had been. What was a thin mattress in the back of his rusty van, the vicious cold of Hollerby woods at dawn, even the cringing but temporary awkwardness of baths and meals in Honey Lane alongside Marianne who had rejected him? Every humiliation could have been borne. Humiliation was nothing – if he could have avoided *this*.

Hubris. That was the only word.

Things began appearing in the corners of his remembered vision; looming out of the landscape as he had approached, then vanishing as he whizzed past. Tall structures of tapering criss-cross steel, with discs and oblongs and spikes clustered around their tops. One – then another – then another – then another – never identical, never dissimilar, never too close together, never too far apart.

Masts. Masts along the main road routes – put there in great concentration, because of demand, and because motorways and dual carriageways often went through marginal places; industrial areas, a city's edge. And along with masts, people in cars, so many, all around him, on Wi-Fi, on their phones.

He had driven for hours through an RF haze.

So you thought you were so clever. Just nip down the A1, take time out in this handy detached vicarage. Find a nice detached house in Northington. Finish your PhD.

Ha. Ha ha ha ha. Ha ha ha ha ha.

Around him, the room itself, the house, the village, the whole world seemed to pulsate, to shake, to rock with silent waves of laughter at the casual dismembering of his plans.

CHAPTER 20

'Oh Tom – I'm glad you're up again. How are you feeling? I'm planning to make dinner early tonight, because there will be a Bible study group here later this evening.'

His mother, slim and compact, light on her feet, had come out of her study and begun to mount the cream-carpeted stairs between leaf-patterned walls. Tom, suddenly panicking, stared after her. He tried to speak, but all his throat produced was a strangled, croaking cry. The brute instinct for physical survival took over, and he ended up shouting too loudly, and too roughly: 'Mum!'

She stopped at the curve of the stairs.

'What is it, Tom?'

'The...Bible Group...' he stammered. 'How many people?'

'Oh, about twelve, I think...' surprised. 'Did you want to...join us?'

Twelve. He swallowed. His mouth was dry.

'Mum. Something happened. I've got worse. I – found out this afternoon. I react now – really quickly, really painfully – whenever I just pass a person with a phone. If I was here, with twelve...'

'Tom – well – this is something new...'

'I know. I absolutely didn't expect it. But...the condition can progress. Will you...could you...ask them to turn off their phones?'

His mother stood on the staircase facing away from him, lit from below by the glow of a lamp on the hall table, very still and poised on the balls of her feet. With a crash the central heating turned itself on; inside the pipes, gurgling began. His mother revolved slowly and walked back down the stairs.

'I...can't, Tom. I just...can't do that.'

In his stomach, a sensation of dissolution, of being drained away downwards, through his feet.

He tried to stand his ground.

'If you told them about me, explained what's just happened...'

She had stopped on the second step, so the stair gave her height. 'It's the way the world is, these days. People expect it – they expect to be connected. Some of them have children or elderly relatives. They're happy to come to Bible Group because they know they can be easily in touch. And...we look at different commentaries, on Bible apps...there are so many useful resources...'

He felt himself sliding down a scree slope, his

fingers scrabbling for a hold. 'Would it not be possible just to…to ask? If they don't want to, they don't have to…but they might be okay with it, they might not mind….'

She stepped past him, her face averted, and walked back through the open door of her study. Between the shining cage of the home gym and the shelves of theological books and the felt-covered board pinned with notices about forthcoming parish events she halted with her back to him, as though caught in a force-field.

'I…have worked so hard,' she said. 'I get alongside people. I embrace what they value in their lives.'

A hiatus, as though she'd temporarily run out of charge. Then, re-energised, gesturing with one arm, 'The Church is so often seen as old-fashioned and out-of-touch. I'm working hard to combat that. I'm new here, Tom. I want people to know I'm on their side.'

Now she faced him. 'Please don't ask this. You can see, can't you, in my position – I would be putting myself against the whole direction of today's society, the whole trend of modern life…'

Tom could not argue. Here – all around them – was the dream she'd waited years to pursue. Years she'd toiled away in accounts departments while he'd been growing up, studying, in the evenings after he'd gone to bed, not the mysteries of the Trinity or the argument from design, but modules with hard percussive names like *bookkeeping transactions* and *elements of costings*, little rigid blocks she could pile up, slowly and prudently, so that one day she could climb them to a better-paid role.

She hadn't gone to uni, although she'd had an offer, and everything had been in place – because she had got pregnant with him. She had been such a quiet, sensible, academic teenager, had never even had a boyfriend before that uncharacteristic summer fling. His father – a charismatic itinerant Australian who, according to Janet, could charm the birds out of the air – had subsequently vanished. Everyone – her parents, her teachers, her friends, had wanted her to have an abortion or at least have the baby adopted; but she had absolutely and doggedly refused. There had been terrible rows, she'd told him; eventually she'd left home to get some peace.

'What time are these people coming?' he said.

'Seven, until nine.'

Twelve phones, two hours. There was no way he could stand it. Outside, the evening was cold, dark, windy and wet; the chances of coming across other people were slim.

'I'll go out.'

The instant agony on passing a mobile phone went away, thank goodness – it must have been a function of his particularly sensitized state. But he still had delayed and cumulative reactions. He avoided the main routes within the village and wandered as much as he could in the surrounding countryside, along less frequented footpaths and lanes. If he saw a human figure approaching, he accelerated to a rapid walk then a short sprint to get past it as fast as possible, or – when he had the option – swerved off before it reached him and took a different path

He was intensely lonely. He longed to sit in the pub with friends, relaxing, chatting. Failing that, he would have settled for stilted interactions with acquaintances, or for simply being in a crowd with strangers, not knowing or speaking to anyone, but sensing the presence of other members of his own species, feeling the warmth of the herd.

Sometimes the craving became overwhelming. He would walk back to the vicarage down the high street rather than by the back way between hedgerows, so that he would pass people, and exchange a smile, sometimes a chat. 'How's your mother doing?' they often asked, for she was held in high regard. But for the few crumbs he gathered he always paid.

He often thought about saying something. At night, when he couldn't sleep, he would go over alternative phrasings in his mind, wondering which were better, clearer, most persuasive, least bizarre, least likely to offend. He would stand waiting for the right gap in a conversation, the words warmed and ready on his tongue.

But something always held them back. A wary sense that, when he crossed that line, there would be no retreating over it again; people's perceptions of him would from that point onwards be irreversibly altered. Old norms, flaking and crumbling, were easy to spot. 'Marriage is between a man and a woman' – that used to be a natural law, indisputable, a self-evident truth, inherent in the meaning of the word. Now you could marry the person you loved, and only a few diehards would argue that preferring your own sex was a mental sickness to be cured or a sin to be renounced. But new norms crystallised as old ones fell away, and those new norms were hard and pure and strong, invisible to all except the few who smashed against them: *it's the way the world is, these days.*

Anyway, it was obvious his mother did not want him to come out as a reactor. Partly it was loyalty that kept him silent, loyalty to her desire to be accepted, to make a good impression in her new role. That, and loyalty's dirty little cousin, need. He hated it, but he was now dependent on his mother. The vicarage was far from perfect; people came there often, singly or in groups. But it was a refuge, it was warm. There was nowhere else for him to go. He would be her clever, reclusive boy, recovering after a stressful time, so hard-working, so immersed in his subject, no time for fun.

He spent more and more time in his room on his

laptop, attached to the internet by a long black snake of network cable and to the mains by an electrical flex. He had explained to Ed about his increased sensitivity and that he needed time to recover before he made the journey back; in the meantime they agreed that he would start, as best he could, writing up parts of his thesis. He seemed to reach out to his previous life across a huge dark chasm that plunged through the centre of England. In leaving it he had passed unwittingly through a one-way door which had softly shut behind him, flush, without a handle to grasp.

He tried keeping in touch with friends, but their smiley, gregarious photos and updates reinforced his sense of isolation. 'I can't do that,' he thought, seeing a group selfie of some mates at a gig. 'And I can't do that either,' seeing a picture of physicists at a conference. And in response to the announcement that two of his school friends were now an item: 'God knows if that's ever going to happen to me again.' He stopped following Marianne. As well as Green Week and the anti-bypass campaign she appeared to be busy saving the hedgehog. 'Perhaps if I'd had a cute snout and been covered in prickles?' he wondered wryly. Probably not. Hedgehogs' freedom to roam, and thus their ability to survive, could be restored, it seemed, by everybody cutting small hedgehog-sized openings in the bottoms of their garden fences and gates. A simple straightforward undertaking, if you had the right sort of saw, causing no inconvenience to anyone.

Obsessively he emailed Kevin about the experiment. 'Kev – what are they doing? What's happening with the review?'

'I'm doing all the exposure sessions we've got booked in up till Christmas,' Kevin had replied. 'They're worried we'll lose participants, if we mess them about. We're also asking the participants how they feel twenty-four hours afterwards. That was my idea – and the Prof went for it. How are you doing, anyway? I'm really sorry about the phone thing.'

'Kev – it's still not going to work. They need to STOP IT NOW.'

'Tom, calm down. These things are like oil tankers – takes a bit of time to get them to change direction. There is going to be a Steering Group meeting sometime in the New Year to reconsider the research design – you know what it's like trying to get anything in people's diaries at this time of year, especially senior people, and there are a lot of those on the Steering Group, including people from outside. I'm writing up our presentation as a paper to put to the group. So don't worry. It sounds like you've got enough on your plate trying to get your resilience back to where it was before.'

'I am worried. I've emailed reactorrights explaining they should tell all the remaining reactors they absolutely shouldn't take part. LET ME KNOW

AS SOON AS YOU KNOW ANYTHING ELSE.'

'Stop yelling at me, Tom. I'm doing my best.'

On the reactorrights site there was a link for metallised material that blocked – or at least significantly reduced – RF. Originally developed by the military to protect sensitive communications equipment from the enemy, the electronics industry now used it to make RF-free clean rooms for testing kit. Per metre, the material was eye-wateringly expensive. Tom used the last juice on his credit card to order a canopy that would hang like a futuristic mosquito net over his single bed.

It billowed from its box on the morning that it arrived in shiny, flexible, semi-translucent folds, silvery, like an evening dress. Balancing on a chair, Tom drilled holes upwards into the ceiling, rammed in four rawl plugs and screwed in four hooks, one at each corner of his bed, to support the loops at the canopy's top corners. A separate sheet went under the mattress and joined to the canopy edges with metallised Velcro. There was also a green and yellow earthing wire, which clipped to the canopy at one end with a crocodile clip, and at the other went into the earth pin of one of his bedroom sockets.

He stood back to survey what he had constructed. It certainly didn't do much for the interior décor. It looked as though some sort of weird alien space pod with four small horns had landed in his bedroom, eaten the bed; and extruded something green-and-yellow across the carpet. A thought wormed into his mind: 'Marianne would have a fit,' and longing reared in his stomach, but he laughed it down. She couldn't even cope with basic weirdness; this was the advanced level. There was a vertical Velcro-sealed slit in the centre of one side; he ripped it open and climbed through the gap, carefully pressing the edges together before throwing himself back onto his pillow. He could cage himself now, when people came to the house. It was stuffy inside. There was a metallic smell, like the scent of blood.

One evening towards the end of January he'd been on the net for several hours. He started to notice a strange pain in the bones of his face, and sharp prickles around the sockets of his eyes. 'I hope I haven't got flu or something,' was his first thought, and after another half-hour he switched off and went to bed. But no snot or coughing developed. The next morning, after an hour on the computer, the painful sensations were there again, and, across his vision, tiny flares.

Tom dropped his hands from the keyboard and sat motionless, staring at his screen. Sheer icy horror swept through his body, stopping his diaphragm, congealing his bowels. 'No,' he whispered. 'God no, this can't happen.'

But he had known, all along, that it could.

He had read it on the reactorrights site back in the kitchen at Honey Lane and had deliberately swerved his mind away. Because the possibility that he might be a Phase 1 reactor had been terrifying enough.

Any device powered by mains electricity produces low-frequency electric and magnetic fields. And if the device includes more complex electronics, such as a transformer, or a fluorescent tube, or a screen, it produces mid-range radio-frequencies as well. Phase 2 reactors become sensitive to some or all of these frequencies. They start to have difficulties with a wider range of electrical and electronic equipment, not just devices communicating wirelessly. Some only develop symptoms relating to particular equipment. Others start that way, then find they have gradually to abandon most, or all, of it.

Tom reached down a trembling hand to the socket where his computer was plugged into the wall. He switched the power off. He sat on the chair at his desk for a long time facing the dead machine. He felt flattened, as though punched several times by an invisible fist. 'This cannot be happening to me,' went through his mind, again and again; 'I will not let this happen.' He wanted, more than anything, to turn back time, to have the chance, just one chance, to live the last few weeks over again, in the light of what he knew now – no, in the light of what he had already known, but had put aside, because of his desperate loneliness, his need for connection, his yearning for a sense of normality. 'How could I have done differently?' he asked himself angrily, 'How could anyone?' But he knew that given the chance he would have managed it, been more continent with his computer use, not let himself go on and on for hours.

He put his head in his hands. There seemed to be an intricate sadism at the heart of this condition; it played with you, it led you on, it gave you hope; it used your own instincts to destroy you. You thought you'd found a way to ride the beast; and it would trot forwards obediently for a while, until you felt a noose tighten round your throat, and you were dragged off backwards, and you found that all along your pleasant journey you had been quietly hanging yourself.

That night Tom dreamt that he was in a hospital and he was being prepared for an operation. He was strapped into a plastic chair by green and white-clad medical staff. His legs were bound to the legs of the chair, his torso to the back. His arms were stretched out in front of him, so that his forearms rested flat on a table. The nurse in charge rolled back his sleeves and, using thick webbed straps, tied his arms to the surface so they could not move. Everything in the room went dark, except for a pool of light falling on his arms. Tom watched his fingers flex at the edge of the circle of light. Then there was a roar in the darkness behind him, as though an enormous motor was starting up, and he saw a chainsaw coming at him out of the dark, the shining blade live and turning, wielded by a doctor in a mask. He suddenly knew what the operation was to be: it was an amputation – they were going to cut off his arms at the elbow. He began to writhe and twist in the chair, frantically straining against his bands. But the knots were efficiently and professionally tied. The blade came closer and closer, hovering above his shrinking flesh, lining itself up for the strike. Tom screamed and kept screaming. He woke up to find himself thrashing at damp tangled bedclothes, inside the metallic walls of his cage.

There was a discreet tap at his bedroom door, and a few moments later his mother came in, a hazy shape on the other side of the silver membrane. 'Tom,' she said, her voice concerned. 'Is everything all right?'

Tom lay back on the pillows. How do I answer that one, he thought. Everything's fine, Mum, except that I can't go anywhere or see anyone, I'm terrified, and my one lifeline to the world might be about to be cut. But instead he smiled tiredly and said, 'Just a bad dream. Don't worry, I'm okay now.'

His mother came over, opened the Velcro slit and reached in, stroking his head. 'It must have been a bad one,' she said. 'This isn't like you. You were usually a good sleeper, when you were small. Do you remember when I carried you to see the moon? You always liked that.'

I wonder where things went wrong, Tom thought to himself after his mother had gone. He let his mind loop back through the years to the boy he had been, mad about music and science, full of hope for the future. Was there a point when the seed of his turning had been sown, something he'd done, somewhere he'd been, some way that he could have acted differently? Or had it always been there, some systemic, perhaps genetic weakness that, in fortuitous conjunction with the particular course taken by human society over the last few decades, would seal his fate? So much about the condition was still mysterious. Nothing that you did or didn't do seemed to make it more or less likely. It was a random misfortune, like being struck by lightning – but a misfortune the world persisted in telling you hadn't happened, couldn't happen, wasn't real.

Tom made a resolution, the next morning. He was only at the start of Phase 2, had just wet his feet in the shallows. He could turn the tide, if he abstained now.

Could turn the tide?

Would. He would turn the tide.

He ripped apart the Velcro strip to exit from his cage and stood barefoot on cold carpet looking round his white monk's cell. The grid of the window was ruled like an iron grating across a featureless wintry sky. On the spindly-legged table sat sleek black temptation; closing it, he moved it to one side and piled files on top.

Three weeks. He would stop using the computer entirely, for three weeks.

His mother did not need to know what he was doing, or not doing, in his room. His eyes fell on the small white bookcase which stood against the wall along from the desk. Books. He could ask her to get him books, from the library in the nearby town. Thrillers to relax with, he would tell her. so he could avoid too much screen time. And physics books, so he could pretend he was still working, 'reading round the subject'.

After six days, his existence felt so thin, so nearly transparent, he was surprised to see his hands and arms were still solid flesh; amazed that he could reach for a mug and grasp it without his fingers sliding through its hard, real, definite substance, so much more convincing than his own. On his solitary walks he no longer allowed himself even the occasional indulgence of brief interaction; there was too much to lose. Before, he had worried that his avoidance would appear suspicious, or rude. Now he almost believed they would not see him at all, that he had faded so much as to be a mere perturbation of the dim February light, that if he did stop to greet anyone, they would glance about, politely puzzled, searching for the source of the sound.

Playing his guitar made him feel most real, but

could not be indulged in too much while his mother was at home. Cradling the curvy instrument on his knee was like having another body to hold against his own, a body which murmured resonantly in response to his touch. Together they undertook the task of learning by ear the songs played on the radio during those weeks, songs played over and over again, a thin slice of musical time Tom would come to know weirdly, intimately well.

At last the weeks of abstinence were over, his mother still in happy ignorance, the empty days and hours successfully pushed through. Full of enthusiastic hope he opened the laptop, but the reaction had set in, even swifter than before. He had sacrificed and sacrificed to the great Digital God – but it had not been enough.

A new thought flared like a dark flame across Tom's mind, a thought he had known existed but which he himself had never had before: *if this is to be my life, I do not want to live it*. Even when the first intensity had subsided, raw burn marks remained, the record of savage initiation.

The next day he did not get up until half-past ten. His mother had gone out by the time he wandered downstairs in his pyjamas and dressing gown and slumped in the kitchen, eating bowl after bowl of cereal, while flicking mindlessly through a copy of the parish magazine. He jumped when the doorbell rang, tried ignoring it, but it shrilled forcefully and repeatedly. 'I suppose I'd better answer it,' he thought. 'It's probably a delivery.' But it was one of the parishioners, a large woman in a purple anorak with a dripping golf umbrella, because outside the rain sliced down in oblique streaks.

'Good morning, Tom,' she said, moving forwards. 'Eleanor Fletcher. We have met before. May I come in? I hope I am not interrupting your studies. I'm a little early, I'm afraid. I'm here to see your mother at 11 o'clock about the fracas relating to the flowers.' Tom stood aside as she powered down the hall. He cursed inwardly. He could be polite, make her a cup of coffee, and get exposed to her damn phone, or he could be rude, leave her, go upstairs and get into his cage.

He suddenly realised he would do neither. He had reached a point of sufficient desperation; he would release the words he had held back for so long. Following her into the kitchen he said, 'I'm afraid I'm going to have to ask you to switch off your phone, if you're going to wait in here.' Eleanor Fletcher's eyebrows shot up. 'Good gracious,' she said. 'What an unexpected request. But I shall certainly do so, if you wish it.' She fished around in her anorak's capacious pockets until she found her silver phone, and then poked at it frowningly until it died. Tom immediately relaxed. 'Thank you,' he said, almost effusive with gratitude. 'Thank you so much. Would you like a coffee or something? It's pretty wet out there. And there are biscuits.'

'Coffee would be most kind,' she said. 'It is an extremely miserable morning. But I think you should also tell me how you are, and what is the business with my phone?'

Tom set two mugs of coffee on the table, pushed the biscuit tin over to Eleanor and sat down. He wondered briefly what his mother would feel about him coming out, but then he thought: Eleanor Fletcher asked me a straight question and I'm going to give her a straight answer. 'I'm a reactor,' he said. 'Have you heard of them?'

Eleanor, who had just taken a bourbon biscuit in one powerful hand, snapped it in two with a loud crack. 'Well!' she said. 'How extremely...unfortunate for you. I am shocked. Why on earth hasn't your mother said anything? How long...has it been going on?'

'Since...last year.'

'And is that why you've come back?'

'Yes. My girlfriend threw me out. How do you know about reactors? Most people don't.'

'Ah,' said Eleanor. 'Well, as it happens, there is a campsite nearby, near Herrington Down. The farmer there is Cuthbert Dimmock. He is a former lover of mine – rather peculiar in some ways, but a thorough-going gentleman. He has allowed some reactors to camp on his land. There is a small valley with no signal. You might like to go and say hello.'

Tom opened his mouth in astonishment. He felt as though the rainclouds had suddenly whisked away and the sun was shining through the kitchen window. He wanted to jump up and plant a kiss on Eleanor's large, sensible face.

'But...' he stammered, 'but...that's amazing. I had...absolutely no idea.'

'It's not publicised,' said Eleanor. 'It's a private matter. It has to be kept small, unofficial and under the radar, as it's not a registered campsite. But I don't think they'll mind you knowing. Of course I shall keep your own situation confidential. They've been there for a few months.'

'I'll definitely go,' said Tom, erupting from his chair, full of renewed energy. 'Hold on – you can show me where it is.' He rushed into the hall, found the Ordnance Survey map that he had been using on his walks and spread it on the table. Eleanor put on her spectacles and peered. 'There,' she said triumphantly. 'B road to Walpham, minor road off, then turn left, then there's a rough track. About seven miles.'

The rattle of keys in the front door signalled his mother's return. Tom swept up the map, and turned to Eleanor. 'Thank you,' he said. 'You don't know what this means. I was...well, I was feeling pretty low.'

'I wish you luck,' Eleanor replied gravely.

CHAPTER 21

Tom bumped his van along the track which wound its way into the downs. The rain had stopped and the sky was overcast, but there was a wild, warm, excitable wind, gusting in different directions. The trees on each side were losing their stark winter outlines, and becoming fuzzy with buds. Dark tangles of blackthorn were seasoned with generous sprinklings of tiny white flowers.

The track finished at a wooden fence with a five-bar gate in it.

Someone was sitting on the gate.

Tom parked on the verge twenty metres away, so as not to appear too intrusive, and walked towards the gate. The figure watched him intently. He saw that it was a girl with long loose dark hair blowing in the wind, and a straight dark fringe, who was wearing skinny black jeans, an oversized black sweater, fingerless gloves and biker boots.

Of all the reactors in all the world, he had to bump

into this one.

'Hey,' she shouted. 'Stop right there. Who are you?'

He stopped. 'Sarah – it's me. Tom Jenkins. Do you remember – at Northington? When…you came for the experiment?'

'You!' Her big mobile mouth contracted into a grim forbidding line. 'What the hell are you doing here?'

'Well, you'll love the irony of this, but – turns out I'm a reactor too.'

'You? Ha!' It was a single fiercely exultant expostulation. But her tone relented slightly when she went on. 'Well, I suppose it could be you, as much as anyone else.'

'Yes. I got it wrong. I'm sorry. I said some crap things. I would really like to meet you and the others.'

She grunted, before going on, after a pause: 'Turn out all your pockets, please.'

Startled for a moment but quickly understanding, Tom obeyed, pulling white scraps of fabric from the top of his jeans and navy ones from his jacket.

'And I need to see your back pockets too. Turn round, bend over and show me the shape of your bum.'

Tom stifled a snort of incredulous laughter, blushed furiously, but did what she asked, lifting his jacket and bending forwards.

'That looks OK,' Sarah commented levelly, after

what felt like slightly longer than necessary, and he could hear the smile returning to her voice. 'You can stand up now...but please tell me the time.'

'Nice one,' thought Tom. He ostentatiously consulted the cheap plastic-strapped wristwatch that he had bought when he had had to stop checking the time on his phone. 'It's nearly twenty past two.'

She glanced at her own wrist and gave a brief nod. 'How did you get here?'

'I came in the van...' Tom began, puzzled, jerking his thumb backwards, but then he understood. 'Ordnance Survey map,' he said. '1:25,000. I used it to find my route. I'll show you.' He set off towards the vehicle.

'Don't worry,' Sarah called. 'I believe you. I don't reckon you're carrying.'

Grinning, she slid down from the gate and strode towards him, once again unexpectedly tall and slender, only a couple of inches shorter than he was. She brought her RF meter out from a small shoulder bag and switched it on. There was a very faint hum, and one green light flashed.

'Final check,' she said and moved the meter round him for about half a minute, then did the same around the van. Nothing changed. 'Right – you're clean.' She put the meter away and held out her hand. 'I believe you. Let's forget about what happened before. Sorry for all the faffing about. We have to be careful.'

'I know,' he said simply as they shook. 'I

understand now.'

Sarah certainly seemed healthier than when he'd last seen her; vomit, sweat and blood stains were rarely a good look. Now Tom saw a pale oval face with dark deep-set eyes, brows like the firm brushstrokes of an impressionist painter, a long, bony but delicately shaped nose, and a big curvy mouth. Not in any way conventionally beautiful, but intriguing and alive. Sensing his scrutiny she raised a quizzical eyebrow. 'What are you looking for? The mark of the beast?'

'I'm s – sorry…' stammered Tom. 'It's just…you're my first one.'

'First one what?'

'First other reactor I've met in the flesh since I became one too.'

She nodded thoughtfully. 'Yes. I see. It's a weird experience, a bit overwhelming. Somebody you don't have to explain yourself to, or say what hell you've been through, because they know.'

'Yes…' Tom still stood staring. He was flooded by an extraordinary sense of fellow-feeling, as if the border controls of his soul had suddenly been lifted.

'Hey,' Sarah said kindly, patting his arm. 'Come on, you came here to see our campsite, so let's go and see it.'

She climbed easily over the gate and Tom followed with less agility. They set off along a stony track up a sloping field of sheep-cropped turf. When the ground levelled out, Tom found himself looking down into a wooded valley, with the larger hills of the downs on its other side. The small ridge on which they stood came off the main ridge at a narrow angle, and then curved back towards it, so that the valley was held securely, as though in the crook of an arm.

They trudged on down the track and into the birch and beech trees where last year's leaves crunched under their feet. At the valley bottom there was a stream with flattish grassy patches on either side. Three tents were pitched around it – one blue and highly technical, one older green and traditional and one flowery-printed yurt. There were the remains of a campfire. Sarah turned to her left and gestured to a small white caravan. 'That's mine.' Further downstream a luxurious-looking motorhome gleamed incongruously among the trees. 'And that's our resident millionaire's.'

'Millionaire's?' asked Tom, genuinely surprised.

'Oh, we're quite a microcosm of society,' she laughed. 'You'll see.'

'What about…facilities?'

'If you keep walking downstream a little way, you'll get to a standpipe and a shack with a chemical loo. We take turns dealing with it. If you keep going for about three-quarters of a mile you'll get to the farmhouse. Cuthbert lets us have showers there and use the washing machine, the computer – for those who can - and the landline phone. People who can use the computer order food and stuff for people who can't. We bring gas bottles up here for heaters and stoves, but they're heavy and expensive so we try not to switch things on much.'

'Doesn't it get cold in winter?'

'Very, you get used to wearing lots of clothes. Stanford lets us in the motorhome when it's really bad. You don't know how happy I am to see spring.'

'Where is everybody?' Tom asked.

'Stanford has gone to the farmhouse to speak to his lawyer on the phone. He's in the middle of a really nasty divorce – two small children, stacks of money involved – he worked in finance, owns his own company. Barry may be working – since he's been here, he's felt a bit better and he can manage a part-time job as a delivery driver. Chai is an IT nerd – she does freelance work in cybersecurity. She's probably at the farmhouse on the computer. And Veronica – she's the oldest, she's seventy – is probably meditating in her yurt. They'll all turn up at some point.'

'And you?' prompted Tom gently.

'What about me?'

'If you don't mind me asking – what do you do, how do you live? You said, back on the campus, that you were a nurse.'

She turned her face away. 'I am – I used to be – oh I don't know, I'm still qualified I suppose. I worked in Exeter A&E.'

Tom bit his lip. 'I can see how that would be difficult, once you started to turn.'

'It was awful,' she agreed. 'Hospitals these days – patients' notes accessed on tablets, multimedia centres by each bed, Wi-Fi and mobiles everywhere – and the lights, oh God – the great oceans of fluorescent lights were what really finished me off.

'Anyway, at first I went from full-time to part-time, to give myself time to recover between shifts. But it wasn't long enough, and the hostel was full of Wi-Fi anyway, although I did try shielding my room with aluminium foil. So I signed up as an agency nurse and just did bits and pieces and went back to live with my parents. They were really decent about things – got rid of the Wi-Fi and cordless phones, didn't use mobiles when I was there – they had a detached house with a big garden, and the neighbours were nice and helpful. But I was too far gone, I suppose. I became a full-blown Phase 2 – you've heard of that?' Tom gave a quick nod. 'And then I became Phase 3. I started having to turn the power off at the mains in order to be in the house at all. There is actually something you can do about Phase 3, if you own the property – you can have the whole place rewired in shielded cable and install earthed metal sockets and light switches, and shielded light fittings – and my parents were prepared to do it, spend the money, cope with the disruption – and then...'

'Then what?'

'Then my father had a massive stroke.'

'That's dreadful. What...what happened?'

'Oh, we were into the surreal world of hospital, rehabilitation, hoists, gadgets, home care packages. I couldn't ask them to pull the guts out of the house wiring on top of all that. And I couldn't stay there, turning off the electricity at all hours, when my mother was trying to care for my father. I left.'

'Where did you go?'

'A succession of damp cottages, squats, normal campsites, rented houses that no one else wanted, sometimes sharing with other reactors, sometimes on my own. I was in a house in the Peak District when I came to Northington for the stupid experiment. God I wish I'd never done it – I had been making a little bit of progress but...well, I lost it. Then finally I heard about this place and Cuthbert said I could come. We bought a second-hand caravan, and my mother drove it here with me in it and deposited me. After the journey I was more dead than alive.'

'How's your dad?'

'Still around, amazingly, two years later. But very disabled and needing lots of care. I'd love to go and see him, but...' she spread her hands.

'I know,' said Tom. 'You don't have to explain. It's a one-way street. At least for now.'

They stood in silence watching the stream ripple busily along.

'So in answer to your first question,' she said, eventually shaking herself and smiling, 'I am not working any more. I am trying to apply for benefits, but in our situation they are very hard to get. I can tell you about them, if you think it might be useful.'

'It might. I'm supposed to be finishing a PhD in physics, but...I think I need to take a break. Temporarily, of course.'

'Come and have a cup of tea.'

Her caravan had a sink and a built-in stove at one end, and a fridge to the left of the door. Most of the wall space was fitted out with cupboards and storage hatches in fake blond wood veneer. At the far end two foam-cushioned benches faced each other, divided by a little chest of drawers. The upholstery was lurid pink velour, but interesting throws with swirly patterns had been laid over it to reduce the impact. Along the windowsill was a row of paperback books, and the doors of the largest cupboard were covered with a Blu-Tacked collage of postcards and photographs.

'Cosy,' Tom said, looking round, his head unnervingly close to the curved cream-coloured roof. 'It's amazing what you can get into a confined space.'

Sarah slid the top of the chest of drawers forwards so it formed a small table, and made two mugs of tea.

'It's kind of less cosy first thing in the morning in January,' she said. 'I have to use all my willpower and moral courage to get out of bed.' She took off her boots and sat opposite him crosslegged, wiggling her toes in stripy socks.

'What do you do all the time?' he asked then added quickly, 'If you don't mind me asking?'

209

'I read books and I listen to the radio. I'm trying to learn watercolour painting' – she indicated a sketchbook on top of the fridge – 'but I'm not very good. Veronica is teaching me how to sew. She's got an old-fashioned Singer in the yurt, with a handle. I had some mad idea that I could do alterations and repairs. I write letters. Sometimes I talk to people on the farmhouse phone. I go for a run every morning and in the afternoon I take a walk up onto the downs – that's where I was when I saw you turn onto the track. I do mindfulness meditation. I eat lots of fruit and vegetables. I am composting the camp's uncooked food waste in a black bin back there in the trees, and I plan to dig it into the soil beside the caravan and start a small vegetable plot. Sometimes I get so lonely I talk to the sheep. I keep hoping that I can recover some resilience, even just a little bit.'

'You are a model citizen,' said Tom. 'Apart from the one thing.'

'Oh yes,' she replied gravely. 'The government would approve of me. Except for that.'

'My ex-girlfriend was very virtuous. She would approve of you. Except for that.'

Sarah glanced up with a question in her face, but divining the answer, her eyes widened and she slowly inclined her head.

'Ah.'

'Yes.'

'I'm sorry.'

'I was sorry too, at the time. Looking back, less so. I...found something out. About...well, her, I suppose.'

After a pause, Tom went on: 'It's so weird talking about being ill and horrible symptoms, and all that – because...at the moment I feel – completely fantastic. Better than I've felt for months.'

Sarah's big generous mouth lifted upwards into a curve. 'You're getting it,' she said with delight. 'I wondered if you would. Some do, some don't.'

'Getting what?'

'The rush. The sweetness. The feeling that all the cells in your body are breathing a collective sigh of relief.'

Tom nodded, his grin answering hers. 'Oh yes. Yes indeed.' Physical euphoria coursed through him, almost orgasmic in its intensity; his whole body felt immersed in a warm, vibrant sea, all his accumulated agony cleansed.

They turned as if by one accord to the caravan's sloping windscreen, and looked out along the valley, where through the opening to the west long shafts of late-afternoon sun had split the grey sky, illuminating the left sides of newly budding trees so they gleamed astonishing vivid gold. Higher up on the opposite hills, radiant sheep casting sideways shadows browsed the undulating turf.

'It's beautiful,' said Tom. He could not take his eyes away. 'To look at, and to feel – both.'

'It is,' she replied. 'We are very lucky.'

'Could I come and stay here?' Tom asked eventually. 'I haven't got a caravan, but I do have a tent somewhere at home. I've been trying to rehabilitate through avoidance but it is hard to achieve. All I've managed to do is spend too much time online and start getting sensitive to computers. This place could really do me good.'

'We have to be careful about numbers,' she said, 'we mustn't draw attention to ourselves. But I'll talk to Cuthbert, if you like, and phone you if he says yes.' She felt in her jeans pocket and brought out a pencil and a slim spiral-bound notebook. 'Write your number down.'

'Data transfer complete.' Tom handed them back with a grin.

Suddenly a frenzied banging on the door behind them made the caravan shake. 'Sarah,' a cracked male voice shouted. 'Sarah, are you in there?'

'Oh my Lord, it's Stanford,' she muttered, then louder, 'It's open, come in,' and a broad-shouldered man with a tanned oblong face and a shaven head shoved his way inside.

Tom half-rose instinctively, preparing to make excuses and slink away. Then he sat down again, marvelling at how firmly the equation 'person = mobile' had become embedded in his brain. Stanford stood in the centre of the van, clenching and unclenching his fists, filling the space with burgundy

212

cashmere bulk. Tom smelled a subtle, fruity, doubtless expensive cologne, mixed with rank sweat.

'The goddamn bloody bitch,' he spat.

'Sit down, Stanford,' said Sarah. 'Tell us what happened. This is Tom, by the way. He's in the club.'

Stanford glanced at Tom as if he had not noticed he was there. He nodded and plonked himself on the seat next to Sarah.

'She's going for sole custody. I expected that. But she's also going to deny access. She doesn't want me seeing the kids at all.'

'What?' said Sarah. 'No access at all? That's outrageous – what are her grounds?'

'That the kids not being able to use their tablets and their Wiis when they are with me is,' he switched to a high mocking singsong, 'damaging their education and social development and impairing their ability to make and keep friends.'

'But that's...'

'And I am suffering from a psychiatric disorder for which I am wilfully refusing to seek treatment.'

'Oh Stanford.'

'It's crazy. When we get together, me and the kids, we just do different stuff. I bought board games. And we went fishing. And we went up in a hot air balloon. Ringo and Twilight are fine with it.'

Tom, impaled by a glare from Sarah, managed, by tensing all the muscles in his face and torso, not to laugh.

'Kids are very adaptable,' said Sarah. 'They accept things.'

Stanford dropped his large head into his hands, and gave a long shuddering groan.

'I don't know what Victoria's saying to them now. She was sympathetic to begin with, but she's not stupid. Worked out the likely effect on my earning potential and her social life. Calculated she'd be better off banking what she had. Went to see lawyers, quietly, behind my back. I don't blame her for that. But…I love my kids…'

He rocked back and forth, the caravan shifting with him on its frail supports, his whole body convulsed with dry, hoarse, heaving sobs. Sarah put an arm gingerly round his writhing shoulders.

'It's awful,' she said, 'but it's not over yet. You've got a good lawyer. You can fight for your kids.'

Tom got up and made for the door. He raised his hand to Sarah, then bent it to his ear to signal 'phone me'. She gave him a thumbs up. As he walked away from the shaking, howling caravan, his own legs were buckling. To see a man like that laid low, a man with all that wealth and forcefulness and power. To see him being ground down like the rest of them…. Despite the physical bliss Tom still felt from the valley, he was filled with despair.

CHAPTER 22

'Would it not be easier,' said Veronica, 'if Barry held the inner part upside down, and you, Tom, fed the elastic-linked poles into the pockets from above, as it were, thus taking advantage of gravity.'

'Let's try it,' said Tom, and Barry obliged.

It did work better, and they were soon able to upend the small rigid blue dome onto its grey plastic underside, and stand it on the turf. The old transit van was across the stream, for extra storage; Tom had driven it through the gate and down the track through the trees.

'Now the outer layer,' commanded Veronica. She stood a few paces away from them, erect and graceful in a large green circle skirt and frothy cardigan, with her silver hair in a bun and her ballet-pump-clad feet placed in a right angle. 'It is important to stretch it as tautly as possible, to maximise the waterproofing effect.'

'Is she always like this?' muttered Tom to Barry,

as they spread the flysheet over the dome and evened it out at the sides. Barry, a short, shy, gentle man immersed in a bushy dark-blond beard, shrugged and smiled. He took a handful of tent pegs and began to push them through the fabric loops into the ground. Tom followed suit. 'It's the cheekbones, I suppose,' he said to himself, and indeed Veronica had splendid cheekbones, a Grecian nose, ruler-straight, and cornflower-blue eyes. You could tell she had been a stunner in her youth.

'These things always take longer to put up than you anticipate,' said Veronica. 'My yurt claimed to be erectable in half a day, which was nonsense. The wooden frame was extremely tricky. Cuthbert and Barry had to assist me. But the high roof means I am able to do my morning yoga exercises inside it when the weather is not clement. Ah, I see you've done it. Congratulations! When, Tom, you have unpacked your luggage from the van, I shall fetch champagne.'

Soon Tom found himself lounging alongside Barry, Veronica and Sarah, who had crossed over the stream to join them, as they sat on an assortment of folding chairs in the afternoon sunshine, sipping champagne from plastic flutes. The Pavlovian spasm of anxiety in the presence of other people that he had acquired since his arrival at the vicarage had begun to subside, and he was relishing the sensation of simply being with his own species; he had not done it in months.

He recalled his mother's words when he had told her about his planned move to the Valley: 'But is that really a wise course, Tom? You will be cutting yourself off from the community – from normal life.'

'Mum,' he had said, when he could trust himself, 'if you can talk like that, you haven't got a clue.'

To give her credit, she had apologised, and hugged him, and said she knew he had been going through a very bad time. She was only anxious because she would miss him, and if he believed it was the right thing for him, she hoped with all her heart that the Valley would do him good.

'Would anyone like a Fortnum and Mason's fancy?' Veronica was asking, handing round a flowered melamine plate. 'My hamper arrived last week.'

'Yes, and it's supposed to last you,' said Sarah. 'It's really sweet of you to give us treats, but you shouldn't keep doing it.'

'Nonsense,' said Veronica grandly. Plainly, Tom saw, it was one of her favourite words. She lay back in her folding chair and lifted her elegant ankles in the air, side by side, to contemplate her green ballet pumps. 'I am an old lady,' she went on, although you could tell she didn't believe a word of it. 'I was sixty-eight when I turned, so the government is obliged to pay me my old age pension. Ha! I am also a property owner, and I have let out my gorgeous but entirely useless flat in North London at a reasonable rent. Thus, I have it a lot easier than you young sprigs for the present at least, until I go gaga and they attempt to put me in some ghastly care home where the rooms are monitored by wireless cameras and all the residents are electronically tagged.'

'I don't see much sign of it yet,' said Sarah with affection. 'Did you know you're in the first position in Stanford's Scrabble league? He's keeping a record of all the games we've had and aggregating the scores.'

'That man!' exclaimed Veronica, but her cheeks became pink with pleasure.

'Did you have a nice day off, Barry?' Sarah enquired.

Barry smiled beneath his beard. 'I watched a buzzard through my binoculars,' he said, in a gentle Welsh accent, 'over the other side of the hills. It came down like a stone.' He demonstrated with his hand. 'And I saw another bird I wasn't sure about – it may have been a kestrel, because it hovered and it had pointed wings. I'll need to check it in my bird book.'

'I'm sure there's an app for that,' said Sarah to Barry, with complete seriousness and sincerity, and suddenly to Tom's astonishment all three of them were rocking with laughter, lying back on their chairs and shaking helplessly. Sarah recovered first. 'Sorry,' she gasped. 'It's...sort of a running joke.'

'Yes, very rude of us,' said Veronica, smoothing her skirt. 'I do apologise. Would you like some more champagne?'

Tom, holding out his glass, spotted a movement in the trees on the other side of the stream, and soon a figure came into view bustling along the path that led up the Valley from the farm. Tom saw it was a short Chinese lady with a pudding-bowl haircut, her round form squeezed into tight black trousers and an orange zip-up fleece.

'Hello, you must be Tom,' she said, when she'd crossed the stream. 'I'm Chai. You are a physicist? That's good! We haven't got one of those.'

She dragged a folding chair from her tent, opened it and plumped down into the seat, breathing hard. Veronica handed her some champagne, remarking, 'Chai worked in IT support for a major bank before she turned.'

'I was the best geek there!' said Chai, cheerfully. 'I could fix anything. Everybody wanted me. They were all very upset when I left. There was a massive systems hack one week later – cost them millions of pounds. Oh – by the way, I have the post.' She delved into the inside pocket of her fleece and brought out a sheaf of letters.

'Chai… you didn't actually… you know, deliberately…?' Sarah enquired.

'Of course not. No – I was the only one who understood the cybersecurity setup. The IT Director was totally useless.' She handed round letters. 'One for you, Barry, two for Veronica, two for Sarah, one for me.'

'Tom looks young and strong,' said Veronica. 'He should be able to assist you, Sarah, with the vegetable plot. There will be a good deal of digging involved, not to mention the carrying in of manure and so on. Are you proposing to make use of our own... offerings, as a matter of interest?'

'I...haven't quite worked that one out yet,' said Sarah apologetically. 'I'll have to read up on it in my permaculture guide. By the way, would anyone mind if I went down now and called my Dad on the farmhouse phone?'

'I don't mind,' said Veronica, 'but Stanford may be hogging it as usual. It is either his solicitors or his investment portfolio.'

CHAPTER 23

Tom plunged the heavy spade into the ground, using the whole of his weight to lever it backwards, sensing the strain and crack of roots. He upended a wedge of soil forwards into the waiting trench, stepped sideways and plunged the spade in again. This time it jarred against something hard; he reached down and grubbed out a lump of chalk with his fingers, chucking it onto a pile to the side.

The morning was mild and overcast after a couple of days of intermittent rain, and the earth smelt rich like treacle. They'd been at it for over an hour, he guessed, and they'd still only dug over about a third of the proposed vegetable plot. Marking out the boundaries with sticks and string, they'd enclosed a grassy rectangle about ten metres by five. 'Big enough for beginners,' Sarah had said. They had extracted the lower parts of the camp compost heap – encouragingly crumbly and brown – and spread it on top of their plot, so that the nutritious organic matter was folded into the soil as they dug.

It was good to be doing something purposeful, with other people. He'd only been in the Valley for a fortnight, but already he felt restored, as though he was coming back to himself, blood flowing again to parts of him that had become pale, stunted and numb. He'd joined in the Scrabble game last night – they'd been in Stanford's motorhome, all thick pile carpet, brushed chrome curves, recessed lighting and subtle shades of grey. Veronica had brought a candelabra with five red candles. 'To create an atmosphere,' she had said.

She had put down the word 'AXOLOTL' on a double word score with the X on a triple. 'That is not English.' Stanford said flatly. 'Can't be with letters like that. Take it off.'

'I think you'll find,' in tones of honeyed sweetness, 'that it is a South American amphibian.'

'Exactly. South American. In a South American language. Not English. Take it off.'

'But Stanford,' said Chai, 'English is full of foreign words. If you want to refer to a new foreign thing, you borrow the foreign word. The word becomes part of English. Like panda. Which is Nepali, actually, not Chinese.'

'Who needs to refer to South American amphibians, for God's sake.'

'An amphibiophile,' said Barry into his beard.

'Sounds like a sexual perversion,' Stanford

snorted.

'Axolotl silly questions and you getsalotl silly answers.'

'We'll look it up in the dictionary,' Sarah said soothingly. 'That will give us the answer. Who's got the dictionary, by the way?'

Chai looked sheepish. 'Very sorry – I took it to the farmhouse. Needed to check something for work.'

No one had wanted to leave the blissful warmth of built-in gas heaters to walk a mile and a half in the dark.

'In future,' said Sarah, sighing, 'we should always make sure we've got it before we start a game. Otherwise there's always some sort of row when we need to check a word.'

'I think there's an app for that,' Tom had interposed, and everyone had laughed and congratulated him.

'So are we going to allow it or not?' growled Stanford, reverting to his serious mode. 'We can't sit here all night.'

'I have a feeling it does exist,' Tom had said.

'Me too,' said Barry. 'A bit like a newt.'

'I will indemnify you,' Veronica said grandly, reclining like an exotic bird against the grey. 'If it doesn't exist – which, by the way, it does – I will accept a sixty-point penalty in the next game.'

'One hundred points,' Stanford had stipulated, 'and you have a deal.'

*

Stanford was coming towards them now, taking a sheaf of mail from his Louis Vuitton tan leather shoulder bag. 'Nice work,' he said approvingly. 'Rather you than me. Letter for you, Sarah.'

She stuck her spade upright in the ground and reached for the envelope. 'Thanks. Hey, it's from Lucy. I'd know that handwriting anywhere. I haven't heard from her for a while. Tom, it's after eleven – shall we stop for a break? I think my arms are going to drop off.'

Veronica, emerging from a meditation session in her yurt, fussed over them, setting out folding chairs, making coffee and handing round biscuits.

'Are you going to grow asparagus?' she enquired. 'Fresh asparagus, lightly steamed, served very simply, with lemon butter.' She kissed the tips of her fingers. 'Ah – delectable.'

'Not this year,' Sarah replied, opening the envelope and unfolding the letter inside. 'In my vegetable book, it's marked "difficult". We're going to start with everything that's marked "easy".' She broke off. 'Oh my God,' her voice suddenly drained. 'No.... No.... Oh God.' She stood up so fast that the chair fell backwards, her face as white as the lumps of chalk. She shifted from one foot to the other in frantic uncertainty, looking wildly around. Then 'Perhaps... it's not too late. I'm going to phone. I'm going to phone anyway,' and throwing the pages down she sprinted for the path through the trees.

Veronica slowly knelt down on the turf and retrieved the letter with her silver-ringed, blue-veined hand. As she glanced through its contents, she seemed to grow older in front of his eyes. He went to her side and silently offered his arm; she pressed down hard on him as she climbed stiffly to her feet.

'What's happened?' he asked.

She shook her head. 'I am afraid it is too late. Read it – I can't see that it matters much now.' Shakily, 'I – I am going to rest.'

Placing the letter into his hands she walked away into the yurt, still graceful, still upright, yet reduced.

The ink was black, the writing open and round; it reminded Tom of school.

My dear Sarah,

By the time you get this letter, I will have come to the end of my road. For a while this little bungalow has been a refuge, of sorts, but after what's been done in the village, it isn't any more. I could try to track down another place, another island in the slowly rising sea, but what would be the point? Once you've turned, every place is only ever provisional, and the effort needed to find the next one is greater.

You've been a wonderful friend, truly, you're one of the reasons I've kept going so long.

Please remember: there is nothing you could have said or done that would have changed my mind.

This world and me – we can't be made to fit. One day, perhaps, if recognition comes, things might be different. But I can't wait that long. I've been this way for ten years.

Goodbye my dear. Be lucky as long as you can.

My love,

Lucy

He stood without moving for a long time, the letter in his hand. Beneath the slowly interpenetrating greys of the mottled sky, sudden swift perturbations of birds reordered themselves in the encompassing trees. The campsite was silent and empty, abandoned coffee cups and chairs and spades making a strange tableau beside the hopeful brown strip of newly dug earth. He had a sense of being full of something he didn't want to spill: an intense awareness of the difference between life and death, an extreme consciousness of being on one side of the divide. But he was acutely conscious too of the thinness, the flimsiness of the barrier: a flap of skin, a few bowls of blood.

He seized the spade and started to dig, with frenzied energy. By the time Sarah trailed back through the trees, he had turned over another third.

'The phone rang out,' she said in a level voice,

staring at the ridge of the downs. 'It just rang and rang. So I called another friend. Lucy's done it. She died two days ago.'

She began to shake with terrible, juddering regularity, as though a pneumatic drill pressed into her. Tom hesitated, not sure what he should do in a situation that was new to him, but that he realised with a twisting sick certainty would not stay new for long. He walked over and put an arm round her trembling shoulders; she didn't flinch. 'I'm so sorry,' he said. 'It must be a shock.'

She made a strange writhing movement.

'How did she...if you don't mind telling me...'

Sarah sniffed and rubbed her eyes with her sleeve. 'You should know,' she said. 'Lucy was quiet and organised and understated and dry – but she had style. She used to love flying, in her old life. She jumped off the church tower, a particularly tall one. She would have flown, for a few seconds, before....'

'Whew...' Tom whistled. 'I don't think I'd have had the guts.'

'The tower was where they'd put the repeater mast to improve the mobile reception.'

'Oh. I see.'

'She'd written to the Parochial Church Council, told them what it would mean for her if they did it, that she was too far gone to try to move again. Perhaps one or two of them had a small pang. Of course they didn't change their plans.'

'Will – anything – come out at the inquest? About her being a reactor?'

Sarah shrugged. 'Might do, might not. In any case the coroner will say there is no hard evidence that reactors exist, there will be suggestions that living as a nomadic hermit the way she did was a sign of mental illness, everyone will say how very sad it all is, and the world will move on.'

A bright-eyed robin perched on the handle of Tom's spade, then hopped onto the newly dug soil to look for worms. From the downs came the single long bleat of a sheep, then a quavering, ironic reply.

'Okay. How many?'

'Oh Tom, I'm sorry. You're – you're so new to this.'

'Just tell me' – taken aback by his own brutality. He hadn't meant it to come out so harsh. But he had to ask. She made a limp gesture of resignation.

'Every few months, you hear of someone. Sometimes it's…someone you didn't know at all. Sometimes it's someone you know of slightly. Sometimes…' – her voice fragmenting – 'it's someone you know quite well. Excuse me.' She turned, her face contorting, ran to the door of her caravan and vanished inside.

So this was the club he had joined. A special club: you didn't have a choice about becoming a member. Very exclusive – people were being enrolled in small numbers, all the time; apparently they were leaving, too. Pressed, gradually, into

228

smaller and smaller spaces, and when the pressure became unbearable, extruded like shit from an anus, mashed and pulped.

Never quite enough people, or quite often enough to disturb the peace of society. Just someone shat out here, someone shat out there; just uncommon enough to stay as individual tragic cases, and make sure no one joined the dots to see the whole.

He had the urge to run; to make his escape from these intimates of corpses and their circle of suffocating hills. To turn his back on it all, run so hard and so fast that he'd burst backwards through time, enter his life before he'd started to turn, by sheer force of will bend his future into a different path.

Madness, of course. The Valley was his best hope to climb back up the arsehole. He was lucky to have found it, should be down on his knees with gratitude. Outside it he'd be a declining tortured wreck.

He picked up the spade again, and began to dig, trying to lose his dark thoughts in action, keep his mind on seeds that would sprout and leaves that would unfold, on life and purpose and growth and the recovery of resilience and not on the flat, final, extended despair that must have led up to that leap, those few mad moments of unnatural, accelerating freedom, the smash of the body into the earth.

*

Everyone had been subdued for the next few

days, as though an invisible insulating layer had been spread over the Valley. People seemed imperceptibly to avoid each other, so that certain topics would not be discussed; when they did finally meet for a Scrabble game, the arguments over trivialities were a relief.

Sarah and Tom broke up clods and raked the surface of their plot. They marked out drills for different vegetables according to Sarah's sketch plan, running taut lengths of string between small vertical twigs. They carefully tore open packets and sprinkled the seed with their fingertips into long parallel grooves scraped into the earth. They were regularly soaked by violently ecstatic rain showers, but then the melodramatic piles of incontinent cloud would peel away to reveal the beaming sun in pure blue gaps of sky; the new-leaved trees hung with sparkling water-beads; puddles gleaming in hollows like round oddments of silk.

One morning they had been planting the potatoes that had been sprouting exploratory white tendrils on top of the transit's dashboard.

'It's going to rain again,' Sarah said, peering up at the sky. 'Let's stop for a break.'

They sat on opposite foam seats in the caravan, muddy boots on newspaper by the door, drinking coffee and eating biscuits, Sarah had taken off her huge woolly jumper; underneath she was wearing a dark red top with a scoop neck. Tom noticed a photograph in a plastic frame on a shelf beside a jam jar of white star-shaped flowers. It showed a person standing in a garden beside a rosebush, round-faced, slight-framed, in jeans and sandals, bobbed blond hair, a hand raised in salute.

'Lucy?' he asked, pointing.

She nodded. 'She sent it to me. Last year, I think. I put it in the frame to make a memorial.'

'She looks nice.'

'She was great.'

'What happens now? After the inquest...there'll be a funeral?'

'I suppose so,' she shrugged. 'But after being a reactor for ten years, she had a lot of reactor friends, and not a lot of normal ones. It'll be quiet. Most of us won't be able to go.'

After the final shitting out, the discreet tidying away. The people who would mourn you did it privately and singly, in out-of-the-way corners. No one came together to weep or howl or rage. They couldn't afford to waste one precious drop of their hard-won resilience, because they knew they clung to the same cliff above the same ravening sea.

'How do you stand this?' Oh God, too harsh, too bitter, what was he thinking?

She looked up enquiringly.

He couldn't help himself. 'How can you just sit there and take it?'

'I don't.'

'I don't understand.'

'I'm not just taking it. I'm surviving – that in itself is an act of defiance. I don't know whether if I was in Lucy's situation I would make the same choice. None of us do. I do know that I'm going on as long as I possibly can. Because when the normal world wants you to disappear, that's the most subversive thing you can do.'

She reached for his hands and gripped them in her own. 'And I'll tell you something else – while I do it I'm going to enjoy every damn thing I can: the taste of coffee and the sounds of birds and the smell of rain and the colours of the sunset. Because for us each small pleasure is a victory, and every one we experience despite the devastation of our lives is two fingers stuck up in their face.'

She spoke with ferocious intensity, fire kindling in her eyes, hair tumbling over their joined hands. Tom stared back at her, feeling himself wrapped around and swept up by her energy. Sarah released him, her face flushed. 'Sorry,' she said. 'I got a bit carried away.'

'Don't be. It was great. Talking of pleasure, may I have another biscuit?'

She gave a great shout of laughter and handed him the tin. 'Sure. Have two.'

They raised their coffee mugs at the same moment with an identical impulse, and then stopped, looking at each other.

'What are we drinking to?' asked Tom.

'To Lucy.' Her voice shook but she controlled it and went on.'And to survival, defiance, and the pleasures that remain.'

Tom repeated the toast and they drained their mugs. Then she lounged back along the caravan seat, her chin raised so that she was looking at the curved cream-coloured roof, and she stretched one leg upwards, pointing a slender foot in her striped sock, and said, in a matter-of-fact tone, 'I don't suppose you fancy having sex, do you?'

Tom jerked upright as though he had been shot; and at the same time felt an erection like a hammer-blow.

'What…now?' he stammered, his voice thick.

Sarah wiggled her shoulders gracefully, still gazing at the ceiling, and said, 'Why not?'

'In that case…yes please.'

She slowly unfolded herself from the seat, so that she was standing before him and he was reaching up with wonder to touch her face when she grasped his wrist and held it.

'Tom, wait, we're in a caravan, there isn't any room. I'll have to put the bed up.' She began to giggle. 'Sorry, bad planning, this part is not going to be very erotic. You go over here.'

She led him to the kitchen end of the caravan, and positioned him with his back to the sink. 'Hold that thought,' she murmured, cupping her hand over his bulging groin as her lips brushed the side of his mouth.

At the other end of the van she bent down, and her bum rose, outlined in black denim, and he watched it come towards him as she dragged wooden slats across the gap between the seats, and he could not resist, had to reach out to touch the smooth curves, feel their firm arcs fill his palms. He thrust one hand gently between her thighs, holding her, claiming her, and she pushed back, warm against his fingers, and moved in delicate circles as she pulled the foam seat backs over the slats. Inside him something that had been dismembered began to reform, twitching its limbs, wanting to dance.

There was a bed now, spanning the whole width of the van. Sarah was clambering round on top, tucking in a sheet, closing the curtains on the mutable morning so the interior was bathed in pink half-light. Finally she lay back breathless and laughing in the middle of her creation, and flung out her arms. Tom applauded.

'Now,' he said, climbing onto the bed beside her, 'Where were we?'

'I think,' she said, reaching for the zip on his jeans, 'That we were about to try something very traditional…'

'…with no secret filming on our smart phones.'

'No naked selfies that get posted online.'

'No rating performance on dating websites…'

234

'No worrying about your social media status.'
'In fact – none of the above.'
'Just good, unclean fun.'
'Oh yes indeed.'

CHAPTER 24

Tom noticed the car as soon as he stepped out of the farmhouse. He'd just tried his first five minutes on a computer (one of the desktops in Cuthbert's office) since he'd come to the Valley six weeks earlier, and was feeling exhilarated – no effects so far – but also cautious. The car was parked at the far end of the yard, and stood out through the cold spring drizzle because it was a particularly lurid shade of blue. It was sporty, an unusual make – not the kind of vehicle favoured by Cuthbert's usual visitors, who turned up, when anyone did, in trucks or mud-spattered 4x4s. He was sufficiently intrigued to take a closer look.

The driver's door opened, and a man climbed out. Stocky, dark-haired, leather-jacketed, gazing around the soggy farmyard in a bemused but jaunty way. Tom stopped in his tracks. It couldn't be. Could it?

'Kev,' Tom shouted. 'What the – what on earth are you doing here?'

Kevin, his confusion vanishing like mist on

a heated windscreen, grinned nonchalantly and sauntered forwards.

'Looking for you, of course.' He added, 'Hey, relax, I know the score. All my tech is in the car. And I switched everything off.' He showed his open hands. 'I'm clean.'

'Oh – that's great. Thanks. Like the car, by the way. Yours?'

Kevin glowed with pride. 'All mine, mate. Well, mine and the finance company's.'

'So – how's the research project going? Have they changed it?'

A strange compound expression passed over Kevin's cheerful face. 'That's what I need to talk to you about. That's why I've been sending you emails and messages.'

'Oh...Kev, sorry, I...'

'Yes, I know that *now*. Why didn't you tell me where you were? Eventually I found your mum online, and she said you'd gone cold turkey on the computer but you weren't with her any more and she was pretty cagey about telling me where you had gone, because apparently no one's supposed to discuss this place, especially not on the net, but eventually I rang her up and persuaded her that I was genuinely a friend of yours and that it was urgent.' He paused to take a breath, then added, 'Okay, so now I know you got allergic to the computer, had to go and live in a tent, blah blah blah. But you could have written me a sodding *letter,* or phoned. I'm not Marianne, in case you hadn't noticed.'

Tom felt prickly with shame. 'You're right. I'm sorry. I should have. I got kind of terrified about becoming a phase 2 reactor, and then I heard about the Valley and got caught up in moving here and well…trying to make the best of it. Anyway, you're here now, which is great. Come and I'll show you our camp.'

They set off along the path through the trees. Tom assumed Kevin would start talking straight away, but he was uncharacteristically quiet, glancing around restlessly at the trunks that lined up like dank columns on either side. Their feet squelched in unison until Tom said, 'OK, Kevin, spit it out. What's happened with the research project?'

Kevin stopped walking and turned to him, clutching his arm. 'Mate – there's bad news. And there's good news. It's complicated. I'm not sure what you're going to say….'

'Right,' Tom decided. 'Guess what – Sarah is here too. Let's go and talk it through in her caravan.'

'Sarah?'

'Yeah – you remember, tall girl, threw up all over the testing room.'

Kevin said, 'Actually, quite a lot of reactors have been doing that. And worse.'

'I took her to the trees.'

'Oh. Yes – I do remember.'

'Well...anyway...we kind of got together. Yesterday. In the caravan.'

Kevin whistled and nudged him in the ribs. 'So – not pining for Marianne then? Actually, that's kind of good, considering what...' He tailed off.

Tom snorted. 'I'm pretty sure she's not pining for me.'

Sarah had put the gas heater on, and the atmosphere was foetid, the caravan windows slimed with condensed breath and steam. She placed three plastic mugs of tea on the fold-out table, pushing one towards Kevin. He pulled a wad of paper from the pocket of his jacket. 'I've got the minutes of the review meeting here,' he said. 'I'll give you the details – that will be the best thing, I think.'

Tom nodded. 'Go ahead, Kev.'

'The first thing was I did my presentation. Afterwards there were a few questions, and then this research fellow who did a lot of the work on the research design – Dr Daniel Bennell from the School of Public Health (we're a multidisciplinary team) – began a long spiel about transparency and full disclosure. He is this small, weaselly guy with a moustache who never uses one word when fifteen will do, so I was sitting back waiting for Prof Arrowsmith to cut him off until he said, "And that brings us to the role of Tom Jenkins in the instigation of this review."

'I'll read you what happened next: "Dr Bennell said that in his paper Dr Corden credits Tom Jenkins simply with assisting with the equations which purport accurately to articulate the reactor experience. He informs us that Tom Jenkins is currently undertaking a PhD here at Northington in the theoretical physics department.

'"However Dr Corden has failed to disclose several material facts. Firstly, in November, Tom Jenkins prevailed on his supervisor Dr Ed Torrios to have the university Wi-Fi system switched off in the area of the physics department around his office. In conversations with Dr Bennell, Dr Torrios has confirmed Tom Jenkins' recent anxious and distressed state of mind. Secondly, at the request of his then partner Marianne Klinghoffer, Tom Jenkins later took part in the experiment, as a member of the reactor group. Ms Klinghoffer, concerned about Tom's increasingly erratic behaviour, felt it would benefit him and their relationship to test whether his claims regarding his reactor status were correct. Dr Bennell has spoken extensively to Ms Klinghoffer and expresses his gratitude for her co-operation."'

Marianne? Marianne had talked to this random stranger about him? Tom felt as though a bone had jammed in his throat.

Kevin glanced up. 'I'm sorry you have to hear this.' He went on reading: '"Dr Bennell reminded the meeting of the concept of cognitive dissonance, the extreme psychological pain which people experience when confronted with evidence that conflicts with strongly held belief systems to which they have also committed themselves through action. The foundational text in this research area is of course *When Prophecy Fails* by Leon Festinger and associates (1956), a study of a sect in Chicago led by a Mrs Dorothy Martin. Martin claimed to be in communication with superior extraterrestrial beings. Her followers believed that the Earth would be destroyed on a particular date, and before that, a flying saucer would arrive to rescue them, the true believers – who had left jobs, homes and partners and given away their possessions in preparation for their departure. When the prophecy failed to materialise, Martin received another message: because of the dedication of the group, God had decided to save the world from destruction. The group then went on to proselytise with increased enthusiasm."'

Flying saucers? Aliens? Where was he going with this?

Kevin went on: '"Dr Bennell drew an analogy with Tom Jenkins' likely situation as he faced the first of his test exposures – the start of a process which could well lead to the discrediting of all his claims and the related loss of status in his personal and professional life. Realising that he was unable to discern whether there was a signal or not, and thus under extreme psychological stress, Tom Jenkins rationalised quickly that there must be something wrong with the experiment, and his ingenious mind set to work. The result was an account of reactors' reactions which means that for all practical purposes *they can never be proved wrong*. In addition, he secured his justification for abandoning the exposure session and therefore not putting his belief system to the test.

'"Dr Bennell added that the equations in Dr Corden's paper might well put colleagues in mind of the ancient Ptolemaic system for explaining the observed movements of the planets, stars and sun, whilst keeping the Earth at the centre of the universe. A highly complex and creative series of rotations within rotations was proposed, which did in fact deliver planetary positions approximating to astronomical observations. However with the sun correctly enshrined at the centre of the solar system, this huge and creaking machinery became embarrassingly obsolete."'

'God, I should have been there,' Tom said. The muscles in his face were so tight he could barely get the words out, his hands were balled into fists. 'God, I should never have left. I should have kept on living in the woods in my van, freezing my backside off, putting up with Marianne's sticky pity. Then I would have been there to make Bennell choke on everything he said.'

'Yes, he's a jerk, I know. Anyway, the next bit is me: "Dr Corden asked whether Dr Bennell was arguing that because someone believed they were a reactor, they were for that reason unable to make any form of valid objective critique of our experiment.

'"Dr Bennell replied that if someone believed they were a reactor, we knew they entertained at least one delusional belief."'

'But that's…'

'I didn't let him get away with it. "Dr Corden queried this, as throughout the period of the study, before the results were in, those conducting the study were supposed to be neutral and evenhanded as to whether a person who believed they were a reactor was or was not correct. Dr Bennell had apparently made his mind up in advance.

'"Dr Bennell acknowledged that he should have chosen his words more carefully and did not in any way prejudge the outcome. However he reminded Dr Corden of the experiment's baseline condition, or null hypothesis, which was in line with the current scientific consensus: RF radiation does not have significant nonthermal effects on biological systems. Ergo reactors do not exist."

'I remembered what you'd shown me, Tom, all those papers showing nonthermal effects, all those scientists who don't get appointed to the official advisory groups who create the "current scientific consensus" in the first place. But I didn't think it would help to get into that with Dr Bennell. So the minutes go on: "Dr Corden stated that it was this type of prejudice which made Tom Jenkins ask him not to disclose his reactor status. In any case the equations were only one part of the critique, which also encompassed the extremely high level of reactor dropouts, the severe symptoms they experienced, and the discarding of their results. These observations resulted from Dr Corden's own direct experiences carrying out the testing. None was predicted or envisaged in the research design, which had now come into contact with reality and needed to be changed."

'Oh, there's pages of argument here. How would our sponsors react to revamping the research design? (Answer: not well.) Such an important piece of research – a great honour for our university, hugely embarrassing if it was discredited. Difficult to imagine what an alternative research design could look like, which we could actually persuade people to take part in within reasonable financial constraints. Finally, someone asked, "Where is Tom Jenkins now? Could he not come and explain himself?"

'I remember at that point Dr Bennell shot me a sideways gloating grin and said, "Unfortunately, according to my discussions with Ms Klinghoffer, Tom Jenkins is now on extended sick leave. He was last known to be living wild in the woods."'

'Wow.' Sarah gave Tom a slow appraising look. 'He was certainly out to get you.'

Kevin flipped to the final page. 'Here's Prof

Arrowsmith summing up: "Everyone had made very valid points and worthwhile contributions. It was important to bear in mind that this was the first major research project in this new, complex, emerging field, and the study team wasn't going to claim we had got everything right. All we could do was strike a fair balance, respecting the work that had already been carried out, while being very open and upfront with our caveats and qualifications about its limitations in the final paper."'

'But…'

'Yes, Tom, I know what you're going to say. But wait – wait until I've told you the next part.'

'What next part? The whole thing's obviously a stitch up.'

'*Wait.* Anyway, I was gutted for those last couple of weeks of testing – moving about like a zombie, stretching my mouth at each participant, thanking them for giving up their time. I kept wondering what to do, wondering whether I should go direct to the ethics committee, trying to get hold of you.

'Then, finally, one Friday evening, it was over – the last one had been done. I sat at my desk, staring at nothing. I got through two jumbo bags of crisps, stuffing them automatically into my mouth. The place was really quiet, just the eerie humming of the servers and the lights. Pitch black outside the windows – everyone else had gone home. I was supposed to be going to the Hat and Feathers for a drink but I couldn't summon up the energy – I felt like my arse had taken root in that chair.

'About 9 p.m. I started opening the data files. The numbers scrolled past my eyes and I imagined zapping them with laser guns like in a computer game – all those pointless, meaningless numbers which I'd gathered with so much effort and which had made me inflict so much pain. I don't know what I was thinking, really. Sabotage? Wipe them all? A few clicks and I could flush them down the digital toilet like the pile of crap they were.

'In the end I didn't do anything like that. What I did was start to play around, do some basic analysis of the data using the statistical software tools. Perhaps I was trying to prove to myself how useless the whole thing had been.

'Remember what we were asking the participants to record – severity of their various physical symptoms on a scale of 1 to 10, then their judgment as to whether the signal was strong, weak or sham. Well – for all of these, there was no significant difference between the controls and reactor group.'

'I could have told you that last year,' Tom said.

'I know. But *wait*. We also asked the participants to fill in a standardised psychological well-being questionnaire during the session, and we scored their answers under five different measures. Well – for three of these measurements – anxious, hostile and calm – I found a significant result.'

Kevin sat back, beaming beatifically around the van. Tom and Sarah looked at each other and shrugged. 'Significant how?' Tom asked.

'Oh come on, Tom. Where's your expensive mathematical education gone?' His voice was growing warmer and he was beginning to wave his arms. 'When exposed to a real signal compared to a sham signal – *whether or not* they think it's real or sham, and regardless of what physical symptoms they are or aren't having – reactors are more hostile, more anxious and less calm than non-reactors, to a degree that is statistically significant – meaning unlikely to be the result of random chance.'

'You...you found something?' Sarah's voice was so faint and breathy, Tom could hardly make out her words.

Kevin was bouncing his head up and down, like a toy dog on a dashboard, his grin unzipping almost round to the back of his skull. 'I haven't said anything to anybody else yet. We haven't officially started the statistical analysis. But I just had to come and find you...'

'Kev, are you sure? Did you check?'

'Of course I did. Looks like *something* starts to happen with reactors during an exposure slot, even if it doesn't reach a conscious level.'

Tom gazed at his friend in his jeans and leather jacket, with his Tasmanian devil scarf and his terrible lairy socks, and tried to open his mind to the wonder of it, to this most unlikely guardian angel.

He spoke slowly, his words flat-footed with astonishment. 'You mean that totally flawed experiment…'

'Might save you after all. Yes.'

'But…Kev – you don't know what this means, for me, for all of us…'

A calm, bright, straightforward future unfurled before his eyes, in which he could speak, ask for help, be believed. The old life waiting for him at the other end of England opened its arms.

He was leaping up to go and tell the others when he felt Sarah's strong hand press down on his thigh, forcing him back onto the seat.

'Wait. Don't say anything yet.'

'Why not? Don't you get it? This is the dream, what we've all been waiting for, the best present we're ever going to get.' And Kev was the one who'd brought it.

'We should wait until it's official. Kevin, do you know how long that will be?'

'A few months? Something like that.'

'Why?' Tom said. 'What's going to change? The data's the data. Science is science.' He had shaken himself free, suddenly wanting to be outside the van's constricting walls, running, chasing a ball down a pitch towards an open, welcoming goal.

'Tom, I have a strange feeling about all of this, and I've been in this game a lot longer than you. If something happened, something changed...' She glanced behind her out of the window, where Stanford stood stiff and motionless, apparently hypnotised by the rippling stream, his expensive navy wool back to them, his shaved head bowed. 'God, it would be too cruel.'

'Okay, let's keep it quiet. But nothing is going to change. Numbers don't lie. Kev, I'm on my way back, mate. This just confirms it. I tried the computer at the farmhouse this morning, for five minutes, and so far I'm fine. This place is doing me so much good – I just need to stay here a bit longer, get the computer and the mobile issue sorted. Hey – when I get back to Northington, we could get a house together. It will be like old times...except with a bit more cabling...'

Kevin grinned. 'No problem, mate. I can cope with a few bits of wire.'

CHAPTER 25

That was the week that summer first showed itself in the Valley, the long cold rainy spring suddenly packing its bags and departing hastily in the night. Each time Tom looked at the trees, shy baby leaves seemed to grow bigger and brighter, as though thousands of tiny parasols were being stealthily opened to make a great lush canopy of green. The air itself seemed changed into a different substance, soft and sweet as butterscotch, rippled through with the fluting notes of birds.

The campers gratefully divested themselves of warm layers, hung their washing to dry on ropes stretched between the trees, reintroduced their bare feet to the earth. Veronica spread a large oriental rug on the grass in front of her yurt, and practised her yoga outside; Chai joined her with Tai Chi. Barry bought himself a bigger van, one he would be able to sleep in, if he got well enough to venture back to Wales. Tom and Sarah worked on the vegetable patch, earthing up the potatoes around their dark leafy haulms to stop the tubers turning green, and thinning radish and lettuce and beetroot seedlings which were sprouting in frothy green rows.

Only Stanford remained wintry, trudging back and forth to the farmhouse like a walking vat of impotent agony. Victoria was insisting that he had not fully disclosed his assets, which left him in a quandary. If he did disclose them, it was extremely unlikely that he would be left enough by the court to buy a detached, isolated house in the countryside. And that was the kind of house he would need – if he was ever to live in a house again.

From: Tom Jenkins

To: Kevin Corden

Hey Kev, I can use the computer for 30 minutes a day now – how cool is that? – so here I am, back on email, at least for short periods. It's like getting a leg out of plaster. God there's a lot of crap in my inbox.

It was really great to see you. Thanks for coming.

Yours

Tom

From: Kevin Corden

To: Tom Jenkins

That's fantastic mate. Don't overdo it. Keep off the porn, gambling, cat videos. It's easy to get sucked in.

Am meeting the Prof on Tuesday to talk about the data analysis. 4 p.m. in her office.

K

From: Tom Jenkins

To: Kevin Corden

Shame I can't be there – just to see her face…!

From: Kevin Corden

To: Tom Jenkins

Tom – I saw the Prof.

I'd better tell you everything that happened. I'm still reeling.

At first she was all smiles and encouragement – keen to show that the little episode of the review was over and forgotten. So pleased we were 'all pulling in the same direction'. So important for her researchers to share their concerns with more experienced colleagues, and not get sidetracked by extra-mural conversations.

I knew what was in my laptop, so I smiled and nodded and agreed with everything she said.

I showed her the first two sets of numbers.

She pursed her lips and nodded in a regretful, sympathetic 'how sad but this is just what we expected' kind of way. Then I showed her the well-being numbers. Her eyebrows went up so fast I thought her spectacles would come off in the backdraft. She exclaimed, 'Oh! I don't think that can be right,' and took the laptop off me with both hands. She started scrolling through the data, typing in commands. After about five minutes, the clouds lifted and she sat back, looking relieved, and said, 'Now that is easily explained.'

I said I didn't see why it needed to be 'explained' at all, but she started being patronising about remembering my undergraduate statistics module, and, specifically, what can happen when multiple statistical tests are performed on a single data set.

I remembered quite well, and I didn't like where this was going. Basically when multiple tests are run on the same dataset, the likelihood of identifying at least one falsely significant result increases with each additional test performed. So to correct for this, the bar is set higher for any individual result to be considered significant. There's a name for this – it's the Bonferroni correction.

(Who was Bonferroni? I hear you ask. Answer: Italian probability guy.)

Anyway the Prof said, 'Now we have five different metrics here – anxious, energised, calm and so on. So we should be dividing by five, shouldn't we? Which sets the bar much higher; and when we do that, these apparent differences between the so-called reactors and the controls are no longer statistically significant.' She'd magicked them away.

The thing is, I'd considered all this Bonferroni business but decided against it, for pretty good reasons. I tried to explain that these different parameters – feeling hostile, feeling anxious and so on – are pretty likely to be highly correlated. Because a person feeling anxious is also likely to feel hostile and uncomfortable, and – well – not calm. So the five parameters that we're testing for are not truly independent. And in cases like that, doing the Bonferroni correction makes it much more likely that the null hypothesis (which is that reactors don't exist) will be wrongly confirmed.

She told me she judges differently. In her view a Bonferroni correction is entirely appropriate.

I'm really sorry, mate. I argued and argued but she's not shifting.

Kev

From: Tom Jenkins

To: Kevin Corden

Kev – this is an absolute disaster – you've got to make this public. Your original presentation, and your original data analysis.

Sarah says there are a handful of sympathetic journalists who might be able to help.

I'm going to do some online research. I'll find you a name and contact details. It's got to come from you, you're the one on the inside, you're not a reactor.

From: Tom Jenkins

To: Kevin Corden

Here's the journalist

Rosario Weissman 09769 969771

It's life and death, for us.

T

From: Tom Jenkins

To: Kevin Corden

Kev

Haven't heard from you – did you decide to meet her? How did it go?

T

From: Tom Jenkins

To: Kevin Corden

Don't keep us in suspense, mate! Did you contact her, and what happened?

Tried ringing – loads of times – but you didn't answer.

T

CHAPTER 26

The wind swept up from the fields and hedges, full of the sweetness of growth, and the stunted hawthorns which studded the ridge above the Valley had covered their dark twisted branches with white capes of flowers.

The savage irony of the seductions of spring.

Tom had left voicemail after voicemail but no message had come back. What the hell was Kev playing at? And what should I be doing? Tom asked himself furiously. Driving up there in the van to see if Kev is okay? I'd be wrecked before I got to the M25, lose everything I've gained from being here.

Yet the whole future hangs on what happens next.

His brain went round and round like a flywheel without a belt, unable to gain traction on any compelling course of action.

As he sat among the swaying hawthorns and the darting birds Tom became aware of a different, more ponderous movement. From the belt of trees lower down the slope, a figure had emerged, toiling like a large black beetle up the stony white scar of the path.

'Kevin!' Tom shouted and waved, full of relief. Kevin twitched a hand in feeble acknowledgement; he didn't look up. When he reached the highest part of the ridge his face was shining with sweat, but his hair, Tom noticed, was limp and unslicked. He stopped about two metres from Tom, still looking at his feet.

'Kev – am I pleased to see you. What happened? Hey – sit down – the grass is dry.'

Kevin turned away as though to admire the view. 'Mate, I'm in deep trouble.' Kevin's voice, but somehow smaller, curtailed, as though part of him had been fenced off. He hauled his jeans back up round his waist; here too he seemed reduced, some of his comfortable roundness gone.

'Why – what's happened?'

'The university have been monitoring my emails. They can do that, apparently, if they think I'm about to commit a breach of trust.' He glanced over one shoulder with a convulsive writhing movement. 'I shouldn't even be here, but I had to come and tell you myself. I parked...away from the farmhouse. I walked...'

'Here Kev – have some water...' Tom handed over his metal flask.

Kevin took a long swig, then lowered himself awkwardly to the ground. He sat a little way in front of Tom and to one side, so that Tom saw only a quarter profile, not the whole of his face. 'I got summoned. To the Head of Ethics. Panelled room. Desk like a mortuary slab. All the blinds were drawn...'

Shuddering, he went on, still in those strange diminished tones: 'He was a small deadly bloke with a pointed white beard and a whispery voice. Basically they would be within their rights to sack me, he said. Prof Arrowsmith had been so impressed with my hard work, and my rapport with colleagues and experimental subjects, that she had been on the point of recommending me for a contract extension.

'Until what he called "recent events".

'And then he said, "And of course there is also the matter of the complaint."

'"What complaint?" I asked. Tom – honestly, I swear, I had no idea what he was on about. They'd dismissed it out of hand, he said, hadn't even thought it worth bothering with, but now, looking back, perhaps they had been too hasty, and might have left the university open to criticism in the future for failing to investigate thoroughly.

'"Investigate what?" I was nearly screaming, by this point.'

Kevin twisted to look directly at Tom, and his face was a terrible full beam of misery. 'Some woman, Tom, one of the control group. Said I put my arm round her when I was making sure she was comfortable in the testing room.'

'Did...' Tom began to say but Kevin swept aside his pathetic response. 'Did I? Didn't I? *I can't remember.* It doesn't seem likely – we all get drilled in this stuff. But some of the participants were nervous. So – just about, possibly, I suppose...'

As he spoke, he'd been snapping stems of grass; now he flung his handful into the wind, small green darts whipping chaotically through the air. 'Can't you see? The truth doesn't actually matter. The point of all this was to show he has the power.'

Tom grimaced in sympathy. They had chosen skilfully, these psychologists, exercised subtle insight; this was just the accusation to touch Kevin in his most tender spot, make him at once the most uncertain and most ashamed. Tom shuddered at the grinding humiliation that awaited his friend.

Kevin went on. 'I sat there in a state of shock. What scared me more than anything else was realising just how far they are prepared to go. It was like he'd casually opened his jacket and shown me the flash of a blade.' He heaved an enormous sigh. 'This thing's too big for me. I can't fight it. I'm really sorry. That's what I came to say.'

Tom felt something begin to crumble inside his chest. When he managed to get words out they were strangled and hoarse. 'So you're giving up? You're not going to help us? You're – going to let them *win*?'

'Can't you see?' Kevin said tonelessly. 'I haven't got any other choice.'

'And the paper that's finally published – your name…'

'…will be on it. Yes.'

'How can you do that?' Incredulity was making him shrill. 'You know it's meaningless…'

'Things aren't that black and white.'

Tom began pacing up and down, gesturing animatedly. 'Kev, I don't understand. Right from the beginning, you had doubts. You didn't like what you were doing to reactors. You were worried about the dropouts – while I was being an arrogant tosser and telling you to get on and zap the loons. You believed me straightaway, when I told you what had happened to me, unlike…well, unlike other people. Kev, you've been on our side for longer than I have.' He stopped pacing as a new thought gripped him and glued him to the turf. 'You know it's real, don't you? You haven't…changed your mind?'

Kevin was still sitting with his knees bent up in front of him, head bowed. 'I know it's real,' he confirmed. He sounded very tired. 'I still believe you. All of you.'

Tom was pacing again. 'So then, logically…' He mimed a series of steps leading to an inescapable conclusion.

'Because I would be flushing my career down the toilet. God, Tom, you know how hard I've worked, what a struggle it's been. The message couldn't be clearer: keep on as I have been, and watch myself get slowly destroyed.' He glanced up at Tom, as though hoping to reassure him. 'I'm not planning on staying, not after this. As soon as I can I'll be looking for a job elsewhere.'

Bitterness flooded Tom's mouth. 'So that's what it comes to. You sacrifice your principles and you keep your career.'

'Tom, mate, put yourself in my shoes, for half a minute. Imagine it's your career that's on the line. Would you walk away? Choose a life pulling pints at the Hat and Feathers? When you know you've got the potential for so much more?'

Tom was standing in front of him now, buoyed by a ferocious updraught of pure rage. He felt agile, light on his feet, itching to put the boot into the soft plump spineless shape below him which had once been his friend, to kick in the head, the face, the ribs, the stomach, until it lay collapsed and moaning on the grass.

'Okay, so you might end up back in the Hat and Feathers. You'd lose a lot. But you'd still have a job. You'd be surrounded by people. At the end of your shift you'd go back to a house, with lighting and heat. You could stop off at a café, buy fish and chips. Text your friends, arrange to meet up. Go to the cinema. Go away for the weekend. Do you know what that's called, Kev? That's called a *life*.' His voice was deforming into a terrible sobbing roar. 'That is freedom. Compared to what happens to reactors, that is nothing' – he drove his heel into the ground – 'that is nothing' – his heel smashed down again – 'that is *no sacrifice.*'

Kevin had shuffled backwards during Tom's tirade, towards the dubious protection of the hawthorns. The sharp spice of their blossoms gave the air bite, as though it had been smoked. He pushed himself shakily to his feet. 'Okay, I'm going now,' he said. 'I'm sorry you feel like that, but I reckon I'm not surprised. I'm not supposed to communicate with reactors any more, not for the present, anyway – it was part of the deal. But I wanted to do the decent thing and tell you face to face.'

Tom said nothing. He was overwhelmed by a terrible sense of loss, of another part of his past life being chainsawed away.

'I'm not a hero, Tom, that's all. There's steel behind this thing; I'm pretty sure anything I did try to do would be pointless. I'll make sure the final paper has as many caveats as I can – all we should say based on this experiment is that if reactors' responses are measured in this particular way, there are no detectable differences, but we shouldn't go further than that.' He spread his hands. 'If there's ever anything else I can do to help – money – or computer time – or the car? I could go to the village now, get you some shopping…'

Tom shouted, 'Are you not getting it? The only thing we need is validation. The only thing that threatens us is disbelief. Nothing you can ever do for us can ever make up for the damage you've done. Get out. Get out. Get out.'

He hurled the words like rocks as Kevin crept away down the hill.

CHAPTER 27

'He was brave to come here,' Sarah said.

'Brave.' Tom spat the syllable out, like food that had festered too long in the caravan's questionable fridge. Since Kevin had gone, two days before, the pure fierce fire of his rage had become sour and smoky, complicated by shovelfuls of anguish and compassion and guilt. He had known Kevin so well, kept him company in his struggles, could imagine all his horror at the prospect of everything he'd achieved being systematically, malevolently unpicked. But the stakes – the stakes were so high. Reactors lived – they survived – in that air gap of doubt; Kev's experiment would seal the coffin lid.

'I think you're getting angry with the wrong person,' Sarah said, taking down coffee mugs from the overhead hatch above the sink. 'From what you told me about what they did to Kevin, and looking back over everything that's happened with the experiment, I'm pretty sure that this was always meant to be the outcome.'

'What do you mean?'

'Kevin was right – there's steel behind this. Bigger forces. Nothing – no one – was going to stand in their way.'

'He could have tried. He's a scientist – or claims to be.'

The day had become sombre outside and Sarah didn't waste power by switching bulbs on in the van. In the gloom the flame of the gas tickling the bottom of the kettle glowed lurid blue. When she'd poured out coffee and handed him a mug she said, 'Tom, did you ever ask who is funding the experiment?'

'Kevin told me – right at the start. The government and the telecoms companies. Part from each.'

Sarah settled herself opposite him, long slim legs crossed on the seat. They were both making the most of the coffee, warming their faces with the steam, wrapping their hands around the mugs, two precious points of heat in the dank chill van. On the thin metal roof the rain began clattering like thousands of tiny malevolent dancing feet.

'I know you want to believe science is pure. And maybe in theoretical physics it is. It's all too big or too small – no one's got a vested interest in how black holes behave, except other physicists who have theories about black holes – and presumably soon enough someone will make some new observations and prove them right or wrong. But lots of science is not like that. It's kind of...' – she put down her mug and twined her fingers together – 'enmeshed. With the real world. And the structures of power which exist there.'

'Well it shouldn't be.' Tom continued to glower.

'People have done research into the effect of funding sources on the outcomes of research. I've read some of it, in a medical context. They've shown that when a pharmaceutical company funds research into a drug, that research is more likely to have an outcome showing the drug is effective – which is what the sponsor wants, obviously. Why does it happen? Loads of subtle choices – the study design, what the drug is compared to, whether negative results are published at all. Anyway the point is, we know what the people funding Kevin's study want: no ifs, no buts: reactors don't exist.'

Someone had turned up the rain; in fact they'd jammed the dial on the power shower as far round as it would go. The clattering feet on the roof merged into a continuous roar. In the erratic gusts of wind the van itself shifted uneasily on its tyres and corner steadies, unsure about its continued presence in the open, pondering whether it should scurry to the trees.

All Tom's complicated agony burst out in an anguished howl. 'But *why?* Why does it have to be absolute? Why can't there be a compromise, a middle way? We're not trying to abolish wireless technology, we'd never do that – but we don't need to, except in a few places. Why can't they acknowledge that, with all the benefits wireless technology brings, it also brings with it a small number of casualties?'

He became more animated, as an analogy unfolded in his mind.

'Just like cars.' He gestured through the streaming window towards his transit van. 'No one's going to stop driving cars, they're too useful and convenient. But at the same time everyone accepts that small numbers of random people each year will be killed by them, and a larger number injured, and car manufacturers are always trying to make them safer. No one tells the poor sod splattered across the tarmac that they merely imagined the car that hit them.'

Sarah's face had briefly kindled, but then she shook her head.

'It's not the same,' she said. 'Think about it. Death is final, and injuries heal, and the injured can continue to live in society. Suppose out of all the people who travel in cars each year, a small number developed a condition where continuing to associate with the rest of society was screaming torture. How low would the odds have to be before you got behind that wheel?'

'They could create reservations,' Tom argued, still in thrall to his vision. 'Special RF-free zones like the Valley where reactors could go and regain some resilience, or sleep there at night so they could go to work during the day. Or live there forever, if they were really bad. It would be like farmers leaving wildflower strips at the sides of their fields, so that insects and birds can thrive alongside their crops.'

Sarah gave a twisted smile. 'Sadly we live in the age of the Human Rights Act, and Disability Equality. So if this condition was recognised and your neighbour installs Wi-Fi and you have to leave your wife and kids and go and live in a reservation, you might have a good case for arguing that this breached your right to a family life. And at work a reactor could reasonably ask for a wired computer and a shielded Wi-Fi-free space. We'd be like worms in a cheese, Tom, can't you see? We'd nibble the whole thing away from within.'

Tom saw an enormous, shining, quivering cloud, humming with connections between all its various parts. Slowly at first, tiny black spots began to appear on its surface, at random, like lesions on a brain, and the spots grew more numerous, and began to coalesce; there was more and more calm empty blackness, and less pulsating light.

He let out a long breath. If reactors ever got the power to do that.... If they ever got the power to do that, something else would happen too, more subtle, but more far reaching; and as he thought of it, he flushed hot then cold with self-disgust, that he could have been so naïve as to believe that the result of Kevin's experiment could ever have been shifted, that it could ever have been more than a baited trap.

If reactors were real, they were living breathing proof that RF radiation had important effects at levels far, far below the current official safety standards, because the current safety standards only acknowledged thermal effects. People would start paying attention to the research papers that existed, listening to the scientists who'd written them, asking why the advisory groups were not taking them into account. Current safety standards would be found to be too lax to protect public health. The government would be forced to introduce drastically lower exposure limits, for everyone, everywhere.

What would become then, of the glorious shining hyperconnected future, proselytised by tech titans and the politicians swept up in their wake: bigger and better wireless bandwidth, sensors and transmitters embedded all over the everyday world; smart cities, surveillance systems, everything connected to everything else; every lamppost, every pavement, every washing machine and toaster a little digital sub-vampire, sucking, sucking, sucking data for the great analytical behemoths of the cloud?

What would become of it? It would not take place.

'So we are impossible people,' Tom murmured, 'leading impossible lives.'

Sarah nodded. 'And we have to remain impossible.'

Tom faltered then, his natural resilience collapsing before the hugeness of the forces against them, the eye-watering agglomerations of money and power. The ubiquity; the public approbation; the addictive convenience; the problematising of *friction* in the gratification of any desire. People had fought battles against corporate denial in the past – against tobacco companies and asbestos suppliers and pesticide producers. The struggles had taken years, and they'd each had to deal with the same old playbook: co-opted scientists, the capture of government regulatory bodies, obfuscatory research.

No one had ever had to fight such an all-encompassing foe.

Seductive voices whispered in his head: this is the future. This is the inescapable direction of human history, inevitable, ever since the man from Motorola made the first mobile phone call in 1973. You can't stop it, and you shouldn't want to. Don't be selfish, think of the triumph of your species as it strides onwards towards mastery of time, space and distance – indeed towards the transcendence of all limits, even death itself. As with every great evolutionary leap, some are sadly left behind. Why fight it? Why give yourself the stress? Survival of the fittest – that's a natural law.

Tom watched raindrops running down the window being ripped apart by the gale. Was this where it ended? Ever since he'd first realised he was a reactor he'd carried something inside him through all his ups and downs, something which had never abandoned him – the small wriggling tadpole of hope. *Surely they've got to recognise it eventually. Truth and decency must prevail. They can't just leave people to rot*. He searched inside himself for that wriggling sign of life. He could not feel the tadpole move.

Coma. Or the rigor of death.

What was left? A long private game of defiance, evading the monster for as long as each of them could, in which any virtuosity they showed would be entirely unacknowledged: no one outside would care, or keep the score. Already he could feel the unwholesome condescending glutinous pity that would spread over them like syrup when the results were known. He could picture Marianne's earnest, reproachful oh-Tom-I-knew-it-all-along face.

Marianne. He hadn't thought about her in weeks. Yet here she was – and she was suddenly talking in his head. Glowing brown eyes, high silvery voice. One of their old arguments about activism and climate doom. 'The future – it's not out there already. It's not fixed. It's not set. It's the outcome of millions of actions we're all taking, every minute, every day.'

'Fuck inevitability.' Apparently he'd said it out loud. Sarah, standing at the sink, rinsing out mugs, turned round. 'Sorry?'

'Fuck this future we are being sold – it's an illusion. It's only there if you keep your eyes half closed and keep your good little blinkers on so you only look at what they let people see. The future isn't set, it's still under construction – no one knows how close a tipping point might be. If we don't fight back, we're letting down all the people who are going to turn in the future – more and more of them, every year – and all the people who don't become reactors but who'll suffer health problems that they shouldn't, because governments aren't taking nonthermal effects seriously.'

'I know that, Tom. I'd fight if I could. But how?'

'They give us bad science. We've got to fight it with good science.'

'What sort of good science?'

'What do they say about reactors? We have no detectable physical abnormalities to account for our symptoms. Ergo they must be psychosomatic.'

She nodded dully as she stowed the mugs away. 'Yeah. That's what they say.'

'So it's simple – all we have to do is find one.'

'Find what?'

'A physical abnormality. One that we all share. It's got to exist. It's just that no one's looked hard enough.'

'That's...all we have to do.'

'Yes.'

'Tom, how on earth...'

He grinned up at her astonished face, his heart lifting for no reason beyond the restored sense of agency that crackled through his veins. A road stretched before him, a road to follow – no matter how soon it became lumpy and potholed and twisted out of sight. 'At the moment, I have absolutely no idea.'

CHAPTER 28

At the farmhouse Tom didn't even open the file where his unfinished PhD lurked, full of holes like an amateurish half-knitted scarf. Every minute that passed now was time lost, time in which Kevin's experiment crept its way, like some new-hatched monster, towards publication, passing through data analysis, writing up, signing off, journal submission, peer review. At every point it would grow longer claws and tougher scales, a shinier patina of respectability.

Instead, Tom plunged straight into the web. Links half-remembered from the reactorrights site bubbled up in his brain. He found the site again, typed and clicked and scrolled and clicked, tabs stacking up like battlements across the top of his screen. Scientists. Scientists who were on their side. Scientists who might have theories about what was going on with reactors. Theories which might crystallise into hypotheses. Hypotheses that could be put to the test, turned into a rigorous experiment, with real reactors, in the real world.

Hypotheses that could be tested FAST.

After the storm, they'd splashed out around the soggy campsite and fished the others from damp tents to meet in Stanford's motorhome, where Tom had told them his idea. 'I don't know if it will work,' he'd confessed, 'but it has to be worth trying. But I've only worked up to 90 minutes online per day.'

'I will take time off my cybersecurity work,' Chai had said. 'If you tell me what to do, I can take over from you each day for another two hours.'

'I can give you half an hour,' Stanford had offered. 'That's my limit. I'll phone the kids, not try to do video calls.'

'As you all know, my dears,' Veronica had said, sweeping an arm in an elegant drooping velvet sleeve, 'computers and I just don't get on at all any more, sadly. What I will do is keep you well supplied with nourishing treats as you search. I will take boxes of mixed nuts and Fortnum's biscuits to the farmhouse office directly. I am quite able to use the telephone, of course – if you wish me to phone up any of these scientists and exercise persuasive charm...'

Tom wondered how Dr Yuri Grigoriev of the Federal Medical Biophysical Centre in Moscow, for example, would respond to Veronica's particular persuasive approach. Perhaps he might like it.

Tom clicked on a list of scientists who had attended a conference in London. More names, tipped into the file of possibilities.

Scientists who had signed a letter to the US regulator demanding a safety review of wireless technology. 259 scientists petitioning the United Nations and the World Health Organisation, calling for exposure guidelines for RF to be made tougher. Scientists from 44 different countries including the USA, Canada, India, Russia, Israel and France, associated with many respected academic institutions. Tom harvested names from the UK.

Most of the scientists Tom was collecting had been researching nonthermal effects – on animals in a lab, or in cells, or in epidemiological studies of humans. Some had drawn on their research to come up with theories about the mysterious condition of reactors. But the theories seemed no more than that. He was skimming through publications by one neurologist on the list who seemed to have no relevant research interests when he came across a short comment the man had published about an article in the *Journal of the American Medical Association*. The title of the article was 'Neuroimaging Findings in US Government Personnel with Possible Exposure to Directional Phenomena in Havana, Cuba.'

This looked boring and of no conceivable relevance.

Tom was about to pass on, but then something twitched in his memory.

Havana. What had he heard about Havana?

Havana *syndrome.*

The US diplomats in the Embassy in Cuba! They had complained of strange, disabling symptoms – including pressure in the head, dizziness, visual and auditory disturbances. Some staff had recovered, but for some the symptoms became permanent. 'Directional phenomena' was a coy euphemism for what was suspected to be beams of radiofrequency radiation. 'Directional' because the diplomats seemed to sense it coming at them from particular directions. Sometimes it seemed to be turned on. Sometimes it was off.

Tom opened the comment from the UK researcher, a Dr Sharifi, based at Oxford. Among a lot of technical beard-stroking about brain-imaging techniques lurked this sentence: 'These results suggest that similar techniques could potentially be constructively employed to investigate the growing phenomenon of reactors, who claim they suffer disabling physical reactions to radiofrequency radiation at the power levels used by modern communications technology, a condition frequently dismissed as psychosomatic.'

Could it indeed?

What had, in fact, the results of the *JAMA* study been?

Tom clicked frantically to find the original article. Forty Havana cases had been compared with forty-eight healthy controls, selected to be of similar educational and social background to the embassy staff. The brain-imaging results for the Havana cases were different from the results from the control group. But no one appeared to be arguing that the stress of being stationed in a communist country had somehow altered the structure of their brains. The abnormalities were associated with these mysterious 'directional phenomena' – i.e. exposure to weaponised radiofrequency attack.

The alarm went off on his watch. Tom smacked its button down. He was on the scent of something – he could sense the tingling in his nostrils.

Chai put her head round the door of the office. 'Okay,' she said merrily. 'Step away from the computer. Right now. And I hope you haven't eaten all the best biscuits.'

'Okay, boss.' Tom sighed. 'But first, let me show you something.' Chai came over and he pointed at the screen. 'This Sharifi guy. Track him down. We need to get in contact. And start finding out about brains.'

CHAPTER 29

Dr Sharifi gazed round from his place of honour in Veronica's best, most gloriously floral folding chair. He was a slender, graceful man in an elegant charcoal-grey suit, a white shirt with cufflinks and a mauve silk tie. His long-toed leather-soled brogues were powdery with dried mud after he had negotiated the uneven track from the farmhouse. 'Consultants' shoes,' Sarah had whispered to Tom. 'God, they take me back.'

The reactors, in jumpers, fleeces and irregularly washed hair, sat in an eager circle around this tailored, showered emissary from civilisation.

'I did put together a research proposal,' he told them, in a gentle, soothing, slightly melancholy voice. 'It seemed a worthwhile area, particularly in the light of the American study. Occasionally over my years in clinical practice a patient claiming to be a reactor would be referred to me. All the usual neurological tests and scans would prove inconclusive; it was frustrating for both of us. There was little I could offer them apart from onward referral to a psychiatrist. They generally didn't come back. I believed that something might be discovered, if I could collect together a…batch…' He gazed round the circle again, with an abstracted, speculative air, and Tom thought to himself, 'He is counting heads – or rather brains. He can hypothesise six, and they interest him…'

He asked, 'What exactly was your proposal?'

'First, each participant would have a series of blood tests to rule out all other diseases that can cause similar multisystem complaints.' Irritated shuffling swept round the circle; the reactors had all, in their lives before the Valley, provided blood samples sufficient to feed several hungry vampires. They had grown used to the refrain of *normal normal normal* until they'd come to hate the word.

'Next, each participant would have a regular MRI scan to rule out structural abnormalities such as brain injury or tumours. Then they would have a functional MRI.' He tilted his head tentatively. 'Perhaps I should explain the difference?'

'It is safest to assume abject ignorance,' Veronica informed him, 'on all our parts, except Sarah here, who is – was – is a nurse, and therefore understands medical terminology.' Dr Sharifi glanced at Sarah and gave her a nod of professional acknowledgement.

'Functional brain MRI is a relatively new technique. A whole series of MRI images is taken one after the other and then these multiple images are combined by a computer. The aim is to measure the activity and connectedness of different areas of the brain, by detecting changes in the flow of blood around it. Often, it has been used to examine what happens in the brain when people undertake particular tasks – for example when they move their fingers, certain areas of the brain light up on the scan. In this study I would compare the results for the reactor group with the scans from a group of normal healthy controls. I should add that my Institute already possesses such a control group of scans – fifty of them – which were collected two years ago as part of a different research project. My intention was to use them as a baseline and simply to recruit and scan twelve self-identifying reactors…'

Tom asked, 'So what happened to your proposal?'

Dr Sharifi dropped his long-lashed eyes, examined the wildflowers in the grass. 'It was turned down. There is no funding available.'

Silence. The unconcerned gurgling of the stream.

'How much would…' Tom, Chai and Stanford had all spoken at once, like a chorus in a play.

'I would not charge for my own time. But there is a cost to book the scanner at the hospital in Oxford, pay the staff to operate it, and to run the computer analyses afterwards. You would need to pay as if paying for private healthcare.'

'How much…'

'For each participant, about four thousand pounds.'

'And you need...twelve?'

'As a minimum – yes.'

Forty-eight thousand pounds.

Dr Sharifi moved his head slowly up and down. 'I am sorry. I cannot see how it could be done for less.'

Stanford said sharply, 'And this is based on what – a hunch?'

'A hypothesis,' Dr Sharifi gently corrected. 'But you are right. It is an experiment. I cannot guarantee that any common abnormality would be found.'

On the slopes of the downs, a sheep raised its mournful quavering voice; another replied in a lower, more ironic key. So this was what it came down to, Tom thought. The purity – yes, the naivety – of his original vision – good science galloping towards them on a white horse – had ridden into the mud and mire of the world.

Money. And money that, should they somehow manage to scrape it together, (and he himself was now worth less than zero, his PhD suspended, credit card debts swelling) would be staked – like a desperate gambler mustering his last chips – on a single spin of a wheel.

Most reactors didn't have any money. And if they had it they kept it close, because it gave them options if they suddenly had to flee. He would be asking them to tear away their futures for one man's speculative idea.

Raising his eyes he glanced stealthily around the group. Barry, sunk in his blond beard, knees drawn up to his chin, held a wildflower carefully between his fingers, turning it so he could watch a beetle crawl. Stanford, uncomfortable in a folding chair that tipped his bulk backwards, wore wraparound shades which hid his eyes but did not conceal his scowl. Chai had her hands clasped over her stomach, feet swinging, an alert expression on her face. Veronica was elegantly arrayed, in a pale straw hat with a curvaceous brim. The hat was trimmed with a silk scarf matching her eyes, which focused like two blue lamps on Dr Sharifi, cool, intense, opaque. Sarah had stood up and turned away to contemplate the sunlit ridge of the downs. Her black back was rigid.

Veronica broke the silence. 'Doctor, you will understand, I'm sure. Your proposal is interesting but expensive. Money, invested in this study, cannot be used again. It represents an opportunity cost.'

Dr Sharifi spread his hands. 'Of course. Please...I quite...'

'The money isn't the only thing,' Sarah burst in, hair flying as she swung back into the circle. 'I can't quite believe you've not thought about it.'

'Thought about what?' Tom asked.

'Every reactor who takes part will have to put their head – their *head*' – she put an emphatic finger to her own – 'usually their most sensitive part – for at least – what – one hour?' – turning to Dr Sharifi, who confirmed it with a nod – 'into a strong magnetic field. We are all here because we are sensitive to various parts of the electromagnetic spectrum. Magnetic fields are part of that. Getting to and from the hospital will be risky enough, although at least Oxford isn't too far away. But what an hour in that machine will do to us – sorry Dr Sharifi, I'm not intending to be rude – but we haven't got a clue.'

Tom swore. Caught up in the exquisite satisfaction of debunking Kev, this central element had escaped him.

He stood up. 'There need to be rules,' he said. 'On who should take part, and who should not. For each reactor, different risk/benefit calculations apply.' He put his arm around Sarah's shoulders, squeezed them. 'You absolutely shouldn't. Nor should any other phase 3. The rest of us – the five of us here, and the others we will need to recruit – have all got to make our individual choice. Yes – Dr Sharifi's proposal is a gamble two ways. We could end up poorer and sicker, and all we would have proved is that – hey – yet another diagnostic technique has failed to detect any abnormality. But if we do nothing, in a few months we'll be officially proved to be deluded anyway. Everything will get harder. We've been searching and searching for weeks and this is the best proposal we've found. It's our chance to fight back. Yes, we might fail, but at least we will have tried. So that's my choice – I'm going to take part.'

'Paid for with what?' demanded Stanford. 'Individual choice ain't relevant. Nothing happens without the money. Forty-eight thousand – it happens. Less than forty-eight thousand – nothing.'

'I know that. I'm saying –'

'If you're assuming I'm going to bankroll the whole thing, you can stop right now.'

'From each according to his ability, to each according to his needs,' Veronica cut in, with her sweetest smile. 'That was Karl Marx, Stanford, but I don't imagine you are much of a fan.'

'You sell your flat in North London then,' Stanford shot back. 'That should more than cover it. Job done.'

'Don't be ridiculous. That flat is my income and my security in old age. To deprive myself of them would be the height of imprudence.'

'Yeah, and if I start spending capital sums on maverick research projects, I get proved to be a lunatic, and I lose my kids. That might not mean much to you – I haven't seen much evidence of family ties – but my kids mean everything to me.'

Clownish patches of red disfigured Veronica's finely chiselled cheekbones and an uncharacteristic cloudiness dimmed her astonishing blue eyes. 'How dare you…. How dare you…. You vile man. You know nothing about my family or my situation.'

'So? Tell us, instead of lording it over us with your Fortnum's hampers.'

'Just because I try to maintain general morale, and keep a stiff upper lip, and don't emote all over the place like some ghastly character from EastEnders…'

'I always thought I'd like to be a dad,' Barry murmured. 'Take the kids camping, teach them about birds. Find things in the woods. I don't suppose it will happen, now.' He ended with a wistful shrug, and in the silence that followed Tom thought: that's the most about himself I've ever heard him say.

'This life is shit for all of us,' Sarah said, after the silence had settled. 'None of us chose it; we've all lost things we cared about. We need to stick together, not wind each other up or try to outbid each other in suffering.'

Chai wriggled off her chair, holding up a hand. 'I think what we should do is thank the doctor for coming here and discuss his proposal amongst ourselves.'

Veronica, recovering her poise, flared her nostrils at Chai's assumption of her chairperson role: 'Well… naturally….'

'After he has gone,' Chai clarified, in case clarification was needed.

Dr Sharifi rose in some confusion. 'Of course. Forgive me. I will leave you now. You have my contact details, if I can answer any further questions…'

'I'll walk you back to the farmhouse,' Sarah said, and they went off together into the trees.

'I accept,' Veronica conceded, 'that it was unseemly to start squabbling in front of the doctor. But really, Chai – the first doctor to show genuine interest in our predicament (and such a good-looking one) – did you have to see him off like that?'

'Yes, I did,' Chai replied with spirit. 'You were embarrassing. And also – I think this worry about the money may be…unnecessary.'

'Seems pretty damn necessary to me,' Stanford growled.

Chai gave one of her calm sunny smiles and folded her hands across her stomach. 'I think the telecoms industry will fund this study.'

'The telecoms industry? Are you mad? This study is the last thing in the world they'd want to pay for.'

'It is only fair. After all, we are risking our health, and we need our money. They make huge amounts of money from RF technology. Their shareholders and chief executives get huge payouts.'

'Yes, but the bastards won't give any of it to losers like us.'

'I didn't say they'd fund it intentionally,' Chai said, serenely swinging her legs.

'How…' Stanford stopped, his mouth hanging open.

'Chai…I can see where you're coming from,' Tom said, as jigsaw pieces clicked together in his head, 'but…is…that…really a good idea? Supposing you…'

'I'm pretty sure I won't. I've been outwitting the bad guys for years. It will be a stimulating personal development opportunity.'

'Chai, you are brilliant,' Veronica said, reaching out to give Chai's shoulders a sudden hug. 'I have utter faith in you.'

'Small amounts will be transferred, from various accounts, in different ways. Nothing big or splashy. Do you know how much mobile banking fraud costs each year? And how much of that do you think is ever recovered from the fraudsters?'

Tom blew out his cheeks. 'I can see why the doctor mustn't know anything about this.'

'No. The poor lamb would have frightful scruples,' agreed Veronica. 'One can tell he is the ethical type.'

'Does that mean,' Tom ventured tentatively, 'we should start thinking about…recruitment? Who's going to take part? I could contact reactorrights, get them to put something on their website asking for volunteers….'

'You might as well put it up in lights,' Stanford snorted. 'Do you want the whole telecoms industry to know what's coming?'

'Come on, Stanford – even if they do know, what can they do?'

The man was in one of his glowering, immovable moods. 'I don't trust them. I say we stay covert as long as we can.'

'Covert's great, as far as it goes, but it doesn't get us extra heads.'

Unexpectedly, Barry spoke up. 'Most of us know at least one other reactor. And they know other ones. We can use the landline and write letters. We'll ask them to pass it on. Don't stress, Tom. It's better, like this.'

CHAPTER 30

News of the study spread, quietly diffusing from the Valley on telephone wires and in envelopes loaded onto Royal Mail vans. Reactors in houses, in squats, in camper vans, in tents, in subtly different phases of the condition, responded with excitement when they heard that it was happening; with trepidation when they realised they were being invited to take part.

Tom went to the farmhouse every day to collect the post. He ran back to the campsite with the letters and distributed them, watching nervously as they were opened and read.

'Has anyone said yes? Is there anyone I can add to the file?' He had a blue ring binder where he kept records: details of people who had been contacted, their negative or positive replies.

The first week, pickings had been thin. A meek artist acquaintance of Veronica's, who lived in the dead spot at the foot of a Cornish cliff and made sculptures from driftwood gathered on the shore, signed up. 'She generally takes my advice on such matters,' Veronica had said, passing the letter offhandedly to Tom. A friend of Sarah's, called Wayne, was the next to accept. 'We lived together in the squat,' she told Tom, 'he's a lovely guy,' and Tom felt an uncomfortable prickling of curiosity about what exactly that might mean.

No one else had replied. 'They're in survival mode. They need time to think about it,' Sarah said to Tom, trying to keep him calm. 'None of them will be in easy circumstances.'

'Every week counts,' Tom muttered, scowling. 'Don't they understand?'

'Some of them volunteered for the Northington experiment. Like I did. Once bitten, twice shy.'

'This is completely different...'

'Only in certain ways.'

'Come for a walk,' she said, the next afternoon. 'There is nothing else you can do, for the moment, now the post has been. For God's sake put that file away. It's a beautiful day – let's go up on the downs.'

The white path made them squint because the sun bounced off it straight into their eyes. Heat had been building for several days, and now it surged up from the land itself as well as hammering down from the burnt-out sky. The short springy desiccated turf was studded with intense and desperate blooming: twining mats of birdsfoot trefoil sewn with bright blobs of yellow; small scabious, like flattened purplish pom-poms; milkwort's deep unexpected blue. Above the flowers hung a second, living, airborne carpet – the shimmering dance of pollen-crazed insects – butterflies, hoverflies, wild downland bees.

Tom and Sarah had waded through the buzzing to the far end of the ridge, ascending the little hummock which formed its highest point. Below them, baking land rolled, a symphony of green: darker lines of hedgerows dividing neon fields, fuzzy verges following the curves of lanes, bubbling clots of trees. Tom could almost hear the vibration in the air, the frenetic activity, every blade and leaf stretched up to drink the rays, the intense, passionate communion between the green and the unmediated blue.

Shading his eyes he looked south towards the horizon through the preternaturally clear still air, and saw a distant shimmer in the chink between two hills.

The sea.

'Oh!' Sarah gasped, when Tom pointed it out and she clapped a hand to her mouth and stood silently on the top of the mound, staring, as a tear snaked down her cheek.

'Hey – what is it?' he asked.

She laughed and shook her head vigorously as though to shake herself dry. 'Oh – you know what it's like – you go on day to day, and then suddenly – wham – something gets under your guard. Ridiculous really.' She sighed. 'I haven't seen the sea for – oh – so long. I used to go sailing – did you know that?'

'No, I didn't,' replied Tom, smiling. 'What sort of sailing? Not that I know enough about it to understand the answer.'

'My dad taught me. We had a boat at Topsham. A cruiser, *Wayfarer*, 32 feet. We sailed to France and up the west coast of Scotland. There was a wonderful feeling of freedom. I was pretty good actually. I only capsized once.'

Turning resolutely through one hundred and eighty degrees she took his hand. 'Come on,' she said, 'is there any shade round here? We'll cook if we stay out in this sun.'

Slightly below the ridge on its right-hand slope, a voluptuous indentation formed a U-shaped hollow. Hawthorn trees crowded round it, their gnarled trunks growing at crazy angles on the steeply sloping sides, their deeply lobed leaves like tiny open hands. The hawthorn petals had gone; only the swollen round centres of the flowers were left, modestly green, preparing to bask and ripen over the months ahead.

Scrambling down the slope, Tom and Sarah flung themselves gratefully onto the stubbly grass, in dim, stuffy, tree-smelling warmth, and looked out at the crisp edge shapes of shadows, rigorously patrolled by the ruthless sun. They began to kiss, drowsily at first, then with more urgency. Somewhere high in the radiant blue above the leaves, a skylark bubbled its endless effortless ecstasy.

*

Afterwards Tom rolled onto his side and watched her for a while. Her eyes were closed, her mouth gently smiling, her arms flung untidily behind her head. Over the grass her hair spread out in a dark sunburst. In another life, he thought, where neither of them were reactors – would they ever even have met? And even if they had, they'd have been different people, normal, happy with their gadgets; they would never have become these exiled selves. Perhaps they would never have noticed each other, would simply have smiled politely and moved on.

Sarah opened one eye and squinted at him. 'I can feel you thinking,' she said. 'What's up?'

'If I hadn't turned up,' Tom blurted suddenly, 'would you – would you just have slept with someone else? I mean – there isn't a lot of choice, in our position, is there?'

'Oh for goodness' sake,' said Sarah, laughing. 'No, I would not have. Exactly which of the others did you have in mind for me? Barry? Stanford? They really aren't my type.'

She brought her arms down, rolled sideways, and twined herself gently around him. 'Come here, Thomas,' she murmured, as though her mouth was full of honey, 'stop thinking about possible worlds. Remember what we said – let's enjoy what we can in this one.'

*

After four weeks and eleven positive replies, including the five of them from the Valley itself, everything went quiet. Tom's mind was spinning like a washing machine, tumbling his thoughts into twisted schemes. Eleven. How could they stop at eleven? They were within touching distance. He had to find the twelfth.

Kevin. He'd have names and addresses on his reactor database. Should he – Tom – grovel and ask for his help?

Madness. Couldn't be trusted.

Sarah. Surely – for something so important.... If he explained it was the only way?

No. Absolutely not. God knows what it might do to her.

Finally somebody rang the farmhouse, left a garbled message on the answering machine. When Tom rang back he turned out to be a contact of a contact of Barry's, a wild man of the back roads, one of the roving campervan crew, who picked up his post only erratically and spoke in an abstracted drawl as though his eyes were permanently fixed on the distant horizon. 'Hey, yeah, you can sign me up, man. That Oxford place – I reckon I can swing by.' Tom was dizzy with relief. Later Barry told him that the man used to be in fashion PR, always had the latest trainers, holidayed in Ibiza, had been surgically attached to his phone.

Tom's file was complete. He phoned Dr Sharifi and told him the news, arranged to send the details of the other participants. Dr Sharifi had looked into the booking of slots on the MRI machine. 'There is no availability until September, I am advised,' he said. 'Also, I presume the five of you will wish to come all together, on the same day?'

'It would make transport easier,' Tom acknowledged.

'There is a whole day free on the tenth.'

Tom felt a rushing, sucking sensation, as though he had been travelling down the sloping rim of a funnel, and had suddenly reached the vertical pipe. Everything he has been doing had been leading towards this point; why would he stop? Yet knowing that he still could was a clot of unexpected resistance he had to deliberately, consciously push through.

After a pause he said, 'Okay,' and, taking a long breath, 'Let's go for that.'

As he put down the phone he crashed it out of line with its cradle because of the shaking of his hand. He noticed churning in his bowels and tightness in his chest and wondered if this was how gamblers felt, as they gathered their chips to place a final one-way bet.

CHAPTER 31

'Let's have a party,' said Veronica, with decision. 'A party to celebrate the end of summer. We should have the party now, while we are all feeling good, before we go on our little jaunt. We may possibly not feel so inclined, afterwards. We shall have a bonfire, and toast good quality sausages. We shall invite Cuthbert, and Stanford's children, if their cow of a mother allows them to come, and your mother, Tom, although she may be busy, being a vicar, and your mate from the couriers, Barry – presumably he could be persuaded to leave his phone in his van? Sarah – you and I are a long way from home and my daughter isn't speaking to me anyway, because she thinks I am insane, and one of Chai's brothers is in Edinburgh and the others are in Mauritius – she is Sino–Mauritian, as you know. So that will be it in terms of guests. Now – let us consider the rest of the food and drink...'

The last day of August began warm, rainy and dull, but by the evening the clouds had been swept away, and the sun shone with a clean golden beam. A small bonfire crackled on the sward beside the stream, and the campers and their guests sprawled on rugs and folding chairs, eating sausages, and potatoes baked in the embers, and salads from a variety of plastic containers, and drinking wine ordered in by Veronica. Veronica wafted, clad in quasi-druidical white kaftan over wide trousers, with silk flowers in her hair, filling people's glasses and pressing them to eat more food. Stanford, who had been reading SAS survival manuals and *The Dangerous Book for Boys*, put himself in charge of the fire, and the fire, knowing what was good for it, obeyed.

The lazy sun eased itself behind the curve of the hills and long soft shadows crept across the grass. Bats flitted across the clearing, half-seen perturbations in the gloom. Ringo and Twilight ran about, barefoot, exuberant, turning cartwheels and paddling in the stream. Janet arrived late, after a parish picnic. She put on her best social manner, and made good use of her beautiful voice, but Tom sensed that underneath she was ill at ease. Veronica breezed up to her, shook her by the hand, and exclaimed, 'Vicar, how marvellous to see you. Most unusual to see the Church taking any interest in our predicament.' Janet mumbled something about it being a 'very difficult problem indeed'. When he introduced her to Sarah she said, 'Sarah – how lovely to meet you. Tom's told me so much about you. You're a nurse, isn't that right?'

And Sarah, who had had a couple of glasses of wine, said loudly, 'Well I used to be a nurse, Reverend Jenkins, but now of course my highest goal in life is to be a no-good benefit scrounger.'

But in general, everything went smoothly. Cuthbert, an understated, weather-beaten man with a beaky face fringed with grey beard, had a long talk with Chai about commodity prices. Barry's mate was very taken with Sarah, and sat beside her staring and saying, 'Wow, man, it's like….You really get to talk to people, know what I'm saying…no phones…you really get a connection, man…'

After they had finished eating, Veronica told Tom to fetch his guitar. 'We should all sing something,' she declared.

Tom sat down on a folding stool and plucked the strings to check the tuning. 'What do most people know?' he asked.

They sang a few rounds of 'London's Burning' and 'Row, row, row the boat'. 'Far out,' said Barry's mate. 'Like, actually making your own music?'

Veronica held up her wine glass. 'I have an idea. Let us play "reactor songbook" - an *hommage,* for those who do not know, to the fine Radio 4 programme *I'm sorry I haven't a clue.* Everyone must think of songs that are relevant to our lifestyle…or can be made relevant with slightly altered words.'

Stanford muttered to Barry, 'That woman has to turn everything into a bloody parlour game.' But he started thinking furiously, determined not to be outdone.

Chai leapt to her feet. 'I got it!' she cried. 'Tom, do you know Gloria Gaynor?' She flung one arm upwards, flexed her tubby bottom to the left and then the right, tipped her chin defiantly and in a high-pitched but tuneful voice, began to sing.

Tom had found her key by now, and joined in with the chords, and everyone else was clapping in time to the beat and singing too, if they knew the words and even if they didn't, they soon worked out how to join in the chorus. 'I will survive!' they sang, and Chai gyrated her hips and worked her arms, and then shouted, 'Hey! Come on! I'm the fattest person here – the least lithe – why am I the only person dancing?' before seizing Cuthbert by both hands.

Even Stanford stood up from the fire, and jigged stiffly from one leg to the other.

After Chai had sung the whole song through three times, and been loudly applauded and received several catcalls, and everyone had collapsed exhausted onto the ground, Veronica smoothed her kaftan, adjusted the flowers in her hair, moved to the centre of the gathering, and announced, 'I have one.' Tom looked up enquiringly, fingers poised. 'I'm not sure if you will know it, Tom,' said Veronica. 'It is from the musical *West Side Story*. "Somewhere" – a very beautiful number. But perhaps you can pick it up. An E would be helpful.' Tom plucked the note, and Veronica began in a dramatic, vibrating contralto, one draped arm extended, her eyes half closed.

She was a dreadful old ham, Tom thought, and not totally in tune, but as she sang, stillness fell on the group, and the yearning of the reactors for a place where they could just be seemed to flow out of each of them, and join together in a swirling column, and move slowly upwards with the smoke of the fire into the fading sky.

When the song was over there was a moment of silence before the applause. Veronica gave a deep theatrical bow. Sarah got hesitantly to her feet. 'I've sort of got one,' she said. 'I had to change the verse, but the chorus is good. You've all got to join in.' She whispered in Tom's ear, and he gave a snort of laughter, nodded violently, and started to play the octave leaps of the introduction to Pulp's biggest hit.

Sarah, tall, gangly, swaying slightly, walked a few paces away, spun round, hair flying, and fixed him with her gaze. She sang:

'He came from Hants he had a thirst for knowledge
He studied physics at Northington college
Til Wi-Fi
Made him fly
He told me that his mum was clergy
And that he had a weird allergy
So had I
And in thirty seconds time he said...'

And with a huge roar that echoed round the

Valley, everybody else joined in.

'I want to live like common people…'

Tom, looking round as he strummed, saw Sarah hold out her hands to Janet, and the two of them dancing together. He saw Stanford swinging a shrieking child on each arm; Barry's mate showing Chai and Barry how to throw shapes; Veronica and Cuthbert attempting a tango. A slim wink of a moon and a couple of inquisitive stars appeared in the deep velvet of the sky, and Tom thought: this is what we become adept at, we reactors – keeping our minds ruthlessly on the present moment, turning methodically away from the future, averting our eyes from the chronic provisionality of our lives. Whatever happens in the days to come, we can bank this, we will have had this time.

CHAPTER 32

Wheels whirred over tarmac, methodically eating the road. Unseen vehicles passed by; Tom tried to distinguish the smug whoosh of sports cars, the laborious overhauling of small-engined hatchbacks, lorries' extended thunderous roars. When the motorhome slowed, he found himself straining forwards against his seatbelt, then he was pushed backwards as it accelerated again.

He could see nothing, but being on the road was still exhilarating. He relished the rush, the forward momentum of his body, the glorious, luxurious extension of his existence through space and time, after it had prowled unwholesomely for so long around a single patch.

They'd RF-proofed the motorhome as much as they could, taped foil over the windows, and hung a big rattling sheet, made from lots of pieces stuck together, directly behind the driver's seat: the aim was to get as close as possible to a continuous metal box, though it would be far from perfect. Pinpricks and edge gaps let in thin slivers of light; in the gloom Tom could see Stanford and Barry strapped in opposite him, and Chai in the seat to his left. Veronica, breaking the rules, was lounging on the fixed bed in the back.

Barry and Stanford looked as though they were blasting into space on some sci-fi mission, their faces shrouded by metallic mesh headnets of the kind Sarah had worn when he had first seen her, that sunny day on campus, last year, a century ago. Chai did not wear one; she said they made her feel worse, and Tom knew there were other reactors who found the same – not surprising, the manifestation of sensitivity being so individual and idiosyncratic. He himself had one in his pocket, to wear when he entered the hospital itself. No one was speaking; they seemed to be zoned out, conserving their strength. The place smelled of Stanford: expensive fruity aftershave, real leather accessories, slightly obsessive cleaning, whiskey, the rancour of divorce. No windows were open because of the foil; they were using no aircon and no lights, to avoid any extra electrics beyond the basics required to move.

The motorhome slowed down again, then speeded up. Sudden braking preceded a crawl. 'Where are we?' he called to Cuthbert through the foil.

'Junction between the A34 and the A4142,' was the reply and Tom thrilled to the romance of the words, to the intense glamour of the normal.

Finally, they slowed right down to a stop. A lumbering turn left. Then right. Must be off the dual carriageway. Stop – start; stop – start – urban driving. The high-pitched peeps of a pelican crossing. Impatient honking of car horns. Young happy voices beyond the foiled windows, suddenly shockingly loud and close – teenagers, agglomerating on their way to school. The slam of brakes and a muttered curse from Cuthbert. Another sharp turn to the right. Quieter – less ambient noise. A gentle pulling up, the yank of the handbrake, the engine off. 'We're here.'

Tom yanked open the side door and after the near darkness of the journey the muted daylight of the moist grey morning was blinding to his eyes. He stepped down onto the tarmac of a huge car park, extending in front of him and off to the sides. A couple of hundred metres away loomed an interlocking jumble of boxy buildings, examples of utilitarian architecture from the 1970s onwards as more and more capacity and specialisation had been jammed into the hospital's site.

Cuthbert had parked next to a belt of conifers in the middle of a sea of empty bays. The plan was for everyone to stay in the van except when it was their turn. Tom was going first; it seemed the responsible thing to do. If something horrible happened to him inside the machine, or directly afterwards, the others could change their minds and head for home. Cuthbert had climbed down from the driver's seat, was walking about stiffly in his ancient waxed jacket. 'Good luck,' he said, shaking Tom's hand. 'Don't worry. I'll look after them. Stanford will set up the loo.'

Tom began to walk towards the rows of different coloured cars. People were getting in and out, phones held to their ears. More people came out of the hospital, hunched over, thumbing. In his pocket he ran his fingers across the crispy texture of the metallic headnet.

Put it on.

Put it on, you idiot.

But Tom hesitated. As he approached the hospital, he found it a peculiar thrill to walk among normal humans; to walk amongst them with no one knowing his secret, neither his secret nor his plan. He sensed their glances slide over him, snagging on nothing unusual: a man in jeans, trainers, backpack, curly blond hair longer than most. But, chancing to look up, he spotted a cluster of antennae giving spiky one-fingered salutes from the highest part of the roofscape. He pulled his headnet on, revealing his alien self. Immediately, heads began to turn.

When he arrived at the MRI reception, he removed the headnet again so he could smile at the nurse and tell her his name. 'Oh. One of Dr Sharifi's specials,' she said, with a sour look, as she tracked him down on her computer. 'I suppose you'd better come with me.' She set off down the corridor on her soft-soled lace-up shoes at such a pace that Tom had to lope to catch up before she vanished round a corner. She gestured into a side room where there were curtained cubicles. 'Take your clothes off in there, please, except for your underwear. Put on the hospital gown. It fastens at the back. Make sure you put watches, earrings and anything metal in the plastic tray. You don't have any other metal in your body – metal joints, pins, shrapnel and so on?'

'No.'

She smirked at the scrunched-up headnet in his hand. 'Just your tinfoil hat, then.'

'I'm sorry?'

'Oh, only my little joke. I'll leave you to get ready.'

Definite hostility. He could sense it. Should he say something? 'Excuse me, my condition is just as real as the other conditions you're used to dealing with, and a lot more socially isolating. Dr Sharifi takes it seriously and is trying to understand it better.'

He would sound like a sanctimonious prick. General principle of life: don't antagonise someone who is about to shut you in a big metal tube. If the thing worked, she'd know soon enough. Her and the rest of the world.

Inside the scanner, the curved metal roof of the tube was only centimetres from his face. He closed his eyes, trying to relax. They'd put a little button into his hand, telling him that if he couldn't cope any longer he could press it and they'd get him out. But then of course the whole scan would have to be started all over again.

Don't press the button.

Soon the cacophony began. Thumping, banging, shrieking, whirring, clattering, clanging, hammering – one after the other, and then all at the same time, like a psychopath in a cage full of power tools gleefully going berserk. The incredible noise was from the motors producing the strong magnetic fields and rotating them to different angles in relation to his skull.

The scan was due to last an hour, but it was impossible to tell how much time had passed. He decided to tell himself that the thing was endless, to deaden his anticipation each time the noise appeared to abate.

When he started to truly believe that it *was* endless, that something must have gone wrong, time had reversed itself, or the nurse had decided that the world would be improved with one less timewaster in it – suddenly it was over and he was sliding out.

Dressed again, he'd walked to the reception desk and thanked the nurse. 'Tomorrow, we have a young man with a suspected brain tumour,' she remarked, with pointedly deliberate emphasis.

*

Barry had left for his scan, and come back, and Chai had gone off for hers, before, in the stuffy dark of the motorhome, Tom began to feel less cheerful. Something was starting on the top of his head, a crawling, tight sensation. Since he'd come to the Valley, he'd managed to avoid it, but now it had returned, dragging him back in time to Northington, and all those cat-and-mouse games.

No longer crawling. More of a straightforward ache. Pushing downwards into his brain. Spreading out over his skull.

Oh, here were all its quirks and nasty habits, just as he remembered. It was like finding out he was sharing a house with a former housemate whom he had hoped very much never to live with again.

How much? That was the interesting question. How much resilience had he built up in the Valley? How much had they all built up?

He shifted round on his seat, trying to establish a good position for his head, but this no longer seemed to exist. Cuthbert was reading one of his favourite classic novels in the front of the van. He had brought six plastic road cones with him, piled garishly in the front seat, and had placed them in the parking bays around the motorhome to discourage anyone else from parking too close. Every so often Tom heard him open the driver's door and climb down to check on them, stretching his legs with a walk round the car park; so far the instinct to obey pointless bureaucracy had apparently worked in the reactors' favour.

Chai yanked open the side door. 'Goodness, that nurse was snarky,' she commented, clambering up the steep step as she held a cardboard tray of coffees high. 'Look everyone, I couldn't resist. I went past one of the hospital coffee shops, and I just had to go in. I got one for everyone. Here, Stanford, take yours with you. Good luck!'

'Thanks,' Stanford grunted as he stepped out onto the tarmac, his silver headnet stuffed in the pocket of his leather jacket. Tom had a last look at his grim determined face, teeth set, brows pulled together, before the motorhome door slammed shut.

Chai chatted on as she handed out the coffees. 'I used to love my daily posh latte, when I worked at the Velvetbank headquarters in Edinburgh. And I always had a blueberry muffin as well. That's how I got plump, I expect. Oh I was a proper working girl! But I was a geek, so I didn't have to be corporate all of the time, and say "process" and "vision" – just now and again, you know? I had a special suit for those meetings, Karen Millen, beautifully cut, very slimming for the behind.' She slapped her rump and then sat, sipping her coffee slowly. 'I had a Dilbert calendar on my desk, a new cartoon every day. Oh, my team loved Dilbert, he made everyone laugh. Sometimes the cartoons were very very apt, and we'd keep them and pin them to a noticeboard. Then the Chief Executive came on a rare visit, and saw them, and I was told I was encouraging cynicism and resistance to change.' She chuckled. 'But my team was always a happy team. And very effective!'

Veronica remarked from the far end of the vehicle: 'Well, my dear, your latte seems to have given you a positively Proustian experience. I refer of course to the famous moment in *A La Recherche Du Temps Perdu*' – she pronounced the French with lipsmacking perfection – 'where the narrator takes a bite of madeleine (a type of small cake) and is transported back to his childhood. Unfortunately, hospitals always make me think of giving birth, and that is not a pleasant memory, in my case. A very long and unnecessarily extended labour, I now believe.'

'How old were you when you had your daughter?' Chai enquired.

'Twenty-four,' Veronica replied. 'I had been married for a year, and already I was rather wishing that I wasn't. It had seemed a good idea at the time – Gerald was an investment banker, older than I was. He simply oozed connoisseurship: how to buy the best wine, eat in the right restaurants, secure the most exclusive villas, employ the best interior designers. Find the best pyjamas, even (apparently they are made by Snodgrass of Sturgeon Street, if you are the slightest bit interested). It felt thrillingly sophisticated at first, like existing inside a padded, velvet-lined, temperature-controlled bank vault. But I found I was not really interested in *the best* –

I wanted to experiment. Unfortunately one of my experiments – I think my daughter Annabel was nine at the time – involved posing as Botticelli's Venus for the undergardener in the summerhouse at our villa in Tuscany (he was an art student from Milan and we had become friends discussing painting – one of Gerald's criticisms of me was my tendency to talk to *the staff* – just because I made the effort to learn Italian, and he would merely say "Grah-ziay" in this ghastly British accent which made my toes curl up inside my sandals). Anyway, Marco persuaded me he needed the practice, and promised to give me some painting lessons myself. Subconsciously I must have known what the outcome would be: the heat, the flowers, the intense gazing, the vicarious caress of the brush round one's intimate parts. Suffice it to say that we were caught spectacularly *in flagrante*. Gerald had invited an important colleague to the villa for a couple of days; the blasted man arrived a day early and had asked Gerald to take him on a tour of the grounds. I think Gerald found the humiliation worse than the basic infidelity (he was not averse himself when on executive trips overseas). Anyway, there was a frightful row. Gerald made me out to be a wicked, abandoned woman, a depraved corrupter of youth (the undergardener was twenty-one for goodness' sake, quite capable of thinking for himself, and Annabel had been well out of the way, on a trip to the beach with some English neighbours) but he claimed I was unfit to care for my child. I won back custody eventually. And now – well, sadly, it seems, Annabel, although a feisty, intelligent woman, has inherited from her father a deep veneration for the conventional. I am beyond her pale.' A sigh gusted from the back of the van. 'The duties of grandmother to her daughter Izzy have been ably taken over by Gerald's second wife, which is sad, because Izzy and I got on very well. She wrote me wonderful letters, for a while; but at that age people fade from your consciousness, if you neither see them in person nor interact digitally. I blame her not at all. Were you ever married, Chai?'

'No,' Chai said serenely, swinging her legs, hands cupped around her latte. 'I have always been independent.'

The voices swirled on. The sealed darkness of the van, the tension of the enforced waiting, the sense of being removed from all usual routines, together seemed to have the effect of a confessional. For a while Tom listened, tried to follow, forcing his focus away from his body as his heart began to jump as if it wanted to burst out of his chest and all he yearned for was to spread himself like jam over the grey-carpeted floor.

Stanford returned, carrying a bacon roll he'd obtained from some hospital eatery, and with a copy of *Men's Health* under his arm. The salty greasy whiff of bacon filled the van. 'Thank goodness it is my turn

313

now,' Veronica sniffed as she glided towards the side door.

Only one more hour to go.

For a while Stanford chewed, surreptitiously licking from his fingers every last molecule of grease. Beside Tom, Chai had gone quiet, put her coffee aside, lain back in her seat with her chin tipped up. Opposite, Barry had curled up like a small animal, his shaggy bearded head supported on one arm, his breathing intentionally, consciously regular and deep.

At last, a good fifteen minutes after they'd expected her, Veronica returned waving a pale pink carrier bag. 'I apologise for holding us up,' she declared as she climbed in. 'But one might as well be hanged for a sheep as for a lamb. I know I will pay, later, but I have indulged myself in the clothes shop – you must have passed it, just to the left in the main corridor. By no means a classy establishment in any way – most of the stuff was absolutely frightful – pastel acrylic cardigans and T-shirts with sequined puppies. But oh! – to browse again! I bought a tiger print scarf. Oh – and I have lodged an official complaint about that nurse. I informed the administrators that she is in clear breach of their equality and diversity policy. Ha!'

*

Tom turned onto his side in his sleeping bag,

burying his face in its warmth. He thought he'd identified a night and part of a day since they'd unloaded themselves from the motorhome and stumbled to their various beds. But time had gone strange, bending itself into distorted shapes: long, indeterminate stretches where he whirled away through supercharged, disconnected thoughts, and periods where he lay gasping with pain, having to focus on making it through each interminable second without screaming.

No one else was doing much better; the silence told him that.

Occasional bleating came from faraway sheep; desultory birds called; there were rustles in the trees. Soft rain drizzled now and again on the outer skin of the tent. But the arguments and bustle and banter had stopped, leaving a human-shaped hole in the soundscape. Tom thought: this is what the camp would sound like after some disaster: an eviction, or a massacre.

Some vague time later, footsteps approached his tent. 'Tom?' Sarah unzipped the inner door and pushed a large plastic bottle inside. 'How are you? I've brought you more water.' He rolled onto his back. 'Thanks,' he said, grinning up at her. 'Still not great. But at least I've stopped believing that life would be better if someone would just amputate my head.'

'Hmmm.' Sarah frowned. 'No – sorry – that procedure's contraindicated in this case.' She nudged the bottle towards him. 'You should keep drinking.'

Tom propped himself on his elbow and poured water into a mug. 'What's going on with the others?'

'Oh, they're all having their own particular reactions. Veronica's got heart palpitations, nausea and dizziness, and hideous tinnitus, she says. Chai's bladder has given way. I found a big container for her to use as a commode in her tent. Barry and Stanford were pretty poleaxed, but are starting to surface and ask for cups of tea.'

'That's encouraging, I suppose,' said Tom, as he lay down again.

'It's a bit like being back on A&E, actually,' Sarah said. 'Only a lot quieter, and without mains plumbing.'

CHAPTER 33

Here it was. Schrodinger's email. Like Schrodinger's cat.

Schrodinger had hypothesised a cat in a box, sealed in with a radioactive element, a radiation detector, and a vial of poison gas. If the element emitted a particle, the detector would detect it, break the vial and kill the cat.

At the quantum level, it is impossible to determine a particle's position until it is observed; more than impossible, actually, because it is the *very act of observing* which causes the particle to select one position rather than another. So, if quantum logic is followed through, the cat in the box is both alive and dead. Until, of course, you open the box.

Here was the box:

To: Tom Jenkins
From: Dr Sharifi

Date: 31 October

Subject: Results

Oh so casually, Tom's index finger rested on the left button of the mouse, his fingertip tingling, growing warm. Just the smallest, most minimal pressure, and he would end this current superposition, where all futures still shimmered, gloriously possible. By the very act of observing he would concretise one future, quite possibly the one in which their sleek, furry, strokeable hope lay stiff and cold and dead.

Drawing in a deep breath, he clicked.

Dear Tom

The lab has sent the images produced from the scans. As you have all been so generous in funding the research, perhaps we should take a first look through them together. Maybe you can contact me to arrange some sort of presentation? The images will be best seen when displayed on a screen.

With kind regards

Yours sincerely

Dr Sharifi

Consultant Neurologist

Curse the man's scrupulous professional detachment. 'Yes, whenever you like, some of us can

318

watch on the farmhouse computer,' Tom banged out in reply.

Thank goodness, that was still true. The five of them who had gone for the scan had recovered over the last few weeks, their individual levels of resilience slowly rebounding to the places they had been before the trip. Once again, the Valley had shown its power.

'As I explained,' Dr Sharifi said, when he came, 'the images are built up from a number of different MRI scans of each subject, using various techniques. I will open the images one at a time.' He sat to one side of the monitor in the farmhouse office, groomed, clean, his graceful fingers draping over the mouse. Tom, Barry, Chai and Stanford were crammed together behind him, their backs against the outside wall. On either side of them, old crimson curtains covered the windows against the cold November evening. Two bulbs in decaying paper lantern shades hung from the high ceiling, giving a milky light. Veronica hovered outside in the hall. 'I may not be able to go near the screen,' she had said, 'but I shall judge from the reaction of the crowd.'

'Here is the first, Subject A. Male, aged 24.' Tom saw the outline of his own head, grey against a black background, surprisingly recognisable from the slightly crooked nose and long chin. A paler grey line ran from the bridge of the nose up over the top of the skull, widening down the back of the neck; similar pale grey covered the front of the neck and the chin. Soft tissue, Tom surmised, in contrast to the inner, darker areas of bone. Three roughly horizontal stripes denoted the top three neck vertebrae, and tucked between them a grey ascending tube, which bulged like a bud on a stem when it reached the centre of the head.

Within the skull, darker lines indicated the kinks and crenellations of the brain. Inside the brain itself, like areas on a photograph which had been overexposed, were three misshapen blotches of white.

Dr Sharifi indicated them with his hand. 'This does not mean that there are actual white patches in the brain,' he cautioned. 'The white areas are a representation of where this brain diverges from the normal, as represented by the brains in our control group.'

'I'm – not normal?' Tom asked. 'In what way?'

'Perhaps I should first explain the concept of brain networks?' Dr Sharifi said. Along the row of reactors, a ripple of nodding passed like a wave.

Dr Sharifi went on: 'As our understanding of the brain advances, the idea that individual brain regions are responsible for specific cognitive functions is becoming increasingly superseded. What we are seeing, with new brain imaging techniques, are several separate brain regions, which may well not be structurally contiguous, working *together*, and when different groups of brain regions are active together – what we call functionally connected – different cognitive functions result.'

'So – more of a team game than an individual sport?' asked Tom.

'You could express it in that way. There are various ways of defining these different brain networks – it is still very much an emerging discipline – but one commonly used is the default mode network, which is linked to thinking that is not directed towards a specific task, to memory, and to the general ongoing activity of the brain.' The doctor clicked to reveal explanatory notes from the lab. 'And that network would seem to be the one concerned here.'

'What's strange about mine?'

'When this brain was in the default mode network, there was more functional connectivity between different brain regions involved in the network than would normally be expected. This is known as hyperconnectivity, which has been shown in other studies to be a common response to neurological injury or disease.'

Tom felt himself and his fellow crammed watchers stiffen, as though they were hounds who had detected the first faint scent of blood.

Drawing a silver ballpoint from the inside pocket of his suit, Dr Sharifi used it as a pointer, touching the front part of Tom's brain just above the eye. 'To be specific, there is hyperconnectivity of the anterior component of the medial orbital frontal area. Orbital refers to the eye sockets. Medial is an anatomical term, meaning closer to the body's midline. The brain is divided down the middle, into two hemispheres.' He made the image revolve, so that the division became visible. 'So the medial orbital frontal area is the part closer to that middle gap. The anterior component means the part of that area close to the front of the body.'

'Let us now look at Subject B.' On the screen Barry's head appeared, pulled down into his neck, with a heavy jaw. Four irregular white patches, one just above the eye socket. A couple of dots above that. A larger patch towards the back of the skull. 'Here we have abnormality of the default mode network, with increased hyperconnectivity of the anterior component. In this case, there is also decreased fractional anisotropy in the corpus callosum, the large bundle of nerve fibres that connects the left and right sides of the brain. (Fractional anisotropy is a measure of how much fluid diffuses in one particular direction rather than equally in all directions. In this case it diffuses more equally than one would expect.)'

It's the same, Tom thought. Part of it is *the same.*

'Subject C.'

'Ooh, that's me!' Chai burst out, nudging Tom hard in the ribs. 'Look at my nose.'

Dr Sharifi gave her a mournful look. 'Subject C,' he repeated. '48-year-old woman. Note the hyperconnectivity of the anterior component of the default mode network, plus decreased flow in the bifrontal lobes.'

Tom's face was starting to tingle. Wait, he told himself firmly. Too soon. Much too soon.

Subject D: Stanford's forceful, squared-off brow. Out of the corner of his eye, Tom saw Stanford lean forward, scowling in concentration. More white spaces, clustered in two main areas. Dr Sharifi's slender silver pen stroking the screen: 'Hyperconnectivity of the anterior component of the default mode network, decreased fractional anisotropy in the corpus callosum.'

The world had shrunk to this close, musty, dingy room, the dark faded wallpaper, the shabby milky lights, the phalanx of filing cabinets facing them from the other side of the table. The doctor's melancholy, modulated voice spoke on.

Subject E: 70-year-old female. Veronica's classical profile, her ruler-straight nose.

'...loss of white matter tracts in the left posterior perinatal lobe. Abnormal default mode network with hyperconnectivity of the anterior component of the medial orbital frontal area.'

They were starting to deduce what to watch for now, on the shining oblong of the screen; what words to be alert for, as their eyes followed the hypnotic tracings of the silver pen.

Subject F: 60-year-old male. Hyperconnectivity of the anterior component of the default mode network....

Subject G: 42-year-old female. The same.

Seven out of twelve. They were more than halfway.

Movement bled out of the room, the watchers becoming still, intent, scarcely breathing, taking in the smallest scoops of air. The clock squatting on the mantelpiece tick-ticked.

Subject H: the same.

The doctor himself now no longer languid, his movements sharper, tighter, his voice edged with excitement.

Subject I.

Tom closed his eyes, clenched his hands. Thought about his mother's God, wondered if he should enlist Him in their cause, start praying now, even though he'd never prayed before, make some sort of deal with the Master of the Universe: if this comes out right...if this comes out....

It was the longest, most agonising penalty shootout he had ever had to watch, and in this game there were no second chances; every shot had to go in. Beside him, Stanford turned and laid his forehead against the cool wall. Heat was powering off his body, and the stench of sweat.

Subject J.

Subject K.

On Tom's other side, Chai's legs folded underneath her and she slid down the wall until she sat on the floor next to his feet.

This next was the last. Surely, surely it could not go wrong now.

Subject L.

Tom's eyes flew to the front of the skull, and the white patch was *there* and Dr Sharifi was smiling as he spoke the magical, mysterious, incantatory words and Tom looked away and looked again to make sure it was not a hallucination created by intense longing or a random flare on his retina and it was still there and in his veins a warm, bright substance began to flow, spreading through his chest and his arms and his legs and his brain.

'So does that mean…?'

'Yes. A positive result.'

Tom seemed to take off, float up towards the ceiling from the threadbare carpet, all the ropes of misgiving that had tied him for so long suddenly slashed through. Stanford, next to him, mouth agape, face shining with sweat, gave an uncharacteristically feeble fist pump. Chai was cross-legged on the floor with her head in her hands, sniffing back tears. And Barry turned to Tom, grinning so broadly it burst straight through his beard, and Veronica flung open the door of the office and, striding up to Dr Sharifi, declared, 'Doctor, nothing any of us can ever say can ever express the enormity of what you have done for us. We are all in your debt until the end of time.' Like an exotic bird alighting in swinging cashmere plumage, she folded down onto one knee and kissed the doctor's hand.

Dr Sharifi gave his melancholy smile. Withdrawing from Veronica's grasp, he turned to the computer, closing it down and pocketing the USB stick in his graceful unhurried way. 'I am pleased that there is a positive result. It is the best we could have hoped for from this type of study. However we need to be very conscious of the study's limitations. It is a small study, indicating the need for further research. It gives us no understanding of the causal connection between the abnormalities shown and the hypersensitivities experienced by reactors.'

Tom said, 'I know all that. But – it's a start, isn't it?'

'I very much hope so. And I must thank you, all of you, for finding the funds and for taking part.'

'What happens now?' asked Stanford.

'I will be writing a paper for submission to *Annals of Environmental Health*, which I believe is the appropriate journal. It may take some time to be published, as there will be a process of peer review. I will keep in touch with you about the publication date.'

Would it be before or after Kevin's, Tom wondered. That would be out of his control. But it didn't matter. I'm coming for you, mate, he told Kevin, in his mind. One way or the other, I'm coming for all of you.

'Now I must drive back to Oxford,' Dr Sharifi said. 'It is quite late.'

They accompanied him to his car, a sleek, low-slung black Audi, and as they were thanking him again in the dark chill yard under the accusatory beams of the security lights, Stanford, who had been eyeing the leather seats and the twin exhausts, blurted, 'You're a successful man. Why are you doing this?'

'Excuse me, I don't quite understand.'

'This. Helping us. Helping reactors.'

Dr Sharifi turned slightly away, gazing beyond the circle of light and into the blackness beyond, which was absolute, the clotted dark of moonless rural night. 'Yes, I am a successful man,' he said, when he turned back. 'But I am also a man alone, and a man living a life he did not choose. Let us say I feel kinship with inconvenient minorities. Good night.'

The Audi accelerated sweetly away along the empty lane, its taillights observing the reactors like receding red eyes. Inside it, tucked in the internal pocket of the doctor's elegant suit, the USB stick with its startling contents hurtled away into the night.

Tom felt his insides quiver beneath the jubilation, with a watery sense of foreboding.

Chai was pulling at his arm. 'Tom, it's freezing. We should go back and tell Sarah. She'll be so happy.'

'Yes, the poor child will be on tenterhooks,'

commented Veronica, adjusting her furry scarf and Russian hat, and taking her torch from her coat pocket. 'Thank heavens, our gamble has paid off.'

CHAPTER 34

On the fifteenth of November Tom told everyone he was going for a walk; he didn't say where he was going. He had made a promise to himself, when he had first come to the Valley, that this would be the month when he would undertake his experiment. It was a private thing; it might work, or it might not. He said nothing because he didn't want expectations or commiserations, or to be the cause of general hope or despair.

At two o'clock in the afternoon, he set off along the track to the high ridge, as he had done so many times before. But this time he forked off to the right. He walked quickly over the small shoulder of downs to the gate where, nine months ago, he had first come in.

He climbed over the gate, crunched across a stretch of grass, gravel and loose stones, felt the shock rise in his legs as his feet hit tarmacked lane. He began to stride along, relishing the smooth uncomplicated surface that rolled under the soles of his boots; he lifted his eyes to the distance without worrying about uneven ground. The day was bright, with an uplifting breeze. The lane snaked between rolling fields, hemmed in by hedges on each side which were studded at regular intervals with tall beech trees, their leaves a shimmering mix of gold, orange and green.

He filled his eyes with the view. Trees, and hedges, sheep and sky – oh, he'd seen them every day in the last nine months. But not these ones! These were new. He feasted his eyes upon them, as though he was a vampire, who, after years of feeding on one victim, had come upon fresh flesh.

He came to the T-junction where the lane joined the minor road, turned right and started walking in the direction of the village. Round the next blind bend, a roar built to a crescendo, and a shiny red Mercedes rushed at him, a perfectly bald man at the wheel holding a phone to his ear. Tom stepped briskly into the rough grass of the verge as it flashed past.

He kept walking, drinking in the world. This afternoon might prove to be a brief and reckless jailbreak, not to be repeated, or it might be the start of day-release, but whatever the consequences he might as well enjoy it. He passed a long gravel driveway, with a sign that read 'Cowdleston Manor', and peered along it to catch a glimpse of a substantial house. A few fields on, a piebald horse put its head enquiringly over the fence. Tom paused to stroke its nose.

Aha. At last. This was going to be interesting. A layby on Tom's side of the road, a wooden 'public footpath' sign pointing across the field. A woman coming along the path towards him, in her sixties, probably, short spiky white hair, purple anorak, black cocker spaniel bustling at her feet.

'Good morning,' she hailed him. 'Super weather, isn't it?'

'Oh yes, it's lovely,' Tom replied, with a smile, adding mentally, 'And I expect you're carrying, my dear.'

Further on, he passed a teenage girl in a slouchy silver parka texting furiously as she tramped scowlingly along; she did not acknowledge Tom in any way, just manoeuvred expertly round him as if she had her own set of radar sensors. Then as he came nearer to the village, he passed a man dragging his poodle, oblivious to its desire to investigate smells as he conducted a forceful conversation with the Bluetooth device in his ear.

The road went over a low bridge over a sweet little river. On the parapet a couple were leaning backwards, taking a selfie.

At the outskirts of the village Tom came to a halt. For his first experiment he had probably done enough. He gazed at the road in front of him, which would lead eventually to a pub, and a church, and shops, and houses nestling in increasing intimacy. In his solar plexus he felt the pull, the ancient human

331

instinct for community, so strong, suddenly, so overwhelming, that he'd taken three unconscious steps forward before coming to his senses. He forced his feet to turn 180 degrees, forced them to step, one in front of the other; to repeat the movement, until they had borne him away from temptation. All the way back to the Valley, he felt the village behind him, calling.

That night in his tent – nothing. Just normal, uninterrupted sleep. The next morning – still nothing. Head – unbruised. Heart – steady. Eyes – clear. He ate breakfast with mounting excitement. Could this possibly be? Wait, he instructed himself, it hasn't even been twenty-four hours yet. He forced himself to get through the day, acting normally, resisting the urge to jump in the air, or break into song. By 2 p.m. the urge became so strong that he volunteered to clean out the chemical loo; he trundled the tank of turds along the path to the farmhouse with absolute joy. Surely if anything was going to happen, it would have started by now.

Finally, at 6 p.m., he banged on Sarah's door.

'Oh my God, Tom, that's totally fantastic!'

She'd erupted off the foam bench, grabbed him by the elbows, and they'd done a wild waltz up and down the centre of the caravan. Then, still gripping his arms, she had stared at him with shining eyes. 'So

– tell me again…. You made it to the village?'

'Yes.'

'And you passed people with phones?'

'Yes.'

'And – you still don't have a reaction?'

'Uh-uh.'

He swivelled his head slowly from side to side, his grin so wide it was hurting the muscles in his face.

'Wow,' she breathed.

'The power of the Valley,' Tom said.

'Oh yes indeed.' And after a few moments, almost shyly, 'What are you going to do now?'

'Wait a few days, then try the same thing again. See if I get the same result. Then – well – push the boundaries, I suppose, little by little, trying a bit more each time. Oh Sarah,' he enfolded her, hugging her close. 'I know it's a tiny step, and there's a long way to go, and nothing is guaranteed, and out there the world's not staying the same, things are getting harder for us all the time, but – just to feel the turn of the tide, the reversal of the direction of change – this, and the computer as well – it shows it can happen, that I could get back.'

'It's wonderful,' she murmured. 'I'm so pleased for you.'

Something in her voice, as she said it. A single cracked note of anguish, swiftly and carefully suppressed. He sat back and scrutinised her.

She flicked her eyes away, at first, then brought

them back and held his gaze, daring him to ask.

'You've been here longer than me.' An almost imperceptible nod. 'Did you...have you ever...' Oh God, how could he not have realised.

'Have I ever tried going out? I did. In July. To see if I might be your twelfth. I'd been here for nine months – I thought it was time to try something. It didn't work.'

He tumbled words into the silence. 'Sarah, that was then, it doesn't mean it will never happen. You told me yourself you were in a terrible state when you got here – a full-blown Phase 3. Much worse than I ever was, and for longer. It will just take more time, that's all.'

'Ah yes,' she said, staring out of the front window into the darkness. 'Time. That's all.' After a minute she shook herself. She rose and moved round the small interior, closing the pink curtains and switching on more lights. 'Tom, look, don't worry about what's going on with me. I'm waiting another year before I try again – that's what I decided. But this is fantastic news, we should celebrate with' – she peered into a wall cupboard – 'hey – tinned tuna and pasta... and yet more home-grown courgettes. And tell me – sounds like you picked the same route that I did – did you see the piebald horse?'

CHAPTER 35

'Roasting,' remarked Veronica, 'whilst giving unmatched crispness and tastiness to meat and potatoes, is extremely demanding on the gas. And the vegetables would have to be steamed separately. I have therefore opted for Boeuf Bourguignon.'

She stood among Stanford's granite-effect worktops and brushed chrome units, wearing a frilled apron and stirring a huge cauldron-like iron pot. Tom inhaled the rich flavoursome steam, letting it warm the insides of his face.

They were in a small pod of warmth in an expanse of frozen land. Beyond the fogged windows the sun, just past the meagre high point of its feeble winter arc, blazed brilliant but heatless in the lurid blue of the sky. Everything earthbound – grass, old leaves, stark branches, voided stems – showed pastel through a thick furring of frost, strangely delicate in a season so cruel and raw. Tom thought of the long cold nights when he lay next to Sarah hatted and socked under layers of blankets and coats, and if he woke in one position hardly dared rearrange his limbs because he knew that one millimetre beyond his body-shaped patch of heat, the bed would be a slab of ice. Between the nights were short anaemic days where the air snapped in the nostrils like taut wire and the overwhelming preoccupation was *the gas*: tapping the metal cylinders to see how much was left, lugging in new ones and lugging out the old; endless trade-offs – cold now, warm later? warm today, cold tomorrow? And as well as the heat, there was water and light: 12-volt batteries to hump to the farmhouse to be recharged, water they'd collected frozen uselessly in its container.

'Chai, please will you pass these round.' Veronica was ladling the stew into deep white bowls. Tom clasped his hands round the minimalist curves, absorbing the blissful warmth.

'Mmm, this smells delicious,' Sarah said. 'Thank you.'

'The secret is putting in enough red wine,' Veronica replied. 'I found some cognac in the cupboard and added that as well. I was sure you wouldn't mind, Stanford, it being Christmas.'

For a moment Stanford looked as though he might explode, but his bulging eyes retreated into their sockets and he grunted, 'Sure.'

'I think I might like this better than proper Christmas dinner,' Barry said, as he collected slivers of bacon with his spoon. 'It's got all the best bits in one bowl.'

'And no sprouts,' added Tom.

'And much less washing up,' said Sarah.

'I would encourage everyone to lick their bowls,' said Veronica. 'That will make washing up easier still.'

Chai looked concerned. 'These are deep bowls, Veronica. That will only be possible for people with long tongues.'

Veronica gestured magnanimously. 'Well, whatever can be achieved....'

'What's for pudding?' Stanford enquired.

'A very large box of chocolates,' said Chai. 'Sent to me by a grateful client.'

'And I have a Fortnum and Mason's fruitcake,' Veronica interposed. 'We can eat both as we play Scrabble.'

Tom looked round the table at the contented faces, mellowing and relaxing as they consumed hot food. Winter out here, unplugged from civilisation, was tough, there was no denying it, but already they were past the solstice; the black tide of darkness had turned, was oozing infinitesimally back down the slopes of the day. And even through the worst rigours of the season, when they all yearned for pipes and wires and switches, central heating and insulated walls, the Valley kept working its magic; the reactors – except for Sarah – had picked their way back towards the world. And inside each of them glowed, now, their animating secret – the results of the study, and their prospective publication, the promise of a new, more hopeful year.

After that momentous day in November, Tom had walked out of the Valley again. And again. He had had no reaction. A week later he had got into his van and driven to the vicarage to see his mother; he had stayed for an hour. On his next visit, he walked down the High Street, past Christmas displays and colourful lights, staring at the multitude of faces as though he had just come back from Mars. So many people! He didn't plan to go into any shops, but had stumbled on an open-air craft market, a small huddle of covered stalls, where he'd seen a dark red scarf, long and sinuous and velvety, and bought it for Sarah, nearly dropping his credit card in the gutter because he was so fumbling and out of practice with transactions. He had hurried back to his van in a dream, marvelling at having got to such close grips with normality that he had carried off a piece in his hand.

'So have you planned your trip yet, Barry?' Sarah was asking, and Barry's eyes lit up under his shaggy blond brows. 'I'm driving to Wales on the 30th and coming back on New Year's Day. I'll sleep in the van in a field near my sister's house – it's quite low RF, she says. I'll get to see my sister, and my mum and dad, and my auntie Nella, and the cats. D'you know,

I've missed the cats....'

'That's amazing,' Sarah said. 'You must be looking forward to it.'

'I hope it works out for you, mate,' Stanford said.

'The first of any of us to try a night outside!' Chai exclaimed. 'You are our pioneer.'

'I have a New Year's resolution for you, Stanford, now you are also becoming more resilient,' said Veronica. 'As you know, I now lead a yoga class every Saturday morning in the village hall. Lights off, phones off, no fitness tech on pain of immediate expulsion (I detect it with my meter). You should join us – we need men.'

'Not my thing,' Stanford replied. 'I do weights and pull-ups and so on right here. Gym equipment folds out of the hatch back there.' He pointed along the motorhome's central area. 'Part of the design.'

Veronica sighed theatrically. 'As ever, you are missing the point. At my class you will have the opportunity, whilst building strength with flexibility, to meet the opposite sex in a low-RF environment. Where else are you going to do that?'

Stanford became brick-red, rigid and furious. 'Just back off, Veronica, for God's sake.'

'I am only trying to help. I would have thought you would want to get over that ghastly Victoria.'

'With some yoga bunny who's going to scream with horror when I tell her I can't use a phone? What's the point? Tell me that.'

And that was the rub, Tom reflected. If you looked in one direction, back to the mud you had emerged from, the progress you made was exhilarating. But if you turned and looked the other way, towards your former life, tiny and indistinct on the horizon, the distance still to travel was devastating in its enormity.

CHAPTER 36

Tom woke in the caravan, his body snug under the duvet, his head contrastingly cold. The air in the van was slimy and chill, like a wet wipe laid over his face. Condensation had formed a stealthy trickle down the wall behind him, and a corner of his pillow was damp. Through the curtains feeble early light was leaking in and birds were starting to tune up in the trees. Sarah was still asleep, curled on her side with her back to him, her breathing soft and regular, her hair flowing across the bed like a dark splintering tide.

Recollection loaded with a snap into Tom's drowsy brain, and his stomach tensed. Second of March: for a month the date had been flashing in his mental calendar, the slice of time on which all his efforts had been trained.

Now at last it was *now*. It was today.

His heart began to race, fuelled by a cocktail of apprehension and excitement. Reaching for Sarah's tiny old-fashioned radio, he buried himself under the duvet and jammed the speaker to his ear. Weather forecast. Time signal for 6 o'clock. Headlines: a government minister refusing to resign. A new drug that might slow the progress of Alzheimer's. Improvement of broadband in rural areas. Having your pizza delivered by drone.

In short: the world continuing on its usual course.

Tom twisted the silver knobs, burrowing through static from station to station just to make sure; all he heard were different angles on the same basic themes.

Nothing there. Well – that was probably to be expected; anything else would have been a coup. At least they were getting out there first – still no sign of Kevin's study – ha! Tom rolled out of bed and dressed himself, pulling on his parka, boots and hat. 'Mmm?' Sarah murmured interrogatively.

'I'm going to see what's online,' Tom said.

Outside, in the grey dawn, the grass was filmed with moisture and the air full of the aftermath of rain. As he squelched towards the farmhouse he met Stanford coming back, carrying under his arm the dismembered pink parts of the *Financial Times* which he had delivered there each day. 'Nothing in here,' he told Tom, tapping the paper with his free hand. 'Cuthbert's been to the shop for *The Newsblast*. He's checking it now.'

The Newsblast. Tom's stomach, already tense, contracted into a dense ball. *The Newsblast* was the big one. Other parts of the media had got the press release, and reactorrights was planning a social media campaign, but they'd contacted Rosario Weissman the sympathetic journalist, and she'd landed a commission for an article for *The Newsblast's* health and science section, including an interview with Dr Sharifi.

Tom hurried on, finding Cuthbert in his kitchen in a fug of bacon and egg, gold half-moon reading glasses perched on his beaky nose. *The Newsblast* was laid out on the big table in front of him as he methodically scanned the pages.

'I'm sorry, Tom. I can't see anything here. I'll look through it again, in case I missed it.'

What was going on? He had to get online. Most likely they had delayed the article, had too much other news, were publishing it another day. Tom swerved next door into the office, flung himself onto the computer seat, drummed his fingers with impatience as the elderly tower ground into life.

Email from Rosario Weissman. Single word title: Spiked.

Dear Tom.

I'm totally furious. All that work and the ******* editor pulled it. 'Not really the line we take' or some such bland bullshit. I get the strong feeling he got sat on by someone higher up with their eyes on the bottom line (editor was pretty enthusiastic when I first proposed

343

it). Most of the advertising money comes from telecoms companies or social media/internet giants. They can't afford to piss them off.

Better luck elsewhere

Best

Roz

The tight knot of anticipation in his gut was gone. Instead, a void, a hollow emptiness, from which something vital was draining away.

He shook himself. Better luck elsewhere. At least, there *was* elsewhere. Who read newspapers any more, anyway? He typed words into a search engine: reactors, fMRI scans, Dr Sharifi. Was served merely the abstract of the article itself in the journal *Annals of Environmental Health*, solitary, academic, virginal, untouched by evidence that any other outlet had picked it up.

Try different keywords: brain, abnormality, scans, radiofrequency radiation, Oxford.

The result was the same.

Tom blinked at the screen, sat back for a few seconds, then plunged directly into social media, searching for the information that reactorrights was supposed to have posted. But it did not seem to be there. What the hell were they playing at? He'd spoken to Olaf at reactorrights, who'd sounded competent, on top of things, a guy you could trust. Tom fired off an email. 'Olaf – where is it? Can't see it anywhere. Will post it myself, now, but you need to get it out there from you.' When he'd done, he switched off and sat staring at the dead screen, his brain wrestling with what had happened, trying to fit parts together as though it was a particularly fiendish calculation.

The first evidence that reactors were real, when, before, they had been assumed to have a psychological condition.

That was news – wasn't it?

Okay – he shouldn't expect every outlet to pick it up, but...*nothing?*

The bell of the landline phone made him jump. He snatched it up. 'Hello?'

'Tom?'

'Yes?'

'It's me. Olaf.'

'What's happening?'

'I posted it, just like I said I would. But – it's just – vanished. Gone.' His voice was faint and breathless, like an eyewitness to an atrocity who needed treatment for shock. 'Gone?' Tom was incredulous.

'I suppose...social media companies...take down posts...sometimes...'

'Yes, but they take down posts about child porn, or neo-Nazism, or – I don't know – calls for people to be lynched. Not this sort of stuff. This is science.'

'It's gone,' Olaf repeated.

'Wait a minute,' commanded Tom, dropping the

receiver on the table. He fired up the computer again, logged on to his social media feeds. Refreshed them, closed them, reopened them.

Shook the mouse. Closed his eyes. Reopened them. Closed them. Repeated all of it, over and over, in a hyperactive effort to align his real and virtual worlds.

Fruitless.

With a trembling hand he lifted the receiver from the table. 'Olaf?' He could hardly speak; something had him by the throat.

'Yes?'

'My posts have gone, too.'

PART 3

CHAPTER 37

He was in his tent in his sleeping bag, in tight, foetid, unchanged clothes. Curled on his side, he needed to move, because his knee was sore, but he could no more shift himself two inches than he could have flown to the moon; the necessary connection between his will and the world had fused, utterly burnt through.

Time had gone limp and shapeless, days hanging loosely around him like wet sheets that would not dry. Other people walked about outside the tent, talked to each other in subdued tones, went on with their day-to-day lives. How did they do that? Doing anything at all seemed the most absolute, inconceivable enormity. He felt detached, marooned, his tent a desolate island, and he wanted it to be like that, to stay like that forever.

Rustling. The fart of a zip.

My brain is screaming. Why can't they hear?

A draught of fresh air tunnelling through the fug.

'Tom?'

Go *away*.

Sarah crawled in. He could smell her – musk, Gore-Tex and lemons. She manoeuvred herself until she sat cross-legged beside his head.

'Tom – you have to stop this.'

No response required.

'You have to stop feeling guilty.'

Now that was not logical. He twisted round on his sleeping mat. 'I am guilty. I failed.'

'You didn't fail. The study exists. That was because of you.'

'Existence is nothing.' He turned wearily back to his former position, let his eyes fall shut once more.

'Okay, no one covered it, the other day, but we can keep thinking about ways to use it. We were sliding down a slope, Tom, and now we've jammed in an axe. We can start to climb back up.'

'I should have realised what would happen.'

'Why?'

'Because it was obvious, to anyone who thought about it for more than two seconds.'

Sarah sighed. 'Tom, I know you want to find the answer. The key that will unlock it all at once, solve the whole terrible mess. I don't think it's going to be like that. It's going to be chaotic and drawn out and bloody and take God knows how long. But...to have taken the first step...' He could hear the grin warming her voice. 'It's like the difference between zero and one – like you told me once, it's infinite.'

'I don't want this reality.'

Gently she rubbed his arm, over and over, with quiet firmness, as if she were stroking a cat. 'I know. I've felt the seduction too. But you can't, Tom. You have to hold on.'

'Why?'

She found his hand, grasped it, lowered her head so that her hair tickled the side of his face. 'Because if you don't, you'll become exactly what they want you to be. We have to stay sane, very very sane, so we can keep working out how to survive.'

'Okay,' she went on, after he had said nothing for a while, 'I'll go now. But please – think about what I said.'

After a few days of rain, the clouds had broken up and the afternoon sunbeams warmed the Valley with the first real warmth of spring. The door of Sarah's van was open, and from inside came the click-click-click of an ancient sewing machine as she mended rips in clothes, interspersed with quiet curses when she tangled the thread. High up in the large suntrap cabin of the motorhome, Stanford was deep in the pink sheets of the *Financial Times*. Veronica, having unrolled a large crimson oriental rug on the grass outside her yurt, was teaching Chai how to do the Cobra pose; the two of them were lying on their fronts and rearing up in parallel arcs, an incongruous pair, one long and graceful, the other short and plump. Barry was watching them, smiling into his beard as he cleaned his van with a bucket and sponge.

In the vegetable patch Tom shuffled forwards on his knees between rows sown with fennel, parsnips, and carrots, where the ground was fuzzy with the first green froth of growth. All he needed to do was find the weeds between the seedlings, grasp them in his hands, rip them out of the earth. And that was what he wanted: to stay low, very low; to meet no one but worms, and speak to no one but worms, never to lift his head up out of the dirt again.

A shadow fell across the lines of seedlings. Tom, glancing up, found Cuthbert standing at the edge of the plot in his ancient cap, shoulders hunched inside his Barbour jacket, staring fixedly at the far ridge of the downs. Sarah came down the steps of her van. 'Hey Cuthbert, how's it going?' she asked, and for a few moments he gave no sign that he had heard, just continued to stand as though he had been planted into the soil, a gaunt brown tree among the tussocks of grass. When he turned slowly towards them, Tom saw devastation in his face, the bony features standing out as though his skin had been vacuum-sealed against his skull.

'The post came,' he said. 'I have had a letter.' He half-lifted a sheet of paper that he held crushed in his hand, but then let his arm drop back to his side.

'Cuthbert, what…' Sarah began, but he shook his

head helplessly and gestured round the camp. 'You should probably all hear this.'

The others were converging as Sarah ran to collect them, abandoning what they had been doing, sensing on the air that something was afoot. Tom stood up awkwardly, conscious of the activity around him but still gripped by a deep detached weariness which he could not push through.

When everyone was assembled Cuthbert smoothed the paper and held it out in front of him. 'From the local Council. There has been an application for a mast.'

Stillness came on the little circle as the people who formed it turned to stone; a pool of deathly immobility among the hopeful bustle of spring.

Stanford was the first to speak, his voice coming out scratchy, at an unaccustomed high pitch. 'Wh – where will it be?'

Cuthbert pointed to the ridge on the Valley's north side. 'Up there, along to the left, just beyond the clump of hawthorn trees.'

'But Cuthbert, I don't understand,' said Sarah, who had turned very pale. 'How can they put a mast there – that's your land.'

'That bit isn't,' Cuthbert replied bleakly. 'It belongs to the sewage works in the next valley. The sewage works is on council land.'

Tom gazed upwards to where the short-cropped grass met the sky, and tried to picture the thing in place, the futuristic warrior in grey spiked armour raking the Valley unceasingly, tirelessly with its beam. Everything would look as it did now – the clear gurgling stream, the trees just coming into leaf, the birds whizzing and perching as they staked melodious territorial claims – but for the reactors it would be utterly changed, a haven violated, a habitat lost.

He had believed he stood on solid ground, could give way for a while, in the Valley's calm embrace. Now under his feet the land itself seemed to bulge and fissure, preparing to crumble away.

Chai was the one who asked, 'How long have we got?'

Cuthbert studied the letter. 'Fifty-six days.'

Eight weeks.

Tom's mental fog evaporated, leaving cruelly lit, sharp-edged reality.

He glanced across at Sarah, who had turned from the group, her shoulders contorting, her hands clamped onto her mouth to muffle any sound.

We have to stay sane. Very very sane. Because we need to keep working out how to survive.

To find another haven like this one, when they were getting rarer by the day; to work out how to travel there without getting iller en route. It would be hard for all of them, but it would be fifty, a hundred, a thousand times harder for her.

Veronica's crisp voice cut in on his thoughts. 'May

I see the letter, please, Cuthbert?' She pulled it from his grasp.

'Ah – as I thought. There is the opportunity to make representations. It probably won't do any good, and we will all of course wish to pursue alternative plans. But we should fight for the Valley. It is precious – both for us, and for reactors in the future.'

'The thing will be overlooking my land,' Cuthbert said. 'I will write to the council in my capacity as landowner. And I will talk to my councillor. It could surely be moved elsewhere.'

'I agree.' Chai waved her arms at the surrounding scenery. 'There are many hills in this area. The mast does not have to be on this one.' Her face creased into a puzzled frown. 'In fact if they want to improve mobile services in the places where there is population, other sites would actually be better, I would have thought. Sheep do not yet use mobile phones.'

'What do you say, Stanford?' Veronica raised her eyebrows, her tone challenging. 'Do we fight?'

'The bitch is going to love this,' he muttered, his lips twisted as though some foul taste clogged his mouth. Then business-like again: '60:40 resource split. 60% to find somewhere else, 40% to stop the mast. I'll sign a letter to the council, if you draft one.'

'I will ask some of the people in the village to write to the council,' Veronica declared. 'I am becoming well known there through my yoga classes. But what we really need is some respected member of the community who can go and speak directly to them on our behalf.' She brightened. 'And in fact we do know someone. Tom – you must ask your mother.'

His mother. Of course. A vicar. Ideal. The obvious person. Yet thinking about the actual asking made a cold crust of reluctance form across his skin. Her anguished words played in his head: *You can see, can't you, in my position – I would be putting myself against the whole direction of today's society, the whole trend of modern life.*

But qualms and scruples went the way of all his other feelings: tossed overboard as self-indulgent luxuries as his small craft foundered. To save Sarah and to survive himself: these were the things that mattered. And there was no time to waste. In extremis, it was amazing how life simplified.

He nodded. 'I'll drive home and see her straightaway.'

'Look at me,' he'd told her, simply, in the end. In the vicarage kitchen, he'd stood in front of her, among the familiar mugs and plates; the shelf of cookbooks; his school photographs, all ears and teeth. He'd stood there tanned, upright and muscular, unmistakeably healthier than the pain-wracked, desperate person who had quit the vicarage the previous year. 'This is because of the Valley. This is what the Valley has done. Not just for me – for all of us. If we save it, I'll keep getting more resilient. If we lose it, I'll end up back where I was, or worse. I'm sorry, Mum, that it's come to this, but you've got to help us. It's our only hope.'

She had looked at him, her angular face softening, and had seen, he suspected, her son, in abeyance for a while in the Valley's healing absence, one day soon walking out of it, cured, reborn, triumphant, ready to step back into his place in society, and do her credit in the eyes of the world.

It might just happen. There was still a chance.

'If there was any other way, Tom,' she had said quietly, sighing. 'But I suppose there isn't?'

'There isn't.'

'I will do it.' She held herself straighter, set her shoulders back. 'You must tell me carefully what you want me to say.'

Tom threw his arms round her. 'Thanks Mum, you're the best.' She hugged him back, for a short while, then briskly stepped away, consulting the calendar that hung on the wall. 'Today is Saturday,' she said. 'I will contact the council on Monday morning and see what I can arrange with the Planning Committee.'

CHAPTER 38

Tom bounded up the steps of the caravan and burst inside, arms full of Ordnance Survey maps and pages printed from the web.

'Look, Sarah, I've been researching where we might go – if the worst happens, of course.'

She had been sitting writing something on a pad; she covered it quickly as he approached. Since the day of the letter she had been in a strange mood, subdued and uncommunicative, going for endless rain-soaked walks on the downs by herself. He'd assumed she was quite reasonably fearful about the future; he'd poured all his energy into finding a way out.

He put down his pile on the table and sat opposite her. 'Wales and Scotland are the most likely places – and the Yorkshire Dales. In fact that would be the most handy for me to get back to Northington in the longer term. I'd travel there and investigate first, so you'd only have to make the journey once, and...'

'Tom...please stop,' Sarah said. 'Stop a minute.'

'Why? What's the matter?' Her tone pulled him up short.

'Tom – I've been thinking. A lot. I've decided – I'm not going to run any more. I'm sorry.'

For a few seconds he was utterly paralysed, staring in silent horror at her calm, determined face, before he seized her by the shoulders and pulled her towards him, shaking her, yelling, 'No...No.... God Sarah, you can't, don't do that, don't do that, don't leave me, not like that. I know people reach the end of the line, but you haven't, believe me, you haven't, I won't let you, there's more left for you in life.'

'Tom, Tom, stop, get off me, you've – you've got the wrong end of the stick.' She fought clear of his arms.

'You said you were going to...kill yourself.'

'*No.*'

Tom threw himself backwards onto the foam bench and let his eyelids close, felt the adrenalin seeping away. 'What did you mean, then?'

'There's only one place where I can be normal. It's a place where there are no masts and all RF devices are banned. A place where the authorities don't want any RF noise, they want things quiet, because they're listening.'

'Listening?'

'Listening to all the radio waves in the universe. Tom, I didn't mention it before, because it never seemed important, but...I am an American. I was born there when my dad was on an academic exchange. I've got dual nationality. I can go back.'

'You can go back.'

She turned to him, clasping his hand with both of hers.

'I'm so sorry. I've been over and over it in my head. It absolutely breaks my heart, but oh God, think about it – I'm so much further down the slope than you, so much further gone. I have to be realistic – my options are running out. Together, the places we can go will always be so limited compared to what you could do on your own. In America – well – they've got this giant radio telescope, the largest one in the world, and round it there's thousands of square miles of quiet zone, deep in the mountains. There are only a few thousand people living there, under the wireless restrictions, and some reactors have moved there already, and...oh Tom, if I can only get there, I can stop running, and really get better, and maybe be able to work again.'

Tom sat back and stared at her. Then he almost laughed.

'Look...I hate to put a damper on things, but... how are you proposing to get there? You can't go within spitting distance of an airport, and even if you did get as far as the plane you'd pass out or throw up with all the Wi-Fi and devices, and somehow I don't reckon you can afford a private jet; even if you could, the thing would be full of electronics. It would be wonderful if it could happen, but it's not a practical proposition.' He reached out to embrace her. 'Stick with me, Sarah. We'll find a way, I promise.'

But she dodged aside to elude his grasp. 'I can get there,' she said fiercely. 'I know I can. I'm going to sail.'

When Tom's lungs had resumed their function of taking in air and he could find no reason for doubting what his ears had conveyed to his brain, he said quietly, separating each word from the rest as though placing weights to hold her down, 'Sarah...you – are – clinically – insane.'

'I am not.'

'You are. You will drown.'

'I will not. Well, okay, I might.'

'Yeah, you might.'

'There's a risk, I realise that. But...I told you, I used to be good. It's like riding a bicycle. It will come back to me. And the phone mast won't go up straight away. I've got time to prepare.'

'You never sailed across the Atlantic and you never sailed that far on your own.'

'No – no I didn't.'

'So you are insane. Or suicidal – despite what you said.'

'I am *not*. Neither of those. Tom, can't you understand – some things are worth taking risks for – calculated risks. I've thought and thought about it, and...about what might happen if it all goes wrong and…well…as somebody or other once said, sometimes it is better to die on your feet than live on your knees.'

He foundered, then, assailed by equal and opposite forces, that met in the middle like two huge waves and utterly engulfed him. Oh God – what she'd said, this crazy plan, this final break for freedom, it was everything he loved about her: her realism, her courage, her defiance, her clear-eyed view of the future.

Everything he loved?

Yes – loved. And he knew, at that moment, that here was someone he fitted together with, better than Marianne, better than anyone else before. Someone he had fallen for, in the Valley's calm parenthesis, where his whole aim and purpose had been to leave, leave it and her behind, to get back to Northington and finish his PhD.

Now she was calmly leaving him.

Because she was right: he hadn't admitted it to himself before, hadn't wanted to, had dashed around putting up a smokescreen of bustle and plans. To find somewhere else as good as the Valley to be her haven, and get her there without some catastrophic loss of resilience – the probabilities were vanishingly small.

She was finished. And she knew it. He wasn't. She knew that too. The curse of differential recovery, which had sent him on ever more frequent and longer excursions into normality, whilst holding her in chains.

If he was in her shoes, if he were brave enough, if he knew anything at all about sailing – he would probably do the same.

If – if – if.

The relentless forking of reality. It was almost audible now, in these extreme times, a click – click – clicking in his brain.

If the mast didn't happen…if the mast could be moved – she wouldn't have to go. If the mast could be stopped, she would stay.

He put his head in his hands, and more strongly, more intensely, more wholeheartedly than at any other time in his life, he threw a hotchpotch of prayer, and will, and supplication out into the universe, for whoever or whatever was there to be moved or swayed by it, focussed so fiercely on one single outcome that it seemed to blaze from his skull.

He opened his mouth to speak, and stopped, started and stopped again, tasting each time the insipid inadequacy of his words. He examined her face, her deep-set eyes under her straight dark fringe, her quizzical eyebrows, her wide, mischievous mouth. A face that he had grown to know so intimately in all its quirks and changing moods, that had laughed and kissed and cried with him, that looked back at him now with love, but also through him, and past him, with the beginnings of a steady resolution, to new vistas where he did not play a part.

Not to see her again.

Never to see her again.

He couldn't accept it.

There had to be a way.

He felt the pressure all around him, squeezing him tighter and tighter, mashing his flesh onto his bones.

The answer slid into his mind like the solution to an equation; as soon as he saw it, he could not understand how he had not seen it before, it was so obviously present in the problem's component parts.

He wanted to laugh out loud, but he held himself back. Instead he took her hand, lifted it briefly to his mouth.

'Marry me, and we'll go together.'

She jerked back against the seat cushion as though he'd electrocuted her. 'Marry you? Tom, are you serious? Have you gone completely mad?'

'Yes.... No.... Look, I'm completely serious. I love you. I hadn't realised it before.'

She stared at him for several seconds before she lowered her eyes and slowly shook her head. 'In any other circumstances, Tom – in any other time and place – I'd say yes in a moment, my dearest boy.'

Other circumstances? What did she mean? It was the obvious solution. Why couldn't she see it? 'So say it now.'

She was squirming on her seat, shifting one way and the other. 'Tom, look – I can't. I...know I said I could sail the Atlantic, that I used to be good.... Well, actually' – her words tumbled out in a sudden rush – 'it's quite likely that I won't manage it and I'll sink the boat and...then you'd end up dead and I'd never be able to live with myself.'

'You wouldn't have to live with yourself,' Tom pointed out. 'You'd be dead too.'

Her mouth quirked into an unwilling half-grin.

'Okay, okay, point taken. But the principle of the thing still holds. I can't take you to your death when... when you haven't reached the end of the road. You're getting better – you've been doing day release into normality. If you find another haven, who knows how far you might go.'

'Might,' he cut in, almost savagely. 'How far I *might* go. Havens are getting harder and harder to find – unless you hadn't realised that. We all have to make our own judgements. You've made yours – why can't I make mine?'

'Because...because you'd be making it early, because of me. You're doing so well, you could make it back. To Northington. Just like you were saying – get back to the university, finish your PhD. Have your career, the one you always wanted, making sense of the universe...'

Tom was pacing the constricted length of the van.

'Yeah, I might. Perhaps. If I was lucky. And then what? Living on the edge, clinging on, trying to fight for recognition when at any moment I could become a refugee again. And – knowing what I know now – keep on modelling what black holes get up to, billions and billions of light-years away, when something so big is happening right here, on this planet, right now – this huge invisible distortion of the integrity of science by a massive agglomeration of interest and power. I want to keep fighting, and fight from a position of strength. So thanks, but the universe can go hang. I'll take my chances with the sea.'

At the kitchen end he swung round, fiercely folding his arms. 'And talking of chances – look me in the eye, and tell me the odds aren't better with two.'

She tried, she tried, it was a valiant effort, but she couldn't hold his gaze. Biting her lip she swivelled her head to stare at the downs.

'I may know sod all about sailing,' he went on, softening his tone, 'But I know about sleep. You can teach me enough, surely, to keep an eye on the boat, while you get some kip. That has to be better than trying it alone.'

'Yes, it would be better,' she flung back, 'of course it would, what do you expect me to say? But you're doing sleight of hand with your arithmetic. Two lives end up in jeopardy, not one.'

'Two lives get a moonshot at normality. You're forgetting the upside, and the upside is – well, oh God, it's huge. Oh Sarah' – he was across the space between them in a single bound and kneeling on the floor beside her – 'if we can pull it off – just imagine how totally fantastic it would be.'

Their faces were so close, he saw the film of tears in the corners of her eyes. She began to stroke his hair, moving her fingers carefully back and forth, abstractedly watching the patterns she made. Outside, birds were going berserk in the trees, spinning long, smooth loops of melody, or intercutting with shorter, harsher motifs. On the downs, newborn lambs tried out their fragile voices and their mothers made full-throated replies. An engine started up; Barry getting ready for work. A high-handed comment from Veronica provoked murmured objections from the rest. In the warm private box of the van, a small travel clock ticked, measuring out neat portions of time; but there did not seem to be any movement forward, just the same recycled moment, poised, quivering, on the brink.

Tom felt reality start to pull; he readied himself for the fork.

'Okay,' she said, leaning forward and kissing him. 'Okay – you win. Perhaps I ought to say no, but I can't. Whatever happens, it'll be so much more fun, with you.'

He wanted to leap up and punch a hole through the roof. Pulling Sarah to her feet, he grabbed her round the waist and in the small space between the table, the fridge, the loo and the cooker, they danced until the caravan started to rock on its corner steadies, and Sarah gasped, 'Stop…stop…we're going to tip it' and they collapsed against each other.

When they had recovered Sarah asked, 'What do we do if your mum achieves some sort of miracle and the mast is stopped?'

'Marry me anyway,' Tom replied. 'Of course we should get married. I'm an idiot for not thinking of it before.'

'D'you know,' said Sarah thoughtfully, twisting a long strand of hair round her finger, 'I've never actually heard of reactors getting married. You usually hear about them getting divorced.'

Tom put his lips close to her ear and murmured, 'So let's do something wildly subversive,' and she gave one of her great shouts of laughter and folded him in her arms.

CHAPTER 39

He was rinsing coffee cups at the caravan sink at eleven the next morning when he saw his mother come out of the trees. She was wearing her smart navy trouser suit and moving fast, full of determination, with a bulging plastic carrier bag gripped in her hand.

When she banged on the caravan door, she scarcely waited for an answer before pushing inside. As she passed him Tom smelt the tang of nervous sweat. Her cap of hair was dishevelled, her beige cheeks scalded with angry unnatural patches of red. Sarah half rose from her seat with words of welcome, but Janet ignored her, upending the carrier bag onto the table so its contents tumbled out.

Newspapers. Loads of them. Tabloids, broadsheets, left, right and centre. What on earth was she doing? It looked like she'd bought a full set.

His mother picked one up, opened it and folded it back to highlight a particular story. She slapped it onto the table, before picking up the next. She still did not say anything. In the silence the pristine newsprint crackled and crunched, and the surface gradually became tiled with thick wadded rectangles, crawling with leggy black type. Tom stepped across to read, and the words sprayed up like acid in his face.

'Phone mast allergy "in the mind".'

'"Reactor" allergy dismissed by scientists.'

'Study puts mobiles in the clear.'

'"Wi-Fi sickness" is techno-fear, scientists show.'

His guts contracted. He snatched a paper at random and skimmed the article beneath the headline. There it was – Kevin's study: the name of the university, the name of the professor, the confident, reassuring conclusions. In every paper. Because, of course, this was the story that everyone wanted to tell.

He imagined eyes all over the country scanning the story in print and on the web; ears hearing it on the radio, in cars, in living rooms, on trains, minds that had for the most part never heard of reactors absorbing it, accepting it and filing it away.

Minds that would be primed, now, if a reactor ever spoke out. He felt their judgement, the cumulative judgement of that anonymous mass of strangers, a million tiny swipes against his skin.

Sarah was nudging him, hissing, 'Tom, make tea, now,' and he floated from the table, laying hands on the kettle in a weird, disembodied state, having to think hard to remember the basic sequence of moves. Sarah was talking gently to his mother, putting an arm round her trembling shoulders. 'It must have been awful,' she said, and his mother gave a convulsive nod. The calming warmth of fragrant steam drifted up from the tea; for a while they all just sat there and inhaled it, hands clasped around the mugs, until finally Janet began to speak.

'There were three of them in the room. A member of the Planning Committee, a Planning Officer, and a man from the telecoms company. Everyone was very polite. I went through what you'd told me, Tom, talked about the situation of the people in the Valley, how avoidance was helping them get better, how just moving the mast a little way could make such a big difference, how Dr Sharifi's paper indicated a shared physical abnormality...and then...'

'What happened then?'

'Oh, the Planning Committee man smirked, reached below the table for a newspaper, shoved it across at me and said, "Unfortunately, Reverend, you're a little behind the times." The telecoms man said, "We don't dispute that your son and his friends have genuine health issues" – oh, his eyes just oozed concern – "but science has now shown conclusively that they are making a misattribution regarding the cause." And they all agreed that it was "quite natural" that I felt compassion for these unfortunate people, but perhaps I needed to "step back a bit" and consider if by "supporting them in their mistaken beliefs" I might be doing more harm than good.'

'That sounds hideous,' Sarah said. 'I'm really sorry. What did you say after that?'

Janet raised her shoulders and let them fall. 'I can't remember. What could I say? I did my best, I truly did. I tried to say what you'd told me, Tom, about problems with the research. But it is impossible, it is no use, it is like trying to find a handhold on a wall of glass.'

So much for Kevin's caveats. Tom had known – he had known all along – that whatever nuance was put in the research paper would be utterly lost.

He said, 'The reports are not true, Mum. The condition is real, you know that.'

'Yes Tom, I know that.' She sounded infinitely tired, beyond all normal forms of exhaustion. They sat in silence, the supply of words run dry, the bold black headlines sneering up at them, cocky and conclusive. After a while Sarah reached out and turned one face down, then began to pile the others on top of it, so that slowly the stories disappeared; with the muffling of the words, the psychic flaying became less acute. His mother took a comb from her satchel and smoothed her disordered hair, fished for a powder compact and restored her beige, unblemished face, spritzed her neck and wrists with lightly scented spray. 'Now I have to be going,' she said, her poise returned. 'I am due to visit a centre for the homeless in Cornchester, and join in serving lunch. It is such an inspiring place – truly changing lives.'

Tom watched her walk briskly into the trees.

Sarah touched his arm. 'Tom, you know it was only ever an outside chance.'

'That we could stop the mast?'

She nodded. 'And this whole publication thing is awful timing, especially with your mum getting tangled up in it – but it was going to happen at some point.' She tried to smile. 'And hey – at least we have plan B.'

Plan B, the crazy plan, the wild hypothetical Atlantic-crossing alternative. It flopped down with a bump on reality like an ungainly seabird, jolting him into an appalled realisation that this was now the way forward, this was what they were going to do. Somewhere in his brain in a small watertight compartment he must have kept alive some faith that there would be another way. He braced himself to lift the last hatch, and let the ocean in.

The reactors sat in a semi-circle around Veronica's wood-burning stove, a black, bow-legged, pot-bellied creature venting its waste gases along a pipe like a stiff tail that passed out through the wall of the yurt. Candles set in storm lanterns stood haphazardly about on a table, a chair and the floor, casting twisted shadows on flower patterns as night rain splattered the fabric of the roof. The centre of the dome, traditionally open to the sky, was sealed by a clear plastic disc, so that the reactors were watched from above by a single moist black eye.

'We must try to focus on the positive,' Veronica said, breaking a long silence. 'This engagement is wonderful news. The Valley is lost, but we shall at least have one last party. May I ask the happy couple where exactly you are proposing to tie the knot?'

Tom and Sarah looked at each other.

'Er – we hadn't thought.'

'I am sorry to pour cold water on your plans,' Veronica went on, 'But there may be difficulties. I cannot, for example, see how Sarah could get to the registry office in the centre of town.'

'But…the law's changed now, hasn't it?' said Tom. 'We could have a civil wedding somewhere else.'

'You still have to go to the registry office in person to register, a certain number of days prior to the ceremony,' Veronica replied. 'I know this because I took care of my adorable granddaughter when my daughter and her prospective third husband drove there in her second husband's Jaguar. That was of course in the days when she was still speaking to me.'

In Tom's stomach, something twitched itself onto the alert. Surely – surely after all they'd been through to get to this point, there couldn't be some final obstacle in their path.

Chai said, 'That has to be the general rule; I see that. But there must be exemptions for health reasons. People get married in hospital when they are dying.

And at home when they are housebound.'

One of the logs in the stove split apart with a sizzling crack.

'Good luck with that. Medical evidence...' Stanford almost spat out the words. 'That's what they'll ask you for. A "report from a doctor" about "the nature of your health condition". And of course, there's not a cat in hell's chance that you'll get it.'

Sarah slammed her fists into the floor.

'God, how could we have been so presumptuous? How could we think – just for one minute – that there might be just one social institution we might actually take advantage of. Oh Tom' – desperate tears were streaming from her eyes – 'I'm so sorry – if the Valley was going to be here for years, I'd go to the registry office with you tomorrow, get wiped out, take the hit, roll back down the slope, start at the bottom again – but we've only got weeks, weeks to go before I'll need everything I've got...'

Tom grabbed her, pinioning her as she writhed in his arms.

'Shhh. It's not your fault,' he whispered. 'None of this is your fault.'

A cough from Veronica interrupted them. 'Actually, there may be an entirely different approach to the problem. And I have been very remiss in not thinking of it before. You can get round the registration business by simply getting married in church.'

'In church?' Sarah lifted her tear-stained face.

'A vicar can come here and arrange it all. Banns – licence – whatever.' Veronica swept an arm out grandly. 'As for the actual church – that may prove more complicated. The one in our nearest village has been converted into a delightful period residence and the one in your village, Tom, unfortunately, is in a built-up area close to the high street. I do not know about any other churches in the vicinity.'

But there had to be other churches. Sarah was starting to wilt again, he could feel her weight dragging him down. Come on, he told her silently, almost shaking her, don't give up on me now. 'Want to find your nearest low-RF church for that special occasion?' he said, into her ear. 'Download our exciting new churchometer app. More than fifty thousand religious institutions, rated, tested and scored.'

'Oh ha ha,' she retorted gruffly.

'I've passed a little church, on my walks,' said Barry. 'Right in the middle of nowhere. Looks like it's mostly kept closed up, but the board said it is open for services once a week between Easter and Harvest.'

'But this sounds most interesting,' exclaimed Veronica. 'Barry, you must get your Ordnance Survey map and show us. I will fetch your boots and anorak myself.' She whirled towards the entrance to the yurt.

With the map spread out on the floor between them, Barry moved his torch over an area a couple of miles to the north of the Valley, and then directed it at a black cross perched on a black square alongside a meandering back road, with mixed woodland enclosing it on two sides. 'There. That's where it is.'

'This could be perfect,' Tom breathed. According to the map there were no other buildings nearby. No spiked lines of pylons marching across the landscape.

No masts.

Veronica was tracing boundary lines with an elegant forefinger. 'And look,' she said, 'Tom – it's inside your mother's group of parishes. What could be better? As the vicar in charge, I'm sure she will oblige.'

CHAPTER 40

'So I went to see the church first thing this morning – it's called St Peter's – you must know it – and it's great, really low-RF…'

'Tom…stop. Please stop for one moment. I need to make sure I've understood you. You are planning to marry…Sarah.'

'Well yes – who else?'

'And sail to America in a small sailing boat.'

'It's the only way she can get there.'

They were in Cuthbert's high-ceilinged, sash-windowed office, where the large square computer table took up most of the space and metal filing cabinets of varying sizes formed a bar chart against the back wall. Beside one window was an old leather wingchair; Janet perched on the edge of the seat.

'Tom, Tom – this is impulsive madness. You need to stop and think things through.'

'What things?'

'That there might be…alternatives.'

'Like what?'

'You've done so well in the Valley, really worked hard, built up your resilience – I'm proud of what you've achieved. Now we should be looking to the future. I've still got the wired equipment in place at the vicarage, and I could do something about the meetings, move most of them to a different venue. It's time for you to come home.'

He couldn't help himself – his skin glowed, his limbs relaxed, he was overwhelmed with sensuous memory. Oh to live in a house again. Central heating that warmed the room before you got out of bed. A bath right next door, with hot water that kept on running. Unlimited electricity that rushed to do your bidding, if you reached out your hand to flip the switch.

But there were other memories too, scalding him like steam jets as they rushed up through his brain. Crouching in his cage on his bed as people chatted and laughed in the hall downstairs, silently screaming at them to get on with it, get on with it, get the hell out. Those innumerable, dismal, haphazard walks, bouncing like a billiard ball from human contact. The hours and hours plugged into his laptop, chasing normality, while his body quietly but momentously metamorphosed from Phase 1 to Phase 2.

'Would you tell people, this time?' he asked. 'Would you let me come out?'

She screwed up her eyes, as though he'd switched

on one of the desk lamps and angled it into her face. 'Don't you think, that – perhaps – after those newspaper articles, it would be best not to? Best for you, Tom. People can make very harsh judgements.'

'No,' he said, 'it would not be best.'

'If it would make the difference, Tom' – she swallowed hard – 'I will talk to them. I'll talk to them today.'

Tom shook himself. The whole thing was irrelevant, a distraction from the business in hand. 'I can't come back, Mum. Whatever you do in the house, whatever you tell people. I can't come back because Sarah can't come with me.'

Janet sliced her hand downwards in a burst of impatience but she caught herself in midair; he watched it mutate into a smooth controlled movement.

'Sarah is a lovely girl' – she had turned on, suddenly, the full force of her beautiful voice, wrapping him in warm velvet, so he wanted to lie back luxuriously in its folds – 'but she is in a very bad state.'

'She would be. She's a reactor. Like I am. It's a fairly crap life.'

'Not like you are, Tom, not at all. You're not describing things accurately. You're a scientist – I'm surprised at you. You told me yourself there are different levels of sensitivity. You are on your way back to normality. She…is not.'

'Mum, that's just contingent, down to luck. I could easily have ended up like her. I still could, in the future. There's no merit in it – I was lucky enough to have the Valley at a particular point...'

'But nonetheless, Tom, things are as they are.' Her voice flowed smoothly on, like a stream round a boulder that lay in its course. 'It is a tragedy, but we have to accept it. There is just no way she can function in the modern world.'

'So I should abandon her and let her sail alone?'

She winced. 'That's too harsh, Tom. What I mean is don't get carried away by – oh, some misplaced chivalrous impulse. We are all dealing with extraordinary things, outside the range of most people's experience. Sometimes it has to be right to salvage what can be salvaged.'

And he could hear Sarah saying the very same words, saying them and even managing to smile: 'Tom, that's fine. It's OK. You can change your mind. We all have to do what's best for ourselves, when we get to the vanishing point.'

'I can see that you care about Sarah very much. But you are talking about crazy, foolhardy risks – and for what gain? After all we've been through' – her voice fractured, anguish clawing the velvet into rags – 'how can I lose you now?'

'Mum – Mum.' He rushed across to her. 'Hey – there are risks, of course there are. But Sarah's a good sailor, and I'm – well, I'm going to try and learn.

And the upside – oh, the upside is huge. No more scurrying, and hiding, and uncertainty, and fear. If we make it, we will be free.'

'And what happens to your research, everything you've worked for?'

Tom watched a tall, slim, blond-haired boy, both him and not him, pass across the landscapes of his dreams. He watched him get his PhD, closing his hand with elegance over one small puzzle-piece of reality; watched him publish a paper in a well-respected journal, speak at an international conference, have colleagues to argue with, be part of a team. He watched him travel the world; visit Australia, land of his mysterious father; play his guitar in the outback under the stars.

Perhaps he was out there somewhere, this other self, in one of an infinite number of possible worlds, a world where in some subtle way his body had been different – either that, or the history of the last fifty years. 'Enjoy it all for me,' he silently told him, and watched as the figure moved into the distance, getting smaller and smaller, until just before it vanished it lifted a hand to wave.

He shrugged. 'In another life, Mum, but not in this one. I'll wash dishes or chop wood or whatever I have to do, I suppose. And we'll keep fighting for recognition. When we're settled, you can come and visit. And we can Skype, that'll be no problem – they've got the internet, it just doesn't follow you about.'

Janet was leaning forward, her hands pressed together as though in an act of prayer. 'And supposing you make it, Tom, you and Sarah, have you thought about...children? About the risk – if you are both reactors – of...passing the thing on? It would be a terrible thing to do to a child.'

Tom's eyes were suddenly filled with tears, and he could not trust himself to speak. He saw a small boy with tousled blond hair and Sarah's dark ferocious eyes, stretching out a hand towards him, and he was reaching out, desperate to take the hand in his, but the boy was being carried away by a swirling black current, further and further away, and although they were both reaching out beyond the furthest limits of their endurance, their fingers never touched.

His legs felt weak; he looked round for something to hold, gripped the edge of the table, manoeuvred himself until he was leaning against it. Nobody knew, he told himself furiously, that was the problem, there ought to be more research, to work out what was actually going on. Collect DNA samples from a large group of reactors, compare them to the DNA of normal people. See how often people who were reactors had a child who became one too. It should all be really scientifically interesting. But who would ever look?

'I don't know, Mum, I haven't thought about it. There are too many other things to get through first. But can't you see – this condition has taken so much from me, I can't let it take love as well.'

'Oh Tom – love – love can come and go. This is a huge commitment, and you are still so very young....'

'I'm older than you when you decided to have me. You knew your own mind, and you didn't get swayed. Give me credit for knowing mine.'

Behind him, the dark wooden door had not been fully closed; in the corner of his eye, he saw it move inwards in a smooth arc.

'Well, here I am,' Sarah said, walking into the room. 'The tainted one herself. Should I ring a bell, perhaps, so that people know I'm coming, and shout "unclean, unclean"?'

On the vicar's beige unblemished cheeks, a brief efflorescence of red.

'I was picking up my laundry,' Sarah said, swinging her rucksack off her back and propping it against the wall. 'I overheard. Sorry.'

She stood in front of Janet, feet planted well apart, arms folded; suddenly she dropped to one knee and thrust her face in close. She began to speak, softly and confidentially, her voice like a knife under a duvet.

'Look at me, Reverend. Smell me – I haven't washed for a while. I breathe air just like you do. I eat food. I've saved lives, because I can give injections and sew up wounds. I have parents who love me, just like you love Tom. I had dreams and hopes and fears and ambitions – and do you know what, I still do.'

Janet had recovered herself. She didn't recoil from

the unexpected closeness, just pushed her own chin fractionally forwards and held Sarah's gaze.

'I am very sorry you overheard our conversation. It must have been painful for you. I was trying my best to take a practical, realistic view, find what's best for all concerned.'

Tom stepped across to Sarah, and helped her to her feet, and they stood together hand in hand in front of the vicar on her leather chair. Janet was looking from one of them to the other, her emotions unreadable behind her bland beige mask. Come on, Tom urged her in his mind. Just say it. Don't, after all we've been through, put another obstacle in our path. I know it's difficult for a non-reactor to understand. If you haven't lived the contradiction in your own body, felt your own screaming incompatibility, you can never quite believe there isn't a way out.

There isn't a way out.

This is the only course for us.

At last, Janet nodded, sighed briefly, then stood up. 'Yes,' she said. 'I agree. I will arrange for you to be married in St Peter's, if you are absolutely sure that your mind is made up, Tom. I can't say I will do it with pleasure, but I will do it.'

'Thank you,' Sarah told her, lifting Tom's hand to her mouth and softly kissing it. 'I will do it with very great pleasure indeed.'

*

'Oh Tom, I'm sorry,' Sarah said, after they had heard the front door close. 'Do you think we would have got on, your mum and I, in another life? I mean, if you and I – somehow – hadn't turned?' Her face clouded. 'But in another life it wouldn't have mattered, I suppose.'

Tom replied, 'You said it to me once yourself: stop thinking about possible worlds. She just said yes – that's the important thing.'

'We're going to be married?'

'We sure are, babe. And in the cutest little church – grey stone, with a funny fat-bottomed tower. Metal grilles over all the windows, to stop people breaking in, I suppose, and huge ivy leaves going rampant over one end, and when I peered in, I think I saw a mouse.'

Sarah laughed. 'It sounds gloriously, fabulously Gothic. Wildlife will help swell the congregation, and I'll wear my dark red dress.' Her mouth fell out of its glorious curve, and set in a more sombre expression.

'Tom – I need to ring my parents – and tell them and…sort out some other things.'

'I'll take your clothes back to the van.' Tom shouldered the rucksack. 'See you later. Good luck.'

*

She didn't come back for an hour, and when she did she came in from the bright optimistic morning like a vampire, her skin pale, her eyes scribbled with red.

'They'll let us have *Wayfarer*.'

'Well, that's good.'

'They're going to get it out of storage and send it to Black's boatyard – Nick Black who owns it is an old friend. I can liaise with him about what needs doing to make it ready for the crossing.' She shifted her gaze, looking out of the front window towards the ridge of the downs. 'They won't be using it again.'

'No. Realistically, I suppose they won't.'

'They're really pleased about the wedding, though. More than pleased…gobsmacked, actually.' She gave a sharp dry laugh. 'They'd given up on me finding someone since I became a reactor. And I think they understand – I hope they do – about having to go away.'

She crumpled onto the seat beside him. 'I can't believe it's come to this. Leaving Mum to cope and… not seeing Dad again. He's going to die, Tom, he's getting weaker and weaker.' Her voice cracked. 'I feel so utterly and completely useless, but if I stayed, there wouldn't be anything I could do. I'd be stuck in some random part of the country, talking to them on the telephone, and becoming a refugee, over and over again.'

Tom stroked her hair. 'Just think, if we make it, how cool it will be, on the phone to your parents, telling them what we've been doing, all that normal stuff…'

'Yes,' she said, smiling up at him through glistening trails. 'They'd enjoy that. Oh – I forgot to say. Mum's coming to the wedding. She'll get a 24-hour carer for Dad.'

'Hey – that's great.'

'And Tom – you do realise…about the wedding.' She sat up abruptly and faced him. 'We can't spend any money at all, and all our wedding presents have got to be cash?'

'Damn.' Tom thumped the table. 'And here I was really wanting that diamond tiara and chocolate fountain. Don't be daft, woman. Of course I know that. You shouldn't even be thinking about weddings. Leave that to me and my mother, and Veronica. Get on with planning our voyage. There's not much time left.'

CHAPTER 41

Later that afternoon, he had loped back along the track, intending to phone his mother and hold her to her promise, tie her down to details like time and date. He was making for the farmhouse door when someone sidled up behind him, saying tentatively, 'Tom?'

'What?' He leapt round.

Kevin stood there, fingering a leather key fob with both hands so it hung protectively in front of his groin.

'What the hell are you doing here?' Tom shouted.

Kevin bowed his head. 'I came to say I was sorry. About the way the study appeared in the press. It was...bad.'

'Oh. That.' Bad? Bad was the understatement of the century.

'I tried, Tom. I tried to put caveats in. Talk about the limitations of the research. The impossibility of drawing firm conclusions. But...the press release had less nuance. And then the articles...' He winced.

'Kev, I told you how it would be. Didn't I? Way back?'

Kevin sighed. 'I know. You were right.'

'The only thing to have done was to have killed the research stone dead. Discredited it from the inside. Only you could have done that. You didn't.'

Why was he even here? Lurking uneasily, a big soft blob, shifting from foot to foot. The thing was done, there it was, casting its shadow over the future. There didn't seem anything else to discuss. 'Look, I thought you weren't supposed to "associate with reactors" any more.' His tone was mocking. 'In case you got the taint, and it poisoned your precious career.'

'I'm not at Northington. I moved on, like I said I would. I've just started a job at Southampton. Not too far from here...'

I expect Prof Arrowsmith's glowing reference helped with that, Tom thought bitterly, and was about to throw some cutting remark to this effect when he stopped. Relaxed his face. Drained the acid from his voice. Filled it instead with something treacly and warm.

'Oh? That's good news, Kev. What are you doing there?'

Kevin stared for a few moments in surprise. (Did I overdo it? Tom thought anxiously, was that screeching U-turn a tad too obvious?) But then Kevin's whole being began to relax and fill out, as though having been squashed into two dimensions he was slowly springing back into three.

'It's a project about attention bias in people with anxiety disorders. How they get their attention stuck on exactly those things that make them most anxious.'

'Sounds interesting. And uncontroversial.'

Kevin nodded his head rapidly several times. 'Totally uncontroversial. Anyway, I thought I'd come and...' He trailed off again, eyeing Tom uncertainly, trying to read his mood. Tom thought: he needs absolution badly. Blessed, his whole life, with the gift of being liked, he cannot cope with its opposite, just has to keep returning to rub ointment on the wound.

'Well – as you're sort of in the neighbourhood...'

'Yes.' Kevin was eager. 'Only an hour away. How are things in the Valley? I want to help, you know.'

To the left of the farmhouse door, a weatherbeaten wooden bench stood between a couple of terracotta pots planted with daffodils. Tom went over and sat down, gesturing for Kevin to join him. Side by side. Like old times.

'Kev, the Valley's finished. We're all having to leave. We have to be out of here in seven weeks.'

'But – what happened? Has Cuthbert...'

'They're putting a mast up,' Tom stated. And we might have stopped it, he went on silently, if it hadn't been for your piece of so-called 'science'.

'Oh no. I thought – I'd thought you would just stay there, until – you got better.'

Tom leant forward, rested his forearms on his thighs, studied the gravel of the yard as he slowly shook his head.

'But...that's terrible. Where will you go?'

'I don't know,' Tom said. 'There are fewer and fewer places. The maddening thing is, I have been getting better. I'd been playing with the idea of going back to Northington. Finding a place in the hills, commuting in. Now...' He shrugged.

'And Sarah?'

Tom shrugged again. 'Even worse, for her.'

Side by side. Like old times. Companionable. He let the silence between them bleed out.

Kevin said, 'I know it's not the same as a haven, but, surely – money would help? Let you put down the rental deposit on a bigger, more isolated house? Or – rent a field from a farmer, who was willing?'

Oh yes, Tom agreed, stretching back on the bench, closing his eyes against the golden beams. *Stay very still, it's happening just the way you wanted.* They still had to find somewhere suitable, hunt it down, but money gave them options, money would help.

Kevin put an impulsive hand on his arm. 'Tom, since I've been earning properly, I've been putting money aside. Saving for my own place. It'll take years of course, but everyone knows you have to start early these days, plan long term, if you want a mortgage. I've got about £3000. You can have it.'

Tom opened his eyes wide, let his jaw go slack.

'Kev – that would be…totally amazing. Do you really mean it?'

'Course I do, mate.' Kevin gave his old, trademark, relaxed, ebullient grin. 'You start paying me back, when you're Dr Jenkins of the Physics Department at Northington, world expert in black holes.'

Oh yes, Tom said, as he sat at one remove inside his head, an operator at the controls of a drone. That would be when he would pay the money back.

The sun sank below the treetops on the far side of the road; the black silhouetted branches became a huge iron cage containing fire. 'It's great to see you,' Tom told Kevin. 'I wish we could talk more, but you understand – we're kind of pushed for time here. There are masses of things to sort out.'

'Oh yes, of course.' Kevin stood up. 'Of course I understand, mate. Hey – I'll transfer that money tonight.'

'You're a real friend. Thanks again. Bye.'

Pushing open the farmhouse door, Tom heard Kevin scrunch away across the gravel, and something seemed to detach itself from his body, step out of his flesh and walk like a zombie after his lost comrade, wanting one thing with a horrible tight-focused hunger: the time before, the house they'd shared, the laughs they'd had. And the pull of the zombie self was so strong he swung round and shouted, 'Kev! Come back.'

Kevin turned quickly. 'What?'

'Keep the money. It was a kind offer. But I won't be coming back to Northington.'

'Why? Where are you going?'

'Sarah and I...' He tried again: 'Sarah and I...'

We'll be in America. Or we'll be dead.

He didn't want to explain the details, have somebody else apply the prudential calculus of normal people, gasp and stretch their eyes.

'Put it this way. Where she goes, I go. And it won't be Northington, or even England. We need to find her a proper haven and I'll get whatever kind of job I can. I'm sorry, I shouldn't have let you think something different. For the sake of – well, the way we were, before all this stuff twisted us apart.'

Kevin was quiet for a while. Then he said, 'Tom, I'm going to transfer the money anyway. Just – take it.'

'But...I was bullshitting you.... I can't...'

'It doesn't matter. When I said what I said about Northington – it's because I didn't want to let it go. I didn't want to believe it wouldn't happen for you. But I'm not stupid. I know the future is bad for reactors and nothing is guaranteed. I don't want the money back.'

CHAPTER 42

I

'Tom, I need books. I've got to read stuff about Atlantic crossings.'

'I need a book too. Something like *Sailing for Dummies* would probably do the trick.'

'Do you know, I think that actually exists.'

'Good. Look – I'll see what the library in town can order in, before we start buying anything.'

'And I'll ask my dad. He's got shelves of sailing books; I'm sure there are relevant ones in there he could get posted to me.'

II

'I think we'll have to go via the Azores.'

'Oh?'

'Well...the easiest way to go – the route most people take on their first crossing – is to leave in late summer, head south to the Canaries by October, wait there until the hurricane season finishes in December, then sail south to pick up the trade winds which carry you across to the Caribbean. Then you stay there for a bit and head up the east coast of the USA when the worst of the winter has passed. It's long, but it's easy because you're going in the direction of the prevailing winds and currents all the way. But...well, you can see why it doesn't work for us.'

'Leaving too late. And too much hanging about on islands en route, in who knows what RF levels. Can't we just head straight across?'

'Well, we *could*. The route that's shortest in terms of distance goes straight across to Cape Cod. But you're battling headwinds all the way across, and you're sailing against the North Atlantic current. You can sail a route that goes further north to try to avoid the storm track and get more favourable winds, but that just increases the risk of getting involved with icebergs and fog – especially earlier in the summer when we need to travel.'

'Okay, that sounds definitely bad. What's the alternative?'

'Sail south west towards the Azores, then west towards Norfolk, Virginia – which is the port nearest where we want to end up, if we want to sail up Chesapeake Bay to get as far inland as possible before we have to transfer to a car. Exactly what we do will depend on the location of the Azores High – that's a big area of high pressure that sits slap in the middle of the Atlantic, and it moves about a bit. We might go closer to Madeira. But it looks like our best bet. The downsides are variable winds near the Azores High – we'll need to take extra fuel in case we get becalmed. And there's a slight risk of...'

'A slight risk of what?'

(Pause) 'Tropical storms.'

'Tropical storms? Do you mean hurricanes?'

'It would only be the very start of the hurricane season. Things only really get going in August.'

'Great. Fantastic. I'm getting kind of surprised that anyone's ever sailed the Atlantic at all.'

'Tom, you know they have. Loads and loads of people, from the Vikings onwards. It's just a matter of managing the risks.'

III

'Veronica, would you look at my list? I don't know much about weddings, and – well – I might have missed out something crucial.'

'Certainly, Tom. I would be delighted. Let us see.... Ah. Yes you have. A fairly serious lacuna, I should say.'

'Oh God, I thought so. What is it?'

'The ring. Or rings, if that is what you would prefer.'

'Bother. Oh well, I expect there are cheap rings out there.'

'Don't be ridiculous. If a thing is worth doing it

is worth doing properly. Here – have these. I shall slip them off now. This silver one with the guard will probably fit you, and this one with the green stone for Sarah. You can get them adjusted as necessary; I will pay.'

'Veronica, we can't...you can't just....'

'Nonsense. Take them. I have so many.'

IV

'I'm writing back to Nick. We've got to decide what sort of electronic equipment we can cope with, and what we'll have to do without. Most sailors these days are permanently attached to internet weather updates, chart info on tablets, GPS and so on, but...'

'...we can't be.'

'No. We can't. But people have been sailing for millennia before these things were invented. My dad taught me to navigate using a sextant, and a compass, and to plot our course on a chart; every sailor should do that, he'd say, because if you're relying on electronics, and they get waterlogged, or the batteries fail, you will have absolutely no idea where you are.'

'D'you know, the US Navy is starting to train new recruits in traditional navigation again after a twenty-year break. I read it in the paper the other day. They're worried that some cyber or electronic warfare technique could knock out their comms completely, and then you'd have these huge warships blundering about blind.'

'Ha! Us and the US Navy. How cool is that? Anyway – we'll take a handheld GPS. We can keep it switched off most of the time and just check in now and again to make sure I haven't taken us wildly off course. And a radio. That only needs to be on when we need to transmit, and in busy shipping lanes, but then it's receiving not transmitting. And the antenna will be fixed at the top of the mast, well out of the way.'

'Hopefully we can cope with that.'

'Other bigger ships will have radar, of course. The Atlantic's pretty large though. In my books, people describe not seeing anyone for days and days.'

'Days and days...'

'And we'll take an emergency-position-indicating-radio-beacon. It doesn't do anything unless the boat capsizes and it makes contact with water. Then it will send a distress signal via satellite.'

'In those circumstances, I'd be quite happy to transmit.'

V

'Tom.'

'Hi Stanford. How's it going?'

'Look what my estate agent sent me.'

'Let's see. That bit looks like a long damp concrete tunnel. And that room – that's amazing, it's straight out of the 1960s.'

'It's a nuclear bunker. It's for sale.'

'Stanford, are you serious?'

'Of course I am. Built for the Cold War. Fifteen feet underground. You enter through a concrete hatch on the surface. Also there are six acres of agricultural land in Lincolnshire included in the lot. Needs modernisation, obviously, but...'

'It would certainly keep out RF..'

'Damn right it would. I'm telling you – this is the future. Going underground. The guide price is a lot less than a house. Reckon I'm going to settle with Victoria. Give her what she says she wants – if she stops all this crap about access. Bitch will be gobsmacked. I'd pay to see her face. Then I'll bid for this place. Get it done up like a secret superhero HQ. Ringo and Twilight will love it.'

'Wow. You will be the world's coolest dad.'

Strange twitching in the lower part of Stanford's face, as though a subterranean burrowing creature was preparing an unprecedented trip to the surface. The man was *smiling*.

VI

'Another letter from Nick.'

'Thanks…. Oh…sounds like we're getting there…. Oh, Tom – he's sent a photograph. Look – there she is – that's *Wayfarer!*'

Smooth, gleaming white, the mast absurdly tall. An arm that stuck out at right angles which he now knew was the boom. Metal railings running reassuringly all the way round the deck. Tiny rectangular windows. He tried to imagine what it would be like, to clamber down into that cramped cabin, sit there, sleep there, day after day after day, boxed in by walls too robust to burst out of yet too fragile to protect, cradled and battered by the huge indifferent waves.

VII

'Ladies and gentlemen, I have an announcement to make – if you would care to gather round.'

Veronica had come from the path through the trees; now she stood in the middle of the campsite, beaming, palms together, her right foot poised elegantly against her left calf.

'We're all ears, Veronica,' Tom said.

'Come on, tell us,' Sarah urged. 'You look like the cat who's got the cream.'

'I have a job.'

'A job? What sort of job?' Stanford sounded suspicious.

'I am the new resident yoga instructor at the Altnahuglish Personal Wellbeing Centre and Wellness Retreat.'

'Where on earth is that?'

Veronica waved a hand. 'Somewhere north of Ullapool. I expect it will be absolute hell to get there and I will have to pay Highlands rates for my Fortnum's hampers. But, my dears, the *point* is that Altnahuglish is at the cutting edge of the latest trend in wellness therapies among stressed-out white-collar workers. Digital Detox is its USP.'

She beamed round at them in triumph, positively radiating smugness.

Tom asked cautiously, 'How does that work, exactly?'

'Clients must hand in their gadgets – all of them – and they are locked away in sweet little metal lockers for the entire length of their stay. There is apparently a small amount of Wi-Fi in the office area for the use of staff, and there is some mobile reception but it is extremely patchy. I shall live in my yurt in the grounds (for sound spiritual reasons) and lead classes outdoors – if it is not raining or infested by midges – or in the wellness studio.'

'That's amazing,' Sarah said. 'How did you pull it off?'

'I lied,' Veronica said grandly. 'Of course. I had to agree to be interviewed over Skype – so I am starting to feel pretty lousy now, and will go to bed soon, but it has (thank goodness) turned out to have been worth it. Naturally I said nothing about being a reactor. I went on about mindfulness, clarity and focus, living in the moment, truly appreciating one's natural surroundings, deep conversations, meaningful interpersonal relationships, passionate living and enhanced spiritual awareness – all as a result of abandoning my smartphone. Oh, and I also knocked six years off my age and told them that Chai was my acolyte. So she can come too.'

'I created her online presence specially, in preparation for this interview,' Chai explained. 'Veronica has many followers, you know. And they all say such positive things.'

Veronica dropped an elegant curtsey, and smirked.

'So you're both sorted,' Sarah said. 'That's great news. How are you getting on, Barry?'

Barry was looking miserable, his head bowed. 'I'll have to pack in my job. I can only do it because I've got the Valley to come back to every night. I've tried to find somewhere like it round here, but there isn't anywhere. I'll have to pack it in and go back to Wales. At least my family is there.'

'What will you do there?' Tom asked. 'Have you found somewhere you could stay?'

'Not a permanent site. There are wild places in the mountains where I can park for a couple of nights before anyone notices, and then move on. That's what I used to do, before the Valley. At least I've got the van now. I can go to my sister's for washing and so on.'

'If I get that bunker, mate,' Stanford said, 'You can come to me.'

CHAPTER 43

Sarah was wearing her dark red dress, in some sort of
stretchy velvet, with tight sleeves, and a scoop neck,
and a long flowing skirt. Tom had teased her about
wearing her beloved biker boots underneath, but she
had actually found some old black ballet pumps, and
her dark hair was pulled up on her head and spiked
with a huge artificial rose.

She began to giggle as she approached the van.
'Oh Tom, it looks fabulous – positively bridal.... Lift
it up as I climb underneath, to make sure I don't rip
anything...' He'd adapted his bed canopy, attached
it to the roof to make a shield for the passenger seat.
Gathering up the silvery swathes, he held them high
as she ducked below his arm and settled herself in.

'The cutting edge in transport for today's highly
sensitive reactor bride,' he said. 'We'd better get
going. It's nearly quarter to.'

They began bumping slowly up the track over
the small shoulder of downs. As they turned on to

the main road, Sarah said, 'I must look pretty strange under this net. I wonder what people are going to think.'

'That we're members of a slightly odd conservative religious cult?' Tom suggested. 'Women have to be kept in translucent coverings when in public.'

'Or I've got a contagious disease, and you're taking me to hospital in a pop-up isolation tent. Or hey – I'm actually completely insane. I could howl and bang on the window and scare passers-by witless.'

'Whatever turns you on.'

'Oh, who cares...' Sarah was pressing her nose to the side window, pulling the fabric taut across her face, gazing in ecstasy at hedges, fields, cars, trees, tractors, houses, cars and people as they flashed by. 'Look Tom – the world! The world!'

The tiny church was very plain inside, its walls whitewashed, and the dark boxy wood pews uncarved. The human congregation was small, and clumped together at the front near the altar. Tom noticed a tall woman in a fitted green dress, her dark hair striped with silver like a badger's fur; she smiled at him with Sarah's smile. But the other rows were not empty. At regular intervals along the polished wood benches, photographs stood, propped up against the upright backs. They seemed to be photos of people – old, young, middle-aged. Beside each photo was a single flower – a red carnation, a pink gerbera, an orange lily. 'Oh!' gasped Sarah, putting her hand to her mouth. 'Oh Tom…. Look…they've done it for us! Isn't it wonderful?'

Tom gazed about in amazement. He'd never seen an arrangement like this before. He thought they'd decided not to have flowers, except a few wild ones from the Valley. He whispered, 'Who are the people?'

'The others. Other reactors. The ones who can't be here. To show they're with us in spirit. Of course it's usually done for reactor funerals,' Sarah went on as Tom took her arm, 'but hey, Thomas, what did I tell you, we're breaking all of the rules.'

'Start the music.' Veronica's voice cut through from the front of the church, where she sat half turned on a pew, a vivid eruption in fuchsia pink silk and an enormous matching hat. 'They have arrived.'

Chai pushed a button on a small battery-operated CD player, and 'The Arrival of the Queen of Sheba' filled the nave with its slowly-building regularities, its inexorable momentum of joy.

CHAPTER 44

Later that afternoon, the picnic in the Valley was in full swing. Folding tables were spread out on the sward, bearing pies and dips and bowls of salad, crusty breads and strange cheeses from Fortnum and Mason, fried dumplings, a huge pile of cupcakes, chocolates and early strawberries – everybody, according to their own tastes, had contributed some food. Crates of beer and wine cooled in the rippling stream, and the guests were sprawled on folding chairs or on blankets in the shade, shoes kicked off, ties and jackets removed, waistbands loosened, chatting to each other, or simply communing with the warmth. It was one of those pure blue days, absolute and glorious, when simply to look up was to catch your breath with wonder.

Tom was standing beside one of the tables, idly considering a fourth cupcake, when Sarah slipped her arms round his waist from behind, and whispered lasciviously and ticklishly into his ear, 'Come for a walk?'

He twisted his head, found her mouth and kissed it. 'OK, where to?'

'Up the hill. To our hollow. To say goodbye.'

Casually they wandered away from the campsite until they reached the path that led onto the downs, where, hidden by the trees, they began to stride upwards with more purpose, hand in hand. At the start of the ridge, they slowed, looking round at the view that had, in all the months they'd spent here, never palled: the muscular shoulders of downs, bulging under their tight sheaths of turf; the lusher, tree-filled valleys with their hedge-lined fields; the clusters of houses along the twisting ribbons of roads, where moving vehicles glinted, catching the afternoon sun. They were approaching the clump of hawthorn which grew around their hollow when Sarah suddenly pulled at Tom's hand. 'Hold on,' she said quietly. 'There's someone talking. And I think they're on a phone.'

They stood still and listened. A male voice, caustic yet amused; that one-sided pattern of speech then silence, speech then silence for which reactors learned to be subconsciously alert.

'Yeah, mate,' the voice was saying. 'I'm up here now, doing a quick site survey. That little local difficulty? It'll be sorted, no worries.'

Silence.

'Ha ha...ha, yeah.'

Silence

'Yeah...we could have, quite easily.'

Silence.

'Yeah, coverage would have been just as good from the hill at the other side of the village, if not better. Did quite a lot of work on that option actually...but then we heard on the grapevine.'

Silence.

'Oh, absolutely...the right decision to move it...best not to let these things get going, if we can, mate...Start to fester...get talked about – and that particular bit of private enterprise...yeah, that was unfortunate....'

Silence.

'Sure...well, not long now until we lance the boil...ha ha...they'll disperse PDQ, I'd guess.... Can just about see them from here, actually – look like they're having some sort of party.... Okay mate, see you back at base. Cheers. Bye.'

Halfway through the call, Sarah had begun squeezing Tom's hand; she was now gripping his fingers so tightly that he thought they might snap. Slowly she turned her head towards him, her face rigid with shock, and mouthed, 'Did you hear that?'

Tom, himself hardly able to speak, stiffly inclined his head. He had assumed – they all had – that in the insouciant exuberance of telecoms expansion, the Valley was just collateral damage – devastating for the reactors, but not deliberately so.

Looked like they had been wrong.

Something else was going on: something purposeful and directed.

They were being *cleansed.*

And what had the man meant by a 'particular bit of private enterprise' being 'unfortunate'? What sort of enterprise? It was difficult to get a business started when you were a reactor. Veronica's yoga classes could hardly have been any sort of threat.

It hit him then. Dr Sharifi and his research. The enterprise that he – Tom – had initiated. Someone had done more than just ensure the research had no publicity. They had identified the doctor's presumptuous accomplices, and taken revenge.

The man came round the bend in the path, stowing away his phone. He started briefly when he saw Tom and Sarah, still hand in hand, standing transfixed across his way. 'Afternoon,' he said to them, giving a frowning nod, and moved onto the grass to make a detour around them.

He was a broadish man of medium height, with brush-cut brown hair and a face-hugging beard. Sarah stepped in front of him. 'Hi,' she said pleasantly, although Tom could hear the tremor in her voice. 'Lovely up here, isn't it?'

'Oh yes...lovely,' said the man.

'You must excuse us,' Sarah went on, laughing

slightly and swinging Tom's hand. 'We've just got married this morning. You should congratulate us.'

'Really?.... Well...congratulations then. Fantastic. Yes.'

'Do you have a partner? Or any children?'

'Er...yes, I do. I've got a wife. And a daughter.'

'How lovely,' said Sarah. 'And how old is your daughter?'

'She's eleven.'

'How lovely,' said Sarah again, simpering, still swinging. 'You do know it can happen to anybody, at any age, don't you? Children too – and nobody knows how or why?'

'I'm sorry...I'm not with you. What can?'

'I wonder how you'd feel,' Sarah went on, casually, still smiling, 'if it happened to your own little girl?'

'What happened?'

Sarah dropped Tom's hand. She thrust her face close to the man's and spoke with sudden quiet menace.

'That every moment she lives in normal society becomes total screaming agony. And if she wants a chance of feeling better, she has to go and live in one remote, marginal place after another, always moving, always under threat. Until the day when she knows she can't stand it anymore, and she makes a nice little noose out of the cord of her Barbie dressing gown, and she slips it over her sweet little...'

'You bitch!' screamed the man. 'You fucking

411

reactor bitch. How dare you? How fucking dare you?'
His left arm shot out and hooked round her neck. She
doubled forwards with a cry as he yanked her head
down. His right hand came out of his jacket pocket,
holding his glowing reignited phone. 'Call Peterson,'
he told it tersely, and as it powered up and began to
transmit he clapped it to Sarah's head.

She started to scream and thrash from side to side,
but the man had her in a headlock, squeezing her
throat as he held the phone in place. He was laughing,
as he talked to the person at the other end of the line.
'Just a little local difficulty…' he was saying, 'Nothing
to worry about… just bear with me for a bit…keep
the connection, it'll be sorted.'

Tom grabbed the man from behind, trying to
pull him away from Sarah, but he used his feet to
kick backwards into Tom's knees. Sarah's screams
were breaking up, her breath growing ragged. Tom
released his hold, moved round to the side of the
struggling pair, and mentally measured the distance
to his target. No time now for half-measures; only one
course; take it. He swung his arm back and punched
the man on the point of the jaw.

The man crumpled onto the turf, releasing Sarah's
neck as he fell. She stumbled forward and lay huddled
on the ground, sobbing. The phone bounced to Tom's
feet. He picked it up, turned it off, and put it in his
pocket.

On legs like columns of jelly he walked over

to Sarah and knelt clumsily down beside her. 'I'm so sorry,' she was gasping, over and over again. Eventually she pushed herself up into a sitting position, and rubbed her hands over her face. 'Are you okay?' Tom asked. She nodded. 'I think so. My neck's sore.' She touched it gingerly. 'As for the resilience, we'll just have to see. Tom, I was a total idiot. I shouldn't have provoked him. I just got so angry.' She glanced over at the man sprawled motionless among the wildflowers. 'The big question is, how okay is he?'

Slowly they both stood up, instinctively reaching for each other for support, moving like sleepwalkers towards the man. Sarah squatted down beside his head. She tilted it slightly to make sure his airway was clear, then lowered her ear to his mouth and placed one hand on his chest. When she looked up at Tom, her face was flooded with relief. 'Still breathing,' she said, and at her words Tom's whole body sagged with the outflow of tension.

'But I can't rule out any spinal or head injury...' She was putting her fingers into the man's mouth, clearing out fragments of teeth. Tom tensed again. The man opened his eyes and began to groan. Sarah sat back on her heels. She said clearly and distinctly, 'My name is Sarah. I'm a nurse. You should stay lying down, sir, for the moment.'

The man spat blood from his mouth. He muttered, 'Fuck off, bitch,' and rolled away from her but his words were slurred and he immediately winced and brought his hand to the side of his jaw. He sat up and flexed his hands in front of him, checking each finger could move, all the while glaring at Tom. 'This is GBH,' he hissed. 'You bastard – you're going down for this.' Then he tried to stand up, screamed in pain, and fell back onto the turf. As he sprawled, his left foot was turned at an odd angle to his calf.

Sarah said, 'You should let me look at that. It looks like you have a fracture.' She gently raised his trouser leg and felt around the ankle. 'Can you move your foot?' He tried, failed and howled. 'Okay,' she said. 'It's a closed fracture, there isn't any wound. Don't move it any more and don't try to get up. I'm going to go and get help.'

'I don't need your help,' he spat. 'Just…give… me…my…fucking…phone.' He stuck out a hand, and Tom had automatically reached into his pocket and was about to pass it over when Sarah grabbed his arm and pushed it back. 'No,' she said grimly, shaking her head. 'No, I'm sorry, we can't do that. I think in our position you'd do the same. It hurts my professional pride to leave you here, but do you know, it's already taken quite a beating through not having had a job for three years. Come on, Tom, let's go. Fast.' And she began running back along the ridge, pulling Tom along after her.

'Wh…what are you doing?' he panted as they ran. 'As soon as he can,' said Sarah, 'he's going to call the police. You'll be arrested, by a load of officers with police radios, get taken to the police station, questioned and charged. You'll probably be charged with GBH. You'll probably get bail, as it's a first offence. But the RF you'll have been exposed to by that point will most likely have wiped out most of the Valley's gains. Then you'll have to go to court and you could end up in prison. D'you think they'll take any notice in there of bleating about the fluorescent lights or the wireless security systems? Tom, you'd be toast.'

They were within the trees now, scrambling down the track in the sultry, leafy air, blinded as they passed from greenish shade into patches of glaring sun. Tom's shirt was sticky with sweat, and his black shoes, dusty with chalk, skidded on the uneven stones. Sarah had bundled the folds of her dress over one arm, her rose was gone, her hair had fallen loose, hairpins shed as she ran.

'I had to hit him,' Tom said, his stomach churning, his mind reeling into panic. 'You know what he was doing. It was self-defence.'

'Who is going to accept that?' she retorted. 'He'll say he was having harmless fun, just getting me to talk to his friend on the phone. No, we've only got one chance – we can't wait until next week like we planned. We've got to leave, and we've got to leave today.'

They pounded round the last corner and

burst into the clearing. The guests, still eating and drinking, looked up in surprise. Stanford, lying on a rug chatting to Chai, called out louchely, 'Hey, you two, couldn't you wait until your wedding night?' Veronica, elegant in her fuchsia silk on a folding chair, said, 'Really, thank goodness we have done the photographs. You both look as though you've been pulled through a hedge backwards.' Sarah's mother, Helena, seeing her daughter's stricken face, sprang up, saying, 'Darling, what's happened? Something's gone wrong.'

Sarah made straight for Cuthbert, drew him aside, and spoke to him urgently in a low voice, gesturing up towards the hill-top they had fled. His features became rocklike under his beard.

'Cuthbert,' said Sarah, 'you mustn't put any other reactors at risk. This is all my fault. I can't let them get arrested on my account. But…the police mustn't find out about the boat.'

'You and Tom had better get changed and packed,' he said. 'I'll talk to the others, and we'll decide how to handle this.'

Sarah nodded, pushed Tom towards his tent, and raced to her caravan, already pulling down the zip at the side of her dress.

Bent double in the small hot stuffy space, fumbling with buttons that slid from his fingers, stamping

416

away trousers that knotted themselves implacably around his knees. *Come on.* Sweating like a pig, heart still hammering, hands like rubber gloves filled with water. The faster he tried to go, the more of a mess he was making. God – he couldn't even manage this simple thing – how the hell was he going to evade the police?

He was free of the suit. He grabbed a shirt, cargo trousers, trainers, pulled them on; found his rucksack, cast around hopelessly – what did he need to take? God, the lists they'd made – all that prep – pointless now. Clothes, washing kit. *Sailing for Dummies*? A bit late now. Physics textbook? No. Biscuits – yes. Guitar – no. Make a decision. Make any decision. Strap the thing closed. Must go now. He threw himself out of the tent.

Cuthbert, Sarah, Janet and Helena, a compact, murmuring four-headed beast on the path to the farm. Barry, Veronica, Stanford and Chai sitting at the other end of the campsite, in a stiff unnatural line. They didn't need to know what was being planned, safer if they didn't.

Tom loped towards the group on the path. A watery smile from Sarah, as she stepped back to let him in. Cuthbert was talking.

'I don't have my mobile. No one does. So I am going to walk slowly back to the farmhouse and dial 999 from there. To the call handler I will mention jaw and ankle injuries, possibly the result of a fall.

Hopefully they will despatch an ambulance only, at this stage.'

Helena said, 'I'll ring Nick and tell him to sail the boat from the yard to the creek. No – actually I'll ring your dad and he can ring Nick. Then there won't be an obvious link.'

Tom couldn't bear to stand there any longer, waiting for the net to be drawn tight. Any movement, any action had to be better than that.

'Thanks, that's great. Let's go.' He grabbed Sarah, dragged her towards the van. She wasn't coming, kept pulling back, shouting something. What was the matter with her?

'We can't go in your van.'

'Why not?'

'It's yours.'

'So?'

'It's registered to you. When they ID you as the likely assailant they'll put your details onto their mobile handsets and get back the make and registration. Then they'll flag it on the Automatic Numberplate Recognition System.'

He wanted to scream. Of course. Nothing happened just in one place any more. The details would pass almost instantaneously through the pulsing unquiet air, to fixed cameras on motorways and major roads, and mobile cameras in police cars themselves, and the cameras would become a vast quivering web of silent watchers, waiting for the fly to blunder in.

'OK, not the van.' But they had to have speed. More than anything else he wanted the smooth symmetry of a steering wheel between his hands, obedient pedals under his feet, the illusion of inviolability in his own small controllable metal world. He turned to his mother. 'Can we take your car, Mum?'

'Too obvious,' Cuthbert said. 'I have an old landrover that I use on the farm. It's rusty but it still goes. It's in the barn, you can take that. The keys are hanging by the back door in the farmhouse. We will hide the van in the barn instead, under a tarp. They may find it eventually – you should still use the back roads. Best give the van keys to Helena.'

'Okay, thanks. But' – he turned to Sarah – 'what about your shielding? I had it all fixed up in the van.' She waved the problem away. 'I'll just have to rip it out and wear it like a burka. Anyway, there are other things to hide. If they search the caravan they'll find the books and my file of letters and photos from Nick. They'll realise about the boat.'

'Don't worry, darling,' Helena said, 'We'll sort it out. Cuthbert – your house is full of books and files. I expect you won't mind a few more about sailing, slipped randomly among the shelves?'

The unsearchability of the analogue, Tom thought, and in the middle of all the panic and horror, felt the faintest frisson of glee.

He put his hand in his pocket and brought out the

phone. 'There's this too, I'm afraid.'

Sarah jumped back, as though the thing had flicked out a tongue.

'It's off,' he reassured her. He looked round the group. 'He's going to say we stole it. I'm not sure what to do.'

Janet had been quiet up to that point, swaying slightly on her feet, her hands gripping her thin elbows through her fawn linen trouser suit.

Now, as she spoke, something seemed to settle within her. She stood composed, and her voice, always beautiful, found new resonance and depth.

'Give it to me, Tom.' She held out her hand.

'But...'

'I shall be going on a trip. I will be heading to the North – or perhaps to Wales. After about an hour –' she looked enquiringly at Cuthbert, who gave a quick nod, 'I will switch on the phone.'

'Mum, that's crazy. If you do that, they can track it. They'll locate you. The police will come after you.'

'Tom, that is the point. They will think it is you. You and Sarah will have more time to get away.'

What had they done? That encounter on the downs – so brief, so random, just ten minutes of their lives – was growing tentacles that reached out all around, wrapping even now round Cuthbert, Helena and Janet, tying them into conspiracy.

'It's a crazy risk. You could get arrested – charged. What about your job, your position in the Church?'

The tentacles would keep on growing, a slimy hopeless enmeshing.

Janet smiled. He'd never seen her look so certain or so calm.

'That doesn't matter. Really, it doesn't. I want to do this. If I end up in court, I will simply tell the truth about reactors, and that what that man was doing was torture. I will talk and I'll keep on talking, Thomas. I'm good at that. The Church can do what it likes.'

He was still hesitating. The curse of living on the edge, he thought, with savage anguish: we drag others beyond the normal, give them dilemmas they should never have to face; make traitors and martyrs out of the people we love.

Sarah said, 'Tom, we haven't got time to waste, we have to get out of here. She's making a choice. Let her; it might save our lives.' Turning to Janet, she said, formally, 'Thank you.'

After he'd put the phone into his mother's outstretched hand he clung to her slight frame, trying to transmit through his embrace, in a single data burst, all the things there was no time left to say.

Then he and Sarah were running, rucksacks bouncing on their backs, the sun, still high in the sky, sketching their bulky fugitive shadows on the path between the outlines of leaves.

CHAPTER 45

'Turn first right,' said Sarah, from beneath her silver veil, studying the road atlas open on her lap. 'There should be a sign to Middle Wallop.' She pressed her face to the side window, pulling the fabric taut across her eyes so she could peer through. 'Yes – there it is, good. Then keep going, there will be a bend in the road, and a left turn towards Quindlesham.' She added in explanation: 'We're currently avoiding Andover.'

Tom swung the heavy steering wheel as he approached the small black-lettered sign, and they entered yet another country lane, trammelled between hedges studded by tall beech trees that reached out stately arms for the landrover to pass under, as though taking part in a courtly dance. 'You'd never get a satnav to do this,' said Tom. 'Thank goodness you can read maps.'

Sarah laughed. 'Oh yes, special reactor skill, and we particularly like the back roads.' She peered out of the window again. 'Okay – left turn coming up.'

At last, a straight bit. Tom put his foot down. Trees rushed past, and air streamed into the open windows. For a couple of minutes, with the wind in his hair, he felt more like a man on the run, but soon he was forced to slow down again to pass over a crossroads, and follow the signs for Lower Quivery.

'Honestly, who thinks of these names?' Sarah asked, marking the place on the atlas page with her finger.

Tom accelerated again along an open road that followed the brow of a hill. 'I wonder if they've found the van yet – or Mum,' he said.

'We just have to hope we get as long as possible,' said Sarah. 'Turn left at the next junction. No, don't. Stop. Stop.' Tom slammed on the brakes. 'Reverse, quickly, back up this lane, take the previous right.' Her voice vibrated with panic. 'Sorry…I think I saw the back of a police car. Sitting just at the far end of that next road.'

Tom whirled in his seat, his heart pounding, and plunged the landrover into reverse. It bucked backwards up the slope, wildly approximating the bends. 'I hope no one's coming,' he thought. Past the turn, he clanged the huge gearstick back to first, and veered off to the right, the engine roaring. Sarah pulled up her veil, craned round, peering out the back window. 'I can't see anything following us. God, that was close.'

She looked at the map again. 'Okay, we'll try a different approach. Carry on along here, then turn left.'

The sun crept imperceptibly down the blue curve of the sky and the landrover nosed its way around the delicate filigree of minor roads. Apart from Sarah's periodic murmured directions, they were silent. Tom realised – if they were lucky – this would be their last English journey, a stealthy, drawn-out, intimate goodbye.

He slowed as they came to a fork in the road. The sky was still clear and blue, but the shadows were deepening and the light was leaching away. He flicked the headlights on.

'Which way? Puddlesham and Wolkswell – or – there isn't a sign for the other one.'

She was holding the map up to her eyes, peering at it with a torch, rotating it from side to side.

'I'm not sure…. Oh God, I don't know. It doesn't seem to match where we are. I can't see properly under all this – neither the map nor the turnings we've passed.' She started to struggle in the seat, grabbing handfuls of the silver covering and hoisting them over her head. 'Tom, it's no good, I'm coming out.'

'But – ' Tom was aghast. 'You'll get fried. We're nowhere near there yet, and there'll be loads of RF on the way, even on the back roads.'

'If I can't see where we're going, we're never going to get there, fried or not.' She was uncovered now, her dark hair whipped into a frizzy maelstrom, fabric bundled behind her in the back seat. 'And between you and me, I'm already starting to feel the effects of our friend and his little game.' She spread out the map on her knees and bent forwards, holding the torch. Tom saw that her skin was clammy, a strange grey in the half-light, and when she twisted her head to look back along the road, she winced briefly and screwed up her eyes.

'We should go back to that last turning but one.' She pointed back along the road. 'That's where I went wrong.'

He drove now with an unknown quantity on the seat beside him, a raw, fissile thing, the process of decay already setting in. They were going to discover how much resilience she'd built up, by testing it to destruction – until they could reach the protective emptiness of the sea. He was torn, a hundred times, between the desire to hurl the landrover at speed round the maddening blind corners of this endless labyrinth of unlit lanes, and the terror of collision, which would be fatal, unless he could contrive to kill them both outright.

He drove on, with desperate, crazy virtuosity, all senses keyed, until the shining band on the north-west horizon slowly narrowed and dimmed and they were enveloped in the rich blue dark of summer night. His world contracted to the moving stretch of tarmac and verge caught up in the headlights' diverging beams; the thrum of the engine, so noticeable now in the surrounding silence; the sharp fecund scents of earth and plants, made fresh and more distinct by the cooling air; the occasional glimpse beyond hedgerows of a three-quarter moon, surveying their progress with a cold dispassionate eye. Sarah, beside him, was still giving quiet directions; now and then she would lay down the torch and hold both hands up to her head, working her fingers over her skull, or cupping her face in her palms. He knew the gesture intimately, although he'd never seen her make it: the beginnings of bruising, headcracking pain, which craved the comfort of touch.

It was as though they had entered a timeless, tractionless zone, where the world, distilled to basic elements – tree, hedge, moon, accelerate, brake, turn – repeated itself in the same few patterns, with no sense of gaining ground, or putting distance behind them. Once, a deer stared, rigid and glassy-eyed, from the side of the road, before it bounded away into the trees. Once, swinging round a bend, Tom had to swerve to avoid late night walkers, tramping along with a dog in a luminous harness with flashing LEDs around its throat. Occasionally, a car would explode at them out of the darkness, and vanish, like a firework that was spent. There seemed no reason why the journey should ever end.

Suddenly Sarah jerked back with a cry, clapping one hand over her face, twisting frantically to reach her pocket. On the folded-back paper of the map, Tom saw, out of the corner of his eye, a dark spreading stain.

He pulled up sharply at the side of the road and clicked on the overhead light. Blood was seeping between her fingers, tracing a lazy red snake down her wrist.

She found tissues to staunch the flow. Sitting upright, she began to pinch the front of her nose, and said, in a muffled tone, 'I had this before, Tom. I had it at Northington. I should have expected it, I suppose, after…you know.'

She was doing her best to keep her voice under control. 'I'm going to need a towel,' she went on. 'There's one in the top of my rucksack – and here – you'd better take the map, we're just past the crossroads south of Beltham.'

The map was spattered with blood stains, which were making it hard to read, but he found the sliver of blue that was their destination, and his heart gave a bound when he saw that as the crow flies they were only ten miles away.

To get to the creek they had to cross the main river. If they carried on along the back roads, they would zigzag up-stream along the river's eastern bank for several miles before one lane deigned to meander across; there would be a drive of several miles back down the other side.

If they broke cover now, and took the B road,

there was a bridge.

The bridge was very near.

Tom raised his eyes from the map and turned towards Sarah, and as he did so he felt a tingling in the top of his skull, and a politely insistent pressure, as though a gaunt hand with a bony index finger had reached down from the van roof.

Appalled recognition hooked into his heart and tore down through his core. He fought against it all the way. 'It's not the same, it's not the same,' he screamed inside his head, but brute sense memories from the time before the Valley surged up and jeered. This was how it had always begun.

He'd known that on this tortuous marathon he might find his limit. Yet some secret part of him had – ludicrously – hoped.

So – he was not invincible.

Let it go. Chuck away that scarce-acknowledged dream.

The head pressure is an early warning; it's only going to get worse.

Drive. Drive while you still can. Get to the boat by the direct route; or both of you are screwed.

He tried to sound neutral and calm. 'I'm starting to feel it a bit as well,' he said. 'I've looked at the map, and I think we should head for the bridge.'

She'd closed her eyes against the pain. With the hand that wasn't holding the towel she gave a feeble thumbs up.

CHAPTER 46

The road rose in front of him towards the highest point of the arch. White lines down its spine divided him from cars coming the other way – they'd left behind the ambiguity of unmarked country lanes. Beyond the low stone walls on either side was dark empty air, and below, the rippling bulk of the river, insinuating itself between the piers.

On the other side, the shock of civilisation. Houses in rows. Pavements, side streets, streetlights, a pub. The sense of other people, unseen, but close at hand, stowed away in their cosy boxes, sleeping or eating or watching screens.

He drove through as quickly as he could, trying to discount the tapping and digging that came and went on his skull.

At the far end of the village, traffic lights controlled an intersection, and as Tom approached, they changed to red. His was the first vehicle in line. As he waited, two more pulled up behind him, and in his mirror he saw another nose into the main street from a side road and make purposefully to join the queue and over the bonnet he read the word POLICE.

Terror overwhelmed him, more intense and absolute than any he had known. His feet shook on the pedals, the wheel turned glutinous in his palms. His brain was paralysed, poleaxed by catastrophe; when it started to function again it confronted only the horror of decision.

The light was still red.

Behind him, either an ordinary car, conveying bored coppers on night patrol, or a vehicle which contained, Tardis-like, a whole hideous future: slow, deadly enmeshment by the institutions of society, the sucking-away of his resilience by its extended vampire kiss.

He could collapse or faint or vomit in the dock or in the cells; the response would simply be to take him *to a hospital*, a transfer to a lower circle of hell.

And it wouldn't just be him. They'd arrest Sarah, too; his mind sheered away from the result.

He nudged her with his elbow and she opened her eyes. 'Police, three behind. I don't know if they're coming for us. Don't panic, look at the map. This main road has bends. I want to come off onto a side road when they can't see us.'

She dropped the towel in her lap, picked up the torch and the map. Tom braced himself for the lights, the clutch straining at biting point; at the first flick of amber he slammed the gas pedal to the floor.

They sped over the junction, skimmed the road out of the village, plunged into the darkness beyond the limit of the streetlights. The road twisted and turned between rounded hills. Tom snatched glances in his mirror; there was a dark-coloured car behind him, following at a sedate distance. But it slowed suddenly, pulled into the verge, and out of the darkness behind it, a siren screamed, collapsing ambiguity like the drawing of a knife. Nothing left now but brutal clarity. The oldest, simplest game. Hunter *vs* hunted. Hunted cannot lose.

Faster. Faster. Flying now, sweeping round corners. Speed ticking up, higher, don't look, don't care. Drive like the wind.

Sarah hissed, 'Okay. Bend to the right, bend to the left, just after that one, sharp left.'

He obeyed, accelerated, shot round the final curve, slammed on the brake and swerved; ploughed down the narrow lane as far as he dared before he killed the lights where stocky trees, entwining their branches, made a roof.

Behind them on the main road, flashing blue lights swept past the turn.

Tom fell against the wheel, his shirt soaked in sweat, his heart kicking the inside of his chest. 'Well done.' He could scarcely gasp the words.

'They'll be back,' Sarah said, wiping blood from her face. 'We're between the main road and the estuary. We'll just have to keep wriggling through.'

He drove without headlights, the windows wound down to heighten his senses. After the frenzy it was eerily peaceful; apart from the quiet growl of the engine and the rumbling of wheels, the wraparound silence was complete. The moon, higher now, cast an ethereal gleam, showing trees running thickly up the sides of the rounded hills; the air was cool and smelt of fresh leaf. His eyes burrowed into the blackness of the single-track road ahead, searching for unwary creatures or oncoming cars.

In his ears, something starting. The faintest vibration, nibbling at the soft fullness of the silence.

Ignore.

Not nibbling any more – cutting through. A drill, drilling in the distance. Behind them, but not behind them.

Higher up.

Getting closer.

Sarah suddenly gripped his arm, and the explanation ignited inside him as though a match had been set to fuel.

Helicopter.

Shit.

Of course. Why bother with wild goose chases down country lanes? Pinpoint the fugitives from the air, and the cars could easily move in.

Useless to hope they wouldn't be spotted; the helicopter would have an infra-red camera to harvest the tell-tale heat from their bodies and the engine. Would make it shine onscreen as though they'd been painted with gold.

But the police would focus on the car. So if one person left it now, that person would have a chance.

He pulled up at the entrance to a field, a gate with a wooden stile to one side, and he faced her.

'Sarah, listen to me. Before we're in sight of the helicopter, you need to go. Get out of the car and go into the woods and up that hill. Take the map. You can make it to the creek across country – it must be a couple of miles. Sail on your own – you know you can do it, that was your original plan.'

'Tom…I…'

'They don't need to have us both. You know the consequences for you will be far quicker and far worse.'

Her face was anguished. 'But…'

'I love you and I always will. But remember what you said to me – they want us to disappear, every day we survive is two fingers stuck up in their face. You've got a chance to survive. Take it.' He leant forward and kissed her on the mouth. 'Do it, Sarah. Do it for me and for all of us.'

She gripped the handle of the door.

'Go,' he urged her, without words, drilling his message into her overflowing eyes.

She was a nurse, she understood necessity. When a decision was made to amputate, she became calm. She climbed down from the car. Shaking out the towel she arranged it around her neck so that the ends were within reach to mop up the blood. She pulled her rucksack from the back and stood for a moment in the moonlight, one hand poised on the top of the open door, her face an unnatural white mask in the disordered frame of her hair.

'Tom; it will always be you,' she said, almost formally, and he thought: This is the last time I will see her, and he had to hang on to the wheel to fight the urge of his arms to grab her and haul her back.

He'd driven about twenty metres down the road when, glancing in the mirror, he saw her on top of the stile sway, tilt backwards and fold.

He crashed the car into reverse, roaring back towards the gate, found her crouched on the ground over a spreading patch of pale liquid marbled with dark streaks, that stank as it gleamed.

Blood. She was vomiting blood.

When she sat back, she was shaking and running with sweat. He eased off her rucksack and threw it into the car, got his hands under her armpits and half-dragged her to standing, so that he could manoeuvre her into her seat.

'Shit, Tom,' she said, lying back. 'So much for your intrepid seafarer.'

He began driving again, from sheer habit and instinct, and lack of any other plan. In the sky behind them, a dot of white light appeared like a hyperactive trainee moon; it moved purposefully towards them, shredding the peace of the valley with the cacophony of blades.

Sarah said: 'I don't want to be caught.'

Tom stared into the blackness, urging the car on. She kept speaking, her eyes fixed ahead. 'I know where we are. If we carry on along this road there's a headland near the river mouth. There are cliffs, high ones. And the tide will be in.'

She laid her hand on his arm.

'Take me there. I've lived with this for so long, I know when I've reached the end. Time to drop out of the asshole, and do it in my own way – to fly before I fall, and then sea, and salt, and waves.'

So here it was at last: the thing that reactors sometimes did. The thing that had first crept into his mind at the vicarage, so many months before, that had lodged there, in an unfrequented attic, and had mostly kept its room. Sometimes he'd found its presence reassuring, the thing held back in case the worst happened, the thing kept ultimately in reserve.

It had come out.

Had come downstairs. Stood now in the main room, and it was not soft and grey and kindly, but hideous, raw, stinking, obscene.

Sarah was beside him. She breathed, she was warm, she was a living point of consciousness, a bundle of impulses, experiences and interconnections that was totally unique; one person, but also a world – and the one that made sense of his own. Impossible, unimaginable that it should end. But time ticked forwards, inexorable, unstoppable: the helicopter, steadily, effortlessly parting the night air, eating the distance behind them, their world hurtling towards its vanishing point. His soul stretched on the rack of the contradiction until he thought the inside of his head would rip in two.

Is there nothing else I can do for her?

Is there nothing else?

Only to stand beside her on the cliff edge, embrace her one last time, and watch her go?

Scour every cul-de-sac of memory. Send hunting dogs into the labyrinth. Set it on fire. Destroy it all if that will smoke something out. These are our last few minutes together. The last dregs in the bottle. The last chords of the song. To be so near the end, the candle guttering, burning so low, and yet on the screen in the helicopter, tell-tale heat would glow, radiant, luminous, shouting 'Life! Life!'

It erupted inside him then, a subterranean surge punching into his consciousness with such force that he slewed the car onto the verge, bumping over tussocks of grass, scraping along a hedge with ear-splitting shrieks.

He'd been wrong. There was one last choice.

The hunted vehicle powered up the valley and crested the ridge at top speed. On the other side it charged downhill towards a right-hand bend, where the road turned to run parallel to the cliffs of the coast.

The landrover did not make the turn. It veered off along a track at ninety degrees to the bend, jolting and bouncing wildly over the ruts, heading for the irregular, hummocky edge which would give way abruptly to pure night air. When it approached a dip where a grove of stunted trees had found some protection from the clifftop wind, it went over the lip of a downward slope and vanished.

The helicopter came closer, poised in its cloud of noise, its searchlight burning away the darkness with cold white fire. The two police cars it had summoned closed in like anxious acolytes eager to assist at a ceremony, racing from opposite directions, sirens screaming.

Among the trees Tom and Sarah were crammed onto the passenger seat, his hand on the handbrake release, hers round the handle of the door. Tom checked one last time: all his preparations were in place. 'Now,' he whispered, and as they slid out onto the ground, he lunged to shove the door shut as the car began to roll.

Lights blazing, the landrover erupted from the trees, hurtled down the final slope and launched itself into the void. For a heart-stopping moment, caught between countervailing forces, it seemed to pause, as though, ungainly monster that it was, it might unfurl wings to ride the upward pressure of the air, and soar beyond the grim reach of physical laws.

But it did not. Gravity took hold; the front, weighted by the engine, tipped down, and plunged nose first towards the churning surface of the waves. Vertical water cloaked the impact. When the whole had disappeared, a patch of more ferocious turbulence marked the place, but this soon passed. The sea absorbed the alien bulk, burped, resumed its age-old work of sculpting stone.

Tom stood at the stern rail. At first all he saw was a band of lesser darkness, the slightest attenuation of night. Then the band turned to greyness which seeped up the sky, and Tom gasped as the rest of their world was revealed, though he had known, intellectually, how it must be.

All around their tiny boat – nothing. Nothing but the rolling emptiness of the waves.

And the waves went on to the horizon. And the horizon went all the way round.

Sarah, who had been resting in the cabin, climbed up the ladder to join him, her hair blowing wildly about her radiant, exhilarated face.

'How are you doing?' Tom asked.

'Oh Tom – I can feel it – things are turning around. I was falling apart, but now – I'm coming back to life.' She gave him an oblique, mischievous smile. 'Though I still can't quite believe we made it.'

Tom squeezed her waist as they stood side by side, watching the pale primrose north-eastern glow which was the first hint of what lurked below the skyline. 'Hey – thanks for letting me try.'

In the little grove they had lain under the silvery shielding with a blanket over it to hide its gleam. They had pressed their bodies into the rough grass as insects tickled their nostrils and twigs skewered their ribs, and tried to stay relaxed and cool, cool as corpses, as the clifftop filled with shouts and running feet beneath the rotor blades' clattering roar.

Infrared radiation was part of the electromagnetic spectrum, its frequencies just above the radio-frequency range. Tom's gamble was that the RF shielding would block heat too – or at least for long enough to persuade the police that they must have gone into the sea.

When the helicopter had finally banked away, they had begun to move, quietly, stealthily, down the other side of the headland, towards the creek.

They had an ocean to cross, thought Tom, and a refuge to find, and all sorts of things might go wrong. But madly, crazily, against all odds, they had made it this far; he was going to allow himself the decadent luxury of hope.

The sun came flaming over the curve of the earth.

AUTHOR'S NOTE

All the characters, places, events and organisations in this book are fictional, as is the term "reactor". In the real world, the condition is known as electrosensitivity, or electrohypersensitivity. The categories of Phase 1, Phase 2 and Phase 3 reactor were also invented by me, to capture the way the condition spans different degrees of severity.

I am privileged to have got to know many people who have developed electrosensitivity. I have been – and continue to be – totally inspired and amazed by their incredible bravery, resilience and ingenuity. In a world increasingly saturated with radiofrequency radiation, they must battle each day to survive, while at the same time facing stigma, disbelief and contempt. This book is a tribute to the ones still living, and a memorial to those who have died because of the physical consequences of the condition, or who, reaching breaking point like my character Lucy, have taken their own lives.

The science in the book is real. The experiment in Part 1 is a composite of various "provocation" studies of similar designs, carried out in various research institutions in various countries over several years. Tom's critique of Kevin's study is a composite of some of the points made in critiques of these studies.

The study in Part 2 is based on real research carried out in the United States and published in 2017 in *Reviews on Environmental Health* (reference given below). I am very grateful to the authors Dr Gunnar Heuser and Sylvia A. Heuser and the publisher DeGruyter for permission to fictionalise it.

All the papers, articles, appeals and books referred to are referenced below, with web links. They are just a tiny selection of the research papers that exist showing nonthermal effects of radiofrequency radiation. A fuller list can be found at **www.powerwatch.org.uk**.

The RF-free refuge in the United States where Tom and Sarah hope to settle is based on the Green Bank Observatory in West Virginia, home to the world's largest fully steerable radio telescope. Around it, the US Government has established a 13,000-square-mile National Radio Quiet Zone.

References

Page 85

NASA Report – Electromagnetic Field Interactions with the Human Body: Observed Effects and Theories, April 1981, Jeremy Raines **https://ntrs.nasa.gov/archive/nasa/casi.ntrs.nasa.gov/19810017132.pdf**

Pages 86-87

Esmekaya MA, Ozer C, Seyhan N, 900 MHz pulse-modulated radiofrequency radiation induces oxidative stress on heart, lung, testis and liver tissues, *General Physiology and Biophysics*, 2011, 30(1):84-9. DOI: 10.4149/GPB_2011_01_84. **https://pubmed.ncbi.nlm.nih.gov/21460416/**

Dasdag S, Akdag MZ, Erdal ME, Erdal N, Ay OI, Ay ME, Yilmaz SG, Tasdelen B, Yegin K, Effects of 2.4 GHz radiofrequency radiation emitted from Wi-Fi equipment on microRNA expression in brain tissue, *International Journal of Radiation Biology*, 2015, 91(7):555-561, DOI: 10.3109/09553002.2015.1028599 PMID: 25775055. **https://europepmc.org/article/MED/25775055**

Carlberg M, Hardell L, Evaluation of Mobile Phone and Cordless Phone Use and Glioma Risk Using the Bradford Hill Viewpoints from 1965 on Association or Causation, *Biomed Research International*, 2017, 2017:9218486. DOI: 10.1155/2017/9218486. **https://pubmed.ncbi.nlm.nih.gov/28401165/**

Chen Q, Lu D, Jiang Q, Xu ZP, Effects of millimeter wave on gene expression in human keratinocytes, *Zhejiang Da Xue Xue Bao Yi Xue Ban*, 2008 Jan;37(1):23-8. PMID: 18275115 DOI: 10.3785/J.ISSN.1008-

9292.2008.01.005. https://pubmed.ncbi.nlm.nih.gov/18275115/

Grigoriev YG, Mikhailov VF, Ivanov AA et al., Autoimmune processes after long-term low-level exposure to electromagnetic fields part 4. Oxidative intracellular stress response to the long-term rat exposure to nonthermal RF EMF, *Biophysics* 55, 2010, 1054–1058. https://doi.org/10.1134/S0006350910060308

Hassanshahi A, Shafeie SA, Fatemi I et al., The effect of Wi-Fi electromagnetic waves in unimodal and multimodal object recognition tasks in male rats, *Neurological Sciences* 38, 2017, 1069–1076. https://doi.org/10.1007/s10072-017-2920-y

Belpomme D, Campagnac C, Irigaray P, Reliable disease biomarkers characterizing and identifying electrohypersensitivity and multiple chemical sensitivity as two etiopathogenic aspects of a unique pathological disorder, *Reviews on Environmental Health* 2015;30(4):251-71. DOI: 10.1515/reveh-2015-0027. PMID: 26613326. https://www.degruyter.com/document/doi/10.1515/reveh-2015-0027/html

Saili L, Hanini A, Smirani C, Azzouz I, Azzouz A, Sakly M, Abdelmelek H, Bouslama Z, Effects of acute exposure to WiFi signals (2.45GHz) on heart variability and blood pressure in albino rabbits, *Environmental Toxicology and Pharmacology*, 2015, Sep;40(2):600-5. DOI: 10.1016/j. etap.2015.08.015. Epub 2015 Aug 17. PMID: 26356390. **https://pubmed.ncbi.nlm.nih.gov/26356390**

Kim J, Yu DH, Huh Y et al., Long-term exposure to 835 MHz RF-EMF induces hyperactivity, autophagy and demyelination in the cortical neurons of mice, *Scientific Reports 7*, 41129 (2017). **https://doi.org/10.1038/srep41129**

Kesari KK, Kumar S, Behari J, 900-MHz microwave radiation promotes oxidation in rat brain, *Electromagnetic Biology and Medicine* 2011, 30, 219 - 234. **https://doi.org/10.3109/15368378.2011.587930**

Page 88
Yu Y, Yao K, Non-thermal cellular effects of lowpower microwave radiation on the lens and lens epithelial cells, *Journal of International Medical Research* 2010, May-Jun;38(3):729-36. DOI: 10.1177/147323001003800301. PMID: 20819410. **https://pubmed.ncbi.nlm.nih. gov/20819410**

Adams JA, Galloway TS, Mondal D, Esteves SC, Mathews F, Effect of mobile telephones on sperm quality: a systematic review and meta-analysis, *Environment International*, 2014 Sep;70:106-12. DOI: 10.1016/j.envint.2014.04.015. Epub 2014 Jun 10. PMID: 24927498. **https://pubmed.ncbi.nlm.nih.gov/24927498/**

Official Advice on the Safety of Radiofrequency Radiation, Risk Assessment and Adverse Effects, presentation by Dr Sarah Starkey to Physicians' Health Initiative For Radiation And Environment conference. **https://cdn.website-editor.net/2479f24c54de4c7598d60987e3d81157/files/uploaded/S._Starkey_Presentation_5th_November_2018.pdf**

Joel M. Moskowitz, Effects of Exposure to Electromagnetic Fields: Thirty years of research. **https://www.saferemr.com/2018/02/effects-of-exposure-to-electromagnetic.html**

Page 89

James C. Lin, Science, Politics, and Groupthink [Health Matters], *IEEE Microwave Magazine*. 22(5):24-26, May 2021, DOI: 10.1109/MMM.2021.3056975. **https://ieeexplore.ieee.org/abstract/document/9393739**

Page 134

David H Freedman, Why Scientific Studies Are So
Often Wrong: The Streetlight Effect, *Discover Magazine*,
December 2010, **https://www.discovermagazine.
com/the-sciences/why-scientific-studies-are-so-
often-wrong-the-streetlight-effect**

Page 241

Leon Festinger, Henry Riecken and Stanley Schachter,
*When Prophecy Fails: A Social and Psychological Study
of a Modern Group That Predicted the Destruction of the
World* (1956).

Page 276

**https://ehtrust.org/experts-call-on-fcc-to-promptly-
review-the-most-recent-science-on-wireless-
radiation-to-ensure-protective-safety-limits/**

https://emfscientist.org/

Verma R, Swanson RL, Parker D et al., Neuroimaging
findings in US government personnel with possible
exposure to directional phenomena in Havana, Cuba,
Journal of the American Medical Association, 2019.
Jul 23;322(4):336-347 DOI:10.1001/jama.2019.9269
PMID: 31334794. **https://pubmed.ncbi.nlm.nih.
gov/31334794/**

Gunnar Heuser, Sylvia A Heuser, Functional brain MRI in patients complaining of electrohypersensitivity after long term exposure to electromagnetic fields; in *Reviews on Environmental Health* Sep 26;32(3), Editors-in-chief: David O. Carpenter, Peter Sly, Publisher De Gruyter 2017, pp. 291-299, DOI: 10.1515/reveh-2017-0014. **https://www.national-toxic-encephalopathy-foundation.org/wp-content/uploads/2012/01/functional-brain-mri-in-patients-complaining-ofehs.pdf**

Printed in Great Britain
by Amazon